The
Murderess
Must Đie

The Murderess Must Die

Marlie Parker Wasserman

First published by Level Best Books/Historia 2021

Library of Congress Control Number: 2021941977

AUTHOR PHOTO CREDIT: Gretchen Mathison

First edition

ISBN: 978-1-953789-87-7

Cover art by Level Best Designs

This book was professionally typeset on Reedsy.
Find out more at reedsy.com

To Mark, with love

Contents

Praise for The Murderess Must Die

"A true crime story. But in this case, the crime resides in the punishment. Martha Place was the first woman to die in the electric chair: Sing Sing, March 20, 1899. In this gorgeously written narrative, told in the first-person by Martha and by those who played a part in her life, Marlie Parker Wasserman shows us the (appalling) facts of fin de siècle justice. More, she lets us into the mind of Martha Place, and finally, into the heart. Beautifully observed period detail and astute psychological acuity combine to tell us Martha's story, at once dark and illuminating. *The Murderess Must Die* accomplishes that rare feat: it entertains, even as it haunts." — Howard A. Rodman, author of *The Great Eastern*

"The first woman executed by electric chair in 1899, Martha Place, speaks to us in Wasserman's poignant debut novel. The narrative travels the course of Place's life, describing her desperation in a time when there were few opportunities for women to make a living. Tracing events before and after the murder of her stepdaughter Ida, in lean, straightforward prose, it delivers a compelling feminist message: could an entirely male justice system possibly realize the frightful trauma of this woman's life? This true-crime novel does more—it transcends the painful retelling of Place's life to expand our conception of the death penalty. Although convicted of a heinous crime, Place's personal tragedies and pitiful end are inextricably intertwined." — Nev March, author of Edgar-nominated *Murder in Old Bombay*

"*The Murderess Must Die* would be a fascinating read even without its central elements of crime and punishment. Marlie Parker Wasserman gets inside the heads of a wide cast of late nineteenth century Americans and lets them tell their stories in their own words. It's another world, both alien and similar to ours. You can almost hear the bells of the streetcars." — Edward Zuckerman, author of *Small Fortunes* and *The Day After World War Three*, Emmy-winning writer-producer of *Law & Order*

The Gloom

Mattie

Martha Garretson, that's the name I was born with, but the district attorney called me Martha Place in the murder charge. I was foolish enough to marry Mr. William Place. And before that I was dumb enough to marry another man, Wesley Savacool. So, my name is Martha Garretson Savacool Place. Friends call me Mattie. No, I guess that's not right. I don't have many friends, but my family, the ones I have left, they call me Mattie. I'll tell you more before we go on. The charge was not just murder. That D.A. charged me with murder in the first degree, and he threw in assault, and a third crime, a ridiculous one, attempted suicide. In the end he decided to aim at just murder in the first. That was enough for him.

I had no plans to tell you my story. I wasn't one of those story tellers. That changed in February 1898, soon after my alleged crimes, when I met Miss Emilie Meury. The guards called her the prison angel. She's a missionary from the Brooklyn Auxiliary Mission Society. Spends her days at the jail where the police locked me up for five months before Sing Sing. I never thought I'd talk to a missionary lady. I didn't take kindly to religion. But Miss Meury, she turned into a good friend and a good listener. She never snickered at me. Just nodded or asked a question or two, not like those doctors I talked to later. They asked a hundred questions. No, Miss Meury just let me go wherever I wanted, with my recollections. Because of Miss Meury, now I know how to tell my story. I talked to her for thirteen months, until the day the state of New York set to electrocute me.

We talked about the farm, that damn farm. Don't fret, I knew enough not

1

to say damn to Emilie Meury. She never saw a farm. She didn't know much about New Jersey, and nothing about my village, East Millstone. I told her how Pa ruined the farm. Sixty acres, only thirty in crop, one ramshackle house with two rooms down and two rooms up. And a smokehouse, a springhouse, a root cellar, a chicken coop, and a corn crib, all run down, falling down. The barn was the best of the lot, but it leaned over to the west.

They tell me I had three baby brothers who died before I was born, two on the same day. Ma and Pa hardly talked about that, but the neighbors remembered, and they talked. For years that left just my brother Garret, well, that left Garret for a while anyway, and my sister Ellen. Then I was born, then Matilda—family called her Tillie—then Peter, then Eliza, then Garret died in the war, then Eliza died. By the time I moved to Brooklyn, only my brother Peter and my sister Ellen were alive. Peter is the only one the police talk to these days.

The farmers nearby and some of our kin reckoned that my Ma and Pa, Isaac and Penelope Garretson were their names, they bore the blame for my three little brothers dying in just two years. Isaac and Penelope were so mean, that's what they deserved. I don't reckon their meanness caused the little ones to die. I was a middle child with five before me and three after, and I saw meanness all around, every day. I never blamed anything on meanness. Not even what happened to me.

On the farm there was always work to be done, a lot of it by me. Maybe Ma and Pa spread out the work even, but I never thought so. By the time I was nine, that was in 1858, I knew what I had to do. In the spring I hiked up my skirt to plow. In the fall I sharpened the knives for butchering. In the winter I chopped firewood after Pa or Garret, he was the oldest, sawed the heaviest logs. Every morning I milked and hauled water from the well. On Thursdays I churned. On Mondays I scrubbed. Pa, and Ma too, they were busy with work, but they always had time to yell when I messed up. I was two years younger than Ellen, she's my sister, still alive, I think. I was taller and stronger. Ellen had a bent for sewing and darning, so lots of time she sat in the parlor with handiwork. I didn't think the parlor looked shabby. Now that I've seen fancy houses, I remember the scratched and frayed chairs in the farmhouse and the rough plank floor, no carpets. While Ellen sewed in the parlor, I plowed the fields, sweating behind the horses. I sewed too, but everyone knew Ellen was better. I took care with all my chores. Had to sew a straight seam. Had to plow a straight line. If I messed up, Pa's wrath came down on me, or sometimes Ma's. Fists or worse.

When I told that story for the first time to Miss Emilie Meury, she lowered her head, looked at the Bible she always held. And when I told it to others, they looked away too.

On the farm Ma needed me and Ellen to watch over our sisters, Tillie and Eliza, and over our brother Peter. They were born after me. Just another chore, that's what Ellen thought about watching the young ones. For me, I liked watching them, and not just because I needed a rest from farm work. I loved Peter. He was four years younger. He's not that sharp but he's a good-natured, kind. I loved the girls too. Tillie, the level-headed and sweet one, and Eliza, the restless one, maybe wild even. The four of us played house. I was the ma and Peter, he stretched his back and neck to be pa. I laughed at him, in a kindly way. He and me, we ordered Tillie and Eliza around. We played school and I pranced around as schoolmarm.

But Ma and Pa judged, they judged every move. They left the younger ones alone and paid no heed to Ellen. She looked so sour. We called her sourpuss. Garret and me, we made enough mistakes to keep Ma and Pa busy all year. I remember what I said once to Ma, when she saw the messy kitchen and started in on me.

"Why don't you whup Ellen? She didn't wash up either."

"Don't need to give a reason."

"Why don't you whup Garret. He made the mess."

"You heard me. Don't need to give a reason."

Then she threw a dish. Hit my head. I had a bump, and more to clean.

With Pa the hurt lasted longer. Here's what I remember. "Over there." That's what he said, pointing. He saw the uneven lines my plow made. When I told this story to Miss Meury, I pointed, with a mean finger, to give her the idea.

I spent that night locked in the smelly chicken coop.

When I tell about the coop, I usually tell about the cemetery next, because that's a different kind of hurt. Every December, from the time I was little to the time I left the farm, us Garretsons took the wagon or the sleigh for our yearly visit to the cemetery, first to visit Stephen, Cornelius, and Abraham. They died long before. They were ghosts to me. I remembered the gloom of the cemetery, and the silence. The whole family stood around those graves, but I never heard a cry. Even Ma stayed quiet. I told the story, just like this, to Miss Meury. But I told it again, later, to those men who came to the prison to check my sanity.

Penelope Wykoff Garretson

I was born a Wyckoff, Penelope Wyckoff, and I felt that in my bones, even when the other farm folks called me Ma Garretson. As a Wyckoff, one of the prettiest of the Wyckoffs I'm not shy to say, I lived better than lots of the villagers in central New Jersey, certainly better than the Garretsons. I had five years of schooling and new dresses for the dances each year. I can't remember what I saw in Isaac Garretson when we married on February 5, 1841. We slept together that night. I birthed Stephen nine months later. Then comes the sing-song litany. When I was still nursing Stephen, Garret was born. And while I was still nursing Garret, the twins were born. Then the twins died and I had only Stephen and Garret. Then Stephen died and I had no one but Garret until Ellen was born. Then Martha. Some call her Mattie. Then Peter. Then Matilda. Some call her Tillie. Then Eliza. Then Garret died. Then Eliza died. Were there more births than deaths or deaths than births?

During the worst of the birthing and the burying, Isaac got real bad. He always had a temper, I knew that, but it got worse. Maybe because the farm was failing, or almost failing. The banks in New Brunswick—that was the nearby town—wouldn't lend him money. Those bankers knew him, knew he was a risk. Then the gambling started. Horse racing. It's a miracle he didn't lose the farm at the track. I didn't tell anyone, not even my sisters, about the gambling, and I certainly didn't tell them that the bed didn't help any. No time for shagging. Isaac pulled me to him at the end of a day. The bed was always cold because he never cut enough firewood. I rolled away most days, not all. Knew it couldn't be all. So tired. There were no strapping boys to help with the farm, no girls either for a while.

As Garret grew tall and Ellen and Mattie grew some, I sent the children to the schoolhouse. It wasn't much of a school, just a one-room unpainted cottage shared with the post office, with that awful Mr. Washburn in charge. It was what we had. Isaac thought school was no use and kept Garret and the girls back as much as he could, especially in the spring. He needed them for the farm and the truth was I could use them for housework and milking and such too. Garret didn't mind skipping school. He was fine with farm work, but Ellen and Mattie fussed and attended more days than Garret did. I worried that Garret struggled to read and write, while the girls managed pretty well. Ellen and Mattie read when there was a need and Mattie was good with her numbers. At age nine she was already helping Isaac with his messy ledgers.

I was no fool—I knew what went on in that school. The few times I went to pull out Garret midday for plowing, that teacher, that Mr. Washburn, looked uneasy when I entered the room. He stood straight as a ramrod, looking at me, grimacing. His fingernails were clean and his collar was starched. I reckon he saw that my fingernails were filthy and my muslin dress was soiled. Washburn didn't remember that my children, the Garretson children, were Wyckoffs just as much as they were Garretsons. He saw their threadbare clothes and treated them like dirt. Had Garret chop wood and the girls haul water, while those stuck-up Neilson girls, always with those silly smiles on their faces, sat around in their pretty dresses, snickering at the others. First, I didn't think the snickering bothered anyone except me. Then I saw Ellen and Mattie fussing with their clothes before school, pulling the fabric around their frayed elbows to the inside, and I knew they felt bad.

I wanted to raise my children, at least my daughters, like Wyckoffs. With Isaac thinking he was in charge, that wasn't going to happen. At least the girls knew the difference, knew there was something better than this miserable farm. But me, Ma Garretson they called me, I was stuck.

Mattie

When I got to talk about growing up in East Millstone, I couldn't stop with just the stories about the chicken coop or my weekly chores. Miss Meury, and all the others I blabbed to in prison like the matrons and the doctors, they were keen to hear more. And I had a lot of time, time to remember. I kept talking.

I was ten that spring, 1859. The day stayed in my mind, not because it was different from the other days, but because of the mud. I keep coming back to the feel of that mud. For three days it rained. As soon as it stopped, we went to work in the field. My boots felt heavy. The muck clung to the bottom and sides of the leather. Those boots were pretty worn. I outgrowed them, so I left the laces untied for extra space. With each step, I felt the ooze sink into my socks. Ahead of me in the field, Garret, full-grown now, and Ma, I think she was wearing Pa's pants, they spread the wet lime. Most years Pa slackened the lime first—watered it down so it fertilized the corn seeds, not burned them. This year he just let the rain pour into the bushels of lime he ordered the week before. After that heavy rain, the lime weakened. Pa said we couldn't wait to spread it, even if the weather was foul. I followed Garret and Ma in the big boot prints they made. My job was to harrow the fertilizer into the earth. Ellen, remember she was my big sister, she stayed in the farmhouse to watch the young ones. Ellen wouldn't have been much help in the field anyway.

No one could say for sure how much lime you needed for a field. Some farmers said two bushels an acre. Some said twenty. Pa didn't pay much attention to their advice. He bought what he had money for. That year, it was almost enough. But Ma and Garret could tell the lime was weak, so they didn't spread it too thinly. When the bushels were empty the lime covered all except the north corner. "Nothing to be done," Ma said.

Then dusk came. Pa returned from harness racing in Freehold, stinking and fussing. The muddy track changed the odds. I saw Ma and Garret sneak a look at each other. I guessed they thought Pa's losses at the track might be a good thing this day, to take his mind away from the field. Pa sat hunched over at the table, drinking the hard cider he got in trade. That table, now that I think about it, that table was scratched and dirty. After ten minutes Pa grabbed his pipe and stumbled outside to stable his horse. When he brought the horse around to the barn—it was halfway to the north corner—I watched Garret and Ma, sitting quietly, looking at each other again. They listened for Pa's footsteps. Now I did too. First the steps slowed, then the man half ran, half stumbled back to the house.

"Why d'you stop? Nothing on the north corner. Useless, all you bastards." The same way I pointed like Pa did when I talked to Miss Meury about my plow lines, I screwed up my voice and snarled so she, or whoever was listening to my story, got the picture. I never said how that word bastard stuck in my craw.

Pa started with Ma first. I saw the blood dribble down Ma's nose as Pa's fist moved away. Garret didn't think about protecting Ma. He was strong enough. But he hadn't protected her before and it was not his way to do so now. He just waited for Pa to pivot and redirect the punches. I was third.

As my storytelling improved over the months, I knew I had to balance things out. Miss Meury and the others might think I was fibbing if I overdid the punches and whippings. Sometimes I jumped way ahead to the war, starting with my older brother. Garret Terhune Garretson. Why did Ma and Pa give him such a name? I never knew. He was born in 1842, a year after baby Stephen died and a year before the twins died. He wasn't my only brother because I had Peter too, but Peter came later. Garret was my favorite. Now you know he didn't exactly look after me. No one did that. But he suffered too and that was something.

I never blamed Markus Van Cortland for what happened. Markus was the first of the boys to go to Trenton, to enlist in Company F, 11th New Jersey Infantry in September '62, for nine months of service. Most of the boys in East Millstone and New Brunswick followed Markus. He was sort of their leader, the one the other boys looked up to. And Garret, he looked up to him. I knew Pa didn't want Garret to go. Needed him on the farm. Garret was the strongest of us children. But Garret couldn't wait to leave. He hated the farm, just like me. First, he went with his regiment to Washington, on guard duty to defend the capital. He'd never been away from central New Jersey before. In the first letter he wrote Ma, and there were only two letters, ever, he said his regiment was attached to Abercrombie's Provisional Brigade, Casey's Division. When I read that to Pa, I stretched out the words, starting with Abercrombie's. All that sounded grand when Pa heard it. He even smiled. Then the regiment went on to Aquia Creek, still on guard duty, this time to protect Richmond, Fredericksburg, and the Potomac Railroad. I stretched that out too. Garret wrote one more letter to Ma on December 10th, not saying much, filled with his usual funny spellings. Meanwhile, Markus Van Cortland wrote to me. Markus's letters were longer, with news about the food and the waiting. In his last letter, he's the one who told me the regiment was marching from Aquia Creek to Fredericksburg, with the Army of the Potomac. I found a United States map in the county courthouse, then I circled the spot in Virginia with a pencil. I thought about pocketing the map, but the county clerk was too close. So I stared at the rivers and place names, trying to keep them in my head. Those details were mine. I didn't bother to tell the others.

On December 17th, 1862, a hired hand who worked for the Van Cortlands, Amos was his name, carried the news about Markus to other farms within an hour. I heard Amos ride up to Pa in the stables. I peeked out the window. I saw their sloped shoulders and how close their heads were, and I knew. On December 30th, that same hired hand—I hated that man Amos—rode up to our farm again. Pa was nowhere in sight that day, so Amos knocked on the door with the news. Mr. Van Cortland, Markus's father, had seen the newest casualty list on the front page of *The New Brunswick Fredonian*, tacked up on the front door of the newspaper office. He bought the paper and sent his hired hand Amos to deliver it. I guess Mr. Van Cortland wanted to spread the suffering. Private Garret Terhune Garretson. I don't know if my brother ever made it to Fredericksburg, if he ever saw fighting. It was the typhoid fever that got him. He must have drunk dirty water in his camp. He died on December 27th in the field hospital in Falmouth, in Stafford Country, Virginia, just a few miles from the battle. When Amos arrived, he handed *The Fredonian* to Ma. She read it, walked to the table in the kitchen just like nothing happened, and threw the newspaper down on the wooden top. The sound of the paper landing on the plank and sliding to the edge, that was what I remember. I stared at Amos as he turned around and left, fast, then I stared at Ma, and then I read the casualty column. Didn't need to. I felt blood rush to, or maybe away from, my arms and legs, but I moved on to my chores, alongside Ma. Neither of us said much. When Pa saw the paper, he knew. Didn't matter that he couldn't read—he could read the name Garretson. We had our own hired hand, a vagrant who helped out in exchange for a bunk. No one asked him to spread the word to the other farmers.

I didn't have room left for grief, though I didn't say that to whoever was listening to my story. The news two weeks before about Markus Van Cortland didn't leave room for much else.

Evelyn Wykoff Sutton

It took me a few months to learn that my nephew Garret died near Fredericksburg. I am not reluctant to tell you that I had little sympathy for my sister Penelope. Living out there on a ramshackle farm with that drunkard. What did she expect? I never understood why Penelope married Isaac Garretson. He was a handsome man, but mean, hapless. Penelope could be dour, I knew that, and then she went a married someone even more ornery than her. Those Garretson offspring, there were a lot of them. They had their problems but even that lot didn't deserve their Ma and Pa. And Garret, he was uneducated and crass, like his father, but he didn't deserve to die in the war.

When I thought about not visiting at all, my Christian duty weighed too heavily on me. I took the train from my home in Newark, south to New Brunswick, then by carriage to East Millstone. Penelope must have heard the carriage approach because she was on the porch, waiting, looking thin, with a shawl that wasn't warm enough for the cool day. I followed her past the tiny parlor, into the kitchen. We sat at the table. No cloth, no tea setting. I sat stiffly on the edge of my chair, because, to tell you the truth, I was afraid of getting dirt on my silk dress. Penelope slumped in the chair across the table.

"How are you?"

"Getting by."

I looked around. This was not getting by. I didn't know much about farming, but it was April and I could see when the carriage pulled near that the fields were a mess. I did know something about housekeeping. The only Garretson who seemed to care was Martha. While Penelope and I sat, that girl scrubbed the dishes in the dishpan, dried them, and put them away, though probably no amount of scouring could get rid of the stale smell in that farmhouse. The oldest child, Ellen, she sat embroidering, with that sullen look on her face, and the younger children were running around the house screaming at each other. Penelope never glanced at them.

I came to the farm to pay a condolence call, the minimum I could do for the only one of my kin who had died in the war, so far anyway. I had another plan too, which I kept to myself at first. If I was to help one of the children, and that was my interpretation of my Christian mission, which one would it be? Ellen would be the obvious choice and with her plain face and with all the young men dying in the war, she would never wed. She might have talent as a seamstress and I could help with that. But Ellen, she mirrored Penelope's sadness. I didn't want Ellen around. Tillie, she was ten, she was a gorgeous child. How much could I help a ten-year old? Eliza, she was seven. She was certainly too young.

I looked at Martha, still cleaning up in the kitchen. She was industrious, no doubt. She could read and write. She was sad too, but not as sad as Ellen. I waited until she went out back to toss the water from the dishpan.

"Penelope, you know Philip and I have plenty of room in our house, especially since God has not blessed us. What if I took one of the girls for a few weeks in the summer? Would it lighten your load? Maybe Martha. She would be a help around the house."

Penelope stared at me, then sat up straighter. "Yes, June, after the planting." Neither one of us asked the girl.

Reverend David Cole

I was forty-one years old, already with a receding hairline, when I first met Martha Place, Martha Garretson then. That was during the war, 1863, a difficult time for everyone. Those years I considered my home to be Rutgers College, where I taught fledgling clergy, and my second home to be the First Reformed Church in New Brunswick, a few blocks from the college. I had just enough time to manage the First Reformed's Sunday School. Those years, the war years, it was mostly girls and a few young boys who came to Sunday School. Pastor Steele had the hardest work, comforting families of the dead and burying the bodies that returned home by train. I had the easier job. But on an unseasonably hot Sunday, May 9th—I recall the date because the battle at Chancellorsville had just ended—you know we often have heightened memories of our worst times—I wondered if I was up to teaching Sunday School or handling any other church task. I left the children in the warm schoolroom for a minute so I could prepare the sanctuary for services. I planned to take my students there to pray for the dead and wounded at Chancellorsville. Word had reached me that one of our congregants died on May 5th. He was a promising lad, and two others were in a Virginia army field hospital. As I returned to the schoolroom to collect the students, in the courtyard I saw three girls, the Neilson sisters, and the Roberson girl, trying to cool off. They talked in hushed tones, but not so hushed that I could not hear fragments. "Mud on her dress, filthy hair, walks off." When I entered the classroom, I saw Martha Garretson sitting alone on a wooden bench, face set in a scowl, sweating.

I continued the lessons later that morning, with a plan. I called on the Garretson girl, with easy questions that gave her a chance to shine. When she answered, the other students looked bored, like it didn't matter. That spring I began to pay particular attention to Martha Garretson. She was often absent on Sundays. If she did attend class, sometimes with her sister Ellen, I noticed that both girls continued to sit apart. I don't remember much about Ellen, but I do remember that Martha sat with her eyes half-closed and her mouth strained taut. I would remember her loneliness for thirty-six years, when I could at last perform my clerical duty to lead her to salvation. In the years in between, whenever I thought about Chancellorsville, and the thirty thousand who were slaughtered or wounded or captured there, I also thought about Martha.

Peter Garretson

Pa never gave me a choice. "Harness the horses. Move along. There'll be a crowd." We left East Millstone at 8:00 that morning to make sure we arrived at 9:00 when the New Brunswick prison gate opened. It was a hot day in August 1867.

I knew it was hopeless to ask Pa to stay back with my sisters. I was just thirteen, and I'd never seen a hanging. That was just fine with me. This one would be special, but I still wanted to stay back.

By the time our horse and wagon got near New Brunswick, the crowd nearly blocked the road. Carts, buggies, riders on horseback, walkers. Men, women, babies, toddlers, old folks. Looked like all Middlesex County was there. A week before, the county clerk traveled around on horseback and passed out tickets to the event—that's what they called it—to five hundred people. First, he gave tickets to families of New Brunswick homeowners and then to families on nearby farms. The men who were not around when the clerk arrived tried to buy tickets from the men who were luckier. No one was selling.

When Pa and me got up close to the county jail Pa guided the wagon to a stable, where the hired hand—he lost an eye at Gettysburg—said he was running out of room for all the conveyances, that's what he called them, conveyances. As we walked around the corner to the jail, we heard jeers. We couldn't make out any words. Pa handed over two tickets to the extra deputies Sheriff Clarkson hired for the event, and then they let us into the prison yard. We pushed through to a back corner where Pa recognized a few farmers. I remember the stale air, the reek of the farmers' bodies crowded together. I had about a foot of space to myself. No more spectators could fit into the yard. Even the skies seemed full of spectators because men and boys stood on the roofs of the buildings on all sides of the jail. I was already almost as tall as pa, but not quite. I stood on my toes to see the gallows. It looked simpler than I expected, just two vertical beams and a crossbeam. A jailor threw a rope over the crossbeam, then tied a weight to one end.

"What's the weight for?" I asked. Pa didn't answer. The farmer beside us said, "That's an upright jerker. That's what they call it. Saw one at Fort Mifflin in '64, when they hung a soldier for desertion. You'll see why they call it a jerker soon enough."

Must have been five hundred gawkers on the ground and thirty on the roofs. We all waited in the heat. The men shouted insults until a hush sort of rippled through the crowd, from front to back. "Door's opening," a man announced. I stretched to see. She was a young, stout woman, dressed in brown with a white collar and white gloves. She walked slowly to the gallows, with one priest on her left and another on her right. Her arms were tied together, forced behind her back. Without ceremony, and without expression or words, Sheriff Clarkson put the noose around her neck and adjusted it. The crowd went silent, but not for long. The insults started up again, more vulgar than before. Dozens of boys and men joined in. Slurs against the Irish, slurs against Catholics, against loose women, against body parts. Pa added slurs of his own. After each slur he looked at me, with that little smile, welcoming me into his club or clan. Then the sheriff cut the secure end of the pulley-like rope. Bridget Deignan's body jerked up, then fell, then twisted. So, the maid who stabbed her mistress twenty-five times, bit her on the neck, and set her house on fire, she suffocated to death. The newspapers called the maid an illiterate animal. I didn't doubt her guilt, though someday others would. But I never wanted to be part of such a, such an event, again.

Driving the wagon home, Pa usually stayed silent. This time he went over and over Bridget's last minutes, with comments about what he saw underneath when her body jerked upwards. He was still reliving all that when we got back to the farmhouse. Ma, Eliza, Tillie, Ellen, and Mattie, they were on the porch, ready to listen. Mattie must have been eighteen. Pa kept talking. Now I'm wondering if Mattie remembered that day.

Mattie

Once I got to babbling about my childhood, if I was talking to Miss Emilie Meury or the matrons at Sing Sing, sometimes I talked on about the years after I was grown. Still on that damn farm, still low spirits.

The summer I turned twenty-two wasn't the worst year for disease in New Jersey. But still bad. We watched out for smallpox, yellow fever, typhus, and of course the typhoid that got Garret during the war. There was also scarlet fever.

Eliza was a happy child, the happiest of my brothers and sisters. No one would quarrel with that. She was the youngest, so she had easy chores, which meant that in Ma's eyes and Pa's she couldn't mess up as much as the rest of us. She was not the prettiest. Matilda, Tillie we called her, was the prettiest. But Eliza, with her brown curls and regular features, was still a looker. When Pa listed us girls in levels of loveliness—Tillie, Eliza, Martha, Ellen—Eliza didn't protest, and I knew that list was about the only thing Pa got right.

The farm meant gloom and sweat for me. For Eliza, it was a playground. She jumped over fences. She picked anemone and Queens Anne's lace. She waded in Moore's Creek, caught fireflies. Eliza begged the others to join her, especially Peter. He was gloomy, hardly any fun. I almost never joined in the play either, but Peter and me, we kept an eye out for Eliza when she roamed in the fields. We knew if she was late for supper because she sprained her ankle, or late for evening chores because she stayed undercover in a neighbor's barn, or, as she got older, maybe late because she snuck out with a boy. One night in May I saw she was late, very late. Even ma, who was faraway a lot in her head, even she noticed that Eliza was late. I found her resting, near the creek. The scarlet fever started on Eliza's tongue and spread to her back, then her whole body. After a few weeks, she couldn't swallow. Ma tried a few teas the Wykoffs used. They made no difference. I gathered chickweed, boiled it in oil, and spread the cooled salve on Eliza to soothe the itching. That didn't help either. Eliza was fifteen. I was twenty-two. I'll tell you something. When I was thirteen, I cried at the news of Markus Van Cortland. I didn't cry again until Eliza stopped struggling on May 21st, nine years later.

The next year is a blur for me. Oh, I did read the newspapers—New Brunswick's *Daily Times*, and when I visited Aunt Evelyn, *The Newark Sunday*

Call. So I knew there was a terrible explosion on the Staten Island Ferry. Seventy-two people died. And I knew Boss Tweed got himself arrested for bribery. But not much happened in East Millstone, except for work on that damn farm. Then Ma took sick.

She got what she deserved. I never said that out loud to my sisters Tillie and Ellen. Didn't need to. I know they agreed. Penelope Wyckoff Garretson birthed five sons and four daughters and buried five of them, Eliza just the year before. Maybe Ma mourned, but I only heard her sharp-tongued gripes, gripes against me and everyone else. Ellen and Peter, they could turn sour too, but they didn't get spiteful like Ma. All summer and fall, that was 1872, I watched Ma in bed in that stuffy farmhouse. She twisted in agony and drenched the bed with sweat. Twice Pa called a doctor from New Brunswick. The doctor offered an elixir. It was useless, and he demanded money for the stupid bottle and his visit, both. Pa decided he was throwing good money after bad so he tried the clergy. Pastor Steele from the First Reformed, he'd be free. Pa called him to the farm. The pastor held Ma's hand. You could tell from his look that Ma's hand was dry and cold. She scowled at him. Not sure I blame her. On his way out the door, the pastor reminded Pa it had been too long since the Garretsons were at Sunday service. I heard that and I snarled a goodbye to the pastor. "Blaming our absence for Ma's sickness?" I asked Tillie. After the pastor's visit, Pa stopped trying. I added on Ma's chores, cooking and sewing, and cleaned up her messes.

As Ma was dying, Aunt Evelyn came from Newark, I suppose to pay her last visit. She brought a gown she didn't need anymore and two issues of *Godey's Lady's Book*. Ellen and I studied the book and altered Evelyn's gown to fit Ma. She was thinner than ever, with bones sticking through her skin. We had to close up a lot of seams. Finally, on October 7th, Ma stopped struggling. Ellen helped me wash Ma's body and dress it in the gown. Ma dead wore a much nicer dress than Ma alive. Five days later we buried her alongside her dead children—Cornelius, Abraham, Stephen, Garret, and Eliza too.

A few months later, on a cold winter day, I had my accident. We made our annual visit, you know, the one to the graveyard to pay our respects to the

Garretson dead. We all went—those of us who were still alive. Somehow, I fell out of the sleigh. That sleigh wasn't fancy. Just the body of a wagon on runners, but when I fell either the runners hit my head or the horse trampled me. Couldn't remember the details years later when one of my better lawyers, Henry Newman, grilled me about the accident. Pa and Peter got me to the farmhouse. No one sent for the doctor. Pa was still mad at him for not helping Ma. And charging him anyway. Peter said I was senseless for an hour or two. After I woke, my head hurt and I saw double for a while. The next day I couldn't keep down the food Ellen cooked. It was tasteless. That was the first and last time I was ever sick. After three days I was fine again, aside from a bump and bruise on my head. Peter and Ellen teased me. They called me feeble-minded and a freak. The teasing was no matter. I was busy then thinking about something else.

I couldn't stay on the farm with Pa. Ma wasn't any, well, any buffer, but at least she was another target for Pa's wrath. She used up some of his meanness. By the time of the sleigh accident, Peter was nineteen. A year before he escaped the farm. He moved to New Brunswick to work as a porter at the railroad station. Pa yelled at him that the farm would be left with only girls to do the work. But by the time Ma died, Pa decided it wasn't so bad to be the only man left. I couldn't stop thinking about how I'd escape too. Hire out as domestic labor? The Irish girls, fresh off the boat, they were doing that. Schoolmarm? I did have six years of schooling, more or less. That wasn't enough. The summers in Newark with Aunt Evelyn, I'd had three by then, gave me a better idea, well, a better idea if I could stomach partnering with my oldest sister.

I never liked Ellen. Everyone knew that Ellen's prospects, that's the word we used, were not good. If Pa was right that his girls could be arranged in a line of descending prettiness, Ellen was not only fourth but a far fourth, way behind me. She was twenty-five, so marriage wasn't going to happen. Seemed like all the boys that the girls could've married died in the war. Not only that. We Garretson girls came from a dirt-poor family.

I needed to partner with Ellen. My days would be dreary, but not as dreary as staying on the farm with Pa. I started in on my sister when I recovered from the accident, in January 1873. "You're good at patterns and lace. I can sew, just not as good as you. But you might not be good at making the sales. I learned a lot from my visits to Aunt Evelyn. I can talk to the society ladies, tell them what we can do, how we can copy the fashions. And you know how I help Pa with bills. I tell him what he needs to pay now and what he can stall on. I know the tricks. I can use that the other way too. I can make sure we get paid quick. We can't be seamstresses here at the farm. We need a town."

"You're gonna leave Matilda?" Ellen said. "She'll be alone with Pa."

"Tillie, Tillie, Tillie. I'm tired of fussing about her. She's already keeping company with Sanford. If it's not him she'll find someone else." Sanford Doland was a conductor on the railroad. Peter introduced Sandy to Tillie at a dance in New Brunswick the week before Ma died. He never introduced any of his friends to me or to Ellen.

I wasn't sure Ellen would follow my plan. She mostly snarled. Finally, after Tillie told us she was engaged to Sanford, Ellen started to pay me attention. "I don't know about leaving," Ellen said, "but Pa tells me every day that I'm a spinster, a dried-up crone, a burden. I'd like to show him. Make more money than he does here at the farm." We packed our few possessions, wasn't much, while Pa was in the fields. Hitched a ride to New Brunswick with a peddler. We left without a goodbye. Ellen and I never laughed much but riding with that peddler we jested that Pa would never notice we were gone.

I'd sent word ahead to Peter. He was living in New Brunswick, in an apartment above a railroad station, not the main station where the police would hold my trunk twenty-five years later. There was room enough in Peter's apartment for three. That was the beginning of our dressmaking business. It kept Ellen and me fed, or at least barely fed, for a long time. I brought in business and talked to the ladies about styles—loops, drapes, overskirts and underskirts, bustles. I sewed too, but Ellen had more patience for tedious work.

After we left, Pa's farm went even more downhill. He had an apple orchard, just a small one, and bigger fields of wheat and potatoes. The wheat and potatoes did poorly and sold for a low price. His apples did fine. I heard that the neighboring farms with large fruit orchards had their best years ever. The other farmers told Pa to change over some of his fields to orchards. He wouldn't. Maybe he was too busy betting on the horses to put in the work for a switch. Or maybe he was just stubborn. I didn't care. I was gone from there forever.

Peter Garretson

The other workers on the railroad couldn't understand why I lived with my sisters. Some of those men still lived with their parents, but that was different. Sisters? I didn't fuss much about our arrangement since Ellen and Mattie helped with the rent. Remember, we had that bank panic. Lasted for years. New Jersey was hurt just as much as the rest of the country. The number of train riders dropped, so my wages dropped too. I needed my sisters' share of the rent. It wasn't just that. Ellen and Mattie kept the apartment spotless and they did all the cooking and my laundry. There was one bad side to the arrangement. I heard their nasty words to each other every night. "Why did you say I'd have it done soon? Why did you charge so little? Where are you going to get that color silk? Why didn't you show her how Deborah Rowen messed up her wedding gown? Don't start the blue one until you finish the brocade." My sisters were nasty to me, but they were even nastier to each other. I ignored their bickering for four long years. After all, I grew up with bickering. Then the national railroad strike of '77 hit the East Coast. By that time, I'd gotten promoted, from porter to baggage master. I was responsible for all the baggage on a train that went into New York and back each day. Sometimes I wished I was still just a porter because then no one paid attention to me. But now I had threats on me, threats of beatings, from each side, the strikers and the owners. I didn't strike. I tried to stay in the background like usual. Those years, I was always looking behind my back. I could handle that on my route—I'm a big guy so I look meaner than I am. But when I got home, I had no patience for the bickering. I started to spend more and more evenings away. One of those evenings, I met Margaret and started keeping company with her. She was poor too. But she was nice and gentle, more like my younger sisters than the older two.

I told Mattie and Ellen I planned to marry Margaret. I reminded them that we knew some people who had moved to Asbury Park who might help get them started in a dressmaking business there. Margaret and me, we went out on the town the night we said goodbye to my sisters in 1878.

Mattie

We had friends if you want to call them that, distant relations of my Ma's, who lived in Asbury Park, thirty-five miles away. When we couldn't stay with Peter after he married Margaret, Ellen and I called on that family. They had no extra room, or that's what they said. They led us to a modest frame house on Third Avenue. The yellow paint was peeling and the whole house was sagging east, toward the ocean. We said it would do. We rented the drafty third floor, where we slept, and set up our dressmaking business. Nothing went well. Asbury Park, it was a resort town, or trying to be, but it was just getting over hard times. There weren't many year-round residents. When we lived with Peter in New Brunswick, Ellen and I quieted down our arguments when he got home. He knew we quarreled. He didn't know it was even worse during the day when he was on the railroad. In Asbury Park, without Peter around, we kept up our quarreling. Business was bad too. Nothing much happened in our own lives in those years. I suppose around us, a lot was happening. I followed the stories in the newspapers. But I only remember three of them, because we only remember what comes to matter later. I remember stories about Thomas Edison's inventions. One of them was electric current, but not the variety that would kill me. Another was about Albert Augustus Pope's business with bicycles, and that was a sport I took up later. The third was the Margaret Meierhoffer story. Remember that one? Just fifty miles north of Asbury Park. Even Ellen followed the Meierhoffer story. When we took a pause from arguing we jabbered about that case while we sewed trimmings at night.

"Do you think she did it?" I asked. "They say she was six feet tall. She might have overpowered that bitty husband. The papers said she was criminally intimate with the farmhand, Frank Lammens. Criminally intimate. Ha. That's not what we called it in East Millstone."

I heard Ellen laugh, maybe for the first time in weeks. "Or maybe," Ellen said, Frank shot the husband. "He was bigger too. If Margaret blames Frank and Frank blames Margaret, maybe they'll both get away with it."

"Well, their lawyers are hopeless. I bet they both swing.

I was right. The sentence came down in 1881, two years after Margaret Meierhoffer, maybe with the help of her boyfriend Frank, shot her husband John Meierhoffer. The two lovers were hung, one after the other, in the Essex County prison yard. The hangman used a counterweight-style jerker, like the one a different hangman used to kill Bridget Deignan fourteen years earlier, in New Brunswick. Peter and Pa saw the hanging and told us all about it. I think Margaret Meierhoffer was the last woman executed in the state of New Jersey. Years later I would set another kind of record.

But before that happened my life changed more than I could ever conjure up.

You must know, I gave up hope of ever keeping company with a good man. I even gave up hope of keeping company with a cad. Who would want me anyway? I suppose I was good-looking enough, tall, slender. Shapely. But I felt like a beast of burden, no different from the mules Pa drove to work the farm. Even when I went to Newark—I did that every year or two—I knew Aunt Evelyn wouldn't show me around to the ladies, or the young men, in Newark society. She was a Wyckoff, on my dead mother's side. The Garretsons and the Wyckoffs, they are huge New Jersey families. Mostly the Wyckoffs scoffed at Pa and his gang. We all, well, me and Ellen and maybe Tillie, we picked up on the missing invitations, the insults. Ma knew too. She told us that her kin said we were a few pretty girls, but base, unrefined. That's how Ma explained the snubs. Aunt Evelyn, I'll tell you, she was one of the better Wyckoffs. She was a good Christian. "Just like you," that's what I said when I chattered to Miss Meury or later to Reverend Cole. Aunt Evelyn was charitable too, even if she was a snob and looked down her nose at us. From early on she was keen about the dressmaking business. She said to me once, "Martha, I am proud of the role I played in getting you started." Well, she exaggerated that role. It was me and Ellen whose fingers bled with those needles. But I do have a little gratitude. Aunt Evelyn tutored me, as she put it, on what the society ladies of Newark wore each year. When I visited her, I didn't say much about our few Asbury Park customers. She didn't know we struggled to keep them. Never told her that sometimes we had to wait to be paid for one dress before we could buy fabric for a second dress.

When I stayed with Aunt Evelyn in 1881, I knew to put on my Newark manners and bearing, as best I could. I shopped with her, well, I looked and carried while Aunt Evelyn made her purchases. We went over magazines together, we looked close at the latest fashions. Low-cut bodices. Draped overskirts. A range of bustle shapes. Half my clientele in Asbury Park couldn't afford those elaborate styles. My aunt didn't need to know that.

Now let me tell you more about that summer of '81, that fateful summer is what Reverend Cole called it much, much later. Down the street from Aunt Evelyn's house, two blocks away, there was a small grocery. She sent me there to fetch provisions. Behind the counter, I saw a handsome young man, about my height. He had nice cheekbones and wavy brown hair parted down the middle. A curled mustache. That was the rage then. Still is. He was friendly, a good talker. Charming even. His name was Wesley Savacool. The second time I went to the grocery, I took special care with my dress and my hair. My hair stayed thick until the end, but it was even thicker then. And all brown. The third time I went to the grocery, I found an excuse to hang around. I waited for Wesley to measure something that Aunt Evelyn didn't even need. We started keeping company. I never had a suitor before. Yeah, I had my eye on Markus Van Cortland. And all these years later I think he had his eye on me. I was thirteen, so I can't be sure. And soon he was gone, dust in some godforsaken Virginia battlefield.

That summer I didn't go back to Asbury Park when I was supposed to. I wrote Ellen, "Sorry, I won't be back for a while. Helping Aunt E. Fulfill the commissions by yourself." Wesley was a lot younger than me but I could tell that didn't bother him. Of course, he thought the difference was six years, not nine like it was. I reckoned he thought I came from a family that had money because I stayed with Evelyn Wyckoff Sutton in a nice brick house. Her husband had died by then. Uncle Philip left her well off. And me, ha, I was stupid too. I thought Wesley owned the grocery. Later I figured that he let me think that. But he just worked there, paid by Mr. Hatfield. And Wesley let me think his parents were well-to-do landowners in Sussex County. They were farmers, almost as poor as Pa.

We married in the Belleville Dutch Reformed Church, it's near Newark, on November 8, 1881. Aunt Evelyn, she wasn't happy. She never liked Wesley. The wedding was about as small as could be—just scowling Aunt Evelyn, Wesley's paunchy friend Richard Dorney, and a reverend. I spent more money than I had on eighteen yards of white satin fabric and in two weeks I sewed myself a dress, showing off my talents. I didn't need Ellen to show off. The dress had a pointed waist, off-shoulder vee neckline, three-quarter length sleeves, a rounded-off train, and a flounced skirt with an overskirt. The hourglass shape was fashionable, and it suited my figure. I bought kid gloves. I wore my hair in a coiled knot on top of my head, with a floral headdress. On the day of my wedding, I knew I looked as good as I ever would, younger than my thirty-two years, maybe closer to Wesley's twenty-three years. Or maybe twenty-six years. He changed his own story a lot. I was embarrassed that Pa was not at the church—Aunt Evelyn had written him—but I did not let Evelyn or Wesley know how I felt. I could never be sure if Pa didn't come because he couldn't read Aunt Evelyn's letter, or because he didn't care. I never sent word to Ellen, or even to Peter or Tillie.

Aunt Evelyn

I married well. Philip Sutton was a banker in Newark, and when he died in 1875, he left me with a house and an income. Just no children.

Over the years I tried to do right by my niece. Martha was a smart girl. She could read and do her sums. I built on that. My house in Newark had books and fashion magazines that appealed to Martha, well, at least the magazines appealed. The girl's wardrobe and coiffure improved during her stays with me, and after. Her dressmaking improved too. The dresses she fashioned with that dour sister may not have given the House of Worth competition, but they were more than ordinary. She did not look like a farm woman any longer and could keep a roof over her head.

By the time of Martha's visit in 1881, I thought she would be an old maid. No one was more surprised than me when Martha started keeping company with that grocer, Wesley Savacool. I had little regard for my brother-in-law Isaac, but I felt a duty to inform him about the courtship. Reluctantly, I sent word to Isaac, a warning about Wesley. "Your daughter is stepping out with a man named Wesley Savacool. I do not approve. His income as a clerk in a grocery store is inadequate. Martha believes he owns the shop. I have reason to think otherwise. He is known to favor drink and gambling. I cautioned Martha against him but she is inattentive to me on this matter. I think it best if you add your own word of warning. Also, I must report that she has been staying out late and appears to be overly fond of him. Yours sincerely, Evelyn Wykcoff Sutton." Two weeks later I wrote again, a shorter note, when the wedding date was set. Isaac never answered either letter and never came to the wedding. I thought, unkindly, maybe there was no one to read him my note. I did not bother to send word to Martha's sisters or brother.

Mattie

For the first few years after I married Wes, we lived in Newark in a small two-room apartment above the grocery. One bedroom, one parlor with a stove in the corner, an outhouse out back. The furniture was whatever Wes plucked out of junkyards. My life with him was good for a while, especially, well, I don't mind saying, in that little bedroom. Wes knew what he was doing. I did not, but I was an eager learner. Soon I was pregnant. That lasted two months. Then I was pregnant again. Another two months. Wes didn't care one way or the other. Me, I was out of my mind to have a child. Finally, the third time, I got past two months, then three, then nine.

Harry Ross, we called him Ross, he was born on January 27, 1884. I wasn't afraid of childbirth, not me. That's what I had waited for, and I was always home when Ma birthed the little ones. Aunt Evelyn recommended a midwife. Wes hired a cheaper one. It didn't matter. I suckled Ross, as I had seen Ma do with Tillie and Peter and Eliza. But I knew that Ma never loved that feeling. She never stared at the baby on her lap. I remember thinking, how could that be? Ross was a dear baby, my baby, my baby. I was determined to do right by him. He wouldn't suffer. Remember that. I was not going to let him suffer.

For the first time ever, I was just as good as everyone else. I paraded Ross around Newark in a pram, the one my aunt bought as a gift. I smiled at all the other mamas who were doing the same thing. I wasn't on the farm. My husband wasn't covered in dung. And my only job was to care for Ross and the flat.

Now, if I am honest, I guess I could say I started to get greedy. Anyway, that's what Wes thought. All I could see was that he was stuck behind that counter. We fought. First, I just used words. I needed money, for food, for clothes, and especially for Ross. I didn't want Wesley to call the cheapest quack if Ross got pneumonia or diphtheria. Or scarlet fever like Eliza. I couldn't stop thinking about scarlet fever. I watched Ross for every sign. Pa never called any doctor when Eliza died, let alone a good doctor.

Wes wouldn't give me enough money. He said Mr. Hatfield cut his wages, due to poor business. I knew what his wages were. I did the calculations. I knew Wes went with his pot-bellied friend Richard Dorney to the Waverly Fair Races, that was just outside Newark, and to Elkwood Racetrack, that was an hour away in Oceanport. Wesley told me he always won. He puffed out his chest and smirked when he said that. He didn't come home from the track drunk and swaggering like Pa, so maybe he did win. If he did, why was there no money for me and for Ross?

Five months after Ross was born, when he was just a baby, I took him downstairs to the grocery. I remember, the morning was hot, it was July. I smelled the fruit. Not all of it was fresh. Then I smelled the meat, some of it hanging from the ceiling. Ross was getting heavy in my arms and the smells clung to my head. I saw Wes behind the counter. He was wearing that crisp apron and starched shirt, the ones I ironed for him the night before. His hair was perfect, like he took a few minutes to arrange those curls. I saw him put away canned goods. He did everything carefully. He had all the time in the world. I stood there for a minute, watching his arm go up and down, slow like. Real slow. "Buy him out," I yelled. "That damn Stuart Hatfield. He's barely paying you. You're smart, Wesley, you can do business better than him."

The store was empty. I saw Wesley draw down the corners of his mouth and glance at the door. He worried customers could come in at any minute. Once I started, I couldn't stop, and I knew that he knew that too.

"Shut up, Matt, I'm doing the best I can."

"No. Ask your parents for money. Why don't you?"

I spoke in loud words, and I stared hard at Wes. I had never met his parents.

"Show them Ross and say you need help."

Wes stared back at me. He heard my taunt. His parents were dead or penniless.

"The only way I can buy Stuart out is if I save money. And the way you're spending it that may take a hundred years."

I felt the sweat trickle from my hair to my chin, while Ross grabbed at my breast. I couldn't breathe. Starting with the bread shelves, I struck out my left arm and swiped everything onto the floor. We heard the loaves fall. Then the canned goods. Now the sound was loud. Then I started with the spice bins. It took Wes a few seconds to understand what I was doing. He ran out from behind the counter. He looked like a crazed animal. I thought he was going to kill me. I was still holding Ross with my right arm. I knew what to do. I hit my husband in the eye with my left arm. He stumbled back a few feet, holding his hand to his eye.

I felt clammy but calm. I turned around and left the store. Ross was still in my arms, sticking to my damp dress.

The second time I took Ross downstairs to the grocery that summer, I started with the vegetables. I threw them on the floor with my left arm and stomped them to a pulp with both feet. But this time Mrs. Stauffer entered with her two girls.

"Mrs. Stauffer," come over this way," Wes pleaded. "The customer had a worm in her corn, you know, that happens, and she is taking it out on the store." Mrs. Stauffer stared at me and Ross. He was screaming and twisting in my arms. Then she gawked at Wes. She pushed her children out the door ahead of her and followed them without looking back at the mess.

Wesley Savacool

I lasted four years with the bitch. Four years too long. She was mean, mean to everyone except Ross. She still slept with me, but it was different, not as good. I needed to head west or I might kill her. That was in 1885. First, I planned to stay in Philly with the brother of my pal Richard Dorney. I'd saved money, hiding it from her, well, and from others too. I had just enough to get as far as Seattle or San Francisco. I was always lucky at the races, at least that's how I remember it. Later, much later, that luck led me to a new life.

I knew I should just walk away, alone. At the last minute, I decided not to leave Ross. He was such a sweet kid, even-tempered. And Ross was not to blame for his mother. Maybe I just wanted to hurt her, hurt her bad. So I started off by train with the boy. I waited until a Sunday when Mattie visited her Aunt Evelyn.

"No need to bring Ross with you to Evelyn's. I'll watch him. We'll walk in Branchburg Park." She gave me an odd look. I hardly ever took Ross out. But I guess she wanted time to herself.

Mattie

A few hours of freedom with Aunt Evelyn. I remember it was the day Grover Cleveland became president. And I remember because that was also the third-worst day of my life.

Aunt Evelyn was the only kin I ever saw. Pa was little more than a ghost and Ellen and Tillie were no longer part of my life. Aunt Evelyn didn't turn away, even though I knew she hated Wes. That day we had tea and gossiped about the neighborhood. Then I went back home. The flat was dark and cold. I saw a note on the table. "Have taken Ross to Philadelphia. Will not return. Marriage not working. Do not try to find us."

Fast, I grabbed the butcher knife, put it in a satchel, and ran down the street to Richard Dorney's apartment. Wes's paunchy friend. He had a brother in Philly. I knocked, loud. He opened the door and peeked out. I pushed past him and stepped inside. I drew out the knife. He was too shocked to move. I had it on his fat throat in two seconds. In two more seconds, he gave me the address of his brother in Philadelphia. I ran to Newark's railroad station. Two hours later—I have no idea what I was thinking for those hours—I was in Philadelphia. Took me thirty minutes to find the apartment and three minutes to walk away with Ross. He was a mess. Wes forgot to take diapers, even though Ross was only one year old. After five hours with Ross, Wes knew the baby would be too much for him. My husband did not put up a fight. All he wanted was to move on west.

Thirteen years later, according to the dozen newspapers I read in my cell, none of the reporters got all of the story right. Some said Wes left me. Just as many said I left Wes. Some said Wes went west. Just as many said he died or wrote that I said he died. Some said, and they were right, that Wes and I divorced. Just as many said I should be charged with bigamy along with the other crimes. Not one of the reporters knew that Wes was alive and well, in Seattle, under the name of Wesley L. May. I only found out because much later my lawyer, the one who was more crafty than smart, dug around. When Wes left me, I didn't know about his debts, either.

Within a few months of Wes hot-footing off, life got worse. I took in a little sewing. Mostly hems and cuffs and collars. The dressmakers in Newark were what Aunt Evelyn called well-established. There wasn't much room for a new business. I begged my aunt for help. She had lost patience when Wesley walked away. I knew what she thought. She warned me about him. Now that the worst had happened, she let her anger well up. I deserved what I got. After he left, she loaned me a tiny bit of money, just crumbs, with a smug look on her face. One afternoon I put on a nice dress, one I had just fashioned so I'd look respectable, to visit her and ask for a little loan. I didn't know it would be the last visit. Evelyn took her time offering me tea. She didn't offer her usual pastries.

"My literary club, Martha, the one that meets the second Tuesday of every month. Two of the ladies, Mrs. Patterson and Mrs. Kruger, they took me aside." She was shaking as she talked. "You must know what I am going to say. You overcharged them. When you delivered their sewing, you asked for more money than you had agreed on."

"Well, those repairs, they were more work. Much more work."

"Martha, even if that is true, it doesn't matter. You should have honored the price."

That uppity tone. What did she know about business or being poor? I slammed my cup down. Tea spilled on her white tablecloth. Ross, he was playing nicely on the floor, he started to howl. I grabbed him and ran. I slammed the front door. Didn't say a word.

There was no one else. Peter, my brother, couldn't help. He was married now, with two daughters. I didn't ask him. I'd never ask Ellen. I hadn't seen Tillie in years. I wrote to Richard Dorney's brother in Philadelphia, at the address where I found Wes and Ross. I begged that brother to write Wes and ask him to send money for Ross's food. The man never helped. I knocked on Richard Dorney's door to ask him to write Wes. Richard must have remembered the butcher knife because this time he wouldn't let me in. By the fall of 1886, I was three months behind on the rent. Then two thugs, sharply dressed they were, came to the door. One was Wes's age. But muscular. The older one was about fifty and almost as burly. They demanded the money Wes owed them. I looked at their eyes and saw they were staring down at Ross. He was playing on the floor. I went into my purse. Brought it to the door so they could see me open it. I pulled out all the money and threw it at them. The younger one picked it up from the floor. Counted it out. The old one scowled at me, then at the younger one. The old one said this was one-quarter of what Wes owed them. Maybe he was lying, but I knew Wes had debts. Maybe they were happy to have what I gave them. Don't know. They turned around and left. I couldn't tell if they knew they would not get more, or if they would be back.

On October 24, 1886, I petitioned John McLorian, the poor master of Newark, for relief. Some call it charity. I told him I couldn't support my child. How was I to know that the poor master had a clerk who was married to Aunt Evelyn's maid? The blabby clerk, a self-righteous asshole, told McLorian that Aunt Evelyn should be the one helping me. The black-hearted poor master called me into his office to say his charge was to help people with no other means of support. Not anyone else. So, he discontinued my case. No help. Nothing.

Ellen was the only one left. I hadn't talked to my sister for five years. "Ellen," I wrote, "Wesley left me last year. I have no money. I am coming to Asbury Park tomorrow." I knew better than to ask. And I knew better than to tell Ellen I would arrive with a child.

The dressmaking business, the one me and Ellen started together, was failing when she tried to run it herself. She had talent with pattern making and sewing, I'll give her that. But she couldn't drum up business and she was bad with money, with what Aunt Evelyn and my second husband Will called finances. When Ellen and I were working together I made sure the customers who wanted to place a second order paid first for their original order, so there was money to buy the silks and muslins. Ellen never thought that way. Now that I was going back, maybe I could fix how the business worked. It wasn't going to be easy. It would take months.

I sold my wedding ring for train fare and skipped out on the rent I owed. All my possessions were crammed into two bags I hauled on my shoulder, along with Ross. By the time we arrived in Asbury Park I was drenched with sweat, right through my winter wrap, and Ross was whining with hunger. I'll never forget Ellen's face when she saw me come in with a three-year-old child. She didn't know about him. After an hour, her look, that look of surprise, that went away. Her sour face took its place. In a week, I knew this arrangement wouldn't work.

I'm going to talk through this next part quickly. I can't linger.

I wrote the pastor at the Belleville Dutch Reformed Church, where I got married. He answered me in a few days. The next Sunday I used my last dollar for a buggy ride to the Colts Neck Reformed Church. Not far. I brought Ross along. Hugged him to me the whole way. He sat on my lap during the service, and I saw Pastor Mortenson look at him from the pulpit. After the service, I asked the pastor to talk in his little office next to the church. He was not a kindly-looking man, but he would have to do. He motioned me to the chair in front of his desk.

"I am Martha Garretson Savacool," I said. I had to remember to hold my head upright and to take deep breaths. "I got your name from your friend, the pastor at the Belleville Dutch Reformed Church. He married Mr. Savacool and me, five years ago." With that out of the way, I slumped and cried. First time since Eliza died. Pastor Mortenson put his hand on my shoulder. I told him the rest of the story while he clicked his tongue and asked too many questions. He stared at Ross, who was sitting on my lap. I don't think Ross knew what I was saying, but he knew something was wrong. He grabbed my hand and used his hand to wipe away my tears.

Over the next week, I waited for word.

A messenger arrived at the Asbury Park flat with a letter from Pastor Mortenson. The family—the Aschenbachs—were waiting for Ross. Their home was in Vailsburg, close to Newark. They had just lost a son to illness and thought another child would help them heal. The family was wealthy. Ross would learn their harness-making business and be set up for a profession. He would be fed, clothed, sheltered, and, Pastor Mortenson wrote, loved. In the envelope with the letter was money for train fare to Newark. Enough for round-trip train fare for one person and one-way fare for a child.

Twelve years later the newspapers, again, could not get the story right. When I said, or people I know said, Ross was adopted, some reporters wrote that I had an adopted son. Some other reporters wrote that I put my child up for adoption, abandoning him. No one understood that I never, never, never recovered from that train trip to Newark, from kissing my dear boy goodbye and handing him to Mrs. Aschenbach. If you are counting, that was the worst day of my life. Much later, we'll get to the second-worst day.

Evelyn Wykoff Sutton

You probably think I am an evil woman, refusing charity to my niece Martha. I can never be certain I acted properly. I did seek guidance from my minister in the summer and fall of 1886. As I said, I decided long ago to take Martha under my wing, away from that dreadful farm where her father worked her near to death. I brought her into my home for summers and exposed her to the culture she never had in East Millstone. Well, I tried to. She had a knack for fashion and picked that up quickly. Literature and music, no, she showed no interest. I decided simply to accept her preferences. She and I talked a lot about dress styles and spent time with suitable magazines and walking through the stores that catered to the carriage trade. There was more, too. From my husband, Philip Sutton, he was a banker, I learned a great deal about business, billing, receivables, and so forth, practices that helped me manage my household staff and that could help Martha as a dressmaker.

I didn't see that courtship, if you want to call it that, coming. To this day I don't know if she set her cap for Wesley Savacool or if he had designs on her. I warned her against him. There were rumors in the neighborhood. Even without those rumors, you could tell when you saw him in the grocery. He was a smooth talker, but unambitious and immoral. As I look back on this, I suppose she simply wanted romance, and that I could not offer.

My heart was broken when Martha married that scoundrel. I stuck with her anyway. As long as I could. I learned, again from neighbors, that her behavior in the marriage was erratic. I noticed, too, that she spent money on her own clothes and clothes for her son, though money could not have been plentiful in that household. I can't say I was shocked when Wesley ran out on her. He was a cad but living with a cad was not as bad as the shame of abandonment.

I helped out a bit, until I saw that my money was not going for rent and food. Every time Martha visited, she had on a new dress. She sewed these dresses herself, but she used money, perhaps my money, for the materials.

The final straw for me came when my friends took me aside to tell me how Martha overcharged them. I had persuaded these ladies, they were part of Newark's social set, to hire Martha for small sewing tasks, hems and collars, and such. She overcharged them, both of them. I was humiliated. That's when I spoke to Reverend Vrelandt, explaining what I had done for Martha and how little it helped. In the past, I said to him, you have counseled us in your congregation on love and charity. But my charity has not helped my niece. Reverend Vrelandt took out his Bible, opened it, and read more passages than I can remember. There was the usual passage in Acts 20:35. It is more blessed to give than to receive. And the passage from Leviticus 19:11. You shall not steal; you shall not deal falsely; you shall not lie to one another." And maybe ten more. "Reverend Vrelandt," I said, "how do I balance the teachings?"

"You must reread the scriptures and follow your heart." My heart had hardened.

Mattie

Starting in 1886, after I let Ross go, once a month I made the trip north to the Aschenbachs. They lived in a nice house near Newark. Brick, three stories, carriage house in back. I brought Ross shirts I had sewn and sometimes a toy that one of my customers had no use for any longer. The customers, and there were not many of them, thought the boy was still at home. In the beginning, when Ross was three, he ran to me, with hugs and tears. As time went on, he changed. I knew he would. By the time he was five, he wasn't excited by my visits. When I came to Newark he couldn't play with his friends there, or I'd take him away from Sunday supper, or from trips to the country. The Aschenbachs weren't happy about my visits, but they didn't make trouble. The adoption had been arranged by the church, but not yet by the state. I could see Ross led a good life as he grew up, and I knew that Mr. Aschenbach planned to apprentice the boy to one of his brothers. All the brothers were in the harness business. That was a big business in Newark. At first, I dreamed, you know, that I could get Ross back one day, take him home with me to Asbury Park. The dressmaking business didn't improve enough for that and Ellen wouldn't have agreed anyway. I told myself to give up.

I was sad and alone those years in Asbury Park, between the time I let Ross go and when my life changed, seven years later. I say alone because Ellen wasn't much company. But just as I had followed the news years before, I kept up with what was going on. I was always interested in inventions, starting with the sewing machine, that miracle machine that would make work easier if Ellen and me could ever afford one. And I read about other inventions that seemed like they would help people, not hurt them. Ha, what did I know? That man, Tesla, the one from Serbia, he came up with alternating current. Damned A.C. But here's the worst. An evil man named Alfred Southwick invented the electric chair.

I need to talk more about the electric chair. It's almost all I think about now. In 1889, everyone was talking about the chair. Even me and Ellen. We knew the murderer William Kemmler deserved what he got. He was drunk, in a rage, when he murdered his wife in Buffalo. Reporters called her his common-law wife so I suppose they never married. Drunk husbands murder their wives all the time. Mostly, they hang for it. But Kemmler was sentenced to electrocution, the first ever. You probably remember that it didn't go well. The newspapers reported problems with the alternating current. How they set it or something. The man in charge of the chair—I wish I didn't know his name but it was Edwin Davis—gave Kemmler 1000 volts. He kept breathing. Davis upped it to 2000 volts. Kemmler's skin turned black and burned. Smoke came out of his head. The witnesses smelled sizzling flesh. They heard him gasp. Froth oozed from his mouth. Why do I remember this, long after I read the stories? Maybe because the chair was a new invention. Or maybe I sensed what was coming. Or maybe the picture of Kemmler roasting was so awful that it stuck.

Remember the war between Westinghouse and Edison? Westinghouse pushed for alternating current, while Edison pushed for direct current. The electric chair used alternating current and Westinghouse wasn't happy that his plan would be connected to death. People might think if they used his alternating current they would die. Edison got his way—the chair used Westinghouse's current, scaring customers. Westinghouse was disgusted. So, when he heard how Sing Sing botched Kemmler's execution, he said, "they would have done better with an axe."

Ross Savacool

You're going to ask me if I remember the woman named Martha Place. She gave me up so early that I don't remember her as my Ma. My Mama was Maria Aschenbach. But I know the woman said she was my Ma. I do remember one day, January 28, 1892, the day after my eighth birthday. Mama wouldn't let the woman visit me on my birthday, but she let her come the next day. It was freezing cold. The woman couldn't take me on a walk like usual. Just sat around, not doing anything. The woman brought some shirts she sewed herself. And a toy streetcar. My Mama let me play with the streetcar, but she took the shirts away and I never saw them again.

The woman was nice to me. I never had a problem with her. But my Mama and Papa brooded over us when the woman came. Mama would sew in the next room or Papa would walk behind us if we went to the park. I didn't know how to play or how to talk with all those people around.

Mattie

Anna Mann. She was one of three or four Asbury Park ladies who were reliable customers for me and Ellen. Reliable as long as we charged less than the other seamstresses in town. One day, it was late August of 1893, I was adjusting a long cloak I had delivered to Anna. I was on the floor in the parlor, on a level with the curved Chippendale chair legs, with straight pins in my mouth. My knees hurt even though the rug was plush. I hoped no one noticed the beads of sweat falling on the carpet. Right then Anna's sister Jennie and her brother-in-law Charles arrived from Brooklyn for a visit. Anna heard them knock and told the maid to bring them into the room where I was doing the fitting. Anna didn't introduce me to them, not at first. She turned to welcome them as I kept pinning. After a while, I heard Anna and Jennie talk about Charles's brother, William Place. He lived in Brooklyn too. Seemed like his wife had died, maybe that year. Jennie said he had hired a housekeeper, but the woman had another commitment and couldn't begin for two months. Now William needed a housekeeper, just a temporary housekeeper, to fill in for that time. Funny, I remember that my knees hurt. I kept listening to the Mann sisters talk. Brooklyn. I had never been there. It was far from Asbury Park, but close enough to Ross in Newark. Keeping my head down and my eyes up, I saw that Anna's sister wore a lovely dress, mauve silk, and Charles—like I said he was Jennie's husband, Anna's brother-in-law—dressed fashionably. A fine wool gray waistcoat, and dark trousers. He was a businessman, a banker. I remember thinking that maybe Charles's brother William, the one who needed a housekeeper, was well-off too. Could I leave Ellen? For just two months. Didn't take me long to decide. Ellen could rot for all I cared. I spoke up. I asked a question about the position. Anna understood. She motioned to me to stand. Then she introduced me to Jennie and Charles Place. "Would you consider offering a referral?" I asked Anna. I suppose it was an awkward question, with Jennie and Charles standing right there. Anna nodded, bobbing her head up and down and looking squarely at her sister and brother-in-law.

The rest happened fast. A week later, William Place came to Asbury Park to visit his sister-in-law Anna. She said her parlor, the same one where I had pinned her hem, would be fine for a job interview. I picked my clothes carefully that day. I wore a somber but tasteful green dress, no overskirt. A man about my age and height came into the parlor. I was waiting for him on the settee. At least this time I was not kneeling on the floor in that parlor. The man was slim, good-looking, well-dressed, just as I expected. He had a mustache and dark hair, parted in the middle like I remembered Wes's hair, and curling up on the sides. But his face was rounder, puffier. He smiled just a little when he spotted me. I could tell right away from his expression that he was impressed. I looked neat, like a housekeeper should. For me, I was impressed with him. I had never worked for someone before since dressmaking is piecework. I wasn't sure what I wanted, but this man had money and, well, he seemed stable. He wasn't much of a talker, not then. My salary, he said, would be $16 per month, plus room and board. I would keep the house clean and tidy, purchase food, cook, and do the washing. His daughter Ida was twelve. She attended school in Brooklyn. Caring for her would not take up much time. He went over the housekeeper's responsibilities. The arrangements were fine with me. So I left Ellen, I left Asbury Park for good, and three days later I arrived at work as Will's temporary housekeeper in Brooklyn.

Five years afterward, the reporters never figured out how Will and I met. Some wrote that Martha Garretson Savacool Place met William W. Place in Asbury Park when he lived there. He never lived in Asbury Park. Other reporters said I answered an ad for a housekeeper. Will never placed an ad, never had to. A few wrote that I met Will in my home in Johnsonburg, New Jersey. That's in the northwest part of New Jersey, far from East Millstone. One more said we met in Newark, the night before Thanksgiving. Wrong too. I learned not to trust those stupid reporters. None of them figured out that Anna Mann was the connection. And that lady must have blamed herself forever.

On a beautiful afternoon in late August, I took the train to New York, further than I had ever gone, and, for the first time, I rode a streetcar to Brooklyn. I was forty-four, but I'd never been out of New Jersey until that day. I saw well-dressed couples walking along the paved sidewalks. The small yards looked cared for, with flowers blooming on front stoops. I walked from the streetcar stop to 598 Hancock, between Reid and Stuyvesant Avenues. Such a nice house Mr. Place had, built just a decade earlier. Red brick, two stories above a basement. In Stuyvesant Heights, a grand neighborhood. New rowhouses, fine people. High class. I learned that the neighbor on one side, Mr. Dawson, Jim, was almost as much of a talker as the neighbor on the other side, Mr. Thompson. Thompson's full name was, I'm not joshing, Napoleon Bonaparte Thompson. We called him N.B. when we talked about him, that first year anyway, when we were talking. I learned a lot of gossip when I went into the back yard if one or the other of those neighbor men were out in their own back yards, maybe tending to their gardens or chopping wood. They never seemed to go to any office. Jim Dawson had no wife. N.B. did, her name was Ella, and sometimes she was outside too. She was less of a talker. Anyway, Dawson said that the first Mrs. Place, Laura was her name, had been a frugal lady who helped Will, I called him Mr. Place back then, save enough to move to Stuyvesant Heights. Dawson was an out-of-work bank teller. He talked a lot about money when he told me Place family stories. He didn't hold back from telling me about all those deaths the Places had seen, in this house and the one they lived in before. Almost as bad as the Garretsons.

Will's house was easy to keep clean. On the first floor, we called it the first floor even though it was up a flight of eight stairs, there was a front parlor, a back parlor, dining room, kitchen, and porch in the rear. Nice furniture, pretty wallpaper. Two big bedrooms and a small maid's room were on the top floor. We had a bathroom off the hall, a bathroom with plumbing. Will slept in the front bedroom. His twelve-year-old daughter, Ida, slept in the back bedroom. I was happy in the maid's room. Will warned me that the previous housekeeper was sloppy, but I found little to bother about besides dust.

I smiled when I saw Ida for the first time. She was a lovely child, with small features and thick black curly hair. She was the only surviving child of five, I soon learned from Will and again from Jim Dawson. Will doted on his daughter. He sang with her at the piano. He let her watch when he developed photographs. That was his new hobby. He bought her whatever she asked for. I followed Will's lead. I catered to the girl, cleaning her room first, making sure she had fresh linens, offering to mend. Ida expected my help.

At first, I shopped for the meals, prepared them, then ate alone, either in the kitchen after Will and Ida ate, or in my maid's room. After a week Will asked me to eat with them, at the dining room table. Two weeks later, I waited to wash the kitchen floor until about the time I knew Will would leave for work but could see me from the front hall. I lowered myself to my hands and knees, with a pail next to me. That evening he told me to hire a day girl for the harder cleaning. A month later, Will asked if I wanted to take a walk in the nearby park with him. We talked about Brooklyn, and Ida, and the hurricane in Mississippi that killed two thousand people. I liked talking with him. He was beginning to talk more than when I first met him. A few days later Will had two tickets for a concert. Ida was going, he said, but then she wanted to go to a party with friends instead. Will asked me to join him. I didn't tell him it was the first concert I ever went to. Maybe he guessed. That night I didn't wear one of the plain dresses I cleaned in. Instead, I fixed up a gown, adding trim, and I looked nice. The next morning, he sent a telegram to Caroline Wilson, the housekeeper who was supposed to start in a week so I could go back to Asbury Park. Remember, I was just temporary then. He told Mrs. Wilson her services were no longer needed.

Like with Wes, I had no reason to wait. But I slept in the maid's room, barely big enough for a cot, and it was right on the other side of Ida's room. When we got back home after the concert, I saw that Ida's hat and coat were not on the coat rack yet.

"William, such a lovely concert. Should we end it with a cognac?"

"Excellent idea."

He sat in the parlor, smoking his smelly cigar and waiting for his drink. I brought it in on a tray, one glass for each of us. He drank the cognac quickly, too quickly. Then I left for the kitchen and returned with another.

"There is a cozier place to drink this second one," I said.

Will was not Wes in bed. You don't want to hear about this, I know, but it might help you understand how we got together, or how Will thought about things later. Maybe Will was out of practice, or overeager. He seemed surprised when I reversed positions, but not unhappy. We took our time, but we still finished before Ida returned. The next day I fixed him another cognac. I guess he thought that was our signal. This time Ida was at home, so Will set up a little cot in the basement, far from Ida's room. I remember the sour smell of chemicals from his photography equipment. He kept the bottles in his desk, too close to the cot. I showed him another position too. Six years later I said a little less about shagging to Miss Meury and Reverend Cole, and a lot more to the matrons.

For the next week, I thought every minute about what I would say. How much would I tell him? Nothing? Lying came easily, I didn't even use that word to myself. Or should I make demands since this was my best chance? I went about my household tasks with energy, making sure Will saw that. I wasn't sure what to do.

William Place

Laura, my first wife, died in 1892. By the end of 1893, I was married again, to Martha. I did not think for long about the wisdom of remarriage. It fell into my lap. Martha was good company, kept a clean house, and she got on with Ida. I knew Martha was not well educated, but she enjoyed the concert

I took her to. She could learn.

"Yes, William, it will be my honor to marry you," she answered in a stilted way, with a smile. Then her forehead tightened, and she paused a minute, took a breath.

"There's one thing I need to tell you first. To be fair to you."

I was pretty sure she would tell me of liaisons. In that instant, I tried to decide what I would do.

"You know I was married before. You think that I had no children, maybe that I couldn't have children. I did. I had a little boy, Ross."

I breathed a sigh of relief. She had lost her boy. Well, I had lost my boy too, William Herbert Place, when he was still an infant.

"I had to put Ross up for adoption. He is with a wealthy family in Newark. I see him from time to time. He might visit here once or twice."

I breathed out. A relief. I smiled, patted Mattie on the back, and put the ring on her finger.

That was the biggest mistake of my life. How could a woman put her child, her own child, up for adoption? Cruel. And why didn't I think harder about the boy visiting? Everything was laid out for me then and I was a damn fool. I was thinking that with Martha I had everything—a housekeeper, a stepmother, a, well, I'll say it, a wench. God punishes me.

Mattie

The wedding on November 19, 1893, was simple, a second wedding for both of us. Reverend Ostrander from the Jane Street Methodist Episcopal Church married us, even though Will did not attend church much. I should have been in mourning. My sister Tillie, pretty Tillie, the prettiest one of us, died of consumption a few days before. She was forty. The doctor called it tuberculosis. I didn't learn about Tillie from Ellen. That sister was still sewing in Asbury Park. I learned from a telegram Peter sent. Another Garretson, I thought, to sleep alongside my dead brothers and sister Eliza. Will thought I might want to postpone the wedding a few weeks. No. What was another death to me?

Not a soul from Will's family came to the wedding. They were respectful enough to me when they thought I was a housekeeper. They just didn't want me as Will's wife. Charles Place—the first brother I met—he and Jennie lived close by in Brooklyn, a block east and on the other side of the street from Will. The other brother, Theodore, was married to Laura, the same name as Will's first wife. They lived three miles to the west, still in Brooklyn. I knew Will's brothers warned him not to marry his housekeeper. Not hard to figure that out. At dinner at Theodore's house that fall, when we were all crowded into the dining room, everyone was chattering and the china and stemware were clinking. I went into the kitchen to fetch the salt. Jennie and Laura—the brothers' wives were in the same set and they liked each other—probably thought no one could hear them. But I heard Jennie, say something like this, all fancy words. "Laura, the future Mrs. Place might be an immaculate housekeeper and well-dressed. But I know from my sister Anna and her Asbury Park friends that Martha is uncultured, unsophisticated, the daughter of a poor farmer. Her style is too flamboyant. Let's be truthful, she is beneath us." When I heard that I lifted my chin, pushed up my nose, and entered the dining room again. I did not look at those women.

For a few days, I stewed, waiting for a time to slap back. I knew I would see Will's relatives again at an engagement party for Theodore's son. I told Will he had to compliment me there in front of Jennie and Laura. He didn't need to know why. So at the engagement dinner, he said to them, and firmly like I told him to, that I was good to Ida and that Ida was happy to have me as a stepmother. Jennie's mouth grew tight, like it did when she was annoyed. She said nothing. As I expected, no one in those families—Charles' family and Theodore's family—attended the wedding. None of my kin attended either. Isaac had died a few years before, alone, on that godawful farm in East Millstone. Peter was busy with his job on the railroad. Ellen was still mad I abandoned her.

The night of the wedding I moved out of the little servant's room, to the front bedroom. To Will's bed. The same bed where his first wife died. I tried not to think of that. I asked Ida to help carry my clothes and shoes, I didn't have much, from the little bedroom to Will's. Ida was playing the piano. She didn't get up.

The first year me and Will were married, I was happier than I ever was, well, since my early days with Wes. This was even better—I was living in a brick row house, not an apartment over a grocery. I had a bathroom, not a shack in back. I had money for nice clothes and for fabric. Will liked my housekeeping, or now, I should say my management of the household. Does that sound snooty enough? See, he hired back Helen. She was the maid who worked for the Place family before she made a visit back to her dying Ma in Ireland. Took her Ma a year to die. Now I had Helen for the heavy work. I could live like a lady. And Ida, like I said, was a charming girl, a lovely child.

Within a year she started her bleeding. I came across Ida talking, hushed like, to Helen. Some piece of cloth was crumpled up in Ida's hand. "Ida, come here. You will talk to me about that. I can show you what to do. None of Helen's business." Soon after that, Ida burst out of her blouses. I offered to fashion new ones. She wanted to go to the dressmaker her girlfriends hired. I had to admit, that girl was a looker. She was soft looking, with a shapely figure. Her skin was dewy, not like mine. I had the skin of the hard-working daughter of a farmer. The neighborhood boys noticed Ida. Every time the mail carrier came to the door, Ida got another invitation, to a dance or a musical evening. Or a birthday party. Ida needed a dress for each event. That's what she called them, events. The talk between Will and Ida was always the same, she always got what she wanted. Sometimes I heard them talking when I wasn't in the room. Sometimes I didn't hear, but I could tell from the packages that came later. "Papa," she'd say, "Susannah's concert is in three weeks. The crowd from the church choir will be there. And from the French class." French class. Then, "You can't ask me to wear the same frock I wore to the Sunday school reception."

"Ask your stepmother to make you a new gown."

"Papa, my crowd is hiring Eleanor Cornwall. She knows all the fashions. I am not going to tell them my step-mother is sewing for me."

"How much money do you need?"

The same, every time. But when I asked for money for shoes or a new hat, Will puffed more on his smelly cigar and groaned. "Save that from your monthly household allowance." I needed to skim money from that allowance for other things.

Still, we spent time together, Ida and me. After she came home from school or on Saturdays we shopped. For rugs at Frederick Loeser & Company, shoes at Battermans, gloves at Abraham and Straus. Brooklyn, you know, it's bustling. Shops and people on the sidewalks looking in the shop windows. Streetcars and trains. Not like East Millstone. Not even like Asbury Park. And we went with Will to Prospect Park for picnics and to Sheepshead Bay Racetrack. I pretended I didn't know much about horse racing. Those trips, Will called them outings, they were fun at first. I was having fun, just like the ladies I sewed for the year before, just like the ladies all around the neighborhood, Stuyvesant Heights. Didn't last long. After a year it was so hard to get on with Ida that I didn't like the outings any longer.

Soon Will's brothers and their families turned even nastier to me. Theodore and Laura. Charles and Jennie. Jennie, really Jenny's sister Anna, she led me to Will, but Jennie scorned me, didn't want to be seen with me. Laura was almost as bad. What did they have to be so high and mighty about? Even Helen, our maid, knew what was going on, the bad blood. Helen's aunt did the laundry and cooking for Theodore's wife, Laura.

"Helen, your aunt Irene, the washerwoman. Does she have a free day to help here with the heavy cleaning?" I asked. "Theodore and Laura are away in the Adirondacks this week, right? And we could use the help."

"No mam, they are still in Brooklyn. My aunt is busy at their house."

Helen's face tightened when she answered me. I could see her look. She knew she was letting the cat out of the bag. You see, the next day was Ida's birthday. Will was throwing her a party. Theodore and Laura had made their excuses, sending Will a note that they would be on holiday.

All this sat heavy on me. Will's stinginess, Ida thinking she would get whatever she wanted, Laura and Jennie's snootiness. I managed because I was used to people thinking they were better than me. And getting more than me. I knew how to live with that. But the worst was Ross.

Will knew about Ross. Not at first but soon enough. I told him the day he proposed. I said I wanted Ross to visit now and then, since the Brooklyn house was lovely. On a Sunday for supper. Or for Christmas eve. Will didn't answer, not directly. I thought maybe he was disgusted that I gave up my child to another family. Or maybe he was relieved that the child was not his responsibility, that I would not expect him to be the boy's guardian or whatever you call it. Will just gave me that little smile. I went with that. Didn't say more. I waited until after the wedding, a month after. Then I started.

"I sent Ross, you know, my son, a letter last week, inviting him to Christmas dinner. I heard from him and from that Newark family this morning. He's coming. He'll take the train and sleep in Helen's room. I'll pick him up in Manhattan and take him here on the streetcar. Helen can stay with her aunt for a few days."

Will looked at Ida. I knew he had told her about Ross. I'm guessing he made it clear to her, maybe said it again and again, that Ross lived in New Jersey. Ida pouted with that pretty little mouth of hers. "I've never met him," she said. "Isn't Christmas for family? Papa, did you know about this? Did you say yes?"

I glared at Ida. "He's coming. You will meet him. He's your step-brother."

The holiday did not go well. There was a problem with gifts. Ross didn't bring any. I gave him a few. Of course, I used Will's money. That's one of the reasons I was skimming from my allowance. Then anyway. Will gave Ida lots of gifts. And he gave me diamond earrings—his best gift, one you'll hear about later. But Ross coming without gifts was only the first problem. Remember, in late 1893 Ida just turned thirteen. Ross was nine, almost ten. I know he was an awkward boy, slow to talk, I could see that, and maybe a bit pudgy. I heard Ida tell one of her friends that Ross smelled of the Aschenbachs' harness business. I was not stupid. I knew Ross did not fit into Ida's idea of a family. I didn't care. I loved that boy.

After a few days, I took Ross back to Manhattan and put him on the train to his Newark family. It was December 27, 1893. I marked my calendar for two months. Then I invited him back. I declared this at dinner a week later, after I got word that the Aschenbachs agreed. I knew they were not happy about another trip. The adoption was still not legal then, so they didn't want to anger me. And maybe Ross was not happy about another visit, if he remembered how Ida treated him. Turned out it didn't matter because this time Will spoke up.

"If you want to see him, you go to Newark. Don't have him come here. Ida doesn't want him in the house. She shouldn't have to have him. He's not her sort."

"You're listening to her, and not to me? I'm your wife. I'm the one you married."

Ida walked away from the table, with loud, heavy steps, with her back toward me. Maybe I couldn't see her face, but you can be sure she had a smug smile. She knew Will and I would keep arguing. She knew her Papa would win.

I did not give up. I called on the Aschenbachs. I wanted to explain that my circumstances had improved. I wore my finest dress and I used proper language. I could do that when I needed to. My plan was simple. I wanted Ross back, even if it meant angering Will. And looking back I suppose Ross would have been mad too. The Aschenbachs had taken care of him for seven years. He liked them. I was selfish. Ross was my flesh and blood. He was the only thing that was mine, all mine, and then he wasn't mine.

The Aschenbachs had a fine house, finer than Will's. A maid brought me through the center hall into their parlor. She wouldn't even look at me. Mr. Aschenbach pointed to a chair, across from the settee where he and his wife sat, upright. I sat down, on the edge too. I saw the silver tea set on the sideboard, but they never offered me tea. Not even water. They listened to me talk about Will and the house and Stuyvesant Heights. They looked at each other. Then Mr. Aschenbach looked at me, cold like, fists clenched. He growled, telling me to leave. I don't remember the vile words he used. I never got to see Ross that day. Two weeks later I had a letter from a lawyer, a notification he called it. "The court has affirmed the legal right of William and Maria Aschenbach to raise to adulthood Harry Ross Savacool." And you should know, the lawyer wrote, "Harry Ross Savacool is now named William Aschenbach, Jr." That was the name of the son who died a few months before I gave up Ross. My son was not enough for them.

They took his name away from me too. I could continue to visit, once a month, for two hours. In a separate note, enclosed with the notification, the lawyer wrote that I should be grateful for the visiting provision, which Mrs. Aschenbach had insisted on, despite her husband's disapproval.

Ida Place

I did not need another brother. I had a brother, once. William Herbert Place. Of course, I never knew him. William died at age two, eight years before I was born. I never knew my sister Hattie either. Hattie died at age three, five years before I was born. I did know Edith and Florence. Edith died at age eight, when I was four. Florence died at age two, just a few days after Edith. I was the only one left. Papa could leave for work every morning. Not that he forgot William and Hattie and Edith and Florence. But he had other things to think about, his work and his clubs, those silly clubs. Mama stayed in the house. She tried to protect me from yellow fever and influenza and those mysterious sicknesses that killed my brother and sisters. Then when Mama was forty-two, the yellow fever hit her. She stopped crying and she went to heaven with her children. That was the worst day of my life, my short life. I'd just turned twelve when she died, and then I was alone with Papa. No, I didn't need another brother. I didn't need a stepmother either. That was not my idea.

Especially not this stepmother. She was so terrible to Helen, our maid, that Helen quit. She walked out one day, didn't even wait for the money Papa owed her. That was a year after Papa married the bitch. Sorry, I mostly use respectable language, but not for that woman. Helen had been good to Mama, my real Mama, nursing her and helping take care of me. After Helen left us because the bitch was mean, for three weeks we had no maid. When I got home from school my stepmother put me to work, washing floors and shaking rugs. I complained to Papa. That day the bitch backed off, until the next day.

"You call that clean?" The bitch ran her knobby fingers over the baseboard, stuck them in my face. She almost hit my nose. Then she scolded and snipped. "There's soot and dust in every corner. Don't you see it?"

"I am not a maid," I snapped back. "Papa doesn't want me to do this work."

"You're the most spoiled child in the world. When I was your age I was plowing fields and taking care of babies. You don't know how good you have it."

"My two sisters died while I was watching, five days apart. And Mama died, choking and starving she was so sick. You weren't there. You didn't see. I'm not spoiled. Bitch." That might have been the first time I said the word, not just thought it.

I felt my cheek burn when she slapped me. She swung around and went outside, walking away from the house. I checked the mirror regularly for the next few hours. The redness on my face started to fade. I rubbed it a lot. I wanted Papa to see the color when he came home. The next morning Papa said he would put an ad in the paper for a new girl. Three days later, Hilda Palm came to us.

Mattie

The reporters and the prosecutors knew that Will and me had our troubles. Our problems. They wrote that I was jealous of Ida. Maybe. They didn't see there was a lot more.

Some days I was happy. I was the lady of the house. I was the wife of William W. Place. He was a respected businessman, and like he told me all the time, a member of what he called fraternal organizations. I had a girl to do the hard cleaning. When we had extra wash I could hire a laundress for that too. So I thought it was my right, my right, to inherit the rowhouse if Will died. I knew he met with his lawyer a lot, and that he had a will. Ha. Will had a will. I didn't want to ask him what was in it. One night, probably in 1895, before he went to bed Will took his keys out of his jacket pocket, that's what he usually did, and put them on the top of the bureau. I closed my eyes but stayed awake. I would tell him I had a headache if he waked up and that I needed to find salts. I snuck out of bed, quiet like, and walked to the bureau. I palmed the key. Then I crept downstairs and opened Will's desk drawer. It usually squeaked, but I was careful. It was easy to find the will. I read it three times. I checked the date.

Calamity. I waited two weeks until Will was home and Ida was out with the church choir. I read the newspapers that day, so I had my, call it my pretense. Had a good story, a true story. I closed the parlor window and waited until Will was well into his cigar. The usual cough came. "Will, we've never discussed what will happen to me if something bad happens to you. I know you are healthy, although that cough worries me. Anything can happen. Did you read the paper this morning? The police captured those masked robbers who killed that man, that respectable man, Richard Pope, in a saloon. He was just sitting there, having a beer, and then he was bleeding on the floor. It could have been you. And then what would happen to me? And," I added swiftly, "and to Ida?" Then I waited. I didn't get up from the armchair. I could see Will's eyebrows move back from his forehead. He was thinking about lying. He wouldn't. Will always said that lying was a terrible sin. He never talked about all the other sins. For me, there was a lot worse than lying.

"Ida has been through a lot. You know that. She doesn't remember losing her brother, or one of her sisters. She does have memories of the others. Of their illnesses. And the burials. And then Laura, her mother. Ida deserves a good life. I am leaving her the house."

"William, no. Damn no. You cannot do that. I have nothing. I have lost even more than Ida." His brows twitched and his jaw tightened. I stood, my hands curled into fists. I hit the table.

"You can fry in hell before I will change my mind. Ida is my daughter, my only child."

I was ready. I had a second plan in mind if the first failed. "So leave her the house. But what about your estate?" Again, I knew he could not lie.

"The estate too."

"Write your lawyer. Now. If you leave the house to Ida, leave the estate to me."

Will didn't quarrel that time. He got up from his chair and left the room. I shook with anger. A wife should inherit from her husband. I knew Ida would marry one day. She would not need the house. I needed the house for Ross. I still called him Ross. I would never call him William like they

47

wanted me to. Maybe when Ross could get free of that family he was with, he could come to Brooklyn. And after I died, I could leave him the house.

Because, you see, Ross was always on my mind. Around the time he was twelve, that would be in 1896, I was into a routine with him. I saw him once a month, at least once a month officially, as far as the Aschenbachs knew. As long as the trains ran on a regular schedule it was easy for me to show up at his school and walk with him to his afternoon job in his uncle's harness-making shop. Those were my unofficial visits. Ross didn't look like Wes, thank God. He was still a little stout, but tall, already with broad shoulders, more like my dead brother Garret and my living brother Peter. I never stayed long when I walked with him to the shop. I never showed my face there, never wanted to get into trouble. Those people could make it hard for me. They could stop me from coming. Ross knew he shouldn't tell them about these extra visits, the unofficial ones. Some days he seemed glum. On those days I worried I couldn't trust him to keep secrets. I worried about him, all the time. The Aschenbachs were going to do what they said they would, train him in the leather business. His first job was already in the office, not the tannery. But they had two other sons and lots of cousins. Ross was shy, slow to talk. Did the Aschenbachs see he was smart? Which son would take over the harness business? Probably not Ross. How would he make his way?

Even though I knew it was a lost cause, I didn't give up on Will. Was it out of spite? Or habit? Before every holiday—Easter, Thanksgiving, Christmas—I begged Will to let me invite Ross. I did change one thing. I stopped inviting Ross on my own. I didn't want a scene after he arrived. So we had what you might call a pattern. I asked to invite Ross, Will yelled no, I swore at him, then we would slap each other. Maybe I slapped the hardest. An hour later I would stop talking to the girl, to Ida. The girl was not the child I wanted in my house. Sometimes, after these troubles, Will called for a doctor. Then I'd get a sedative. Will and the doctor called these headache powders. I knew they were stronger than regular headache powders. I didn't fight those tonics and pills and felt sad when the bottles were empty.

William Place

The triangle was uneven. Mattie detested Ida. Ida detested Mattie. I detested Mattie. Mattie detested me. I loved Ida. Ida loved her Papa. That was the shape, we each knew. Even the neighbors knew. And my brothers too. I should have known such a triangle couldn't last.

As an insurance adjustor, I spent my days in the office investigating arsonists, petty criminals, fraudsters. If I suspected serious deception, I hired a private detective, maybe a Pinkerton, to investigate whether some faker had submitted a phony claim. I could have hired one of the Pinkertons I knew to follow my wife, but I never mixed work with my private affairs. It was Ida's idea to hire Fred Fahrenkrug. Fred was engaged to Ida's best friend, Gertrude Hebbard. He was a junior detective for the American Detective Association, a fledgling company trying to compete with the Pinkertons. Fred knew a lot about Martha already, I was sure, through idle gossip with Ida and Gertrude. I faced no danger of revealing anything new to him.

By 1896, after almost three years of marriage, I sought a way out. "Follow her." That's what I said to Fred. "Follow Mrs. Place to Newark and New Brunswick. She must have a lover in one of those cities. That would not surprise me from the, well, the way she was, um, the way she was with me when she was my housekeeper, before she was my wife. If there is any funny business, any skullduggery, and I know there is, then I can seek a divorce." Yes, I was embarrassed to tell Fred that Mrs. Place might not be loyal to me, or that I saw her as a double-dealer. But I could think of no other option. Fred didn't look at me when I laid out the possible betrayal. At the time I thought he was embarrassed too.

Although I had come to detest Martha, if I am honest with myself my second marriage was not without its gratifications. With Laura I had five children, so you know we had relations. Looking back, our coupling, I now understand, had been routine and practical. With Mattie, even after a fight, I was aroused more than ever. Sometimes the harsher the fight, the more the thrill. My behavior shamed me, fueling my desperation to end the marriage. Why am I telling you of my private actions? Because I didn't blame Martha alone for what happened in that row house.

49

For a month, I notified Fred Fahrenkrug every time I learned that Martha was leaving Brooklyn for the day. Fred drew upon the skills he learned in his detective agency, taking the same train as my wife. He sat many rows away from her, with scarfs, hats, and beards for disguise. He was a handsome lad, the most handsome in Ida's circle of friends. His disguises hid his looks well. Martha never saw that he was behind her on her trips to Newark to see Ross, and on trips to New Brunswick to see her brother Peter and his children.

Fred and I met in a Manhattan pub for his final report. "She went exactly where you thought she went," he said. "To visit her son, either at his home or his school, or to visit her brother or niece in New Brunswick. But never anywhere else." Again, he did not look me in the eye. Probably felt badly that he found no misdeeds. I came close to asking Fred to be inventive, maybe for Ida's benefit. Then I remembered that I was a member of the Odd Fellows and the Royal Arcanum, fraternal organizations with standards, high standards, catering to men of integrity. To be honest, those clubs meant more to me than my Christian teachings.

I was stuck with what my brothers called, to my face, an underbred woman. The contrast between my daughter and my wife was stark. Ida read many books, as I did. I sometimes read aloud to Ida. Or she read to me. Martha had no respect for books, not even for the classics. And music. Ida loved music as much as I did. Not Martha, not even church music. And walking. I loved to walk with Ida. Martha thought walking was for errands, not exercise. And hobbies. I loved teaching Ida about photography. I showed her the chemicals and tools I kept in my desk in the cellar, while she watched me work. As her knowledge grew, she could have taken photographs herself. I was not aiming for that. I simply liked the company. Martha had no interests beyond the house—yes, she was proud of my house—and her clothes. Let me say something about her clothes. Martha was a gifted seamstress. She knew fashions. But I was never certain that her clothes fit in with the clothes of the other women in our neighborhood, or the frocks of the women married to the men in my office or in my clubs. Laura, my sister-in-law, once used the word flamboyant. Martha did favor elaborate trims and feathers. I liked that at first. Then I began to wonder if she went overboard.

Mattie

Odd, I know, that two people as mean to each other as me and Ida could love the same thing. Bicycles. I begged Will to take me to the Great Bicycle Exhibition in Madison Square Garden. He said yes after Ida asked too. Even before we got into the Garden the three of us felt the excitement. Street performers leapt into handsprings and cartwheels then held out their hands for tips. Boys selling newspapers on 26th Street darted between a jumble of horse-drawn streetcars that jockeyed for space. We saw the crowd squeezing into the Garden and followed them. We gawked at the huge hall, the hundreds of exhibits. Pennants, shields, flags, and banners hung from the ceiling, from the balconies. Colorful. Never seen anything like it. When we walked down the aisles, looking at one booth after another, salesmen handed us catalogs until we had too many to carry. I read in the newspaper that 120,000 people attended. So many companies. Sterling, Pope, Wolff, Robley, Western Wheel, Keating Wheel. Soon I knew them all. Ida learned their names too. Even Will had fun. He talked to the salesmen about technology and prices. To all those other people in the hall, the three of us looked like a happy family, in Manhattan for an outing. You know, outing was Will's word.

And Will was hooked too. In February he bought three bicycles and two sets of women's riding outfits. That was the only time he matched what he did for Ida with what he did for me. Now we each had shorter skirts, bloomers, gaiters. We could move around in those—not like the stays and tight waists in our dresses. The women's bikes looked like men's bikes, but they had a drop frame for petticoats. The bicycle shop owners called them safety bikes.

Fred Fahrenkrug, the handsome lad engaged to Ida's best friend, Gertrude—Fred taught Gertrude to ride. Then Gertrude taught Ida. Then Ida, grumbling and thinking it would never work, taught me. I was strong, with a good sense of balance. In thirty minutes, I was riding.

I suppose Will was generous with the bikes because he hoped me and Ida would ride together and we'd find it hard to argue while we peddled. Well, it didn't work. We hardly ever rode together. But each of us rode a lot, all over Brooklyn. Ida rode to school, to Sunday School, to her friends. I rode to the baker, the hatmaker, the druggist. When we quarreled, we stormed away from each other on our bikes, riding in different directions. Sometimes I shook with so much anger that I had to work hard not to wobble even though as I said I had good balance. I loved the feel of that bike, my hair flying out of the hairpins and my full sleeves, the style then was full, blowing behind me. For the first few blocks I felt peaceful. Once I rode beyond Reid and Jefferson Streets, to the outskirts of Stuyvesant Heights, I felt free. Later, in my cell, in the Raymond Street Jail, then Sing Sing, I closed my eyes and remembered the wind behind me, pushing me.

Ida Place

I always thought I would marry first. Gertrude Hebbard, supposedly my best friend, shoved her way to the front of the line. Yes, Gertrude was three months older, so maybe she was entitled, but she was not as pretty. Maybe pretty, but not as pretty. She could never do much with that thin hair.

Gertrude's fiancé, Frederick Fahrenkrug, was good-looking, I had to admit. Even better looking than Thomas Gillette. For a year or so, I had my eye on Thomas. He worked with Papa in Manhattan. I saw him there, at his desk, every few months when I had a reason, or invented a reason, to accompany Papa to the insurance agency. As the nephew of the owner of the company, Thomas had prospects. But Thomas partied with a set far from my circles. Debutants and heiresses.

So I decided to stop dreaming about Thomas, to shift my focus. I was happy to be courted by a new beau. Edward Scheidecker was nineteen, handsome, well-dressed, maybe too well dressed. Edward and I stepped out together. We went to dances at the armory. We sang in the church choir. We rode bikes together to Prospect Park. Edward had not proposed yet, not officially. That would come. My friends thought so too.

Edward was genial, easy to get along with. Papa liked him. There was another side, though. Papa asked too many questions about Edward's occupation. Edward was training to be a watchmaker, then decided that was too tedious. He enlisted in the third battalion of the 22nd New York Army Infantry, posted sometimes at Fort Jay on Governors Island. He took me there one day. Fort Jay had a stone retaining wall and a brick parapet. Impressive, like a castle. Other times Edward was posted at Fort Totten in Willets Bay, Queens. That was less impressive. When I told Papa where I was going with Edward, I usually mentioned a church event or a choir event, not the forts where he trained. No need to remind him that Edward was a soldier. For Papa that meant still a private. When Edward told Papa he would be promoted to corporal soon, Papa looked away, that move with his chin down and to the side that he gets when he doesn't believe someone. I hoped Papa wouldn't get in the way of an engagement.

"What would you think of a double wedding ceremony?" Gertrude asked me. "You could marry Edward at the same time I marry Fred."

"Yes, yes, that would be so much fun." I smiled a little. Why did she think I wanted to share the attention on such a day? Didn't she know the guests would look at me, not at her? "I'm worried about Papa. He likes Edward, I think. Who wouldn't? Ed is charming. But Papa frets about me, too much. He frets about a good match." I never mentioned Thomas Gillette to Gertrude. That was my secret, then, when my secrets were meaningless.

"If your Papa doesn't approve of Edward, stop wasting everyone's time. Find a new beau, in a hurry. I still want to have a double wedding. When you get married, you can get out of that house for good. Even though Fred can't prove any shenanigans, that woman is a shrew."

Gertrude and I had been friends for years. She knew and loved my mother, my real mother. When Papa remarried, Gertrude was shocked he chose such a coarse woman. His housekeeper! I didn't mind Gertrude saying those things to me, but I did mind that she said the same things again and again to our friends. Made Papa look bad. I couldn't wipe her slurs out of my head.

That was how things stood on a hot day in early June, 1897, just after Gertrude and I graduated high school. The four of us, Gertrude and Fred, me and Ed, we went to Steeplechase Park on Coney Island. It opened that week so there was a big crowd. We had fun, walking down the midway and eating from the food stands. Gertrude and Ed wanted to ride on the new Ferris wheel. Fred refused. "The ground is good enough for me," he said. I was tempted to try that ride with the others. But I was tempted even more to spend a few minutes on the ground with my best friend's fiancé. "I'll go another time," I said. "I just ate a sausage at that concession and my stomach might go around along with the wheel."

I did not realize that as the Ferris wheel turned, it provided a bird's eye view from many positions.

Edward Scheidecker

I remember that day, a hot day in early June 1897. I paid for two tickets for Steeplechase Park at Coney Island, and then two more tickets for the Ferris wheel. Since my sweetheart Ida didn't feel up to the ride, Fred said he would stay with her. Gertrude and I climbed into one of the hanging cages. As the wheel ascended, the cage wobbled. I reached for Gertrude's arm, to steady her. She soon figured out that she felt safest if she leaned into me and looked down at my hand. I didn't mind. She was a good looker like Ida, though she was a little sweaty that day. But Gertrude was a good friend, had been for years. I had no fear of heights, so while Gertrude was looking at, well, at my lap, I was looking out at the promenade. I saw Ida and Fred from up high, walking along the midway, with the late afternoon sun angling down on them. A few turns later, I spotted them again, this time walking closer to each other. Ida was looking at Fred, intently.

William Place

I thought of myself as a man in control of his emotions, like my father and my brothers. When Mattie was difficult, I said as little as possible. Often, I would stand up and leave whatever room was the site of our quarrel, going downstairs to my photography equipment or up the street to brother Charles's house. Other times, despite my intentions, I failed to control myself and lashed out. I never knew which it would be, and I suppose Martha didn't know either. That day in June 1897, I lashed out.

It was a muggy day, with no cross-breeze in the parlor. During the afternoon at work, I investigated a fire, as usual, but this one was particularly horrible. The day before the fire destroyed most of the buildings on Ellis Island, in the middle of the night. I was called in to consult. Along with two insurance agents from other companies, I took the ferryboat to the island to assess the damage, which the three of us estimated at $900,000. Although my company, London and Lancashire, was not the insurer, the loss appeared so great that a group of us were tasked with assessment. It was dreadful to see the buildings in ruin, but equally dreadful to realize that 250 immigrants, who barely escaped with their lives, lost all their possessions. I was told that one of the newspaper reporters had a different take on the tragedy. "The losses," he wrote, "were chiefly of clothing and personal trinkets, which probably had no great intrinsic value." I made a note to myself to ask the members of one of my fraternal organizations if they wanted to take up a collection for those poor souls. You see, as an insurance adjuster, I knew what losses could mean to people. The members would no doubt value my suggestion, my knowledge. Wonder why they had not come up with it themselves. I mentioned my concern to Martha at dinner. She sat across from me at the table, looking distracted, not listening. I remember thinking she looked old that day. I saw strands of gray, though her dress, as usual, was fashionable and becoming. Then, just as I finished my story about the impoverished immigrants, she brought up Ross again. As though Ida would let that country boy in the house another time. I yelled at Mattie to give it up. I said some things about Ross that I shouldn't have said. I had no patience left.

"The more you ask, the firmer I will be. Ross is not coming back here, not even for dinner."

She stood up, lurched forward, and slapped me. She would say I hit her too. Maybe I did. The origin hardly mattered as the punching turned serious. To be honest, she was the stronger of the two of us. I ran out the front door into the warm June evening.

"She tried to kill me," I yelled to Jim Dawson, who was outside on his front stoop trying to cool off. Jim never asked who she was. He knew. While I stood on the sidewalk, shaking, Jim ran down the street and found a policeman on patrol, Sargent Cooper. I entered the house with Cooper as protection. Martha was sitting in the corner between the hall and the parlor, mumbling. Her foul language embarrassed me. Sargent Cooper arrested her. She was held overnight in the Gates Avenue police station, on charges of physical abuse. That night Ida cooked for me and we played a piano duet together. We were, well, we were giddy. Maybe we were trying to ignore our embarrassment at the turn of events, or maybe we were celebrating because we found a way to put Martha in her place.

The next day I put on my best gray suit, the one I wore to funerals, and I walked to the Gates Avenue police station where I appeared against my wife as a complainant. Magistrate Harriman, a man of about sixty, with a paunchy belly and a no-nonsense demeanor, was in charge. I talked to him, quietly, and I suppose awkwardly, about the hitting, the punching. I explained that on previous occasions Martha threatened to hurt my daughter, my dear daughter, my only living child. I thought that might carry more weight than a story about how my wife seemed indifferent to poor immigrants. Harriman read aloud the charge against Martha and stared at me for a long time. "Mr. Place," he said. "You look like a respectable businessman. You have never been in court before. Your wife has never been in court before. My responsibility is to ask you to reconcile." He turned to Martha. "Mrs. Place, will you promise to end these quarrels? And find a way to handle disagreements more responsibly, and calmly?" Martha stood up straight, with her shoulders back and her head high. I could tell she was damned if she would look humble. She said nothing, but she nodded her head in agreement.

Then Harriman looked in my direction. I knew I had no choice, not this time anyway, though maybe there would be another time. "Magistrate Harriman, I will work with my wife to try to manage our differences without resorting to loud quarrels or physical harm." Martha glared at me as I spoke. The magistrate looked pleased, as though he had accomplished his mission. I didn't bother to disabuse him of that hope. He paroled Martha on good behavior. Then Harriman took me aside, for more of the same.

"Mr. Place. You seem like a good man, a sensible man, responsible too. Don't let this happen again. Don't let your wife take charge of the disagreements. Be the man of the house." Of course, I knew how it looked, to neighbor Dawson, to Sargent Cooper, to Magistrate Harriman. They saw a meek, browbeaten man. What I was, was beaten down. By the death of my children, the death of Laura my wife, and now by Martha. But I was less beaten than they knew. I would use my head, that was the right thing, but my fists were ready too.

I dreaded returning home, with Martha beside me. Ida would be crushed. She was looking out the window of the front parlor, watching us climb the steps to the vestibule. But I had a plan to forestall another quarrel. I would take charge. Use my mind for now. As I opened the inner door to the front hall, Ida glared me and at Martha.

"Ida and Martha," let's get settled and then speak in the parlor. Five minutes later the three of us were seated, erect, all with grim faces, on the parlor settee and chairs. "Ida, your step-mother is paroled on good behavior. She promised the magistrate that she would not provoke me, or you. For my part, I said I would not provoke her. Looking ahead, it will be good to have a separation for a while. I will speak to Mr. Vliet in New Brunswick. You remember him, Ida, he was a friend of your mother's. He owns a clothing store and factory. For years he and his wife have wanted you to visit. Spend six weeks there. Just ignore Martha's brother, Peter Garretson. He lives in that town but it's best you stay away from his family. Have a good time in New Brunswick. Then some of the tension we all feel will cool off. Martha, during this time you have no responsibility for Ida. I will be responsible, only me."

Ida and Martha both smiled. That was a miracle. So with this plan, I separated the women. I knew I would accomplish another goal too. Ida was becoming too close to that Edward Scheidecker. There was something about the lad I didn't like. Brother Charles and Brother Theo, their daughters, almost grown now, were courting too, but they found businessmen, or managers, or medical students. Why had Ida found a watchmaker turned soldier? With the rank of private. It was bad enough that my brothers thought I had married an underbred woman—that's what they called

Martha—now my daughter was getting ready to marry down too. It didn't help that Scheidecker hung around with Fred Fahrenkrug. Oh, Fred was all right for a detective, but he was not polished and never looked me in the eye. Edward was handsome, I suppose, and personable, but Ida could do better. One thing Martha and I shared was wariness about Edward. In one way that was odd, because from Martha's viewpoint the young man was not a step down. Something else was at work here. Ida reported to me that the last time Edward called on her, Martha took him aside and told him to stop his courting because Ida loved her father more than anyone else. Why would she do that? Maybe if Ida married a wealthier man, then Martha thought her own claim to the row house and my estate would have more of a chance. Or maybe she was just mean. Or maybe she didn't like Edward, was watchful of him, as I was.

My plan for that summer worked well, for a while. Ida enjoyed her time in New Brunswick, where Hendricks Vliet and his family made sure she was invited to social events. Ida wrote me, hinting that the young men of New Brunswick were paying her a great deal of attention. I could trust Hendricks Vliet to screen them for suitability. Meanwhile, Martha had a summer of freedom. She visited Ross several times and Peter and his daughter Grace, Martha's favorite. For my part, I welcomed six weeks when I was not dodging quarrels between my daughter and my wife. But one week after Ida's return to Brooklyn, the accusations, and then the silences, and then more accusations, all that started again. I sent Ida to live with Theo and Laura for a few weeks but couldn't ask them to take my daughter forever. None of this was Ida's fault. Who could blame her for loathing her stepmother? The fault was mine, not Ida's.

I had tried the investigation, handled by Fred, then the assertive approach Magistrate Harriman naively required. I had exhausted all my ideas, except for brawn, my last resort.

Ida Place

The summer of 1897 in New Brunswick was the highlight of my short life. At first, I thought I would miss Edward. He hadn't proposed yet, but

I expected him to, maybe when I returned to Brooklyn in September. We wrote a lot, especially me.

I didn't like to deceive the Vliets, my hosts. They were a good family, one of the posh families of New Brunswick. Everyone in town looked up to them. But I was away from Brooklyn, away from the bitch, away from my prying Papa. Yes, Papa was good to me, but he was serious, and sad. Always watching me. I wanted to enjoy myself. The Vliets made sure I was invited to parties and dances. I met a new set of boys who flirted with me, but they were barely out of high school. I was not interested in stepping out with children.

The person I missed most was Fred Fahrenkrug, my friend's fiancé. I was naughty. I don't regret it. When I suggested to Fred that we could meet from time to time in Newark, a halfway point between New Brunswick and Brooklyn, he grabbed at the idea and made it his own, lining up train schedules and reserving a hotel room. I told the Vliets I was visiting a school friend who moved to Newark. Fred told Gertrude he had work there, as he often did. The ninny believed him.

I wasn't sure if I truly loved Fred or if I just felt like being spiteful to Gertrude. Some days it was one, some days the other. In the Newark hotel, in bed, I let him feel my body, firm from all my bike riding and exercise. At first, I didn't understand that I could, or should, feel his body. Soon he coached me. I did know when to stop him, firmly, to clear my soul. I wasn't sure how much longer I could manage that dance.

Grace Garretson

I was surprised to see Aunt Mattie at the front door that afternoon. I hadn't seen her in a couple of years. She looked about the same, tall, slim, sturdy. Her hair was a little grayer than before, but she always dressed nicely. Pa said she thought she should look like an advertisement for her dressmaking business. I knew that since she remarried, she was not doing that work anymore.

"Pa won't be here until almost six when his train gets back to the station and he's cleared out all the luggage."

"I need to leave way before then, you know, to get back to Brooklyn for dinner. But I didn't come to see Peter. I came to see you. What are you now, fifteen? You know, you're just a little younger than Ida, she's my stepdaughter."

I knew about Ida. When I heard from some of the girls in town that the new girl's name was Ida Place, I figured it out. Ida was in New Brunswick for the summer, tossing her black curls at the boys, going to all the receptions I was mostly not invited to attend. I lived in a small house ten blocks from the big fancy house where Ida stayed with the Vliet family. Ida and me, we lived in different worlds, well, almost different. I saw some of those well-off girls in church, the First Reformed. They knew me and they were friendly with Ida that summer. But I was never near Ida outside of church. On Sunday two of those girls brought Ida along to the service. I saw them whispering as they passed me, walking down the center aisle. Ida walked in front of the girls and steered clear of our Garretson pew.

The day Aunt Mattie visited, I was still mourning for my Ma. She was sick for a long time before she died. Aunt Mattie is just checking up to make sure I'm all right, I thought. But I also guessed she wanted news of Ida. And I was curious too. I wanted to know why that stuck-up girl was spending her summer away from Brooklyn. So after I offered Aunt Mattie tea and cookies, we sat and talked. The younger children, the ones I had to look after now, played quietly for once.

"Aunt, I saw Ida Place in church last Sunday. Are the Vliets relatives of hers or something like that?"

"Oh, no. They were friends of Laura Place, Ida's ma. They wanted Ida to spend time with them for years. Will, he's my husband, he thought this summer was as good a time as ever." When Aunt Mattie talked, her fists tightened in her lap. "What do you hear about her? Is she having fun in this town?"

"A lot of parties I hear. But they are parties I'm not invited to—at the big houses on Livingston Avenue or in the Market Square Hotel. I don't see her much."

Aunt Mattie gave me a knowing look, like she understood.

"Are you going to visit her today too?"

"Of course. I can walk there from here, right?" Those fists remained tight.

We talked for a while. Aunt Mattie asked after the younger children and after Papa. I asked her about Ross, the cousin I had seen once or twice when he was little but didn't remember well. She told me he was growing tall and going to school. Then she changed the subject quicker than I expected. She wanted to talk about her bicycle riding. She also wanted to talk about my clothes.

"Grace, are you wearing some of your Ma's dresses? Do you have enough?"

I worried that she thought my dress was shabby.

"No, we gave away all Ma's clothes. Too sad to look at them. I'm getting by. Does this one look out of style?"

"Dear, I was thinking that I could send you some of my clothes, the ones that are still fine, that I've grown tired of. You could just shorten the hems a bit. Your address is 318 Seaman Street, right?" I loved my aunt. I wasn't sure I wanted the frocks of a woman in her forties, but in her own way, she cared about me.

Later that afternoon I pointed Aunt Mattie in the right direction for the Vliet house. I didn't need to watch her walk down Seaman Street to Livingston Avenue. I knew that once out of my sight she would turn left instead of right and head back to the train station.

Mattie

My scheme began on September 20th, 1897—that's what the prosecution claimed ten months later to prove premeditation. It was not so simple. Assistant District Attorney Maguire was right that I started to think about how to end my troubles then. But I didn't settle on a scheme like he said.

Ida returned from her summer in New Brunswick at the end of August. Then Will sent her to Theo's for a while, and then she came back to us. She acted like a princess, made a mess with her trunks and her laundry. I was mad and miserable for a few days. Then it was Saturday, September 18th. Will usually gave me my twenty-dollar household allowance on Saturdays. I told him all the time that twenty dollars barely covered the usual weekly expenses, milk, food, coal, wood, wages for Hilda Palm, the maid. In the past, he never bristled at my complaining or summed up the expenses himself. But he didn't like paying. He didn't give me money that Saturday. I waited two days before I brought it up. On Monday morning, the 20th, I got out my reticule and opened the drawstring wide in front of Will.

"Not on your life," he said. "You have money left from last week. I saw the receipts on the sideboard. No need for coal or wood on these warm days. You can stretch what I gave you last week."

"Bastard. Do I need to steal it from Ida? I know you give her money."

He got up from his chair, pulled out his wallet from his jacket, and grabbed bills. "Here's ten." He threw the money on the breakfast table. In a minute, he was out the door, on his way to work. I don't know if Ida heard us or not. I didn't care.

I stuffed the bills into my purse. Holding onto the banister, I stomped my feet slowly on each stair and walked to the bedroom. I grabbed writing paper and a pen. "If anything should happen to me," I wrote my niece Grace, "please take $200 for yourself and keep the rest for my son Ross when he comes of age." Nothing, then, about how to get the money.

I would kill myself, jumping off the Brooklyn Bridge. I would disappear to the West, as I guessed Wes had. I would pawn the diamond earrings Will gave me. I would murder Will and molder in jail. I would maim Ida and molder. On the morning of September 20th, I dreamed about what I might do. I didn't call my ideas options, or choices, or schemes. I didn't weigh them. I just fixed on each of them. I knew none was right. Then back to the dining room, for two glasses of whiskey. It was 9:30 in the morning. I put on my riding outfit, but not my hat, and biked four miles around Brooklyn, my face to the warm sun, my hair flying out of my topknot. I didn't mail the letter I wrote Grace, not for another five months. It would haunt me long after that.

Between the day I wrote the letter and the day that got me into terrible trouble, we had our last Christmas in Stuyvesant Heights. A holiday musicale, Ida said. Foolish. I never heard the word before. I guessed what it meant, and I was right. Ida wanted her crowd to come over for what she called an evening of singing. Of course, Will agreed. He agreed to whatever the spoiled brat wanted. Ida practiced her music the week before, pounding out those tunes on the piano. She thought they were sweet. They were just tinkling, again and again. Drove me crazy. Sometimes Edward was there, singing with her. Sometimes that friend, Fred. Or Will. They had a few songs they wanted to practice before the musicale.

Will and Edward. Not sure what to make of those two together. Will was not keen on Ida walking out with the boy. Will was snooty, still is, wanted Ida to marry someone above her station, and her station was already pretty high in my eyes. Will never stopped comparing Ida to her cousins, the children of Charles and Theodore. "Carolyn," she was Charles's daughter, "is marrying well, marrying a young shipping merchant. Why can't Ida do better?" That's the kind of thing Will said to me on the days we were talking. Not many of those days. But I knew Will liked Edward, found him fun, easy to talk to. Will was fighting with himself on what to say to Ida. I watched Ida when she talked about Edward, when she got ready to go out with him. She didn't primp much. I wasn't sure she was so keen on him either. Still not sure. I didn't say much about him, at least not to Will.

Back to the musicale. When the date arrived, I knew the plans were fine. Before Hilda went to her room for the night, she laid out the lace runner on the sideboard. She set out china platters. Cakes and pitchers of punch and lemonade. About a dozen young people knocked at the door, in groups of twos and threes, all part of Ida's set. They dressed nicely. You could tell they were happy to be there. It was December, an odd night, warm. Will opened the windows when the house got crowded. He asked me to sit in the parlor, so after a while I did, but I wasn't going to talk to those people. They wouldn't want to talk to me anyway. Then, when Will asked me to serve the lemonade, I heard Gertrude complain that it was not sweet enough. The window was right there, next to Gertrude, half-open. I took the pitcher, leaned out the window, and tossed the yellow liquid into the yard. Then I put the pitcher back on the sideboard, glanced at Gertrude and Ida, and walked upstairs. I didn't run or sulk off. I made sure Gertrude heard each of my steps. Half the guests were too busy talking to notice. A few looked at the window, then at me, then at each other. Will saw. Edward saw. They remembered the lemonade months later. When they told the story, they puffed it up, made it seem even worse.

Edward Scheidecker

I wish I could forget that winter, the worst of my life. President McKinley ordered the USS *Maine* to sail to Havana in January 1898. He wanted to tamp down tensions over whether the U.S. would go to war to save the Cubans from their Spanish oppressors. The boys in my battalion, all we talked about was whether we would be ordered to Cuba to fight. I admit—I didn't want to go to war. I may have looked good in my Army uniform, but I worried I was more of a watchmaker than a killer. After a couple months of training, I knew how to hold a gun, but I began to figure out that I'd rather hold a loupe after all.

I was on edge to begin with. And then, on top of a looming war, I had to keep an eye on Fred. Ha, my friend. He was a detective, so he had a good idea how to hide what he didn't want me to see. But I was not dumb. There were many times when Ida was too busy to practice singing or to walk in the park, when Fred was not around. I know I should have blamed Fred as much as Ida. But Ida, even though I loved her, she always had to do better than Gertrude. If Gertrude had a new dress, Ida bought a new dress. If Gertrude had a bicycle, Ida wanted one. And maybe if Gertrude had Fred, Ida wanted Fred. Or maybe I was just tense about whether I was ready for war, I don't know. My Ma, she was a widow, she liked Ida, wanted me to marry her. When I wasn't thinking about how I'd do in Cuba, I was thinking about Ida.

Mattie

I counted the weeks. Now it was February 5th, twenty Saturdays after the Saturday that I wrote Grace to keep part of my money, some would say fixing my fate. Again, Will needed to give me my weekly allowance. I hated asking for it. The whole business reminded me of my marriage with Wes, who never gave me enough money either and then deserted me.

"If you're waiting for your allowance," Will said that day, "don't. You owe Abraham and Strauss and the milliner thirty-two dollars. You think I don't know? I am going to have to pay them myself because I, yes I, care about our reputation, the reputation of this family. Your allowance goes to cover these debts, this week and part of next. Your full allowance." He had on his haughty voice.

"And Ida, Ida doesn't pile up debts?" I said. "Her clothes, her newest bike, her cab rides? Always Ida. Pretty Ida. She can have anything. Will, with me, you are a stingy shit."

I went down to the cellar to get away from him. Really, it wasn't as bad as it could be. Will thought he was so smart. He didn't figure out why I was short of funds. He didn't see the envelopes. He didn't know I was mailing five dollars a week to Ross. I reckon the Aschenbachs gave Ross what he needed. But I wanted my son to know I took care. Later I would have even more for him, one way or another. And I needed my allowance. From it I would stash away a few more dollars, for myself. Maybe I did have a scheme, like the prosecution said.

The Murder

Mattie

I can remember the day, well, most of it, Monday, February 7th, 1898, down to the minute. That's what they asked me to do. I'll give you the times, as best I recollect.

7:30 in the morning. After Will wouldn't give me my allowance on Saturday, I let two days pass before asking again. As usual. We were all—that is, Will, Ida, me—sitting at the table for breakfast. As usual. Gloomy. As usual. So, see, nothing was out of the ordinary so far. Will was dressed in his serge business suit. I brushed it down for him the night before. He read the *Brooklyn Daily Eagle.* He liked to do that because it covered his face, so he didn't have to look at me. I was already dressed for the day, in one of my older but respectable dresses. I planned to go out. Ida wore her bicycling costume but not her gaiters. Hilda poured coffee, it was too weak, and fed scraps and milk to Trilby, she was our fox terrier, and to Trilby's four puppies. I smelled the toast that Hilda brought in, burnt to a crisp again. Ida didn't care. She slathered her toast with jam. When she ate, a glob of strawberry jam sat on her lip until she licked it away. I ate quickly, a lot. I needed energy for going out or for whatever I would do that day. I knew I had to have money. Ross would expect his five dollars. I set my mind to be direct.

"I need my allowance. I will start to repay what I owe. No need for you to go to the bother."

"I said no on Saturday. I still say no."

Ida smiled at Will. That smug smile.

"Ida knows. She knows you send money to Ross. That's why you can't pay your bills, isn't it? You send my money—my money—to your brat." Will said awful things to me every day, but that was the first time he used the word brat for Ross.

"No. No. I sent him a little gift at Christmas. Of course. That's it." Turning to Ida, "Liar. Why do you lie? Always." Turning back now.

Will was not strong, but he was strong enough to hurt me. The slap grazed my cheek and my jaw. He had never hit me in front of Ida before. Ida stood up, went to the back parlor. Will didn't say anything. He followed her out. I yelled back to Will, "Why do you let her do what she wants? I will give you more grief than you can imagine." I turned to see the two of them, smiling in the back parlor, plotting, looking satisfied.

It's that breakfast I remember most. The rest of the day I remember too, but sometimes I think that what I remember might not exactly be right. There are so many newspaper articles and court records. Gossip too. Some is right I reckon, some not. Most of the time I knew what I was doing. People think I am simple. They are wrong.

Now it was 7:55. That's my best guess. Soon after that breakfast trouble, Will got ready to leave for work. Just like he did every day. At the same time I put on my hat and gloves. Empire Rose perfume too. Will gave it to me when we first married and a little was left in the flask. I stood at the top of the stairs as he walked out the inside vestibule door, then the outer door. I ran down to catch him. Stood on the stoop for a minute.

"Will, give me the money. I will go downtown to pay my bills."

No answer as he strolled down Hancock Street, pretending nothing happened. I went back inside, hid behind the lace curtains, and looked out the parlor window, a full flight above the street. Gave me a good angle. I saw Will, a half-block away, turn his neck to peek back. Ha, he could still do that for, well, for another ten hours.

A minute later Ida came into the parlor. She started to read. Sometimes I thought she read to make me feel bad. I could read, Ida knew that. I read the daily papers. I just didn't want to read all that useless fluff she liked. She put the book in her lap and started to talk. She said she would leave the house for good and I said, no, I should be the one to leave. When I get to this part of the story, I always stop for a minute. The truth is, I told my lawyers or Emilie Meury or Reverend Cole or whoever was listening, I'm not sure if that's what we said or not. I think Ida threw her book at me and then she went upstairs and I followed. Again, I'm not sure because the trouble at breakfast and what happened later drowned out what I said. I do know I went upstairs, slowly, with my hand on the railing. In my mind, I still felt that slowness. I went into my bedroom and started to pack my trunk. I was still doing everything slowly, thinking a lot. Then I remember walking down the hall and opening the door to Ida's room. Ida had slipped into her gaiters and put on the sailor hat she wore when she rode her bicycle. She looked pretty.

"You brat. Why did you lie about Ross?"

"How long have you been sending Ross money? Years?" Ida paused. "Did Papa give you that twenty on his way out?"

"None of your business."

A door creaking. Hilda opening the back door. Holding the laundry basket, trudging outside. I saw her through the window of Ida's bedroom. Hilda's breath made steam in the cold air.

"I hate you—and your bastard." Same word I heard from my pa and hers. Even worse out of Ida's mouth. At that word, she slammed the door in my face. It hit me on the same cheek Will hit at breakfast. I've been hurt worse. But that pain, added to the stinging on my cheek, rolled down into my whole body, down to my feet.

Now it was 8:15. I took the stairs to the cellar, fast. Past the furnace, past the firewood, past the axe. Will's darkroom. I knew he kept his powders, development chemicals he called them, in the small desk. On top of the desk was a glass jar. Inside the top drawer was a bottle of powder, sulfuric acid. No odor. Maybe I grabbed the bottle. Maybe I poured a quarter-inch into the glass. Or maybe I just thought about doing that. When I turned around to leave the cellar, I saw the axe, the one our handyman used to chop firewood. I grabbed it. Something extra.

I walked back upstairs, two flights, slowly, so as not to jostle the powder in the glass. If there was powder there. I held that glass tight with one hand. The axe in the other hand. Then to the bathroom, it was between the bedrooms. Or maybe I never went to the cellar desk. Maybe I went looking for powders in the bathroom for the headache coming on. I added water to the white powder in the glass. No smell. Back to the hall, still holding the glass. And the axe.

I pushed open her door. She was standing there, adjusting that ugly hat on her hair, that curly black hair. In my head, I hear the word "bastard," the word she said two minutes ago. Maybe she says it again, maybe she doesn't. "Bastard" is what I hear. My arm swings up. Eyes, lips. She screams. Collapses. Twists. Hilda, in the snow, through the window, hanging clothes. At the far side of the yard, pinning up Ida's white, stiff bloomers, moving away from the house. Hilda looking up. A minute to finish. I'm swinging. Another scream. Dropping the axe. Ida gasping. Jerking. I'm fixing my eyes on the pillow.

Soon, say at 8:50, I looked out the window again and saw Hilda staring back at the house. I reckoned she heard. She would come inside. I closed the door and went to the top of the stairs. Hilda stood in the hall, at the bottom of the stairs, looking up. I called down. "Hilda, are you there? I need to talk. Come to the front room." I put the axe in a corner, behind me, quick.

"You heard Ida scream?" Hilda didn't even nod, just looked at me. "We were arguing, you know how we do that. And you know I don't get along with Mr. Place. You hear how he quarrels with me. He hit me at breakfast, you saw, like he did before. I'm leaving him today, so we are breaking up housekeeping. I don't need your services anymore. I'll write a recommendation and you can get another job soon, maybe even here in Stuyvesant Heights. Before you leave, I'll pay your wages. But the rest of the day I have errands for you. Finish the laundry. Then knock on my bedroom door—I'll be packing my trunk and writing letters—and I'll tell you where I need you to go." Hilda frowned. Dumb frown. Didn't ask questions.

A minute later I was back in my bedroom. I heard Hilda go out again. I ran down and hid the axe in the umbrella stand near the front door until I could figure out what to do with it. Then I climbed back upstairs. I sat at the vanity table and pulled a blank notebook and pen from the drawer. I ripped out a handful of leaves from the notebook. I knew what to write. Five letters in all. One I had written to Grace months before, on the September day I quarreled with Will about my allowance. Then I wrote a second letter to Grace. Those two letters went in one packet. Then three to Peter. In the longest, I gave him instructions. Buy a nice home. Don't put any money into the old farm. Look after Ross and take him to live with you when he turns twenty-one. Writing that sentence, I pushed the pen so deeply into the paper that it almost made a hole. Keep all the clothing in the trunk for your family. Those three letters went in a second packet. Then a third packet, addressed again to Peter, waiting for my two bank books and the key to the trunk. Also, the baggage check.

Why did I write three different notes to Peter, to put in one envelope? The only one of my lawyers who gave that a minute of thought was the yokel from New Jersey. And even he didn't bring it up until it was too late to do any good. Were three letters to the same person in one envelope enough to point to insanity? Probably not. When I wrote those letters, I don't know if I was insane, but I was crazed. I had thrown that powder in her face, I'd done it, and now I had to figure out what to do next. The train, the trunk, the money, the postage, Hilda, the bicycle.

I wrote a short letter for Hilda. Gave her a recommendation for another employer. I put it into an envelope, along with her wages and a little extra. Better for her not to be angry. Also a note for her to take to the bank.

I was almost done. I wrote a final letter, this one to Mrs. Sarah McArran. Might as well offer the nice woman from the neighborhood, the woman I ran into in the shops, my bicycle, and my rubber plant. Two weeks later one of my smarter lawyers thought my attention to the bicycle and the plant might point to insanity. He never said that to anyone who listened.

Must have been 9:30 when Hilda knocked. She wanted her final orders. "First, go to the post office for stamps for my packets. Here's a quarter. Then go find Mr. Fetzer, he's the railroad expressman. Tell him to fetch my trunk right away and bring it to the depot. You know, the ferry station for the railroad. After that go downtown to get my bank book at the Brooklyn

Savings Bank. Here's a note so the teller will give you the bank book. Hilda, hurry, I need to make the afternoon train to New Brunswick." I said "New Brunswick" loud and slow.

When Hilda left I pulled out from the closet the trunk with the initials W. W. P. on the side. I fashioned labels for the trunk and folded and laid my better clothes in it—three silk gowns, an opera cloak, a sealskin coat, underwear, four pairs of shoes, slippers, eight rings, a gold watch, photographs. I packed them carefully. Remember, I'm a dressmaker. Two days later Detective Mitchell lied when he unpacked my trunk. He told reporters my clothes were thrown in, slipshod like. Lies. Next, I taped the labels to the trunk. On the first label, I wrote a return address, 598 Hancock Street, Brooklyn. On the second I wrote Send to P. D. Garretson, baggage master, train 181, Pennsylvania Railroad Station, New Brunswick, New Jersey, and 318 Seaman Street, New Brunswick, New Jersey. I locked the trunk and put the key in the third packet. I didn't seal the envelope—I was waiting for the bank books and the claim check from Fetzer, the expressman.

Then it was 10:30, or about then. I folded linens. Rearranged wine glasses. Dusted. Kept moving. I heard a small sound, a creak. I listened. Maybe I heard Ida, walking around in the cellar. Maybe Ida was walking.

An hour went by. Hilda came back. Fetzer was hot on her heels. She led him upstairs to the front bedroom. He was not a big man, but broad, used to carrying. He hoisted the chest on one shoulder and brought it downstairs to his wagon. I watched.

Hilda handed me the Brooklyn Savings Bank book. I saw the balance. $213.83. Then I went to a hidden spot in my bureau. I took out my second bank book. This one was for the Howard Savings Bank in Newark. The balance was $1074.08. Will thought I had debts. I had just a few. Ha. I did that to confuse him. I was good at managing my money. Especially when I needed to manage my money to leave him. For years I drained off that allowance for Ross and for myself, just in case.

I can see when I look at you, you're doing the sums in your head. I'll save you the bother. If I skimmed off seven dollars of the twenty dollars each week, well, that's a little more than twenty-eight dollars a month, say thirty.

That's $360 a year. We were married four years, so say that's almost $1500. Maybe I took a little more too, and not from my allowance. I gave Miss Meury or whoever was listening a wicked smile and kept talking.

The bank books, I enclosed them in the third packet. I added in the key to the trunk. Put a stamp on. Hoped it was enough.

Then I saw Hilda eat her lunch. I told her not to bother with mine. She didn't ask about Ida and I didn't say anything. It was already midday and we still had a lot to do. I told Hilda to take the packets to the post office to mail them. But then, damn. That wouldn't work. I forgot to ask Fetzer for a baggage claim check to put in the third packet. If Peter didn't have the check he couldn't claim the trunk.

Now it was about 1:30. Hilda was on her way out the door, to post the packets. I called her back. "Hilda, stupid Fetzer never gave us a claim check. Run back to him and get it. Hurry. Remember, I need to get the trunk on the 3:15 train to New Brunswick. Then I'm going to get on that train too." I repeated the last sentence, to make sure Hilda heard.

More than an hour passed. That damn maid. Where was she? I sat at the little worktable in the kitchen, drinking whisky then wine, whiskey then wine. On an empty stomach. I needed to forget everything. Or did I want to stay sharp?

At 3:00, I think that was the time, Hilda came back with the receipt. "What took you so long? I missed my train to New Brunswick. My trunk is on it and I'm not."

"Ma'am, the expressman was not at his station. He was making his rounds. I had to wait."

"Doesn't matter. I can't fire you again." I knew I should add something about what my plan was now, but my mind was foggy. I took a breath and focused. I made sure Hilda was paying attention. "All right, I will make the next train, the 6:00. It will still get me to New Brunswick in time for a late supper."

A knock. It was the groceryman, at the back door. Hilda had hired him to take her own trunk away for her. She led him to her little room at the back of the house, then she turned her head. We both heard another knock. This time it was the fruit peddler. "We don't need anything today." He looked surprised. "Do me a favor," I said, taking the note for Mrs. McArran and another quarter out of my pocket. "Deliver this to Mrs. McArran, around the corner on your rounds." The peddler smiled when he saw the coin. He nodded and left.

I sent Hilda to the post office again, now with the three packets. At least the girl was fast this time. When she came back she tended to the last of her regular chores. She laid the table for dinner and put the leftover roast out. I watched her and could see she was sneaking looks at me while she was working. I didn't know why—she knew I drank a little in the daytime. I guess I forgot to put away the whiskey and wine bottles. I thought maybe I should clean up now, but that might call more attention to the number of bottles on the table. I needed her to leave. "Let me get your wages. Wait a minute." When I walked upstairs, I heard Hilda in the kitchen, neatening up, opening and closing the cupboards, putting away the bottles. She was busy. Would she see the axe I stashed behind the umbrellas in the stand near the front door? I grabbed the axe on my way upstairs.

Two minutes later I handed Hilda the envelope containing my recommendation letter, along with her monthly wages, plus five dollars. "This is to tide you over." And maybe to forget.

By now it was 4:00. Hilda and me, we both heard the doorbell. Mrs. Sarah McArran. Hilda answered the door. I stayed out of sight, listening.

"Hilda, hello. Much goings-on here, eh. Mattie sent me a note. So, she's leaving William. Says he was always trouble for her. She's going away, or maybe she's away already, and she's leaving me her bike and rubber plant. Oh, and is Ida here? I'd like to see her."

I stepped out from where I was hiding. "Hello, Sarah. Hilda, I'll take care of this. No need for you to help. Just finish cleaning out your room and you may leave." I waited until Hilda walked away. "Sarah, Ida's not here. She's boarding elsewhere now and so she isn't home today. I'll be leaving soon too, to stay with my brother in New Brunswick. Let me get you the bike and that plant."

Sarah McArran thought she struck gold. She took the bike, mounted it, and tried to ride home with one hand, carrying the plant with the other. After half a block I saw her give up and walk the bike.

Then I had two hours until Will returned. Two hours to think. More whiskey helped.

6:14. He was like clockwork. I knew he would be. I sat on the top step of the staircase, near our bedroom, waiting. The police thought they figured it out. I was headed to New Brunswick but when I missed the train, then I was afraid Will would find Ida. What's true is that I was afraid of Will. He would hit me. I wasn't going to let anyone hit me again. I heard the key turn, then heard the door open. Then his step, not heavy. Then no steps for a second. He would be surprised the lights were off in the front hall. They were always on at that hour, always. He walked to the back parlor. "Martha?" he yelled. I knew he would draw a match from his pocket. I heard him strike it. He lit one of the gas lamps, I saw a glimmer from where I sat. He walked to the door to hang his hat and coat on the rack. His back was to the stairs. The axe was in my hands. I stood up and ran down as he began to turn toward me. My dress made a rustle. But I was fast. First on the side of his forehead and cheek. He howled. He ducked. The axe glanced off his head, into the woodwork. He was stunned, just for seconds. He moved to the door. I yanked out the axe and swung again. He put out his arm to cover his head. I gashed him. Then my swing improved. I hit him on the left side of his head just over the ear. The bastard was dead.

But now he was crawling, screaming. Dragging himself through the half-open inside door, to the vestibule. I stood in the hall, holding the bloody axe. His legs were three feet in front of me. Could I hack them off? Yeah, that's what I was thinking. I changed my grip to lash down, then the bastard stood up just enough to open the outer door. He leaned on the railing and yelled for help. I saw a tall, young man, a stranger, start up the front steps. Did he see me? I slammed the door shut and turned the lock, then ran upstairs into Hilda's room at the back. I opened the window and threw the axe into the snow in the backyard.

Now to the front window in my bedroom, looking down. N.B., I saw his thinning hair from above. That damned neighbor dragged Will next door. I never got a break—couldn't even kill the bastard.

Nothing left to do except end it all. I made sure the bedroom windows were closed tight. I fiddled with the gas jets. I dropped to the floor and covered myself with bedclothes. Then I waited. I was still alive. Not enough gas? The smell was sweet, not bad. Did I want more? Twenty minutes, then the sound of men's feet climbing the stairs.

I was tired. I closed my eyes.

Ida Place

Was I any different from my friends with stepmothers? We hated them. Well, maybe I hated more, but mine was a shrew. By the time Papa knew, he couldn't control her.

I called her son a bastard. She went insane. Stunned me. Acid, burning through skin and eyes. Scorching. Agony, for a second. 'Til the axe.

James Desmond

I blame my wife. She's the one who wanted to live in Crown Heights. "It's fashionable," she said to me, "a good neighborhood." So I found rooms to rent on the top floor of a boarding house on the edge of the neighborhood. With two children, it's a squeeze to fit in the small boarding house rooms. 64 Albany Avenue. That's less than a mile southwest of the Place residence. I'm a waiter at Sweet's restaurant on Fulton, in Manhattan. To go to and from work I take the Brooklyn el. Hancock Street is on the path between the el station and my boarding house.

I'll never forget what I witnessed on Hancock on February 7th. I didn't work my night shift. The restaurant closes on Mondays. That's the one day I work a day shift. I clean and sort through the stock of food. I took my usual route home from the station—Reid to Hancock to Albany. I was cold, so I walked fast, but not too fast because I like to look at the block of brick houses on Hancock. I want to own one someday, if I ever become maître d' at Sweets. My wife says the Stuyvesant Heights neighborhood is even nicer than Crown Heights. Walking home, I passed in front of the Place row house at 6:17. I know the time because I checked when I got off the el—it was 6:04—it takes me twenty-six minutes to walk home, and the Place house is halfway. When I looked at the stoops along the north side of Hancock, I had to look twice. The cold wind made my eyes tear. I thought I wasn't seeing right. But I was. A man, about fifty, staggered out the front door and grabbed the railing.

"I've been shot. Help me." His voice trailed off to a mumble.

Blood poured from the man's head, on his left side. I know people around here say Brooklynites are a close tribe, proud of helping each other. Maybe they're right, because I couldn't just walk on. I ran up to help. Behind the man, the front door was half-open, and the inner door behind it was half-open too. In the hall I saw a tall woman, holding an axe. For a second I thought she looked crazed. I wanted to flee. But I knew I was the only one there, right then, who could help. I grabbed hold of the wounded man's arm, to hold him up. I didn't know what to do. Maybe I screamed for help. I remember looking down at my arm, holding his arm, and seeing the blood soak into my coat, my good coat. Funny thing to remember. I took another look behind the man. Now no one was in the hall where I had just spotted the woman. Then I saw another man, about as old as the wounded man, run out of his house next door to help. This second man had thinning hair, a puffy face, a weak mustache, and wire-rimmed glasses. I wasn't sure he was the right person to take charge of the emergency, but I sure was happy to have help. Then yet another neighbor ran out too.

I let these good men take over. Thirteen minutes later I was back in my boarding house, washing the injured man's blood off my coat.

Napoleon Bonaparte Thompson

These days I work as an advertising agent, three days a week, but that was not my first profession. For years I served the Lord as Reverend Thompson, pastor of Baptist churches in Massachusetts, Rhode Island, and New York. Years ago, I lost the support of my most recent congregation in a scandal. Few residents in our Stuyvesant Heights neighborhood know about it. They have not heard the lies, the slander. Only a few know about Mrs. Lillian Swift, an upstanding teacher in Boston, whose reputation was ruined along with mine. The busybodies from the church thought they had proof that Mrs. Swift spent an overnight stay with me in the Pebble House Hotel in Portland, Maine. Fools. If my wife of twenty-five years knew better than to listen to malicious gossip, then my congregants should have known too. Now, at age fifty-six, I live at 596 Hancock, next door to the Place residence, with my steadfast wife, Ella. Like most of our neighbors, the Places call me N.B. No one wants to say my full name, Napoleon Bonaparte Thompson, and no one even believes that is my full name. N.B. works for me.

Will and his first wife Laura, even his second wife, they knew I was happy to help whenever I was needed. I helped Ida when she locked herself out of the house, and I helped Will if he needed to lift a heavy package. Will is a good man. He knows about the scandal and doesn't believe it. Not a spiritual man, no, sadly Will isn't, but a good man. One I was happy to help. And to be honest, I thought Mrs. Place was a good woman. Quick to anger—aren't we all? I talked to her, too, when we were in our yards. The neighbors said she was not very cultured and a little, well, flamboyant in the way she dressed. As if she wanted to raise her station. Some of the older women in the neighborhood didn't approve when she rode her bicycle, with those riding suits. Ankles showing. But I had no problem with her. And my wife Ella had no problem with her.

So that brings us to 6:17 on September 7th, 1898. We have an old grandfather clock that Ella inherited. It needs repairing. Before all this, I thought I'd ask Edward, the lad who kept company with Ida, may she rest in peace, to see if he could fix it. He was trained as a watchmaker, though he gave that up. I had not gotten around to asking him. In any case, the clock chimes late, sixteen minutes past the hour, not on the hour. I heard it when I was eating supper with Ella that night, sitting in our front room. When it is just the two of us, as it usually is, we sometimes sit in the front parlor to eat, not the dining room. We watch people on the street while we eat. I heard the chime, and I said to Ella how I needed to send a message to Edward. Then I took another bite of beef. That's when I heard a shout for help, from a voice I did not recognize. Ella and I stood up and looked down through the window in the direction of the noise. There was a tall, slender young man supporting Will Place on the front steps of the house next door. Will, by God, Will was bleeding about the head. I ran into the cold—didn't grab my coat—to help.

"My wife shot me."

"Let's get him into my house, right over there," I said, moving my head to show the stranger which house I meant.

"No. No. Take me back in," Will gasped.

"You've been shot. We need to take care of you." My second sentence was one I had uttered many times as a clergyman. It felt good to say it again.

I saw the young man look with dismay at the blood on the arm of his coat. Although I was hardly a connoisseur of fashion, I could tell that the coat had seen better days. He looked worried. Must be his only coat. Then he and I both saw James Dawson, the neighbor on the other side of the Place home, run to our aid.

"Can you take over, sirs? I need to get home." I knew the young man was in a hurry to wash off the stain.

"I'm fine, lad. Jim will help me. Just give us your name in case we need it later."

"James Desmond." Dawson remembered the first name, same as his, and I remembered the surname. As Desmond ran off, Jim Dawson and I heard the Place door slam shut and the key turn. By the time we twisted to look, we could see only the locked door.

"Jim," I said, "you go fetch Dr. Richardson and the police. Oh, also, Will's brother Charles. You know where he lives, just down the block. I'll bring Will into the house, my house."

As I grabbed hold of Will, he was slumping, I glanced at the Place house. I saw a woman who looked like Martha in the upstairs window. When her eyes met mine, she darted back behind the curtain. I wanted to stand on the sidewalk and stare, but I knew my pastoral duty. Struggling, I got Will over to my house, almost carrying him into the basement, that was at street level, down just two steps. Ella watched all this from our own front window. The minute she heard us enter the basement door she gathered blankets and set water on the stove for tea.

Soon Jim Dawson returned, with two policemen in tow. I learned they were James McCauley and Cord Wilkin. From the Ralph Street Station, Fourteenth Precinct. They were on patrol close by when Dawson found them. I noticed their long blue frock coats, stretched out on McCauley, loose on Wilkin. Smart looking. Two rows of brass buttons. This was the new uniform for the New York police, for the past month, since January 1st. That's when to my annoyance and the annoyance of half of Brooklyn, our town lost its separate identity, became consolidated as part of New York City. We would be seeing these new uniforms for two days.

Back to my recollections. "She shot me," Will gasped again, now to the patrolmen. His forehead was gushing blood. Also, his cheek and his hand. McCauley and Wilkin were junior patrolmen, probably more used to horse and carriage accidents than gunshots. I saw them look at each other, not happy. We all heard a knock on the basement door. John Barton, I learned he was a new police recruit, he came in. He must have seen the commotion on the street. Probably about a dozen people out there and growing. Looking back, I realize the long night of chaos had begun, more chaos than Hancock Street had ever seen.

"Go run and get Ennis," McCauley said to Barton. "Use the call box on the corner." I noticed a slight smirk between McCauley and Wilkin. Then the two of them left, telling me they were going to tell the gathering crowd to keep back and assuring me they would return soon. I suppose their training did not include medical aid.

The next ten minutes passed slowly. Remember, I was a pastor turned part-time ad agent, not a medic. When Ella walked down the basement steps carrying tea, I grabbed the tray and told her to go back up to get towels. I used the oldest to staunch Will's bleeding. Then I held the towel in my hand for a minute, listening to Will groan. I wasn't sure where to apply pressure. I forced myself to glance, just a quick glance, at Will's scalp. It did not look like a shot—the blood was not oozing out of a bullet-shaped wound. A long cut. I wanted to leave the first aid for Dr. Richardson to figure out. But I knew I needed to do something, so I placed the towel on Will's neck, not his scalp. Thank goodness, Dr. Richardson entered then, with a police officer.

This man's uniform had a striking number of brass buttons. Those buttons were more impressive than his slicked-back hair and scraggly beard. The officer introduced himself as Captain James Ennis, Ralph Street Station. I recalled the smirk between McCauley and Wilkin when they mentioned Ennis's name, but he seemed inoffensive to me. Patrolman Barton followed the doctor and captain inside, and a minute later McCauley and Wilkin followed Barton. I walked to the far side of the basement, to give Doctor Richardson a wide berth. He took charge. He probed the wound, maybe not gently enough because Will lost consciousness. "Are you a relative?" Richardson asked me.

"I'm the neighbor, the next-door neighbor. Napoleon Bonaparte Thompson." Despite my unease at Will's condition, without thinking I automatically added my usual next two sentences. "I know, it's a mouthful. Just call me N.B. A half-hour ago I heard Will scream and ran to help. He says he thought he was shot, but it doesn't look like a gun wound to me."

"Right. A sharp instrument. Maybe an axe." Now Richardson turned his head to Barton. "Go fetch an ambulance from St. Mary's. Callbox should work." Then he turned back to me. "I'll tell you, I am not sure this man will survive. My guess, his skull is fractured. And wounds on his forehead and left cheek."

Captain Ellis yelled at Barton as the recruit walked out. "And John, from that call box, call the Fifty-Fourth too and ask for reinforcements."

I heard another knock on the door. This time it was James Dawson, coming back with Will's brother, Charles Place. The room was getting crowded, especially with Jameses—me and Ella, Will, Dr. Richardson, James Dawson, James Ennis, James McCauley, and Cord Wilkin. By the end of the night, even more men squeezed into my row house. I wouldn't keep straight the names of the policemen, but no matter.

Charles Place looked like he might faint when he saw his brother's pale, bloody face. All of a sudden I remembered the other members of the Place family. "You know," I said, half to Charles and half to Captain Ennis, "I wonder where Ida is. She's usually home at night, eating at home. And where is Martha?" I wondered whether I should tell Ennis that I had seen her in the window. I wasn't certain. Maybe it was the maid, the Swedish girl. Oh, but I was certain enough. "You know, Martha might have been in the house. I saw a woman half covered by the curtains."

"Who is Ida?" Ennis asked. "And Martha?"

"Ida is Will's daughter. His only surviving daughter. From his first wife. And Martha is the second wife." I turned toward Ennis, away from Will. "And none of them get along," I said, stretching my mouth at the corners to talk quietly. "Well, Ida and Will here, they get along."

Captain James Ennis

That morning and afternoon were quiet in the Ralph Street Station. As captain, I supervise the Fourteenth Precinct there—patrolmen, sergeants, and detectives. To be honest with you, we hired a few extra patrolmen three months earlier because we feared that when we consolidated with the New York City police on January 1st, the muckety-mucks might not let us expand. So we had a full precinct that day. Around 7:00 in the evening the precinct dispatcher told me John Barton rang in from a call box. A man had been shot at 598 or 596, he wasn't sure which, Hancock Street. I didn't usually go to crime scenes, I was too busy supervising, but a shooting sounded serious. Although my men were fine with breaking and entering and rows, I wasn't sure they could handle a shooting. I took a patrol wagon to the 500 block of Hancock. A crowd of about twenty people pointed me to the basement door at number 596. I knocked and when the door opened, I saw some of my men inside. They looked eager to see me, even though I was not a popular captain. They blamed me for peeling plaster and leaky toilets in the stationhouse, and maybe for being a little smug. I suppose I was guilty on those charges, but I had been a captain for ten years, and I knew what I was doing about law and order.

The owner of the house, Mr. Thompson—he told us to call him N.B.—related his tale of what he saw in front of 598. "Let's take a look," I said. I swung my arm to direct McCauley and Wilkin to follow me. "The rest of you, wait here for the ambulance." Then I looked around, remembered that Barton was already on an errand or two, and spotted another candidate.

81

He said he was James Dawson, a neighbor. "Mr. Dawson, can you run to the station and ask one of the patrolmen to call the coroner, Dr. Delap? You know, just in case. They have a telephone over there." When I said the word coroner, I lowered my voice and turned away from Mr. Place. He never heard much of anything at that point anyway.

I walked next door with McCauley and Wilkin, past the crowd that had grown to about fifty. My officers tried the doorbell at 598 Hancock. No answer. They tried the handle to open the wooden outer door. Locked. I stood to the side as Wilkin, he's slender, narrow shoulders, he leaned left into the door, and McCauley, he's six feet two and, say, 240 pounds, leaned right into the door. Nothing. Then Wilkin stepped aside, next to me, and McCauley kicked. A second later we saw blood on the tile and mat in the vestibule. An inner door. Locked again. I looked at McCauley. After he kicked in that inner door too, I saw the hall carpet, the part near the door. Bloody.

We sniffed. "Gas?" McCauley said. Later, I described the smell as distinct but weak. "Where's it coming from?" Wilkin said. I wasn't sure. McCauley and Wilkin scrunched their noses. Just then a terrier and puppies ran to us, barking. No time to deal with the dogs. They were harmless.

I knew to be methodical. "Let's start on this floor." McCauley and Wilkin followed me, walking through the front parlor, then the back parlor, the kitchen, the dining room. I saw the table laid for dinner, with a half-eaten roast in the center. Nice furniture, respectable, neat, nothing amiss. "Try the cellar." Again, nothing amiss. "Upstairs."

Now I smelled gas more strongly. We followed the smell to the back bedroom. I think a draft misled us, I don't know. McCauley entered first. A young woman, maybe a girl. She was on the bed, with her feet sticking out from a sheet and her head at the foot of the bed. Stretched out a little to the right. Her face was down on a pillow, soaked with blood. One of the girl's arms rested under her head and the other reached out. The room was a mess. The bottom of a chair, cane I remember, had a broken back that had fallen to the floor. Most of the bedclothes lay on the floor too.

The three of us never agreed completely on what we saw. Deep cuts in the back of the girl's head. Burnt and protruding tongue. Swollen or discolored lips. A thin crust on the lips. Mucous between the top and bottom lip. Bleeding or scarred mouth. Discolored right cheek. Bloated face tinged maybe red or blue. Eyes protruding, or maybe disfigured, or maybe burned. How much blood, well, that would become a point of dispute among us, but the next day I read in Joseph Pulitzer's sensationalist paper, *The World*, that it was a pool of blood. No one is sure what pool means. We did agree that the girl wore a bicycle dress with a black skirt, bloomers, and gaiters, like she was getting ready to go riding. Her clothing was not disordered, I thought, but Wilkin thought two buttons of her dress were unbuttoned. McCauley thought he smelled acid. Maybe poison. In 1898 we had heard of crime scene photography but didn't use it. We relied on our eyes and memories, for what that was worth.

McCauley pointed to a scissors on the bed, near the girl's hands. He started to turn the body over, then glanced at me. I nodded yes. We looked for wounds. Didn't see any. While we looked I heard footsteps and saw two patrolmen I didn't recognize walk in. Must be from the Fifty-Fourth Precinct. They watched us examine the girl. Then I heard one say to the other that they were going to check out the gas smell. A minute later I heard "Here's another," and me and my officers left the body to run to the front of the house.

Officer William J. Maher

It was a quiet Monday, supper time. Nothing much was happening in my precinct, the Fifty-Fourth. Our captain, Gerald Parker, he got a message that the Fourteenth needed help. The Fourteenth and Fifty-Fourth helped each other for emergencies and serious crimes. Parker ordered me to Stuyvesant Heights, something about a shooting, or that's what they thought then. I was happy that our captain told the other Maher, William Frank Maher, to go with me. It wasn't surprising we had two William Mahers in the Fifty-Fourth. Maher was a common last name for us Irish. To keep the two of us straight they called me W.J. and they called William Frank just plain Frank. He was the shorter one.

When Frank and me got to Hancock Street, men in the crowd out front directed us to the Thompson house. In the basement, we saw a doctor tending to the victim who'd been shot or injured in some way. Mr. Thompson, he said to call him N.B., told us three other policemen left a minute earlier to check out the Place residence next door. "Follow them," he said. "I'm not sure if Captain Ennis and his men got into the front door. I should have told them to use the basement door. That one will be open. When I've been in my backyard I've seen Will," he pointed to the injured man, "go in and out, many times, without a key." I saw that the victim, now I knew his name was Will, William Place I learned later, was in too much pain to hear N.B. "Yes, use the back door." Frank and me, we went out N.B.'s basement door, through the backyards to the Place basement door. It opened easily. We didn't know then that Captain Ennis and two of his men had searched the house a minute earlier, so we did our own search. We found nothing. Then we heard footsteps upstairs. I raised my thumb in front of Frank's face. He nodded yes. We climbed to the parlor floor and searched through those rooms too. Nothing but a dog and puppies. Then we climbed to the bedroom floor. From the staircase, we heard voices. I thought they came from the back of the row house. For a minute me and Frank were scared. Since we work out of the Fifty-Fourth, not the Fourteenth, we didn't recognize the voices. But they didn't sound like culprits. We kept going. We entered the back bedroom. Three men crowded around a girl's bed. Frank and me made sort of a second row in back of the first group of officers.

Under normal conditions, the men from one precinct would introduce themselves to the men from another. Not now, not with a beautiful girl lying dead in front of us. Two of the officers who got there first turned over the girl's body. They were gentle, checking for injuries. They put her on her back. Me and Frank tried to nudge our way to the bed, to get a glimpse of the girl. But Frank was slight and I was not much bigger. We couldn't get close, couldn't even catch the eye of the man with the most brass to get an assignment. I thought maybe we should find another way to be useful. I said, "Frank, let's go check out that gas smell." I made sure the man dressed as a captain heard me. I walked back down the hall, sniffing, following the gas. Frank followed me. I could hardly believe what I saw. "Here's another one," I yelled to Frank. "Go back to the other house and fetch that doctor." Frank stopped in his tracks and ran downstairs.

Within ten seconds, the three men who entered the house first—I learned later they were Ennis, McCauley, and Wilkin, Ennis was the captain—joined me in the front bedroom. The room was a mess, chairs overturned, workbasket overturned. A middle-aged woman lay on the floor on her back, between the two front windows. Unconscious. Her head was covered some with sheets or a small blanket and a pillow. The bed looked stripped. A corner of the sheet was stuffed in the lady's mouth. I saw that the two gas jets in the room, they were over the dresser, were pulled down. Gas escaping full blast. The globes that should have covered the jets were broken on the floor. I saw Captain Ennis look at one of his men, it was Wilkin. He was wide-eyed and wasn't moving. "Open the windows," the captain yelled at him. Then the captain bent down to examine the woman. I figured I deserved some credit for finding her, so I did the same. I saw small rips in her dress. All of a sudden, she moaned. Ennis gave orders to his own officers, McCauley, Wilkin, and a recruit named Barton who just arrived, and to me too. We lifted the woman and carried her downstairs to the front parlor, while Ennis watched. She was not light. We laid her on the floor. Her breathing was regular and her color was fine, though she stopped moaning and looked like she passed out. We tried artificial respiration, as best we could, pumping her arms up and down. It was chilly in the house, but we all started to sweat from the hard work.

Edward Scheidecker

I pushed past the crowd in front of the house that night, February 7th, elbowing men aside. In the parlor, I saw four policemen taking turns raising and lowering the arms of Mrs. Place. Nearby, a man dressed with more brass than the others sat and watched. I didn't know it then, but he was Captain Ennis, of the Fourteenth Precinct, Ralph Street Station.

"I'm Ida Place's sweetheart. We're engaged to be married. Where is she?"

Captain Ennis stared at me. After a few seconds, he led me upstairs. He didn't know I knew my way around the house.

I saw the body on the bed, covered with a sheet. Beautiful Ida. My eyes welled with tears. They rolled down both cheeks.

"What can you tell me about her?" Ennis asked. He was clever, didn't offer any unnecessary information.

"We have a friend, I mean Ida and me, his name is George Young. The three of us were supposed to meet at my house at 2:00 this afternoon, to practice songs, songs for a concert. I live less than a mile northwest of here. Ida knows the route. She either walks or rides her bicycle. She never came. We were worried. I had a practice session with my regiment later in the afternoon, so George offered to come here to look for her. He said he rang the bell and yelled but no one answered. When I came back to my house after the practice, George told me he couldn't find Ida. I decided to try, just now." My tears turned to weeping. "Maybe if I could have come earlier, maybe."

Ennis interrupted me. "Do you know any more?"

"Had to be her stepmother. That awful woman. She always told me to give up on Ida, that I was a fool to court her. She said William, that's Ida's father, loved Ida and Ida loved William and there was no room for me. You're not going to believe this, but once she even said that if William only dared, he'd marry his daughter." I stopped for a minute, took a breath. "Trilby, the terrier, and the puppies. They must be hungry. We should feed them. No, wait. I bet that woman poisoned them. No one should eat any of the food in this house."

I saw Captain Ennis staring at me. Yes, he knew I was a good source. Then the captain walked away and gave orders to throw out the food in the pantry and icebox. He said he would remember to ask Charles Place to take temporary custody of Trilby and the puppies. I felt good that I saved them from neglect.

Napoleon Bonaparte Thompson

By about 7:30 on the night of the murder I had been sitting with my wounded neighbor Will for over an hour. What was going on next door in the Place house? None of the officers returned to fill me in. Then my basement door opened, this time without a knock, and I saw the smaller of the two police officers who had arrived after the first contingent. "There's another one, two women," the officer said, in a strange, frantic whisper, trying to ensure that Will didn't hear. "We need a doctor." Dr. Richardson was still attending to Will, swabbing and wrapping his wounds. Ella was standing by, ready to assist.

Just then the ambulance surgeon arrived. Dr. John Gormley. What a contrast between the two doctors. Richardson was about sixty, short and bald. Gormley was young, slender with broad shoulders, and clearly the junior physician. I saw they knew each other. Richardson smiled and did not pull rank. He motioned with his chin and hand. Gormley should quickly examine Will. The doctors whispered their observations to each other. Then Richardson glanced at the officer, the short one, I think he was Frank Maher. We were remembering Maher's report on more mayhem. Richardson quietly gave Gormley the next assignment. "John, go check next door while I finish up with Mr. Place. I'll be over in a minute." Gormley grabbed his bag and rushed out, followed by Frank Maher.

The crisis next door must be even worse than I imagined. I needed to get away to check on everyone. After all, I was an ordained clergyman, not a medical orderly. "Dr. Richardson," I said, "I am a reverend, or I should say, I was a reverend before I became an advertising agent. If you don't mind, I'll go next door too, to see if I can be of assistance. Ella is here, she can help you if you need supplies. And Will's brother Charles too." Dr. Richardson nodded. He looked distracted, trying to fit bandages to Will's round and bleeding head. As I walked next door, I chose the path on the front sidewalk, not through the backyard. I wanted to count the crowd. I saw close to a hundred spectators, shoulder to shoulder on the sidewalk despite the darkness and the cold weather. The next day I read in *The World* that the crowd grew to five hundred by the end of the evening. That paper was prone to exaggeration, but this time the reporter captured the atmosphere. Our block was the eye of a storm.

I walked through the open front door of number 598, into the front parlor.

Several officers knelt on the floor, taking turns raising and lowering the arms of Mrs. Place to try to revive her. Captain Ennis, the only man sitting in a chair, spotted me. "Go upstairs, N.B., and tell us if the girl on the bed is Ida Place. Cord here, that is, Patrolman Cord Wilkin, he thinks it's her. I need to be certain. Watch out for the smell of gas. We opened the windows but it might have lingered." Gas? The captain didn't need to say more. Mrs. Place had tried to kill herself, a sin in the law and the eyes of God.

I climbed the stairs. By now the smell of gas was faint. I peeked into the front bedroom, saw no one except a mess of bedclothes on the floor. I walked to the back. There I saw Officer Barton, standing guard, and Dr. Gormley. On the bed was Ida Place. No question. I noted her position, felt her cold hand—Gormley was holding her other hand—and nodded my distress to Barton. On the bureau, I spotted a tumbler holding barely an inch of colorless fluid. "Funny that no one but you noticed this," Barton said, taking possession of the tumbler. Months later, Mrs. Place would say she dropped the tumbler, but I swear we found it on the bureau.

Returning to the parlor, I saw Ennis still sitting, maybe overseeing the officers moving Mrs. Place's arms up and down. "Yes, oh, yes, the poor girl is indeed Ida Place. I am sure of it. So sad for Will," I said. I felt pleased that although my visit to the Place house might have been due to curiosity, I was able to do some good by identifying the victim, poor lovely Ida, and spotting the tumbler. As I walked back to my house, I wondered whether I should be the one to tell Will about his daughter. Maybe not, but I was certain my pastoral style would be superior to Captain Ennis's. Will was slumped back in a chair, waiting to be carried into the ambulance. Dr. Richardson looked up when I entered. "Good, you're back, Mr. Thompson. Let me go now and help Dr. Gormley."

As Richardson grabbed his coat and bag, I noticed that Charles Place was missing. "Where did Charles go? Is he upstairs?"

"No," Richardson answered while rushing out the door. "Charles just ran home for a minute to tell his wife what was going on. He'll be back."

With no doctors or relatives present, I felt comfortable reverting to my old duties. I put my hand on Will's shoulder, very gently, on the side with the least blood. "Will, I must tell you what I have seen. Ida is in heaven." He had been wincing and weeping all evening with the pain of his wounds. Now, I saw a rush of new tears and wailing. Later, Will would say that he did not hear me. Charles had left the room so there would be no proof, other than my word, of when Will first learned of his daughter's murder.

Captain James Ennis

The woman was faking. I knew that for certain. No harm in us making a good show of trying to revive her. I watched as the officers pumped the woman's arms up and down. They were breathing hard with this exertion when a handsome young man entered with a doctor's bag and introduced himself as Dr. Gormley, the ambulance surgeon. "I'm Captain James Ennis from the Fourteenth Precinct, and these here are my officers, well, two are my officers, Cord Wilkin and James McCauley, and the third is from the Fifty-Fourth, helping out. Oh, the fourth one too," I said, seeing Frank Maher—I was learning all their names—follow Gormley into the parlor. "This woman may be unconscious, Dr. Gormley. There was gas escaping in her room." I could see that Gormley understood I was in charge. He knelt on the floor, motioned to the officers to stop pumping, and checked the woman. Then he demonstrated a more efficient and effective form of artificial respiration but told the officers to hold off while he tried something else. He reached into his bag for smelling salts, which he put under the woman's nose. She coughed. She recovered consciousness, or more likely she no longer hid her consciousness.

Gormley looked at me with a smirk, which I returned in kind. A sham, a faker, we both knew. "We're going to need a second ambulance," he said, with no urgency, expecting me to handle arrangements. "Only because we shouldn't take any chances," he added, with a second smirk, looking away from the policemen.

"Frank," I said to the man from the Fifty-Fourth, "is that your name, go to the call box and ask St. Mary's for another ambulance. No need to run. Dr. Gormley, you should examine the other woman. Upstairs."

From my seat in the parlor, I heard louder and louder noises from the crowd on the street. Turning to look out the window, I saw Coroner Delap arrive, stepping out of his carriage. An enormous, pointy mustache covered the bottom of the man's face. It was well known among the higher-ups that Delap had a record of asking for bribes to change the cause of death, on death certificates, hiding suicides. So far he had weathered the investigations. Delap and I worked together on other cases, without any unpleasantness. I walked down the Place front stairs and shook his extended hand.

"Don't drive the victim away yet, chaps. Let me check him," Delap told the ambulance crew that had just arrived. Then he looked over the crowd gathered in front of both 596 and 598 and gave me a puzzled look. Where was the wounded man, or maybe where was the corpse? I steered Delap to N.B.'s basement door and over to William Place, still slumped in a chair. I handled the introductions. The Coroner seemed most taken with Ella Thompson, or at any rate with her teapot. Eventually, Delap turned from Ella to look at Mr. Place. His face was covered with so many bandages that we could barely see his eyes. Brother Charles sat next to him. Delap examined the bloody man, lifting the bandages to check the wounds, undoing Dr. Richardson's careful work and then replacing the bandages, haphazardly to my eyes. Like Richardson, Delap thought Mr. Place's wounds were serious. "Captain Ennis," Delap said, turning to me so the patient would not hear. "I'm going to plan for the worst and take Mr. Place's ante-mortem statement. Right now." I knew Delap was following every guideline ever issued, guarding what little was left of his reputation. He stood over Mr. Place, waiting until he opened his eyes. "Mr. Place, I am Dr. Delap—can you tell me what happened to you?"

"She shot me," William Place whispered, sticking to his original belief. "I heard a rustle, but my back was turned. Might have smelled Empire Rose. Must have been her."

Delap bent down to put his ear close to Mr. Place's face. Still uncertain, Delap looked at me, frowning.

"Do you mean Mrs. Place?" I asked. "Did you see her?" I knew Delap wanted no ambiguity.

"No, couldn't see." Then the man passed out again. Delap frowned, but looked resigned to hearing nothing beyond this useless account.

"All right, Captain Ennis, get the ambulance crew in here," Delap said. "Let's move this man out."

From the front of N.B.'s house, I watched, along with Coroner Delap and Charles Place, as two of the three-man crew carried Will Place into the ambulance while the third fetched Dr. Gormley. Finally, the ambulance sped off to St. Mary's Hospital. I turned to Delap. "Sorry, Coroner, I think you need to see something next door."

"Damn, I was hoping to warm up with a cup of Mrs. Thompson's tea."

"Another body first," I said.

The crowd on the sidewalk had grown close to two hundred people. I needed to detail a policeman there to control the gawkers. Just then six more officers arrived in a police wagon from the Ralph Street Station. I had not called for them, but I suppose word of the frenzy on Hancock Street traveled fast. I told Patrolman Thomas Baker to stay with the crowd. Then I spotted Officer Frank Moore and Detectives Robert Mitchell and John Becker climbing down from the wagon. I yelled at them to push through the crowd to help in the Place house. It was hard to be heard above the noise on the street. As I tried to gather the reinforcements, I saw Charles Place walk away from both row houses. I stopped him. "I'm going back home, Captain. I will visit my brother in the morning."

"Mr. Place, first I need you to come with me. I have some sorry news for you." I gestured for Delap, Moore, Mitchell, and Becker to follow me and Charles Place up the front stairs to the Place house.

The six of us crowded into the back bedroom, where Officer Barton still stood guard while Doctor Richardson examined the body. "Two hours, maybe three," the doctor said, looking at Coroner Delap. "Rigor mortis is just setting in." His estimate would be nearly forgotten in the days to come.

Looking at his niece, Charles Place gasped but recovered quickly. "She did it. I'm sure she did it. Martha. They were miserable and always quarreling. Drunk. Always drunk. And a temper."

"We can go over this again later," I said to Charles Place. "Not in this room."

Then I turned to Delap—he would take the lead, probably dotting every i and crossing every t. I was right.

"Dr. Richardson, I know you're a good man," Delap said, "but I'd like to examine the body myself." Richardson stepped aside and Delap looked over the girl. He moved her slowly, slower than he needed to, making sure to give the impression that he was being gentle with the body. Then he turned to me. "Captain, I need Dr. Alvin Henderson to assist here. He's the coroner's assistant. Do you have an officer who can fetch him?" I went downstairs, found Frank Maher, and sent the patrolman from the Fifty-Fourth on his final errand of the night. Dr. Richardson, pleased that his work was done, said goodbye.

A few minutes later, Detectives Mitchell and Becker left the murder scene too, telling me they would help as needed back at the station house. And they did. Frank Moore, though, he was the star of the day. "Captain," he said, "come outside with me." As we walked to the yard, Frank explained. "When I searched a back bedroom—it looked like the servant's room—I felt a breeze. I saw that the window was open a little. You need to see what I saw." In the back yard, I spotted an axe in a snowdrift, ten feet from the back wall of the house, covered in blood. Frank picked it up and handed it to me. I grinned and gave him a pat on the back. Then I went inside the house and handed the weapon to John Barton, asking him to bring it to the station.

At about 9:30 ambulance number two arrived. The crew paced up and down on the sidewalk, awaiting instructions. The crowd shouted questions at them, questions they couldn't answer. I told Officer McCauley to let the crew into the front parlor, where Mrs. Place was resting. With help from McCauley, the men carried her down the front steps. The driver took her to St. Mary's hospital, where she was wheeled to a different floor than the one where doctors were treating her husband. No doctor accompanied the ambulance.

A half-hour later, Dr. Alvin Henderson arrived in the Place parlor, where Delap and I waited for him. I had never met the man before. He was in his late forties, I would guess, with the usual mustache and thinning blonde hair. Unlike the coroner he worked for, Henderson seemed happy to be at a crime scene, even late at night. The doctors greeted each other warmly. I dismissed all but two of the officers and stood guard myself as Henderson examined the girl's body, the fourth doctor to do so. The blood from her mouth, Henderson thought, suggested strangulation. "How long has she been dead?" I asked.

"Maybe four hours. She's still a little warm. Only a slight suggestion of rigor mortis." I remember thinking that was odd. At 9:00 Dr. Richardson said maybe two hours, maybe three. It was now 11:00 at night, and Dr. Henderson said maybe four hours. I knew I had been called to the scene before 7:00. She hadn't just died when I saw her.

Following official procedures to the letter of the law, Coroner Delap needed ten men for a quick inquest, to establish the circumstances of the girl's death. By now close to three hundred gawkers, attracted by the mayhem on the street, stood on the sidewalk and front steps, staring up at the house. With all these candidates, Delap had no trouble finding a jury. I watched as he impaneled ten men for an inquest. He swore them in and ushered them upstairs into the back bedroom. Then Delap instructed them to view the body and to look at the mess in the room. Two of the gawkers who formed part of the jury were reporters, a fortuitous event for their newspapers. Another gawker Delap impaneled was Fred Fahrenkrug, though over the course of the next year no one, and that includes me, would ever consider his presence curious. Only later did I learn that this Fahrenkrug fellow was a private detective who was engaged to one of Ida Place's friends.

At close to midnight, Coroner Delap adjourned his makeshift jury. Two police officers found a pine board in the cellar, put it over two chairs, and lifted Ida, now covered with a sheet, onto the wooden bier. Then they too left for the evening. For a short time, quiet settled back onto Hancock Street.

The Tangle

Hilda Palm

Yesterday I lost my servant's room at the Places'. I moved back to the attic room in the boarding house where I lived before, in Crown Heights, a mile southwest of the row house in Stuyvesant Heights. I could afford the landlady's fee for a month. Mrs. Place gave me no notice, but her $5 tip was more than some would do.

At eight in the morning, I heard a knock on the door to my room. Two men in uniform.

"Good morning, miss. I'm Detective John Becker and this here is Detective Robert Mitchell. Can we talk?" It did not sound like a question.

I'd never been this close to coppers. Well, in this case, detectives. I looked them over. Becker was calm. Mitchell, holding his nightstick and cigar, moved from foot to foot. Did they see the color drain from my face?

"Not to worry, miss," said Becker. "You're not in trouble, at least we don't think so. We need to talk about your employer, Mr. William Place."

I set my mind to my Swedish accent. Accent, that's what my English teacher at the Lutheran Church called it. I thought I'd better hide it as best I could. Teacher said I talked better than most.

"Oh, come in. Watch your heads. The ceiling is low." I motioned to the two chairs at the table and moved up a stool for myself.

The men looked around. I was proud that the room they saw was clean, except for the table. It was crowded with newspapers, open to the help wanted sections. In their wool jackets, the men might not notice that the room was chilly. Mitchell started to puff on his cigar. Started coughing too.

"Miss," Becker said, "did you work at the Place residence yesterday?"

"Yes, I'm the maid for them, for three years. Was the maid. Not any longer. I was dismissed from service yesterday." I tried to control the bitterness in my voice, but I'm sure they heard it. Becker looked at his nervous partner. Aside from Mitchell's cough, they were silent for a minute.

"Who dismissed you? And when?"

"It was a terrible day. The missus sent me around on a hundred errands. She expected me to run around Brooklyn, and that was after she told me she didn't need me any longer. But she did pay me my wages, with something extra, and wrote a reference letter."

Becker asked me to describe the errands. I went over my day of dashes up and back across Brooklyn, trips to the bank, the post office, the baggage expressman. When I talked about the expressman, Mitchell interrupted.

"That trunk. Do you know where it was going? And when?"

"To her brother, a train man in New Brunswick. Peter is his name I think. Peter, Peter, Garret, maybe Garretson. She told me to rush so the trunk could make the afternoon train to New Brunswick."

"And when you were in the house, did you see the daughter, Miss Ida Place?"

"Oh, yes, in the morning, at breakfast. They ate everything I made but the missus complained about the coffee. They bickered too." I saw the men look at each other even though I didn't say anything about the slap. Knew not to spread stories about my employers. Bickering was one thing, slapping was another. "Then I washed up. Finished the laundry. I started it before breakfast so there wasn't a lot more to do. And then I heard a quarrel while I was hanging out the wet clothes. Hoping they wouldn't freeze in this weather." Another look, between them, then at me. "Those people were always fighting. I didn't bother myself with it. Why?"

They stopped looking and started talking. Their words didn't sink in. They must be muddled, talking about another squabble, like the one the year before when Mr. Place sent Mrs. Place to jail. They saw I wasn't understanding. "Dead. Dead." They had to say it more than once. When I muffled a scream, then they knew I got it.

Now the two of them asked me questions, sometimes the same questions asked in different ways, about what I heard during the quarrel at breakfast and what I heard when I was hanging the laundry. They kept looking at me. They thought I knew something. The more I cried, the more they stared.

"Ida had everything she wanted, but this isn't right. I never thought the quarrels would end this way." I tried to stop crying. "I didn't know Ida well, even though she was just three years younger than me. Mrs. Place didn't like it when I talked to the girl."

"Did you ever think to find a policeman to tell him what was going on in the house?" asked Mitchell. I winced. They're trying to blame me. Always, always the maid. Becker gave Mitchell a dirty look.

"My daughter is in service too," Becker said. "She works for a troubled family, just a different kind of trouble. There was nothing you could do. Tell me, do you think Mrs. Place could have killed her daughter? They were both in the house at the same time."

"She's a mean lady, that's for sure. Nasty to Ida, and to her husband. She makes threats too. But she wasn't the worst mistress I ever worked for. Sometimes I saw her raise her hand, like she was getting ready to slap me or someone else, but I never saw her hit or do anything like that."

As the men left, I stopped them on their way out and looked at Becker.

"How did you find me here?"

"The neighbor, Mr. N.B. Thompson. He knew that your aunt, Irene Palm, works as a washerwoman for Laura Place, you know, Mrs. Theodore Place. We checked with Mrs. Place, who sent us to your aunt's boarding house last hour, and she sent us here."

I should have known. Nosy N.B.

I went to the attic window to watch the coppers leave. They were talking on the sidewalk, in front of the patrol wagon. Saw the top of their heads. Hard to tell from that angle, but it looked like they were arguing.

I hoped they believe me.

Mattie

I guessed it was before dawn on Tuesday. After the ride in the ambulance, with rough blankets over me, the hospital bed felt snug and safe. I was alive, Will was alive. I didn't think Ida was alive. Why didn't I check? That girl taunted me, tossing those black curls. So I did something. The acid and more.

St. Mary's Hospital. I saw it once before when I rode my bicycle through Crown Heights, almost as fashionable as our neighborhood. Took up a whole square block. At first, the doctors and nurses treated me with respect, even though they thought I was unconscious. I felt good lying still, eyes closed. The doctor checked my lungs, my breathing. I knew he would find me healthy. His respect didn't last long. "She may have inhaled gas," I heard him say, "but couldn't have been much. The police who've been around say she murdered her daughter, or maybe they said it was her stepdaughter, then she tried to doff herself. Or faked it." Listening to him, I knew for sure that Ida was out of the way.

Then they left me alone to sleep. I smelled cleaner and bleach, not too bad, and I smelled myself. I was still in yesterday's dress, with a few small tears in the fabric. Needed to wash up.

The guard sitting at the half-opened door to the ward dozed off. I forced myself to breathe deeply, to think. No one had charged me with anything, not for Ida, not for Will. I could leave, quietly. I sat up and looked at the clock in the corner of the ward. Five in the morning. Put on my shoes. No coat. Crept to the door. Squeezed through and started to walk down the hall. I was silent but the guard felt me brush by. I ran. He caught me. Most days I could have knocked him down, but I must have been shaky after lying on the floor and in bed all that time. The guard's arms were all over me, my waist, my breasts, my face. The nurse on night duty saw the ruckus and screamed for a doctor. She helped the guard hold me down while the doctor gave me something, an opiate, maybe morphine. I never had morphine before, not even with Ross. It felt good. I slept until nine. Missed breakfast.

That morning the police decided to move me. The hospital loaned me clothes, ugly clothes. I hadn't worn anything so unstylish since East Millstone. I threw the clothes aside and asked the guard if I could write a letter. He was the same guard who had tackled me a few hours earlier—still on duty—and he looked sheepish now. When he said yes, I asked for paper. Sarah McArran, the neighbor might help. After all, I gave her a rubber plant and a bicycle just the day before. I wrote her, a big mistake. I asked Sarah to go to Hancock Street to fetch clothes for me. But before I listed what I wanted, I wrote, "The horrible news is circulating. I should prefer death to it. Through Will's threatening I was driven to desperation, but enough, I say no more about him. Go to the house and bring me some clothing." Then I wrote a list of what I wanted—dresses, wrappers, skirts, a fur cape, kid gloves, some other things. I asked the guard to post the letter to Sarah. Then I had a better idea. I asked him to send someone from the hospital to fetch those things from home, along with my cloak and hat. I knew he might say no, but he wasn't sure how to handle a prisoner who was a woman, or maybe he felt bad about touching me the night before. He talked to the supervising nurse and together they asked one of the younger nurses to help. I forgot to tell the guard not to post the letter to Sarah McArran. One of many things that would come back to haunt me.

An hour later the young nurse came back to the ward with a satchel. When I pulled out the garments, I heard the guard tell her to search the clothes for weapons hidden in the pockets or seams and to watch me dress. I guess the guard hadn't turned kindly after all. The clothes in the satchel were just what I had put on the list, but how could the nurse have done this—when she went to Hancock Street she took Ida's cloak and hat, either by mistake or to taunt me. I threw them down. "Not mine. Give these to charity. I'll go without a wrap." I saw the nurse and guard look at each other, a look of disgust.

But when I asked for water and a cloth to clean myself, the nurse obliged. Maybe she smelled me. I ducked under the blanket on the hospital bed and washed as best I could. Then I changed into one of my dresses under the covers, while glaring at the nurse. She was shaking, I saw. Ha, afraid, even here. The woman thought I was dangerous, or demented, or both. I asked for a mirror and arranged my hair carefully in a tight knot at the back. I patted down the wisps. I would not look demented. When I was ready the guard told me to wait in the hospital room while he brought a man upstairs,

Detective Becker. I didn't know it then, but he had just returned from calling on my maid.

Becker looked me over as he walked into the room. He was surprised. He must have been expecting a madwoman. He spent the night before with Ida, I guessed that from listening to footsteps upstairs when I laid on the floor in the parlor. If he saw me that night, he saw an unconscious woman. "Mrs. Place, we are heading to the Ralph Street Station so you can make a statement to Captain Ennis." I didn't nod, just let him take my elbow to lead me out.

Becker drove me to the station in an ordinary open patrol wagon. Without a coat, I was freezing. North on Rochester, out of the nice Crown Heights neighborhood. Then east on Atlantic. North on Ralph. The route took ten minutes, enough time for me to go over my story. Just to myself. I imagined I was telling it to the Captain. I heard a few holes. I plugged those up. Anyway, I thought I plugged them up.

I didn't mind the open wagon, but I did mind the crowd of men and women jostling each other outside the station. Some were quiet, craning their necks to see me. Others were yelling, "Murderess. Murderess." You won't understand this, but I didn't think they could be talking about me. Becker led the way into an office. It was empty except for a young woman, pretty, simply dressed in a gray uniform of some sort.

"Mrs. Place, this is Mrs. Sarah Driscoll, the matron for our Ralph Street Station. I'm going to leave and let her search you while I look for the Captain."

The awful woman put her hands all over my body, my chest, legs, pockets. I stiffened at her touch. I barely heard the woman's apology. Mrs. Driscoll found handkerchiefs in my pocket, took them out, and smiled. With a slight Irish lilt, she said, "We'll get these back to you before long. I doubt any warden would object to handkerchiefs."

She was kindlier than expected and willing to talk. I took my first chance to try out the story. Later I knew that was my second mistake that day, after the letter to Sarah McArran.

"I didn't do it," I said, facing the young matron.

"Didn't do what?" She still looked kindly.

"I didn't kill Ida. I did find acid and throw it in her face, but she was alive when I left her. I didn't see her the rest of the day." When I said "in her face," the matron winced. I added a few more details about that day. "I took the axe to protect myself against my husband. That man and my stepdaughter made so much trouble for me. They talked behind my back. When my husband left for work I took some white powder, or salts, from his desk. I put the powder into a glass of water and threw it in my stepdaughter's face."

"What part of her face?"

I pulled my lips back, not expecting such a question. "Her mouth." I kept talking. "Then my stepdaughter went out and I never saw her again. Later, I got an axe because I knew when my husband came home, he would go for me and I needed to protect myself."

Sarah Driscoll glanced at the door. I stopped talking when I saw Ennis, the Captain in charge the night before. He's the one who sat on his arse giving orders. Since my eyes were closed then, I didn't get a good look at him until the meeting in that office, which turned out to be his office. Nice uniform. But he combed his hair back in an odd way and should have given up on a beard. He walked into his office, along with Detectives Becker and Mitchell and a stenographer. I recognized Mitchell's cough. Probably a cigar smoker like Will. Mitchell was one of the officers, there were a lot of them, who tramped through my house the night before. I never saw him, but I remembered that cough. Turns out he had called on my maid that morning too, along with Becker, but then he went right to talk to Ennis while Becker came to fetch me from the hospital. Mitchell and Becker didn't look at each other.

The stenographer stared hard at me, probably planned to report back to his wife that he had seen the murdering shrew. I gave that look back to him. Once everyone was seated, the Captain did the introductions. He said what the purpose was of that meeting, but I can't recollect. That was the first of what seemed like hundreds of interviews, hearings, inquests, arraignments, indictments, trials. I never could keep them straight. I'm not sure it even mattered. Now the police started their questions.

"Tell us about the events of yesterday and what led up to those events," Ennis said. I didn't realize it then, but he knew to give little away.

I dropped my head down and carried on as I planned. I told about growing up and Wesley and Ross. Then I got to what the Captain wanted to hear. "I struck my husband. I was afraid he was going to attack me. He is critical of everything I do. We had a violent quarrel in the morning. He slapped me in the face. Hard. His daughter sided with him, she always does, and she makes up stories about me, how mean I am to her, lies, and when I went to speak with her, she slammed the door in my face. So I got some acid from my husband's photographic supplies in his desk, and I threw it in her face." I stopped for just a second. I remembered, too late, that I had decided not to use the word acid. My third mistake of the day. Better not stumble. Just move on. "Then I closed the door. After that, I didn't see her again. I was busy with housework. When I went to feed the furnace, I saw the axe in the cellar, and I thought I should have it in case my husband came at me again. When he returned from work, I struck him with it. Then I tried to kill myself. That's all there is to it."

While I talked, Captain Ennis looked across the desk at the stenographer. Now Ennis looked up. "Mrs. Place, had you been drinking?"

"A glass of whisky and a glass of wine."

Then, without warming, Ennis said, "John, pull the parcel out from under my desk. Unwrap it and place it on the desk. Mrs. Place, look at the axe. Do you recognize it? The dried blood?"

"I suppose I recognize that axe as ours." Then I stopped talking. I stared at Ennis until he started to look uncomfortable.

"All right. Now let's talk about the trunk. Your servant, Hilda Palm, this morning she told our detectives that a trunk went to your brother in New Brunswick and the police there confirm it arrived. I'm asking you to give us an order to take possession of the trunk. If you are innocent of murder, the trunk might help you prove that."

"Oh, no, that trunk is mine and it's going to my brother, Peter."

"I advise you to reconsider. Your decision here is not going to help your case."

"No. That's final." I almost spit at Ennis.

"All right. Let's go back to your morning quarrel with your stepdaughter. Miss Hilda Palm heard two quarrels in the morning, one when you quarreled with Mr. Place at breakfast, and one with Ida Place between 8:30 and 9:00. Sound accurate?" I didn't know why the Captain was interested in the timing.

I answered his questions, while Becker made notes for himself and the stenographer rushed to keep up with me. Had I babbled too much? Finally, we were done. Ennis told me to wait in an anteroom. Becker stayed behind for a minute. In the anteroom, all eyes were on me. The officer at the front desk stared and the matron, Sarah Driscoll, watched me pace up and down while we waited for a patrol wagon. Later I learned that Mrs. Driscoll was thirty-two and had been working in the Ralph Street Station for ten years. I also learned that she had a perfect memory.

Captain James Ennis

Five of us were in my Ralph Street office that morning. Detectives John Becker and Robert Mitchell, the stenographer, the matron Mrs. Sarah Driscoll, loyal to the core she is, and the woman. As captain, I frequently had criminals in my office, once or twice even a murderer, but never a killer who was a woman. I listened to her tell us her whole sad history. Her childhood on a failing farm, her marriage to a man who deserted her, the story of her son, and how she had to place him with another family, marrying her second husband. Then she made a confession, but to what? She told us she hit her husband with an axe and threw acid in her stepdaughter's face. The woman is crazy. I showed her the axe that Officer Barton brought over earlier. No reaction, none. A reporter for *The Sun* wrote that we also showed her the riding dress, with dark stains around the shoulders, the dress Ida Place had on when the patrolmen found her. That's impossible. Only the undertaker would undress the girl, and he did not get down to business until later. I was frustrated—I needed a confession. I thought if the woman saw her stepdaughter, she might understand the trouble she was in. She might admit her guilt. I asked Detective Becker to drive her to Hancock Street. That didn't go well either.

The Place murder was not good for me, or for the Fourteenth Precinct. We had been consolidated with Manhattan for only a month, forty days to be precise. I needed good results for John Mackellar, Deputy Chief of the Brooklyn police. He's my boss, and popular among the men. At the time he was under a lot of pressure from the borough of Manhattan to reduce our ranks but was holding firm. Good results with this case could help him out, and in that way help the Fourteenth. And help me.

Deputy Chief of Police for Brooklyn, John Mackellar

James Ennis, Captain of the Fourteenth Precinct, Ralph Street Station, came to see me early in the morning on February 8th. He filled me in on a murder in Stuyvesant Heights the night before. Captains didn't usually call on me, their boss, for a murder, at least not an ordinary murder. But this was a strange case. A respectable woman, married to a respectable man, living in a respectable neighborhood, born in the United States, killed her beautiful stepdaughter. And women don't usually kill, and when they do, the victim is rarely another woman. Ennis knew this was red meat for the newspapers. The journalists would eat it up.

I followed Ennis back to the Ralph Street Station and sat in a holding room while he questioned the woman. I didn't want to be there during the questioning. I didn't want to step on Ennis's toes. He's a good man, a little stuck up but a good man. Knows our procedures. When the interview ended Ennis told me about the woman's story and her answers. He said one of his detectives, John Becker, would swear out affidavits later that day.

I knew what I needed to do next. I rushed by cab to headquarters in Manhattan. In the cab I brushed off my jacket, ran my fingers through my hair, and used some spit to polish my brass buttons. I needed to report to New York City Police Chief John McCullagh—easy to remember his name because it was close to my own. The Chief's Chief, we called him. He had been in his position for just a month, since Brooklyn and all the boroughs were incorporated into greater New York. Eighteen police departments merged into one. That winter we all worked through the uncertainties of the consolidation. Everyone was on their best behavior, sharing information. I didn't want McCullagh to form a bad opinion of the Brooklyn police, or to think any more about cutting our ranks. Fortunately, my part in the Martha Place case lasted just this one day, for me a day of stress.

I had met McCullagh a month ago, at a consolidation ceremony. I wasn't sure he recognized me, but in his office now I kept the small talk to a minimum and laid out the facts. Then I went into the theories circulating at the Ralph Street Station. "Martha Place planned to murder Ida then run away to New Brunswick on the 3:15 train. She sent her trunk there. But she missed the train. That messed up her plans. Then, or maybe as an afterthought—afterthought is the word everyone used in the station—she decided to murder her husband and then run. Maybe she thought she would need to kill her husband to hide her first murder."

"Hmmm," McCullagh said, stroking his whiskers. "If she planned to run away, to New Brunswick, where she sent her trunk, then why did she tell everyone that was where the trunk was going, and that was the train she wanted to take. And how did she expect to hide what she had done if both the husband and the daughter were dead and she was missing?"

I tried control my squirming. Not a good start to the reorganization.

"I see your point, Chief McCullagh. Whatever the truth, our fine prosecutors will get at it. I will meet shortly with John Clark. Yes, another John for our club." I stressed the word *John*, hoping to add some levity. But the Chief's Chief wasn't smiling. "You probably haven't had an opportunity to talk with him yet. John is the Assistant District Attorney for Kings County, Brooklyn, working with D.A. Josiah Marean. They will have their own ideas about the case. I just didn't want you to hear about it first from those damn newspapers." McCullagh nodded, then asked his clerk to escort me out. No goodbye wave. Either McCullagh wasn't pleased at having Brooklyn crimes to worry about, or he thought my inductive powers wanting.

I quickly arranged my third meeting of the day. I sent a message to John Clark, telling him my officers would bring Mrs. Martha Place to the municipal offices at 4:00, to talk with both of us. Then a message to Captain Ennis, asking him to arrange transport for Mrs. Place. I stayed in

Manhattan, visiting a pub or two until it was time.

Mattie

After the meeting with Captain Ennis and the wait in the anteroom, Becker—he looked too smug for his own good—led me outside. The crowd had grown to both sides of the street. Still yelling "murderess." I walked back to the open patrol wagon, looking straight ahead while I buttoned my kid gloves. Didn't want those fools to see me looking bad. I still had no coat but no one cared. Becker drove to the row house. That must have been the plan he and Ennis came up with while I paced in the anteroom. When we pulled up to the curb, I saw a long string of lilies and white roses, smilax leaves too, attached by string to the door. The undertaker had been busy. Holding my elbow, Becker guided me up the icy front steps, into the house, and up the inside staircase. He told me to go into Ida's bedroom. I stood still in the hall, made a face at him. Why should I move? Gentle wasn't working. He shoved me in, with just enough force so I knew I had no choice. I glanced, without moving my face. Wouldn't let Becker know that for a second I saw Ida. The girl was lying beneath a sheet, on pine boards laid over two sturdy chairs. Becker had that look. He was deciding—should he take my head and shove it into Ida's queer face? He decided on the cautious path. He had no idea how to handle me.

"Damn, woman, are you afraid to look at what you've done?"

Now it was early afternoon. I grabbed my own cloak and hat from the rack as Becker led me back down the slippery front steps, into the wagon, more firmly than he led me in. He drove to the Gates Avenue Police Court, east on Hancock and north on Ralph about a mile. I had ridden my bicycle this way hundreds of times, past more row houses, more businesses, parks. Becker said this stop was for an arraignment, or maybe he said "indictment." I can't remember. Detective Mitchell, the one with the cough, waited for us on the curb, looking over the mob on the sidewalk and smoking his cigar. Becker walked up to him. "Wasn't her, Mitchell. Not that gal. Get your mind back to the guilty woman."

"OK. Maybe you're right," Mitchell croaked. I couldn't follow this. Who was the gal? Didn't make sense then and still doesn't.

I hadn't eaten at all that day. "I'm hungry," I snapped at Becker as the three of us walked into Gates Avenue Police Court's shabby reception room. Becker spoke to a matron, who brought out a light lunch of lukewarm soup and tasteless bread. Mitchell told me to eat quickly because Magistrate Lewis Worth was waiting. By the time I finished lunch, around 2:30, the crowd outside took over the reception hall of the station. Mostly women. And some men—probably reporters, judging from their notepads. Police were trying to shoo them outside.

The two Fourteenth Precinct detectives stuck to me like glue. They led me upstairs. This was the first time I had ever been in court, well, the first time not counting that drama when Will had me arrested the year before. I thought it might be time to change, I'll put it simple, from proud to scared. I put my head in my hands and put on a miserable face. That was easy to do. Magistrate Lewis Worth looked me over. I grasped the brass railing in front of his desk. Again, I heard the complaints against me. The judge said it was a formal charge, formal is the word he used. "First-degree murder, felonious assault, attempted suicide." I lowered my voice to a scared lady-like sound. I denied murder and said nothing about the other charges. I decided to repeat myself, so I denied murder two more times, again, in a whisper.

"Mrs. Place, are you able to afford a lawyer?" I looked at Judge Worth, uncomprehending for a minute. Why hadn't I thought about that?

"No. Of course not."

"I assumed as much. It seems unlikely your husband, one of the alleged victims, will offer funds. Under section 308 of the New York State Code of Criminal Procedure, a very generous section that to my dismay goes far beyond the other states, I am obligated to assign you defense counsel. And because you are being accused in a capital case, the state will pay your lawyer. In the chair behind you, to your left, you will see attorney Wayne Knittle. He will represent you.

I turned around. The state will pay for a lawyer? But Knittle? This man, maybe in his thirties, didn't look like he could defend a kitten. He had a baby face, eyes too wide apart, long neck, big ears, receding hair, and a frayed suit. A baby weasel, that's what he looked like. Maybe I could have gotten beyond the way he looked, but the man was shaking, stuttering.

"Sir, if it, if it please the court, I ask you to reconsider. I have never handled a murder case before. The defendant deserves experienced counsel."

"Now Mr. Knittle, it is your turn on the roster for indigent defense. Surely you can take on your responsibilities as a member of the New York bar. You want to stay in good standing before this court, right?" I saw the little weasel nod his head yes. Knittle already knew what I learned later. Worth was sheriff before he was magistrate. He was a no-nonsense man.

"Sir, sir, if you insist, then grant me an adjournment so I can review the precedents."

"All right. Court is adjourned one week, until February 15th."

Knittle left the room, almost running.

Detectives Becker and Mitchell didn't let me out of their sight. They took me through a back door. I had said little, maybe too little, but earlier I said too much. I hunched over, leaned to the left, then to the right. Becker and Mitchell looked at each other. They thought I was shamming. But the reporters saw me slump and that's what I wanted. I read in the papers the next day that I almost collapsed.

The detectives led me back to the patrol wagon and drove for a half-hour, across the bridge to Manhattan, to police headquarters in the Municipal Building. The streets were new to me. I'd visited Will's office in Manhattan once, but that was in the lower part of the city, more than a mile farther south. These buildings were the highest I ever saw, some fifteen stories, and the streets looked more crowded than in Brooklyn. Shoppers, strollers, businessmen. Cranes next to construction sites. Newsboys hawking papers. And even here, even in Manhattan, a crowd waiting for the patrol wagon. Becker struggled to pull up to headquarters because so many people stood jammed together on the sidewalk. Those damned reporters must have spread the word about my whereabouts. By now it was 4:00. Becker rushed me inside. He knew John Mackellar and John Clark were waiting. Later I learned who they were, their fancy titles—Mackellar was Deputy Chief of the Brooklyn police and John Clark was first Assistant District Attorney working under District Attorney Josiah Marean. Marean. That name would be in my life too much in four months.

The offices in the municipal building were nicer than the rooms at the Ralph Street Station or the Gates Avenue Police Court. Paneling. Leather chairs. Paintings on the wall. Mackellar and Clark introduced themselves. They had manners. They did not introduce the stenographer, who looked almost as uncomfortable as the stenographer in Ennis's office that morning. Then Mackellar read from his notes. Explained I was under arrest, "charged with felonious assault and attempted suicide." I said nothing. Then, he added, "murder." When I heard that word I muttered, "I did not do anything of the kind." That was the end of it. Mackellar's head dropped two inches and Clark's jaw tightened. Maybe they thought I would confess and make everything easy. I never saw either man again.

Becker and Mitchell didn't take me back to the Ralph Street Station, but to the Raymond Street Jail. Raymond was a big prison. Scary too. Built from stone. Looked like a church from the front, except for bars on the windows. Later the warden told me, proud like, that the prison was modeled after the fortress at West Point. Didn't mean much since I'd never seen West Point. Becker and Mitchell kept me between them, and we walked away from the main building, to the red brick female annex. They must have been there before because Becker told me this wing had more air and light than the main building. Hard to believe, maybe they were joshing. When we walked in the foul smell choked me. I started coughing almost as bad as Mitchell. Two matrons waited for us inside the door. Then all five of us walked to my cell. It was large, sixteen feet by eighteen is my guess, with barred windows. I saw three beds, but no other inmates. The youngest matron took me behind a flimsy screen and searched me. That was search number two of hundreds of searches I had to put up with. I stood stiff while she put her hands all over me. At least she was efficient, did it fast. Didn't look me in the eye. Then I asked the matrons if there were newspapers. "Are you certain you want to see them?" the older matron said. She scrunched up her face, like the papers were trash. Maybe she knew those papers were all sensational, yellow journalism they called it, each trying to sound more outlandish than the other. More likely she didn't think I could read.

"Of course I do," I said. She brought in a stack, three Brooklyn papers, and four Manhattan papers. I would read them later when I calmed down. I was shaking a little, maybe from the smell, or the search. Then that matron walked away to hunt for the guards. The younger matron stayed, with a good-natured look. Detective Mitchell, coughing, asked if I wanted to say anything more before Becker and he left. Wasn't sure what he meant by more. I sort of forgot what I said earlier that day.

I was deciding how to answer when the older matron came back with the guards. Becker and Mitchell talked to them and then left. Becker waved goodbye. There was no way for me to know he was returning to the Ralph Street Station to write out three affidavits, one for attempted suicide, one for assault in the first degree, and one for homicide, quoting my own words that day. Funny that I thought Becker was the nicer of the two detectives. Maybe he was a kind man, but he thought I was guilty as hell. Claimed he heard me admit to throwing acid in Ida's face and admit to hitting Will with an axe. That's when I was talking too much.

After I slowed my breath, I picked up the newspapers the older matron had set down on the table. Damn reporters. Their stories of the previous day's events rambled and were thick with mistakes. But it was their descriptions of the murderess, that's what they called me, that stuck in my craw. I despised the reporters' interest in how I looked, but at the same time, I sniggered when they didn't agree with each other. "She was 150 pounds, with brown and gray hair" one of them wrote. "Slim but big-boned" another one wrote. "Thin lips, square jaw, beady eyes." "Her nose is long and pointed." "Long sharp nose." "Sharply cut features." "Her chin is sharp and prominent." "Her forehead is retreating." "Small-brained." "Changeless eyes." "Cold face." "Altogether her face is a strange one." Some reporters guessed at my age. "Forty-five." "Short and forty-two." "Thirty-two." I smiled. Forty-nine would be my secret. The reporters never stopped. "Intelligent but not attractive." "Refined but uninviting appearance." "Delicate, refined general appearance." "Fascinating woman." "Underbred." "Handsome and well dressed." "Dashing." "Had a dashing way about her." "Dresses unpretentiously but in excellent taste." "Model housekeeper who did all her own housekeeping." "Immaculate housekeeper." "Frugal." "Seemed capable of exquisite cruelty." "Soulless."

The worst, the one I would never forget, came from the *New York Times*. "There is something about her face that reminds one of a rat's." Or maybe the worst was the Brooklyn *Standard Union*. "She was akin to a female hyena."

Coroner George Delap

The day before, the day of the murder, Captain Ennis looked at me a few seconds too long whenever I said anything about procedures. He saw I was playing by the book. I wasn't giving self-righteous officials the least reason to add anything to those ridiculous charges that I accepted bribes to make suicide causes of death disappear. Even if Ennis smirked a little, irritating me, I had no choice but to be proper. So on February 8th, early in the morning, by telegram I applied to Judge Gaynor of the New York Supreme Court for permission to hire Dr. Alvin Henderson to carry out the autopsy on Miss Ida Place, and to hire Dr. William Moser, a pathologist, to assist Dr. Henderson. Henderson served officially as my assistant, but he wasn't the sharpest. Moser was better qualified to examine the girl's organs, her stomach, to look for poison. By noon the day after the murder, I received a telegram approving my request.

Our team, three doctors, along with a stenographer, arrived at the Place house at 2:00. Police stationed in front of the house did not allow anyone else to enter. Martha Place had already come and gone, in the custody of Detective Becker, so we could proceed in privacy. As Henderson and I expected, Moser found no poison. Working away, Moser said, "an abrasion of the right temple and a deep gash above the left ear, from head to neck. Could have been made by a blunt instrument. Possible that the congested portion of the brain, which looks like a hemorrhage, could have been caused by a blow or a fall, and that could have been the cause of death, but more likely it was suffocation, maybe with a pillow. Eyes are burned. The liquid in the vial would have blinded her, but that was not the cause of death." Our stenographer managed to keep up. Henderson, the nominal head of our team, nodded in agreement as Moser worked. The stenographer captured that nod too. We concluded that the girl's death was due to asphyxia, which the public would call suffocation. For a few minutes, we discussed time of death. We settled on four hours—the girl had been dead for about four hours when the police found her. If they found her at 7:00 or so, then she died around 3:00. That detail never rose high in the minds of the lawyers connected to the crime. Don't know why, but that's not my business. Last thing I need to do while I'm being investigated for bribery is to question the prosecutors, or even the defense lawyers.

Much later it occurred to me that no one ever asked any of the three of us if Ida Place was pregnant. Not Assistant District Attorney Maguire, and not a single one of Mrs. Place's lawyers.

Edward Scheidecker

The day after Ida died, I walked to St. Mary's Hospital, leaving my apartment in the Bedford-Stuyvesant neighborhood of Brooklyn. Even though that sounded a lot like Stuyvesant Heights, and the two neighborhoods were so close that they were almost one, my block was not as nice as Ida's. She used to remind me of that. I walked two miles south, avoiding Hancock Street.

I had a right to visit Mr. Place in the hospital. After all, I'd courted the man's daughter, deceased daughter. And I knew him. We sang together in the Place home while Ida played the piano. Mr. Place was polite to me, maybe not encouraging, but perfectly polite. Ida would want me to check on her father. I didn't realize the stepmother was in the same hospital, but no matter—when I read the newspapers, I learned she had been taken away by the time I reached St. Mary's. At the men's ward, I saw Mr. Place in bed, wrapped in bandages and gauze. A nurse was at his side.

"I'm a relation of Mr. Place's, I whispered to her, smoothing my hair." Nothing wrong with stretching the facts a bit.

"Well, I have good news," she whispered. "The doctors say his wounds are serious, but not life-threatening as they thought last night. It's a compound fracture. I can give you more details if you're a relative." She went on, with a tone of pride. "The fracture is in two places. The axe cut through the frontal bone to the left and over to the nose. Then there was another cut over his left eye that penetrated the temporal bone and joined the other wound in a semi-circular curve. They removed bone fragments, just splinters really. They put in a drainage tube and stitched up his left arm and hand. No need for trephining."

The nurse stared at me, saw the blank look on my face. "No need for drilling into his skull," she whispered, even more quietly. I smiled as though I understood, but she didn't return the smile. Turned back to her patient. I turned to him as well.

"How are you feeling?"

"Eh." Not much of a response.

"The doctors here are good. They seem to be taking care of you, right?" Another "Eh."

"I'm sorry about Ida. Poor Ida."

Mr. Place was already slumped on the bed, but now he disappeared into the sheets. Like he melted. Was it pain? Surprise?

"Mr. Place, didn't anyone tell you? Ida, Ida, she was murdered."

Later that day Theodore and Charles Place learned from the alert nurse that I told their brother about Ida. They wanted to do that themselves, at what they said was the right time. As though there was a right time.

Napoleon Bonaparte Thompson

The morning after the madness, I did not to go to my office. I was tired from the night before and thought I might be of some use in the neighborhood. The temperature was too cold for me to spend more than a minute on my front stoop. I sat for most of the day in my parlor, watching the crowds and activity in the street. First, a nurse arrived next door. The patrolman guarding the Place house let her enter, but she was only there about five minutes. She left carrying a satchel. Curious. Then no activity for a while, aside from a young man in a black coat, hanging a string of white lilies on the Place's front door. Traffic on the street quieted down for a while.

Ella made a plentiful lunch, my favorite sausages, and apple pie, and served it in the dining room. She wanted to get me away from the front window. She had always been less sociable than I was. On that day she underestimated the assistance I could offer.

In the afternoon, more activity. A patrol wagon stopped at 598. Martha Place, looking stern, along with an officer. They walked up the Place front stairs. I didn't recognize the man until I remembered that I talked to him the night before when he asked who else might have been in the Place house. I told him about Hilda Palm since I had seen her hanging laundry in the yard. When the clothes are out there, you know, if I see Ida's bloomers and such, then I try to set my mind to looking away. But I did look back in the afternoon to see if they had turned to ice. I saw Hilda there again, in a hurry, checking on the laundry. She was probably at the Places' the whole day. The officer I saw with Martha, now I remembered his name was Becker. I couldn't guess why he was escorting her into her home. Maybe to pick up clothing. I asked Ella to look. She said Martha was wearing a different dress than the one she wore when they carried her into the ambulance the night before. She was walking on her own, with no trouble, despite the escaping gas yesterday. When I craned my head, I could see her scowl at the top of her front stairs. Must have seen the lilies on the door.

After Martha and Becker disappeared into the house, I stayed at the window. Another officer waited on the curb, shuffling and smoking. Then the first officer and Martha came out after just a few minutes. The two officers got close to each other. The smoker clenched his fists and Becker shoved his shoulder out. I could tell Martha was trying to listen to them. But it seemed to end all right. The one with the cigar relaxed his hands and Becker gave him a pat on the back. The three left in the wagon. A few minutes later Frank Fairchild, the neighborhood undertaker, arrived. He saw the lilies on the door of the Place house too. He nodded his head in approval as he entered. I suppose Fairchild now took charge of the body. Then I saw members of Ida's Sunday school class enter, but they left soon. Their high voices carried through the window. They complained that Fairchild didn't let them see Ida. Half an hour later, more commotion. The Coroner arrived and entered the Place house, along with two other men carrying black bags. Not sure what that was about. While those men were still in the house—it was almost dinner time—the two detectives I saw earlier returned and knocked on my front door. Detective Becker introduced me to the other one, Detective Mitchell. Becker thanked me for leading them to Hilda Palm and reported that they had a fruitful talk with her that morning. "Is there anyone else you suggest we interview?" he asked.

I was ready for this. "Oh, yes, try Gertrude Hebbard or Fred Fahrenkrug. Miss Hebbard is close, just around the corner on Reid Street. She was a friend, maybe a best friend, to Miss Place. And Mr. Fahrenkrug, he's a detective, a private one, is engaged to Miss Hebbard. He was in the crowd last night. I think the Coroner picked him for the jury, but you might have left by then."

That's how Becker and Mitchell might have learned that Gertrude wanted a double wedding and that Fred had carried out an investigation for William Place. I knew about the investigation because Will told me one night in early September, when I knocked on his door after I heard an argument, and after I saw Martha ride off on her bicycle. What I didn't know was that Becker had already listened to what he considered to be Martha's confession, and that night would fill out affidavits swearing to what he heard. He probably needed to digest what I had said about Gertrude and Frank, to decide if he needed to do more or if he already knew enough. He must have decided there was no reason to continue with inquiries. A sensible conclusion, I suppose.

Peter Garretson

Mattie was a lost cause, didn't matter she was my sister. Mean as Ma and Pa, almost as mean as Ellen. When Mattie finally found herself a husband, he was a cad who deserted her. Left her penniless. I was happy when she found William Place, but that turned into a bad match. I knew what Mattie saw in William, but never figured out what William saw in Mattie.

New Brunswick was a small town, so the summer before Ida Place died, I heard from Hendrick Vliet's handyman, Ollie, that a girl named Ida was spending the summer away from her family, boarding with the Vliets. Ollie didn't know Ida was sort of my niece and he never mentioned her surname. Just her looks. He was doing some carpentry work in the train station as I sorted the baggage, and he maybe had too many beers at lunch. He talked about how he liked looking at the summer guest relaxing in the lawn chairs when he fixed the Vliet's roof. Slowly, I began to guess who this Ida was. I remembered that there was a connection between Mattie's new husband's first wife and the Vliet family. Around that time Grace, my oldest daughter, she's sixteen, told me about a girl who was coming to church that summer, who put on airs. Said her name was Ida. That was the name of a cat we had. Grace thought it was funny that Ida had the same look. Grace never said Ida was Aunt Mattie's stepdaughter, so I don't know if she knew or not, but I was getting the picture. A stuck-up girl spending the summer with a posh local family. I suspected Ida and Martha didn't get on.

After wondering about the Vliet's summer guest, I didn't think about Mattie much those months from August to February. Then all hell broke loose. Mattie went from mean to murder.

When I got home the night of February 8th, my daughter Grace was waiting for me at the front door. The reporters would write that Grace was nine, left home alone. The New York people who read the papers would think I was the negligent brother of a crazy murderess. All the reporters had to do was ask our neighbors. They knew who Peter Garretson was—a struggling, hard-working widower, raising four children. Grace at sixteen. Margaret at fourteen, named after my dead wife. Matilda at twelve. Ogden at three. I was tired. And now this.

I knew something was wrong when I saw Grace's grim look as she opened the door. She handed me letters, some addressed to her and some to me. From Mattie. Grace had already read the odd messages and knew what was stuffed in the envelopes—money, bank books, a trunk key, a claim check for a trunk.

Damn trunk.

The day before, on my train from New York to New Brunswick, I handled the baggage as I always did. I lifted boxes, valises, and trunks, and I recorded the pieces as required, and arranged them to fit snug on the train, and then in the baggage room. I had never, never, had a piece of baggage addressed to me. When I lifted one of the wooden trunks, I was dumbstruck to see it was going to Mr. Peter Garretson. There was a return address. Mattie. At the New Brunswick station, I lifted off the baggage, as usual, depositing more than twenty pieces with the station master, Cyrus, again, as usual. I pointed to the trunk. "Cyrus, this trunk's for me. No idea what's in it. Hold it here until I can get a wagon to carry it home. Probably tomorrow, maybe after dinner." I wasn't in a hurry because I didn't care what Mattie sent.

"Must be Christmas late for you this year," Cyrus said. He was just as surprised as I was to see baggage for a Garretson.

The next evening, still standing in the front room, I read Mattie's letters. Took me a while—I was not the best reader. Grace stood next to me, arms crossed, staring down while she waited for me to finish. She said we should sit and then she told the story as best she could, starting off fast. She heard it from the New Brunswick police chief, Francis Harding, who called at the house an hour earlier, just before I returned from work. I knew Harding, he was a good sort. He explained to Grace that a man named Captain Ennis from Brooklyn had telegrammed to say that a trunk was sent yesterday afternoon to Mr. Peter Garretson in New Brunswick, by Mrs. Martha Place. Grace slowed down. Started to shudder. "Mr. Harding said the man in Brooklyn told him that Aunt Mattie murdered her stepdaughter." The wind left me. I was passing out. Grabbed the seat of my chair and felt my head drop to my knees. Grace stood up and rubbed my back. She went on, "This Ennis man told Chief Harding that the trunk should be held in the baggage room of the New Brunswick train station. And, oh, the lawyer. Let me look at the note I wrote for myself." She walked to the table to fetch a scrap of paper. "I'm supposed to tell you Chief Harding talked to a lawyer he knows, Howard McSherry, who told him to tell Cyrus not to release the trunk until its owner agrees, or until there's a court order. McSherry. Is he the father of Olivia, the girl who was in my class?" I knew the name McSherry too.

Now I understood why Cyrus gave me a funny look when I came through the station that evening. No more joshing about a late Christmas present. Chief Harding must have gone to the station earlier in the day to look for the trunk and to tell Cyrus to hold on to it. I was frantic. I was only a baggage handler, but I played poker with Harding, a weekly game I was happy to be asked to join when another man was needed, and Grace went to school with Harding's sons—and McSherry's daughter—until she had to drop out to help with my young ones. Harding and his friends knew I grew up poor, but I thought they liked me. We got along, even though I wasn't part of their set. Now they would know poverty was not the Garretsons' only problem.

My first family, the family in East Millstone, they were dead to me. Some of them were truly dead—the brothers I never knew, and Eliza and now Tillie too. My other sisters were still on this earth, but just trouble. Ellen was sour and Mattie, well, Mattie. Where was she when I needed her? Yeah, first she had come to stay with me when she had nowhere else to go. But then, when my wife Margaret got sick and I had to take care of Grace and Maggie and Matilda and baby Ogden, where was Mattie? Still in Atlantic City with Ellen. Mattie wouldn't have been much help anyway. She cared about Grace, for sure, but she probably didn't even know the names of my others. Now she had gone and done it. Murder. Dragging the Garretson name down. Embarrassing me again.

Grace said she told Chief Harding to return after dinner when I was back home. I wasn't thinking about dinner, but Grace knew she had to feed the three younger ones. We all sat at the table. Grace and me didn't eat a thing. While Grace stared into space and cut up food for Ogden, I read and reread the letters, the ones for me and the ones for Grace. They got jumbled in my head, a mix of strange orders. "Keep the money to buy a new home. Don't put any money into that damned farm. Look after dear little Ross and share with him. Keep $200 for yourself and share the rest with Ross when he comes of age. Take Ross to live with you when he becomes twenty-one. Grace, use the clothes I am sending." I added up the money in the two bank books Mattie enclosed. Just as I got to the sum, we heard a knock. Grace thought it was Harding and opened the door. Instead, it was a reporter from our paper, the *Daily Times*. He told Grace he had gone to Brooklyn that afternoon and had just returned to New Brunswick. He wanted to get Peter Garretson's thoughts on Mrs. Martha Place, the sister. Grace closed the door in his face. I smiled. I saw the satisfied look on her face. She thought my smile was for the way she treated the reporter.

"There's thirteen hundred dollars," I said. "More than I make a year."

"But why?" she said.

I shrugged my shoulders. Then I checked the tops of the letters. All either had no date or the date of February 7th. Except for one. One letter, written to Grace, was dated September 20, 1897. It was one of the neater letters, written in ink.

We heard another knock. Chief Harding. Grace led him into the parlor and scooted the children upstairs. Then I motioned to her to sit with us.

"Francis, I always knew Mattie would be trouble. I'm sorry about this."

"Ah, don't worry, Peter. We all have black sheep in the family. But we need a plan for what to do. The first problem is the trunk. Your sister is not letting us open it. We're keeping it at the station for now. That's what that Brooklyn captain wants. The next problem is that your sister may need a good lawyer if she's not going to, sorry chap, not going to hang." He turned his face away from Grace, lowering his eyes and grimacing with his lips.

"Francis, Grace said you talked to Howard McSherry. He's the only lawyer I know, even a little. His daughter goes to school with our children, right? But I can barely pay for the wood to heat the house this winter. Nothing left to pay a lawyer." I looked quickly at Grace then back at Harding.

"Peter, when I mentioned that I'd called on Howard, that was because I needed advice on releasing the trunk. But let's think about your sister too. There's a complication. The crime, the presumed crime, happened in Brooklyn. Howard can practice law in New Jersey, not New York. Let's talk to him anyway. Maybe he'd like to flap his wings in a serious case. One more thing, Peter. Captain Ennis tells me his detectives there talked to the servant girl who worked for your sister. The girl said she posted letters to you. I need to ask you to hand them over." Shit. I waited for a second, then nodded to Grace. She fetched the letters and motioned for Harding to sit at the table to read them. He took in the dates on the letters, as I had. When he got to the bank books and then instructions about money, he looked at me with a small smile.

118

"Maybe you do have enough money for McSherry."

When all this happened, I was forty-five. The reporters thought I was thirty-six. I felt eighty.

Mattie

Two days had passed since Ida died. The matrons watched me every minute, the younger one in the day, the older one at night. I heard the older one report to Warden Richard Bergen when he made his rounds. I'd spent a "restless night." I wonder what kind of night she'd have if they charged her with murder.

The warden had visited me around supper time the night before. He was young, about thirty, not bad looking except for greasy hair and skimpy whiskers. "I need you to follow our rules but do let me know if there is anything amiss so we can address it." He talked a long time, laying out what would happen next and trying to sound official and friendly at the same time. He knew the reporters would be out here soon, looking for stories about his star prisoner.

That morning I was alone, except for the day matron, the younger one. I worried I had been foolish to make admissions the day before, in front of the Ralph Street Station matron and all those men. My plan then was to admit to everything except killing. Was that right? Now I saw that I needed a lawyer, a good lawyer, someone to tell me what to say, not that fidgety Knittle. I walked up and down the cell, pacing in front of the matron. Her eyes followed me.

Warden Bergen was decent to me the night before, even if he was just trying to protect himself. No harm in asking him. What was he going to do, arrest me? I walked up to the younger matron. By now I knew her name, Mrs. Handy. "Please call the warden for me. I need to talk to him."

A few minutes later Warden Bergen entered my cell. His hair was still greasy. "Mrs. Place, how are you doing this morning?"

"This jail takes some getting used to. But everyone has been kind. I need to ask a question. That judge, Magistrate Worth, yesterday he assigned a lawyer named Wayne Knittle to represent me. Do you know him?"

The warden waited a few seconds before he answered. "No, I don't. The lawyers who are assigned for defense, in capital cases, it's a rotation. And there aren't many capital cases, to be honest. Some of the lawyers are good and some are not. Do you have funds to retain a lawyer of your choosing?"

Now I was the one to wait a few seconds. "I'm not sure. If I did, who do you think is up to the job?"

Warden Bergen scratched his skimpy whiskers on one side. Then the other side. "Well, if I was in trouble, I would go to the top for representation. I would try for Ridgway. James Ridgway. You know the name? He was district attorney of Kings County until last year when he retired. But he's not old, no, in his late forties maybe. Now he's in a law practice, a private firm. It may seem odd to think of a prosecutor as a defense lawyer, but the thing is, these men, they know all the tricks because they have seen them. Not, of course, that any tricks would be needed in your case. But he is smart. A little ruthless too. I shouldn't have said that. Here's an order. Don't repeat what I just said. But ruthless may not be a bad thing for you."

I smiled when Warden Bergen winced. He knew he said too much. Now that I've heard from jailhouse scuttlebutt that the warden is an ambitious man, I think maybe he wanted to rack up credit by sending Ridgway a notorious client. I thanked Bergen for visiting and turned back to my chair so he would go. Then right away I asked Mrs. Handy for paper and pen. In my letter to Ridgway, I said I wished to discuss representation, that was the word the warden used so I used it too. I didn't say one way or the other about payment. The matron offered to have the letter delivered. The warden must have told her to treat me special. Then a shock—three hours later the guard at the door told me I had a visitor, James Ridgway. He was about my age, distinguished-looking, with silver hair. What stood out the most was his suit—the best-tailored suit I ever saw, out of fine wool. The man knew how to dress. Mrs. Handy looked impressed and offered him not only a chair but tea too. He asked me to go over my story, which I now had down cold. I didn't change anything from the day before. I would live with what I said. Live, I hoped.

"This will not be an easy case to win," Ridgway said. "You admit to two heinous acts—throwing acid in Ida Place's face and hitting your husband with an axe. Convincing a jury that you are not guilty of first-degree murder will take talent. And I understand you have limited funds. I would need to take the case on a *pro bono* basis. In other words, I would be paid a very modest fee by the court. Far less than my standard fee. But you know Mrs. Place, you have gained notoriety. I don't mind admitting that the publicity this case will bring intrigues me.

Ridgway gave me hope. That night, for the first time in ten years, I dreamed of escaping. Markus Van Cortland. The boy from the farm near mine in East Millstone. No, he was not killed in Virginia in the war. He was biding his time, scheming how to get me out of the Raymond Street Jail. I had thought of Markus every now and then since that deadly winter, 1862. He didn't age. He was young, beautiful. He knew what to do. He would distract the young matron. He would kill the guard.

Peter Garretson

After Chief Harding's visit to my house, it took another day for that stinking detective from Brooklyn, Mitchell's the name, to get a court order allowing the police to open Mattie's trunk. I was glad for the delay, so I could figure out what to do next. No one thought of me as clever, but even I knew that Harding would share Mattie's letters with Mitchell, and her money might never see the light of day, or of my day. That money was the best thing Mattie had ever done for me, and for Grace. If the Brooklyn police didn't claim the money, and I worried about that, then I would go along with Harding's plan to hire a lawyer, but I hoped to keep at least some of my sister's gift for my family. Five hundred dollars, that's all I would let go for a lawyer. Anyway, that's what I thought. Harding had taken the letters with him, but not the money or the bank books. He probably thought that if I used some of the money to pay his pal McSherry, at least the money would stay in our town, New Brunswick.

Harding wanted to open the trunk as soon as he could, but he needed two of us with him—me, because I was the recipient, and Detective Mitchell who would come carrying the court order from the judge. I couldn't miss a

121

day of work. I rode my train that Wednesday, the train where I was baggage master, from New Brunswick to New York and back again, returning about 5:00. Although I didn't know it, Mitchell was on the same southbound train. Mitchell and me found Harding waiting for us inside the station. The three of us gathered around the trunk. The detective was the nervous type, smoking like a chimney, eager to get to work. Cyrus, the station master, waited off to the side but now he put his hand out for the claim check. After I gave it to him, he hovered in the background, probably getting ready to pass along any gossip.

Mitchell put his cigar down, asked me for the key, and opened the trunk. He was practically drooling as he fumbled with the lock. He wanted a piece of evidence to prove Mattie's guilt. I just wanted to get through this ordeal. In the end, there were no surprises. "Anticlimactic," is the word Chief Harding used. In the trunk, Mitchell found silk gowns, an opera coat, a sealskin coat, four pairs of shoes, slippers, seven rings, one was diamond, a gold watch, brooches, underwear, and photographs of Ross. Mitchell pulled them out, one at a time, frowning at each item. When he lifted out the underwear, coughing over everything, I grabbed the items from his hand and threw them back. He scowled at me. "Come on, Peter, we're just doing our job," Harding said. I thought the clothing was carefully packed, as I expected from Mattie. Mitchell thought it was thrown into the trunk with little care. All three of us saw the trunk offered no clues to the murder.

Harding frowned and scrunched up his face. Was he trying to impress a New York City detective? "If Martha Place planned to kill her stepdaughter and then run away," he said to Mitchell, "why would she send her trunk to New Brunswick, where she would be easily found? Was it possible that she planned to kill herself instead of escaping?" Mitchell shrugged his shoulders. I stayed silent. Cyrus left in a hurry, probably to spread the news about the anticlimactic contents.

Harding had brought Mattie's letters along and handed them to Mitchell. "Detective, Mrs. Place enclosed cash and bank books along with the letters. I told Mr. Garretson he should retain all that for now." Mitchell shrugged, which I took as the best news of the night.

Harding and Mitchell put the trunk on the 6:22 train back to New York. Mitchell rode along with it and would take it back to his captain. We never learned what happened to it next, or to Mattie's jewelry. I doubt Grace wanted any of it, even though she would always be fond of my sister, no matter what.

William Place

I could not leave St. Mary's Hospital. My wounds, though not mortal as the doctors first feared, were healing slowly. John Maguire, the assistant deputy attorney, came to the hospital to see me. It was three days after the savagery. Maguire would expect to see a man crushed by the murder of his daughter and the betrayal of his wife. But I was not an emotional man. I lived through tragedies before and I would do so again. I would show some sorrow, of course, but I would not put on a show for him.

The nurse led two men into the ward. "Mr. Place, I am John Maguire, assistant district attorney. This fellow here is Archie Broome, my clerk. How are you feeling? Well enough to talk?" The nurse brought in two ladderback chairs for the men. She was careful to give Maguire's chair the place of honor, closest to my bed. Maguire was short, paunchy, with a pleasant round face. Broome was tall, thin, serious. They sat down, both staring with apparent concern at the heavy bandages encircling my face.

"My wounds were serious. I have a compound fracture of the skull and my hand was wounded. But the doctors didn't need to trephine, you know, to use a saw to surgically remove bone. I need to stay in the hospital for some time. Will that affect the trial?"

"Before we get to the trial, Mr. Place, I need to take your statement. I am sorry to come here so soon after, well, after you were injured, but the sooner we can talk to a victim, the better. In terms of memory, that is."

I nodded understanding. "I can talk, though I get tired easily. Maybe not tired this morning, though. I had my first coffee in three days." My smile was partially hidden by winding bandages.

"I need to ask, are they giving you morphine?"

"The doctor gave it to me last night, but not this morning."

"Best not to say anything about that unless you are asked. I don't want your statement or testimony called into question."

Again, I nodded.

"Now, let's start at the beginning with who you are and what happened. Don't leave out any details." Archie Broome took out his briefcase, surprisingly fine leather, a notebook, and fountain pen, not so fine. I began. I took seriously what Maguire said, that I should start with who I am.

"As you know, my name is William Place, William W. Place. I live in Brooklyn, Stuyvesant Heights to be precise, at 598 Hancock. I have owned the row house there for ten years. I am fifty-three. I was forty-eight in 1893 when I met Martha. Her name then was Martha Garretson, well, Martha Garretson Savacool. Then, and right up to today, except of course for this time recovering from the wounds she gave me, I work as an insurance adjuster, fire claims mostly, for London & Lancashire Insurance. It's a fine business, international. My office is in a grand eight-story building, designed by a renowned architect."

Maguire started to fidget. Broome kept scribbling.

"My specialty, as I said, is fire losses. So, Mr. Maguire, I have worked with many lawyers settling claims, but I confess I have never met a district attorney before."

"Mr. Place, I am an assistant district attorney. I don't think D. A. Marean would appreciate my sudden promotion. Please go on. We need your version of events."

"You can see I am an ordinary man, in every way, though thinking back I realize Martha believed I was, well, good looking, and of substantial means. Before she met me, she met my brother, Charles, he's a banker, and she learned I had a good occupation. She also knew about my social set, though I'm not sure how much that mattered to her. I am a Mason in good standing. I am a member of the Royal Arcanum, you know, the benefit society. And I was past district deputy of the Odd Fellows Circle, I'm sure you know that one too." I looked at Broome as I explained, "It's a fraternal organization promoting friendship and care of the sick." I looked back at Maguire. "I do not claim to be a member of high society, but I do get together with men who are in the better circles of Brooklyn. I would like to think I have their respect. Oh, and I should tell you about my other interests. I read the newspapers each day, attend concerts, play the piano. Mrs. Place does not share any of those interests, which is one of the things that came between us. She is not a simple woman, but uneducated in the arts. And you are probably curious about my spiritual leanings. I was well enough to read the newspapers this morning, where I saw that one reporter wrote I was active in the Jane Street Methodist Episcopal Church. Another reporter wrote I was a prominent member of the Lewis Avenue Congregational Church. Both reporters are correct. First one then the other." I kept to myself that clergy at each had chastised me for lack of attendance. That was not Maguire's business. "But, I will be honest. I think of myself as a man of science, more than a believer." That much I was willing to tell him. "My hobby—photography—it kept me busy and sane in the years I mourned for my wife, my first wife, and my children."

Maguire was squirming again, his bulk shifting from side to side. He tried to get Archie Broome's attention, but the clerk was still focused on capturing every one of my words.

"God has not been kind to me, Mr. Maguire. Four children lost. William, dead at age one. Then Hattie, dead at age three. Then in the same year Florence, just one year old, and Edith, who managed to live until age eight. It was hardest on Laura, my first wife. Somehow, she survived, for a time, despite the grief. When Edith and Florence were hit with that deadly typhoid, Ida was four."

Maguire stopped squirming and leaned forward when he heard Ida's name.

"Ida kept Laura alive because Laura had to be strong for Ida. And protect her. Then Laura died a miserable death, leaving me a widower. Then I was the one who had to protect Ida. I married Martha because I thought she would be good for Ida. I put aside that the woman lacked education, lacked refinement. I was a fool."

Maguire was smiling, happy I had moved on to the killer.

"But talking about marriage, I'm getting ahead of myself. First, I hired Martha Savacool to be my housekeeper. Nine months after Laura died. I found Martha thanks to the good graces of my sister-in-law's sister, Anna Mann, of Asbury Park. She introduced us."

I frowned and smirked as I said good graces.

"'My daughter is twelve,'" that's what I told Martha five years ago when I interviewed her for housekeeper. "Ida goes to school. You won't have to watch her much, but she will be around in the afternoons and holidays. Do you mind?'" When I said that to her, I assumed she was childless.

"'I took care of my two little sisters for years. I loved them.'" That's what she said to me.

So I said, "'You will love Ida too. She's a sweet child, talented with music, smart.'"

"Looking back, I think I saw Martha hesitate for a second, then smile. I set a monthly wage, which seemed fine with her. All was arranged."

I went on talking, telling Maguire about the wedding. How none of Martha's relatives attended. I considered adding that none of mine did either, but I decided to keep Charles and Theo out of the picture for now. I talked briefly about our first year of marriage, how Martha and I started off in good spirits. Then the painful story of Ross. His dreadful visit our first Christmas. The one detail I left out was that Martha told me about her son before our wedding. I let Maguire think that I learned about Ross after we were married. I was careful not to lie, not to a man of the law, not, it was my creed, to anyone. But I knew Maguire did not have the full picture about Ross, and he wouldn't. Not from me.

The more I talked, especially about how mean Martha was to Ida, the more Maguire looked puzzled. I could see he wanted to know why I was attracted to the shrew. I did add that we had some fine times together, that she kept an orderly house. I knew I had to keep my face, what little Maguire could see of it, placid, composed. Hidden under the bandage, then my scabs, then my skin, then my brain, I could feel my shame. I tried to forget, though I failed, how she aroused me, how she led me. I had not been intimate with Laura for years. For most of that time, we grieved for our dead children. Only I knew the many ways I had been unfaithful to Laura's memory. For Maguire I shoveled on all the details about church and culture and clubs,

126

talking more than usual, too much I suppose. But I needed him to see me as upstanding. I knew for the criminal courts of Brooklyn my own guilt was not central to the crime, or crimes. But for me, it lingered. I read in the *Brooklyn Standard Union* that I had been infatuated with Martha. Infatuated. What a proper word for lust.

Once I got through talking to Maguire about Martha, I needed to take a deep breath to keep going, but this time because of the horror, which he knew about, not the shame, which he didn't. I told him about the days leading up to the murder, then the day of the murder, then the darkness in the hall, then the rustle of a skirt, the faint whiff of Empire Rose. He stopped squirming. Broome had a harder time than ever keeping up. The nurse, the overly attentive one, came in to say I needed to rest, but I explained that I would feel better if I finished my statement. Maguire asked only a few questions, particularly about timing and when I learned that Ida had been murdered and about Wesley Savacool. An hour later we were done. I was exhausted.

Napoleon Bonaparte Thompson

My life remained unsettled. Even the third day after the mayhem, I didn't go to work. I had a funeral to attend.

That morning Ella said she didn't think any more people could fit on Hancock Street. I touched her shoulder to nudge her away from the front window so I could see too. I guessed six hundred gawkers were milling around and I was pleased to see that the *Daily Eagle* confirmed that number, and even more pleased to see that the *Standard Union* raised the number to one thousand. The night before the police removed the white lily garland from the front door of the Place house, I'm sure in an effort to make it harder for spectators to find the house. That failed miserably. Everyone in Brooklyn knew the address.

At 10:00 Sargent Barton arrived with fifteen policemen. I put on my coat and chatted with him for a minute. Chief Ennis had told him to control the crowd at the start of the funeral. I went back inside to the parlor so he could do his job. Despite the chill, I opened the parlor window slightly to listen to him address the gawkers. "The funeral already took place early this morning," he said. "Now go, disperse, give the family some peace." Barton, standing on the sidewalk, and me in the parlor, we could both see the warning to the crowd didn't work. Half the gawkers left, but the other half, rightly suspicious of Barton's words, stayed.

Now it was 10:30. Edward Scheidecker stood in front of the Place house, weeping. He was making quite a show of it. Pastoral instincts intact, I went out to the sidewalk to comfort the lad and lead him inside my own house for a cup of Ella's tea. Ella and me, we assumed he was weeping over his lost fiancé. The story was more complicated. "When I went to see Mr. Place in the hospital the other day," Edward said, "I told him Ida had been murdered. I think I was the first to tell him. Then I said I would go to Ida's funeral, to say goodbye to her. Mr. Place barely spoke to me, he's still weak, but he did say I shouldn't go. I told him he couldn't do that, couldn't stop me. I had to go. He didn't take it back, just said it was up to his brothers. So I called on Charles a few hours later. Theodore was visiting him. The brothers had just returned from the hospital where they heard, first, from the nurse, then from Mr. Place himself, that I was the one to tell about Ida, and that made them angry. They didn't want me to see Ida's body or to attend her funeral. Told me to leave." There was even more to the lad's sad tale. In addition to telling him to leave, the brothers denied ever hearing he was engaged to Ida. They said their wives claimed Ida never spoke of him. "Those Place brothers," Edward said, as he finished his tea and gobbled a biscuit. "They don't think I was good enough for Ida. They didn't think that stepmother was good enough for Mr. Place. And they were right. But they're wrong about me."

I listened. I told Edward to keep Ida in his prayers and thoughts and to forget about Theodore and Charles Place. From our perch at the front window, Ella and I watched Edward walk away, still weeping. The crowd watched too.

I went upstairs to put on one of the suits I wore when I led a congregation. While I dressed, I tried to reason out what Edward told me. Charles and Theodore Place were angry that Edward had been the first to tell Will about

Ida. That wasn't right. I was the first to tell Will, perhaps inappropriately, the very night of the murder when Will sat in my house with his wounds. It's possible my news about Ida never sunk in. After all, Will was in pain, maybe in shock. But if he did hear, why didn't he tell Edward that he already knew? Was he trying to get Edward into trouble? Or were the brothers looking for an excuse to keep Edward away from the funeral? Or was all this a misunderstanding?

Charles Place didn't want Edward at the funeral, but he had asked me to attend. I walked next door, not an easy twenty-foot walk because the crowd had increased again, with huge numbers of spectators taking the places of people who had been chased off by Sargent Barton. A guard positioned at the Place front door let me in the parlor, where Undertaker Fairchild was overseeing the casket. The white lilies that had hung over the front door of the row house now draped the casket, along with other arrangements. I saw a flower wreath, with a note signed by Edward Scheidecker. The Place brothers and their wives must have neglected to read the signature on the note. The four of them stood stiffly in the parlor, along with their older children. Six or seven other men and a few women I didn't recognize entered the parlor quietly, looking ill at ease. Will was still in the hospital, forbidden by his doctor to leave. Reverend Adam of the Janes Street Methodist Episcopal Church led the service, not quite up to my standards but good enough. Then six of the men carried the casket out the door, down the stairs, past the spectators held back by Sargent Barton and his crew, into a white hearse. Three black carriages were to follow, in a procession. Along with Jim Dawson, the other next-door neighbor, I climbed into the last of the carriages, putting the total number of mourners at twenty-two. We were not headed to the cemetery where Will had buried his wife and four children. He was no longer pleased with that location and planned to have the caskets moved once he was well enough to select new plots. In the meantime, Ida would rest in a vault at the Cypress Hills Cemetery.

I had spent some time talking to Charles Place and comforting him on the night his niece's body was found and his brother was hurt. One of the reporters, a particularly entrepreneurial chap, had noticed Charles and me talking. In the next day or two, word got around about the timing of the funeral and the restrictions on who could attend. The reporter tried to speak to Will about the details but the watchful nurse turned him away. Next, the reporter hunted down Charles. After a number of conversations, the Place family decided to ask me not only to attend the funeral but also to serve as the only attendee designated to talk to reporters afterward. I suppose they thought that my years as a man of the cloth, along with my experience as an advertising agent, made me suitable. While I went with the others to the vault, Ella made scones and tea for five reporters who waited in our front parlor for me to return, hopefully with a vignette or two. The only one of my stories the reporters found worthy was the one about Edward. The fiancé, for some unknown reason, was not allowed to attend Ida's burial. That story made it into the papers, but it was soon forgotten.

Mattie

The Raymond Street Jail was godawful for most inmates, but I was getting special treatment. I was notorious, after all. How many women, I should say how many respectable women, native-born like me, married to professional men, are accused of murder and felonious assault? By now I knew the right words.

My first few days in that jail, I weighed the safest plan. I don't mean what I would admit to, I was sticking with the powder on Ida and the axe on Will. I mean how I would seem. I acted, well, unemotional in the hospital and in the Ralph Street Station. Silent, like I didn't care. Then I tried something else, sagging, collapsing at the Gates Avenue Police Court. That didn't feel right either.

I was still thinking about this, four days after they said I killed Ida, when I met Miss Emilie Meury. She gives her time to the Brooklyn Auxiliary Mission Society. Young, thirty-two. Spends her days at the jail. The guards know her. She's the one they call the prison angel. First, I avoided her. She's preachy. Pretty, at least I thought so, with a pert little face and slim waist. But she hides her looks. She wears the same plain gray dress the other missionary ladies wear and she always holds a Bible close to her breast, as though that's going to protect her or anyone else. When she heard one of the older missionary ladies try to convince me to come to the Sunday service, she saw that wasn't working. She tried herself.

"Mrs. Place, we would be honored if you joined us on Sunday."

"God hasn't helped me so far, why should he help me now?"

"When you are in a group with other prisoners, you might feel the spirit more than when you are alone."

I kept saying no. She bowed her head and looked down at her Bible. She was disappointed, like it really mattered.

"I don't want to pray. Won't do no good."

"Mrs. Place, simply come and listen. The prayers of others might bring you peace. And the service will give you a chance to leave your cell for an hour."

I couldn't argue with that. The cell wasn't bad, but I wanted to move, to stretch. So on Sunday, when the guards walked through the halls of the women's wing and asked who wanted to attend the service, I nodded my chin up an inch. They led me and a few other prisoners to the women's service, down the hall, near the entrance. Miss Meury was already in the chapel, along with two other missionary ladies. She raised her head when I walked in and gave me a big smile. I hadn't gotten too many of those lately. We all sat in a circle, on hard wooden stools. The service went on and on, with a reverend leading the prayers and the missionaries joining in. Some of the prisoners joined in too. Not me. I sat quiet like, saying nothing except singing a psalm or two. I remembered melodies from the First Reformed in New Brunswick. The chapel had fresher air than my cell. At the end of the service, as everyone walked out, the feeling that I was alone again rolled over me. For a minute I forgot to act as though I didn't care. My eyes well up. Before I could turn my head away, Miss Meury noticed. She stayed behind to talk, like she wanted to comfort me. What a busybody. The guards paced, then ended our little talk. The next day I read in the paper that I had broken down, weeping, and had to be led out of the prison chapel. That Meury woman must have talked to reporters. I would have to be more careful. Later I realized she may have said a little to reporters, but those men were looking for anything sensational. They added their own drama to her story.

When the guards and me started back to my cell, Miss Meury craned her neck and smiled again. "Can I visit you next week, Mrs. Place?"

"You're not afraid I'll throw acid in your face and hit you over the head with an axe then suffocate you?" I knew better. I just couldn't help myself. But the woman didn't move, didn't flinch. Neither did the guards.

"Mrs. Place, I am here to guide your soul, not to judge you."

Without answering I turned away and walked back between the guards.

For the next week, I stewed about lawyers. Peter didn't visit, but a letter bringing up his name arrived by messenger late on February 10th. It started with the usual fluff—good day and I hope this finds you well. After that, Howard McSherry wrote, "Your brother, Peter Garretson, and New Brunswick Police Chief Francis Harding, have asked me to represent you during your trial. I am not a member of the New York bar, but I can consult. Have you arranged for legal representation? Can we meet on Monday, February 14th? I assume it is not a problem for you that the date is Valentine's Day. I will travel to Raymond Street."

I knew the name McSherry because of my years in New Brunswick. McSherry belonged to the Elks Club and was always getting written up in the papers. He made it to the title of Exalted Ruler. People in town thought of him as a lawyer, thought he was successful. He acted in the Elks' performances, sometimes produced them. Maybe he could bring drama to the trial. That wouldn't be so bad. "Dear Mr. McSherry," I wrote back. "I am in discussions with Mr. James Ridgway, who served as district attorney of Kings County but is now in private practice. He may take on my case. Can you communicate with him to work this out? I must add that Magistrate Lewis Worth appointed a lawyer for me, a Mr. Wayne Knittle, but I do not approve of that choice. I am available to meet you on Monday. I am always available." Warden Bergen helped me with the letter, though he grumbled. He wanted Ridgway, only Ridgway. But even so, the warden posted the letter for me. As long as a flock of reporters was lining the jail sidewalk, Bergen would help with anything he thought was lawful.

Between the time I wrote to McSherry and the time he came to visit me in my cell, the warden brought news from the court. Wayne Knittle had written to Judge Worth, resigning from representation. That little weasel was willing to accept the judge's wrath. Now I had to hire a lawyer, or maybe two, or wait for Worth to replace Knittle. Ridgway was leaning to taking me on. I liked him. He was a no-nonsense man. Maybe McSherry would work with him.

On February 14th, the warden escorted McSherry into my cell. He had dressed for the occasion, in a fashionable topcoat and hat. He looked surprisingly prosperous for a New Brunswick attorney. I asked about Peter, but McSherry wasn't interested in small talk. He was interested in payment, especially if he had to work with James Ridgway.

"Mrs. Place, if I represent you, along with Mr. Ridgway, will you, or Peter Garretson with your funds, the funds you gave him, be paying both lawyers? Equally?" I separated my arms, palms up, noting that I had no idea. "Please look into this," he said. After asking two or three more questions, he took his leave. I know from one of the chatty guards that as McSherry walked out, he stopped to talk to Warden Bergen. The warden told him I had asked Matron Handy to mail a letter I wrote Will, asking to see him, to explain I had done nothing wrong. Mrs. Handy had shown the letter to Bergen for the usual screening. I imagine Bergen and McSherry each shook their heads in disbelief that I would write such a letter. Maybe Bergen warned McSherry—I would be an odd client. A year later McSherry would tell the governor of New York that I must have been insane to want to see the father of the girl I murdered.

At the time I didn't know all that. I was just trying to figure out the money. I expected my brother Peter to visit. Then I could discuss money and payment with him. After all, I sent the trunk to Peter. He was involved whether he liked it or not. And I transferred all my money to him, or anyway, he probably thought it was all my money. He never came. No kin came to see me—not my sister Ellen, not my brother Peter. But Miss Emilie Meury came.

An hour after Howard McSherry left, a guard brought the missionary lady into my cell. I saw the guard, the chatty one, look her over, you know, I mean look her over. Like I said, she was pretty, even if she tried to hide it with that ugly, plain dress. I never agreed to meet with her, but her smile drew me in, and I had nothing else to do.

After we prayed—I could tell she wouldn't let me skip that—I asked about her life. I guess I pried. Did she have a sweetheart? She told me she lived with her sister Julia. Their father was a Presbyterian minister, so the sisters grew up knowing the importance of God, and that stuck with Miss Meury. The Presbyterians had no nuns and of course, she couldn't be a minister. A neighbor told her about the Missionary Society. Soon she was attached to the Brooklyn prisons, welcomed into the Raymond Street Jail to give what she called spiritual guidance to women convicts. That filled her day, she told me. Didn't have a sweetheart. Didn't want one. She said all this in an easy way, not shy, not embarrassed. Then she looked up at me.

"Will you have visitors?"

"Not sure."

"Maybe your brother?" Anyone who read the papers knew I had a brother. "Any friends?"

"Maybe." She didn't need to know I had no friends.

That was the first of Miss Meury's daily visits. Why did I keep talking to her? For most of my time in the Raymond Street Jail, only Miss Meury visited me. I'm not counting the people who had to be there like Warden Bergen and Matron Handy and the lawyers. Oh, and I'm not counting that swindler. I'll get to her later. I didn't think the lack of company would be a problem. But the more time I had alone, the more I would stew about what I had done, or a trial, or a sentence. When Miss Meury came, I sat while she read me scriptures, like the Missionary Society required, but then, quiet like, she asked me how I was. I gave her my usual answer, could be better. But soon I started to tell her about New Jersey, about growing up on the farm in East Millstone. About the work, and about my brothers, and my sisters, and the deaths. She shuffled in her seat and waited a minute before she looked up. When I got to the chicken coop story, how Pa locked me in there overnight, that one really got to her. She took the Bible off her lap and moved it to the chair next to her.

"Have you told any of these stories to Wayne Knittle. Your lawyer? Stories about your childhood might help your case."

"Knittle? He never met with me. Hasn't been here at all. Warden tells me Knittle ran to the woods, got out of it, out of being my lawyer. Now maybe I have Ridgway. Or maybe McSherry. Don't even know who to tell these low-down tales to."

I could see Miss Emilie puckering her lips. Couldn't tell if she was more upset over the chicken coop or the lawyers.

Wayne Knittle

On the memorable morning of February 8th, I was partway through my breakfast when a messenger arrived at the door. He carried an official letter from Magistrate Lewis Worth requiring me to represent Mrs. Martha Place on three charges, including first-degree murder. Worth added an unnecessary sentence toward the end of his letter. "I will remind you that the death sentence is the mandatory punishment for first-degree murder in the State of New York." I was not a well-known criminal defense lawyer, no argument there, but I can assure you that I did know the 1888 criminal statute.

The eggs and coffee my wife served me that morning lingered on the plate as my stomach flipped. I knew I might be called for indigent defense work, everyone was at one point or another. But why did my name rise to the top this time? Most likely the clerk, using a roster in orderly fashion, was simply at the Ks by now. But I would not do this. Not even if Worth reprimanded me.

I could get past the condescension. I knew my education at the Albany Law School was far from Ivy League, and in my solo practice, I defended petty thieves, not high-profile clients. I struggled just to pay the rent on my little office. But I could not get past the execution part of this case. The truth was that I was scared I would lose. For me, the death penalty, whether by rope, chair, or rifle, was obscene. An eye for an eye was a relic of the past. We could do better now.

How to convince Worth to release me from defense duty? I would plead shaky knowledge of relevant law. If Worth thought my background so weak that he had to remind me of the statute, then maybe he understood what would happen if a jury found Mrs. Place guilty. I would appeal, and part of my brief would be my own letter to him in his file, in effect documenting my incompetence. He would be out on a limb too. Following this plan, I wrote to Worth on February 10th. Two days later I received his letter dismissing me.

I did feel guilty abandoning the woman. More than that, I was curious. And even more than that, maybe I couldn't get past Worth's condescension as much as I thought. You'll see that I had a better handle on criminal defense than I let on.

Mattie

I thought I was arraigned on February 8th, but maybe that little performance was not enough because I had another arraignment on February 15th. The day before, Warden Bergen explained to me that an arraignment is a court hearing where an indictment is presented in court and the accused person answers to the charge. Still confounding. This time I dressed for the part. When I packed the trunk the week before, I didn't send everything to Peter. I held back some nicer clothes, the ones the nurse brought me in a satchel that first morning when I sulked in St. Mary's. Here's what was odd—the police never paid any mind to the clothes I held back. If I planned to run off to New Brunswick, why did I leave nice frocks in my bedroom in Brooklyn? No one asked.

In my cell early on the 15th, the younger matron watched me dress. Wasn't her fault. She was required to look. Mrs. Handy was in her late twenties, a little plump, and she'd had a hard life too. Her husband drank a lot and couldn't keep a job. Worse, she couldn't have children. It took me months to learn all that because Mrs. Handy knew she shouldn't talk much to the prisoners. Aside from Emilie Meury, Mrs. Handy would be my closest, well, I can't say friend, but she would be the person who knew the most about me. She stood a few feet away while I put on a stylish black dress, then a plush, black seal cape, and added pearl earrings. I finished off with a large black straw hat trimmed with an ostrich feather, including a black veil covering my forehead. The previous day a new police recruit had brought me more clothes and hats from Hancock Street. Mrs. Handy looked at my ensemble and smiled. Thank the Lord, the Raymond Street Jail had no uniforms for women.

The guards walked me to a closed patrol wagon with a wooden bench along both sides. They called it a Black Maria. I sat on the empty side and adjusted my dress. Opposite me on the other bench two men smirked when I climbed up. The rougher-looking one told me he knew why I was there. Murder. He snickered and kept talking. They were only charged with wrecking a bank in Brownsville, on the eastern side of Brooklyn. The men were dressed in shabby suits, unshaven. Despite the cold weather, the air in the Black Maria was stuffy and I could smell them. I stared back, silent, grateful that the Gates Avenue Police Court was not far away.

My smart dress was right for the occasion, I knew as soon as I saw the big crowd in front. Mostly women, some men. The chant was the same, from all those ugly mouths.

"Murderess. Hang 'er."

On and on. A court officer came to the Black Maria to help me out of the wagon. He told the bank wreckers to wait right where they were until another officer came to fetch them. "Ladies first," he said, ignoring their smirks. "Mrs. Place, I am Court Officer Shuttleworth. We'll make our way right past these gawkers. I call them police court matinee girls. Here we go." What a handsome man, I thought. He hooked his arm through mine, courteous like, smiling. He led me upstairs to a cell set aside for women. The matinee girls tried to follow, but other officers held them back. I waited on a bench while Judge Worth tried other cases, all petty matters according to talkative Shuttleworth. I guessed the bank wreckers would have to wait a while for their turn too. I moved my skirt and hat over my hands to cover my fidgeting. After an hour Officer Shuttleworth took my arm again and led me into the courtroom, the same courtroom I stood in a week ago. It smelled of cigars and sweat. Maybe it did before too but I couldn't remember. I looked around. Sitting in front I saw Detectives Becker and Mitchell and Captain Ennis. Becker and Ennis smiled just a little when I walked in. Sitting in back, I saw N.B. Thompson, that know-it-all neighbor, the evil Place brothers, and stupid Edward Scheidecker. Well behind those men was a nearly bald man, hunched down, hiding. He looked familiar. Could that be Knittle? Why would he be here? Among the whole lot of them, not a friendly face. A wait of another few minutes. Then Judge Worth entered, along with a squat man with a round face, a man I learned was Assistant District Attorney John Maguire. Worth called me to the front. He read the counts against me, all expected by now—first-degree murder, felonious assault, attempted suicide. Two times he asked if I understood the charges. I suppose he thought I was dumb. I answered quickly, but quietly. Worth frowned. I saw him screw up tight his mouth and eyes, like he had a hard time hearing me.

"Are you ready to continue this trial, Mrs. Place? You seem to have trouble expressing yourself."

"I don't know." Again, a whisper.

"Well, let's move to the next issue. Do you have counsel, Mrs. Place?"

"No sir, I do not."

"First I asked Mr. Knittle to defend you. He wrote me to resign, against my wishes. Then I heard Mr. James Ridgway was going to defend you. And this morning I received a telegram from an attorney named Howard McSherry, saying he would defend you. He's from New Jersey, I understand, and not a member of the New York bar. Who is it to be, Mrs. Place?"

Maguire interrupted, looking at Worth. "I have word it will be McSherry, unofficially of course, and that he is trying to arrange to work with a member of the New York bar, maybe Ridgway. I doubt Ridgway will agree—all highly unusual."

Worth looked at Maguire. I saw the judge roll his eyes. Then he looked at me.

I had to speak up, formal like. "I have met with Mr. Ridgway and Mr. McSherry. Both are good men. They are discussing whether they can work together and under what conditions."

"Tell me who you have retained."

"I have not retained anyone yet. I expect to do so soon."

"Then I have no choice but to adjourn this trial so you can arrange for counsel. The trial is now set for February 23rd. Mrs. Place, I will not grant another delay."

Officer Shuttleworth led me through the crowd, back to the Black Maria. I rode to Raymond Street, this time in an empty wagon. The people of Brooklyn may have been curious about the trial that day, but by nighttime, they turned their attention elsewhere. The USS *Maine* sank in Havana, killing 266 men. My crime, or crimes, moved away from the front pages.

Henry Newman

I admired my partner, James Ridgway, for his legal mind. Our firm was lucky to have attracted him. His connections as a former district attorney would be useful. Of course, he never let me forget that he joined us as the senior partner. Ridgway lived the high life. This winter he was vacationing in Palm Beach, away from the cold, at the Royal Poinciana Hotel. He asked me to fill in for him, on a temporary basis, to defend the crazy murderess. Why did he agree to represent Martha Place? Our firm handled a general practice—we did not specialize in criminal defense. He told me that even though the case would not pay a large enough fee to cover expenses, it would make the front page of every newspaper in a fifty-mile radius. "Think long term," he said, looking down his nose at me. "The hubbub in the newspapers will get our name out there, free advertising. The firm already has a portfolio of good clients, but this case will make a big mark. We'll attract a wider range of criminals. Some of them will have money." He told me this before any of us realized how the USS *Maine* disaster would compete with the Place story for the public's attention.

Following Ridgway's directive, I was to work with a Mr. Howard McSherry, retained by the Place woman's brother, Mr. Peter Garretson. McSherry, Ridgway said, would do all the leg work. But McSherry was a yokel from New Jersey, and not recognized by the New York bar. I was wary.

Later I learned that Ridgway waited until March 2nd before sending a notice to the court that he had been retained by Mrs. Place. No one seemed to know for certain who her counsel was—the inept Wayne Knittle, the yokel Howard McSherry, the swanky James Ridgway, or me. I was annoyed, and in my heart, I knew this could not be good for our client.

Howard McSherry and I met in lower Manhattan the afternoon on February 22nd, in a watering hole our firm often used for informal meetings. He was tall, well-dressed, with sparse brown hair and a mustache. I felt shorter than ever, but confident in the thorough review of the case I carried out the night before. To be honest, I had to review not only the slim case record but also the state's criminal statutes since first-degree murder was far from my specialization. McSherry ordered a whiskey, as I did. We began with the usual preliminaries about how we ended up with the Place case. I suspected he was disappointed to be partnering with me, rather than Ridgway. McSherry made sure to mention the many trials he had won, all minor cases by my standards, and certainly they would be minor by Ridgway's standards. A half-hour later, after hearing more than I wanted about the workings of the legal system in Middlesex County, New Jersey, I turned to strategy.

"Howard, have you considered the insanity defense?"

"Yes, that's what the brother, Peter Garretson, suggests. You know brothers—they always think their sisters are crazy. Ha. Says she had an accident in a sleigh when she was younger. Hurt her head. Says she's never been right since. And there's more."

He wanted to say more on insanity, but I cut him off, while his mouth was half-open. "Howard, everyone I know who follows the case thinks we'll try for an insanity defense. But let me take another approach for a minute. Is there an alternative story, an alternative plausible story, we can offer the jury? The police have a simple theory—they think the woman was jealous of her stepdaughter, killed her, then missed the train she chose for her escape, and then, as an afterthought, tried to kill her husband to cover up the first crime. Can we offer a jury something else?

McSherry pursed his lips, looked surprised. "What do you have in mind?

"Well, let me try this one out on you. Maybe the maid did it. That Swedish maid, Hilda Palm, she must have seen what a grand life Ida led. Ida had everything. Hilda's an immigrant from Sweden, she has nothing. She was in the house, or at any rate in the yard that day. I know that from the arraignment two weeks ago—the stenographer's transcript. She must have seen where Mr. Place kept his photography supplies.

"Mmmm." McSherry looked stunned, then recovered. "But remember, Martha Place admits to throwing acid."

"Ah, right, Howard. Let's go with what you said. Martha Place throws the acid. Then let's say she walks out. Maybe later Hilda replaces some laundered bloomers in Ida's room, sees Ida writhing in pain on the bed, and decides to end Ida's misery with a pillow. And here's another possibility. That fiancé, Edward Scheidecker. You know, the Place family distrusts him. They think he overstated his relationship with Ida. Her uncles had no idea she was engaged. And that story the fellow told Ennis on the night of the murder. Scheidecker's story about his friend George Young going to check on Ida when she didn't get to a 2:00 practice session. Sounds peculiar. I bet no one interviewed Mr. Young."

Another stunned look. Another slow recovery.

"Yes, you're right, Henry, but why would he throw acid in the face of his girlfriend? Or hit her with an axe? Or smother her with a pillow?"

"Well, let me try this. What if Martha Place did throw the acid, as you said she confessed doing. Then Edward called on Ida, maybe sneaking into her room while the stepmother was imbibing. Let's say Edward was on the prowl for some courting or whatever you want to call it, and he saw the girl's beautiful face ruined. Maybe he's a callous lad who no longer wanted to marry her so he smothered her. Or maybe he's a kind lad who wanted her misery to end, so he suffocated her."

"Give me a minute to think about this." I didn't want to give him a minute, even though the yokel looked overwhelmed.

"Howard, let's talk about Mrs. Place too. Her actions are not as clear as the reporters suggest. I'm not convinced she ever planned to make that train to New Brunswick. If that train was her escape plan, why did she ask the servant girl to handle the trunk, the trunk with an address on it? Think about it. At some point, the police would find Ida dead, or Ida and William dead, and they would question the Palm girl. The Palm girl, who was sure to have read the label on the trunk, would tell the police that the woman had gone to New Brunswick. Why would Martha Place make it easy for the police to find her? That could be a red herring, to throw us off the scent. Let's say Mrs. Place was planning to escape somewhere else. The police would go to Peter—that's the brother, right, in New Brunswick?—looking for her. He would be dumbfounded and have no idea where she was. But since she had sent her clothes to New Brunswick the police would still think she was there. They'd probably harass Peter, hound him. But to no avail. And then there's the issue of Mrs. Place's letters to Peter and his daughter, and those bank books. If she was planning to hide out in New Brunswick then why did she send all her money to Peter and Grace, for them to keep?"

Did Howard McSherry follow my reasoning? I couldn't be sure. His eyes glazed over as he looked past me.

"Howard, here's my theory. Mrs. Place wanted everyone to think she killed herself. Maybe not in the house. Maybe somewhere else the next day. She wouldn't need much money. She could give most of her savings to her brother and niece. But really, she was going to slip away, west, as her first husband had, Wesley Savacool." Howard stared at me when I said "Savacool." "At least those were the rumors about him. Let's say the woman had kept enough money to get the train from New York to maybe St. Louis, and then maybe to Denver. After all, if she skimmed $1300 off William Place, the money she sent to New Brunswick, then maybe she skimmed more." At that point, neither Howard nor I knew that Mattie kept diamond earrings for herself.

"She would get a housekeeping position," I went on, "save money, then set herself up as a dressmaker. Now we get to William. The police think William was an afterthought. Maybe she decided that afternoon that she had to kill him to cover up Ida's murder. But what if she planned to kill William all along? Then he crawled out the front door, ruining everything. She couldn't disappear, leaving the police to think she doffed herself, because now a crowd would be looking at Hancock Street." I paused for a moment.

"I'm assuming, between us, that she's guilty as sin."

The more I talked, the more wide-eyed McSherry looked. He had stopped drinking his whiskey, and now downed it quickly, saying nothing.

"And if you aren't tired of hearing me jabber, here's something else to think about. I'm trying to invent alternative theories, as you can tell. Another theory could be time of death. Four doctors examined Ida Place right after the murder. The autopsy report hedged on time of death, but the doctors reached a consensus—Ida Place died four hours before the police found her at 7:00 at night. So she died about 3:00 in the afternoon. Here's a preliminary copy." I retrieved a piece of paper from my jacket pocket and pushed it along the table, damp with whiskey circles, toward McSherry. "And by the way, the reporters, who must have been listening in on conversations around the crime scene, covered time of death. One wrote that Dr. Richardson said the girl had been dead for two hours. Another wrote that Delap, the coroner, said the girl had been dead for four hours. The *Daily Eagle* wrote the doctors said the body was still warm. Everything we know points to death in the middle or late afternoon. But Hilda Palm, let's go back to her, she says she heard screams about nine in the morning. How is that possible? Is Hilda Palm lying? You're quiet, Howard. Sorry to drone on. Any thoughts?"

"I'm not sure." McSherry spoke slowly.

"That's the point. We want to make the jury unsure. That's all we need."

I kept going. "And I've been thinking about the insanity plea. I'm sure you've read up on the M'Naghten rule, the questions that are the standard for insanity. Here's how they would apply for Mrs. Place." I pulled another sheet of paper from my pocket. "Did she know her act would be wrong? Yes. Did she understand the nature and quality of her actions? Yes. You see, this is not a dumb woman. She may want us to think she is dumb, but she is not. She ran a dressmaking business. Maybe not successfully, but she managed to feed herself for over a decade, without a husband. And she was smart enough to marry Mr. Place, to marry up I dare say. No one should accuse her of being stupid."

I waited a minute, assessing McSherry's reaction. The New Jersey lawyer's wide eyes returned, slowly, to a steady size. Then, an odd smile.

"All food for thought Henry. Food for thought. Now, while you've been researching the case, I've been doing a little work of my own. Peter, the brother, told me about the first husband, Wesley Savacool. You mentioned him. We took some of the money that Mrs. Place sent to Peter and hired a detective, the best, a Pinkerton. He contacted another Pinkerton, a detective on the West Coast. This second chap tracked Savacool to Seattle. Turns out he's alive though some reporters claim he's dead. Peter thought maybe the husband could provide proof of insanity or some other condition. The Seattle Pinkerton got this letter out of him." McSherry, with a smug look, pushed the letter across the still-wet table. I read it, slowly.

Dear Mr. McSherry,

I don't know how you found me in Seattle. I guess you hired a Pinkerton, a smart Pinkerton. Nothing that he told me or that I read here in the papers surprises me. Martha Place is a shrew. I'm sure she killed that stepdaughter and tried to kill that husband. She tried to kill me too.

When I was a young man, I had no prospects. Just a little education and no money. I caught on with a grocer in Newark, where I worked to earn not much more than my keep. One day I met Mattie, that's what we called her. She was older than me, but friendly, easy to talk to. I thought she was a looker, but now I think that's because she wore nice clothes, dresses she made herself. Anyway, she set her cap for me. We stepped out. After a short time, she told me she was with child. Turned out she really was. I'm from a good family. I knew what to do so we married. She lost the baby, and another one. Then she gave birth to Harry Ross, Ross we called him. That was about the last happy day of my life for a couple of years.

Mattie was always after me for money. Money for dresses, for toys for Ross, for this and for that. We argued. We argued a lot. Once she threatened to hit me over the head if I couldn't make more money. Another time she came into the grocery and pushed provisions off the shelves. I had to close the store to clean up and I had to pay the proprietor for lost goods. She embarrassed me with my friends, too, because she was a shrew to them. She didn't want them in our flat.

I can tell you that she had a temper, but I don't know if she was crazy. She wasn't crazy when I met her.

My name is now Wesley L. May. I married another woman, Annie May. I have two sons, Lee and Arthur. I have a better life. Do not try to contact me again.

Wesley L. May

I had been flaunting my own ideas while McSherry held a crucial card close to his vest. Well, I was amazed. Maybe I had misjudged this man. I looked up and smiled. "Great work. Where does this leave us?"

"Well, probably no help for an insanity plea. I'm relying on you for those other options, Henry."

He could do the digging, but not the strategy.

"Here's what I'm thinking now, Howard. Our goal, our top goal, should be to keep her from hanging. She's admitting she threw acid in the girl's face. But she's not admitting to smothering her. And the cause of death, well, they say it's smothering, asphyxiation. We need to introduce at least some doubt about that. Also, we need to split the charges. If William Place testifies about his wife's efforts to chop him to death, that will prejudice the jury against her for all the other charges. Remember, there are no witnesses to her actions against her stepdaughter. Let's work on keeping the attack on William out of the story."

Howard made no show of protest as I went up to the bar to settle the tab. It had been an odd meeting. I had contributed the most in terms of a defense strategy, but I had to hand it to Howard McSherry. He did bring something to the table. "See you in court tomorrow, Howard."

Mattie

I knew I looked good when I went to the Gates Avenue Police Court last week, so I didn't change anything on February 23rd. I chose the same elegant, black clothing, fixed my hair the same way. I took the ride from the Raymond Street Jail in the same Black Maria, but this time with a different set of scruffy male prisoners. Again, they stared at me and I stared back. Again, the crowd was big and rowdy, maybe five hundred. I was still in the news, despite the looming Spanish-American War. The crowd jeered when the Black Maria pulled up. Shuttleworth, the friendly court officer, was nowhere to be seen. Instead, officers Keyes and McCann rushed me from the van into the holding cell. Keyes was rough and McCann was all business. No smiles this time from the court officers. I stared at the crowd. I was getting used to being the center of attention.

The day before Emilie Meury—I laughed that even the reporters called her the prison angel—offered to keep me company in court for the arraignment and the following day for the inquest. First, I said no. I remembered she liked talking to busybody reporters. But the truth was that I liked sitting with her. Miss Meury said she was interested in my spiritual well-being, and I knew that was true. But that didn't keep her from bringing up other things too—what she thought about people, about the warden, the matrons, events going on in the country. She had a neighbor whose son was on the USS *Maine*. We talked about the inquiry into the explosion and who was to blame. I didn't think Miss Meury was a lady friend, not exactly, but she was company. In the end, I told her yes, it was all right if she sat with me in court. That morning she talked her way into the area just outside the holding cell, where I could see her. Then, after a short wait, Officer McCann brought me into the courtroom and Miss Meury followed. I sat down at a table next to Howard McSherry and a shorter man I had never seen before. They had been waiting.

This time I had counsel. But the delay had cost me. Ridgway was in Florida, soaking up the sun. I was beginning to think he was all show. He sent a note telling me his junior partner, a Mr. Henry Newman, would be his replacement for the time being. Ridgway said not to worry, Newman was a smart attorney. The shorter man at the table must be Newman.

Judge Worth seemed to know what was going on with representation and he didn't look happy. He called Newman and McSherry up to his desk, along with a man I recognized from the week before, Assistant District Attorney Maguire. I could hear them talk. "Mr. McSherry," the judge said, "you are not a member of the New York bar, is that correct?" McSherry nodded. "And you are consulting with Mr. Ridgway, or, more specifically Mr. Ridgway's associate, Mr. Newman, correct?" Another nod. "I want to emphasize that your presence in this courtroom is a courtesy granted by the court." Judge Worth asked McSherry if he was ready to proceed. He answered that he had not yet decided whether to waive the examination of the defendant or to go directly to trial and request an adjournment. I couldn't figure out what was going on. Worth turned to ADA Maguire. Maguire said he was ready to proceed but would agree to an adjournment.

"Very well," the judge said. He shrugged. "I said I would not do this but I have no choice. This court is adjourned until March 2nd." As Officer McCann led me out, Miss Meury gave me a reassuring smile.

McCann saw that the crowd in front of the building now blocked the way to the Black Maria. He requested more guards to help him. They formed a wedge and made a path as the matinee ladies grumbled. With an officer on each of my elbows, we pushed to the Black Maria. I stared at the crowd again, putting on my haughty look. I was alone for the ride back to the Raymond Street Jail. I fretted, confused about what had happened.

Henry Newman

At the arraignment on February 23rd, I met Mrs. Place for the first time in the dingy Gates Avenue Police Court. I should have visited her in jail, but Howard McSherry had done that, and I disliked cells. Unfortunately, the woman looked strong enough to have wrestled and won. The very next day, the 24th, I was in court again, this time in the more impressive Brooklyn Kings County Courthouse. This building I knew well.

Coroner George Delap had organized a preliminary inquest on the night of the murder and had impaneled a jury, but on this day, he was presiding over a formal version, leaving no stone unturned. From the newspapers and gossip in the courthouse, I knew he was under a cloud of suspicion for accepting a bribe. That was still unproven but, in my mind, likely. Delap lived almost as well as Ridgway. I wondered then, and from time to time in the coming years, whether Delap's affinity for bribery was more widespread than officials realized.

Howard McSherry, wearing the same suit he had worn the previous days, met me in front of the courthouse. We were amazed at the size of the crowd lining the sidewalk. Those rowdy spectators knew this inquest was not for the death of a drunken bum, but for the death of a beautiful, seventeen-year-old girl, the daughter of a professional man. I heard the bailiff say he had never faced such a mob scene before. And this was only an inquest, to determine cause of death—we weren't even at trial yet.

Howard and I managed to bypass the crowd. We entered together and found seats. Neither of us had any role in the proceeding, but we needed to observe, soaking up whatever we could use to defend Mrs. Place at the next stage. I spotted Assistant District Attorney Maguire sitting beside Delap, probably ready to help as needed, or perhaps to watch over him. I pointed out Delap to Howard. The Coroner was hard to miss given his enormous mustache. Whispering, I told Howard about the bribery scandal. He showed no surprise. New Jersey must have its own skullduggery.

Looking off to the side, I saw two clusters of people—the thirty witnesses waiting to testify and a jury of seven of the ten men who Delap had sworn in for the makeshift jury the night of the murder. I didn't recognize any of the jurymen, but I listened as the bailiff checked them off, by name, and seated them. The last of the seven was Fred Fahrenkrug, a name I recognized but couldn't place. A minute later I recalled that he was in a *Tribune* story a day or two after Ida died. The reporter described Fahrenkrug as a friend. In a notebook I carried with me, I jotted down a reminder to investigate this oddity. As I shook my head at the idea of a friend as a juror, the court officers allowed about a hundred yapping spectators to squeeze into the courtroom. Neither Howard nor I had ever seen such a spectacle in the halls of justice.

Mrs. Place sat up front, surprisingly relaxed. Howard told me that the good-looking woman sitting at her side was Emilie Meury, the missionary lady he had met on his visit to the jail. I could see the two women chatting. Another pretty woman sat off to the side, with the male witnesses, looking uncomfortable. I guessed she was Sarah Driscoll, the matron from the Ralph Street Station. Next to her was a third pretty woman, younger than the others. Must be Hilda Palm, the maid. Both Driscoll and Palm were on the witness list. Craning my neck to look in back, I saw two well-dressed men, glaring at Mrs. Place. Later I learned their identities—brothers Charles and Theodore Place.

The first witness Coroner Delap questioned was N. B. Thompson. He appeared a little too eager to testify. He bounded into the witness chair, dressed formally. He had a round face and puffy eyes. Clergyman turned ad agent. From one line of snake oil to another. Thompson stated that he told William Place his daughter had been murdered, as Place waited for an ambulance to carry him to St. Mary's. I puzzled over that. If Thompson was the first to tell Place, then why did I read in *The World* on February 11th that Edward Scheidecker, the supposed fiancé, told the police that he was the first to inform Place, the morning after the murder. Either Thompson aggrandized his role, or William Place was too dazed to absorb what Thompson told him that first night. Or Edward wrongly supposed that William's response in the hospital indicated he was just hearing of the murder for the first time. Or maybe *The World* reporter got it wrong. No way to know.

Next James Desmond ascended the witness stand. He was tall and thin, dressed in a suit that had seen better days. In a quiet, shaking voice, he explained that on his way home from work he found William Place bleeding on the front steps of the Hancock Street rowhouse. Desmond testified that when he went to assist, he looked back at the house and saw a woman standing in the hallway with an axe in her hand. I heard gasps from the crowd. Even Judge Worth looked awake at that testimony.

Three police officers came up next. James McCauley was the tall, muscular policeman, the one who kicked in the Place front door. After he found Mrs. Place, he helped carry her downstairs and tried artificial respiration to revive her from what he thought might be a suicide attempt. Then Officer Frank Moore, who discovered the bloody axe. Then Officer John Barton, who safeguarded the tumbler of supposed acid. Just as I was tiring of the police witnesses, Delap called Hilda Palm to the stand. She was an attractive woman, a girl really, twenty at the most, probably dressed in her Sunday clothes. I expected her to have a Swedish accent, but it was slight. She relayed the events of her day on February 7th, repeating what I already knew from the report Becker and Mitchell gave to Captain Ennis weeks ago. The police had shared that report and others with defense counsel. Hilda

Palm had been busy. Breakfast, the laundry, the argument, the dismissal and severance pay, and the endless round of errands relating to the trunk, the post office, and the bank. What I grabbed onto was that Miss Palm insisted she never saw Ida again after breakfast. So Ida Place sustained some of her injuries at the time of the argument, around 9:00 in the morning when the maid heard a scream. But the implication that Miss Place died at 9:00 was just that, an implication. I tore a sheet of paper from my notebook and scribbled a thought for Howard. "Could have died any time after quarrel." Howard looked over the sheet, showed no reaction, and pocketed it.

Next in line was William Fetzer, the expressman, confirming that he carried Mrs. Place's trunk to the ferry. Then Sarah McArran, testifying that Mrs. Place said she was leaving her husband. Mrs. McArran was the proud recipient of Mrs. Place's bicycle. Rubber plant too. Would a deranged and dangerous woman be thinking about her bicycle and rubber plant? Or were such thoughts proof of insanity?

Then Edward Scheidecker. Here was something peculiar, to add to the peculiarities about who informed the father of the daughter's death. Along with the report I had been given summarizing the interview with Hilda Palm, I had a copy of the memorandum Chief Ennis wrote late in the evening on the day Ida Place died. Ennis noted that Scheidecker came to the Place house that night, about 7:00 or so, to check on Ida. I brought this up at the pub when I met with Howard. Scheidecker said that his friend, George Young, had called on Ida at 2:00 and could not gain entry. That's why Edward came later, to see if anything was wrong. But now, on the witness stand, Edward testified that he himself came at 2:00, couldn't gain entry, and so came back in the evening. Maybe an innocent foul-up, I thought, but this was just what defense lawyers looked for—a crack in the story, a suspicious crack. Again, I made a note to myself to look into this further. I had no idea then that I'd never follow through.

When Delap turned to the medical aspect of the crime, at last, the jury perked up. He called to the stand Dr. John Gormley of St. Mary's, the young doctor who first attended Martha Place, then stayed to check on Ida Place. Gormley testified that the girl's face was blue and swollen and her lips were injured. No surprises. Next on the stand was Dr. Alvin Henderson, the unimpressive coroner's physician. He added his own medical testimony, stating that Ida Place died of asphyxia. I looked at the jury. They were still paying close attention. I looked in particular at juror Fred Fahrenkrug. He stared at the floor, his shoulders raised and his face down. The third physician to weigh in was Dr. William Moser, the pathologist Delap hired to help Henderson. Moser explained that he saw a congested portion of Ida Place's brain, the size of a silver dollar. It could have been the result of a hemorrhage caused by a blow to the head, but he could not say whether it was the cause of death or not. With asphyxia you sometimes see hemorrhage from the ear, nose, or mouth, but not always. Asked to state the cause of death, Moser said "Miss Place died of asphyxia and possibly a brain concussion."

Delap was through with the medical experts. Sarah Driscoll, matron at the Ralph Street Station, took the stand. I had heard of maids serving as witnesses, but never a matron. I didn't know what to expect. "When Martha Place arrived," Mrs. Driscoll testified, "she told me about throwing acid in her stepdaughter's face. She took a white powder from her husband's desk and added water to it. Then she got an axe to defend herself from her husband. He had made trouble for her and she was afraid he would hit her again. She told me many times that she was afraid." I heard the observers in the courtroom gasp for the second time that day at the mention of the axe. I snuck a glance at Howard. We had our hands full. The violence shocked the crowd, not the need for self-defense.

Last, Delap called Detective John Becker. He testified that on February 8th, at the Ralph Street jail, in the presence of Detective Mitchell and Mrs. Driscoll, Martha Place confessed to throwing acid at Ida and to striking Mr. Place. No need to glance at Howard again. Our uphill battle was obvious even to the leafless tree I saw out the window.

"The inquest is finished. There will be no more witnesses called. The jury will leave the room to deliberate," Delap said. Court officers led our client to a waiting pen while Howard and I sat in a corridor to discuss what we heard. I should say to commiserate. Two-and-a-half hours later, a court officer walked up to us to say the jury had reached a verdict. We watched him enter the pen to bring Mrs. Place back to the courtroom. Once we were assembled Judge Worth asked the foreman to read the verdict. "Asphyxia and possibly concussion of the brain. We cannot determine the exact cause of Miss Ida Place's death." Delap thanked the jury, then, looking at our client, said she will be held until trial, without bail.

Mattie

Up to now, I've been talking about those godawful weeks in February, and if you ask me, I have a lot to say. But I don't have much new to tell you about goings-on between the inquest on February 24th and the trial late in the spring. Just a lot of court appearances—March 2nd, March 18th, April 11th. Three judges—Worth, Aspinall, Hurd. A lot of fussing, sometimes they called it arraignments, for no good reason. The guards hauled me up and back from jail to court. I always dressed nice for the crowds, my stylish black clothes. But I'll skip all that and tell you what I dwell on about that time. I had lady friends. Mrs. Handy and I talked a lot, especially when the guards were dozing. Then there was Miss Meury. When she visited me in my cell, I let her think I was all right with praying. I wanted the company. I only got mad at her once, when I asked if she thought Ross could visit me. She told me not to think about that until I sought redemption. I didn't talk to her the next day, but I got over it. The Aschenbachs wouldn't let him anyway.

In March, my lawyers changed again. Henry Newman and Howard McSherry, they were good together. They spent time plotting strategies until Ridgway returned from Florida to take over my case and told Newman to scram. So I had to figure out what to do about McSherry. Did I want him or not? First I thought no, but the next day I decided I needed someone who knew my people back in New Jersey, well, who knew Peter anyway. Then that damn Ridgway pulled out. He thought he could garner more attention conniving to recruit a regiment to fight in Cuba than lawyering for me.

For two months, I brooded in jail while my case went nowhere.

Robert Van Iderstine

My turn.

William Hurd, the judge now assigned to preside at Martha Place's trial, wrote me on April 14th to explain that James Ridgway had withdrawn as counsel, leaving the judge no choice but to go down the roster to find another attorney. Me. Wayne Knittle had been the last court-appointed officer for the case, so I suspect attorneys were listed on the roster not in alphabetical order but in terms of when we were admitted to the New York bar. Undoubtedly, Judge Hurd recognized that Mrs. Place would have a credible lawyer this time. Hurd's letter to me was not the usual assignment letter, but customized, full of praise for my legal skills, despite my relative youth. If Mrs. Place were to be convicted and the case appealed, he wanted the appeals panel to see he appointed adequate counsel.

I was more than adequate. Four years ago I started my own firm, with an office in Manhattan. I began to establish a name for myself in political circles. And I became a member of many clubs and organizations—the Crescent Athletic Club, the fraternity Theta Delta Chi, the Citizen's Union Movement. Also, Brooklyn's Plymouth Church, whose first minister was abolitionist Henry Ward Beecher. I served as vice president of the local Republican club, soon to be president. I spoke out against the power of the railroads and for breaking up the dominating political machine in the city. I lectured in favor of organized assistance for the poor children of New York. Given my political leanings maybe Hurd thought I would rise to the challenge of defending a nearly indefensible woman. Maybe I did have one flaw as an attorney. My club mates teased me, claimed I was a boring public speaker. Hurd wouldn't know that, and if he did, he wouldn't care.

I was not thrilled about taking on a *pro bono* case. My paying clients as well as my political and cultural activities kept me busy. But this was a high-profile case, a capital case, one that could be good for business. My name would be in the papers. Up to that point, notices about me and my wife were limited to the social columns.

A paragraph at the end of Hurd's letter disturbed me. After Mrs. Place's April 11th court appearance, she had sent him a message, changing what she had written earlier about dismissing a certain Howard McSherry, a New Brunswick lawyer who had been solicited by the defendant's brother to assist in the case. She wanted McSherry to continue in that capacity. I would need to work with him. McSherry was a member of the New Jersey bar, not the New York bar, so all official work would be done by me as attorney of record. Hurd enclosed a separate note along with the formal assignment letter. He wrote that he was not sure why McSherry was in the good graces of the defendant. But the judge could find no reason to ban him from the courtroom, and even the next month, as McSherry crossed ethical lines, the judge would look the other way.

I agreed to be the next attorney to defend Mrs. Place. I didn't know what had happened to Newman, or to Ridgway, but I could guess. Ridgway, the attorney Martha Place tried to hire herself, liked to sun in Florida, expecting his junior partner to do all the work. I knew this because we had friends in common. Parts of the New York bar, or maybe I should say the Brooklyn bar, or at least some circles of that bar, were a close-knit community. And we all knew that Ridgway wanted to recruit a regiment to fight in Cuba, which was likely to bring him more fame and glory than this darn case.

At the time I received Judge Hurd's notice about replacing Ridgway, Martha Place's defense was in shambles. First, she had Wayne Knittle as an attorney, for less than a day. Then Howard McSherry, always McSherry. Then James Ridgway, maybe, as he boarded a train for Florida. Then Henry Newman, to replace Ridgway. Then back to Ridgway. And now me. A common thief, looking at maybe a month in jail, deserved better.

Unpleasant as it may be, I knew I had to talk with Howard McSherry. After a few telegrams, we agreed to meet the next day, Friday, April 15th. McSherry suggested the same Manhattan pub where I learned he had met Henry Newman. At least, I thought, as we sat over whiskeys, McSherry had taken notes and remembered most of the defense he and Newman had discussed. I shook my head a few times, nodded my head a few times, and made some tweaks. Howard and I got along better than I expected and admitted to each other that neither of us was confident about winning the case. I wanted to make sure he understood that if Martha Place were found guilty of first-degree murder, the judge would have no discretion—the death penalty was mandatory in the state of New York. He understood. Just reminding him out loud of sentencing directives made my stomach lurch. I paid the bar bill and we departed, Howard for the train to New Brunswick and me, glumly, for the subway to Brooklyn. I hoped the publicity would compensate for the strain.

Mattie

Robert Van Iderstine had less flair than James Ridgway. He wore a well-made but understated suit. He spoke softly. Maybe too softly. Ordinary looking. At least he came to see me every week, to talk through the case. When I struggled with his last name—not the Van part, I grew up with Dutch names in New Jersey—but the Iderstine part, he laughed.

"All my clients think Van Iderstine is a mouthful. Let's make it easy. Call me Six."

"Six?" I said. "Why six?"

"The initials of my name are VI. You know, six in Roman numerals." I didn't know, but I liked the sound of the new name. Van Iderstine was Six to me from that time on. Aside from the laugh about his name, Six was all business. He told me he had done criminal defense work before though it was not his, specialization. Something he added next didn't sit right. Working with Howard McSherry was an irregular arrangement. When he said that I gave Six a sour look. He softened a little, said Howard knew the details of my case at this point better than anyone, and that was all to the good.

Back to court on June 6th, with my new lawyer for the first time. Much ado about nothing, again. Judge Hurd, looking tired and pale, started but didn't get far. ADA Maguire told the judge what I heard the day before through the Raymond Street Jail grapevine. Dr. Henderson, the doctor who signed the autopsy report, was recovering in St. John's Hospital from an appendix attack. He couldn't be a witness. And one of the police sergeants who was also a witness was recovering from the same operation. The crowd in the courthouse laughed at the coincidence. Even I had to smile. Hurd adjourned the court until the first Monday in July. Thought he was so smart. The first Monday in July was the Fourth of July.

Back on my cot in the Raymond Street Jail, I understood, at last, that Markus Van Cortland, the farm boy from East Millstone, was not coming to lead my escape. He had tried, many nights when I slept, but he had been too weak. I turned my attention to that cad, Wesley. Yeah, he behaved shamefully, and he abandoned me and Ross, but we loved each other once. We made love, we made Ross. I pleased him in bed, I knew that. Maybe he would remember the good days and return to save me. He would know more than Markus. Wesley was sly. He would bribe the warden. He would seduce the young matron. He would get me out.

Emilie Meury

Aside from Sunday, my quiet day, I spent mornings at the Raymond Street Jail in the crowded part of the annex for women known as general population. I tried to talk with each of the women, those who would sit with me. I forced myself to ignore a great deal. The women didn't bathe much or clean their cells. One stole her brother's earnings, twice. One lifted shoes from a shop. One failed to care for her infant son. Three or four were accomplished swearers. And so on. Their stories were forgotten, of no interest to anyone but me. None of them faced the prospect of execution.

In the afternoons I walked to the quiet part of the annex to see Mrs. Place. Her cell was large and smelled fresher than the rest of the wing. Like the other women prisoners, she wore her own dresses, but they were of good quality to begin with and she kept them clean. Despite the relative comfort of her cell, this woman yearned for company. For one thing, of course, she faced the possibility of a mandatory death sentence. But I don't think that was the first thing on her mind, not that spring. She was happy to see me, happy to talk. And she did talk. Her entire story, from birth to imprisonment. She liked to talk about herself. I wondered how many chances she had to do that in her life. At first, she showed no interest in prayers, though from time to time she sang a psalm with me, while Mrs. Handy and the guards listened and sometimes sang along. As the months went by, I couldn't decide if Mrs. Place's interest in scriptures grew or not, but she seemed to accept the spiritual part of our sessions together, almost as though prayer served as a gateway to talking about herself, or a gateway to connecting with me.

I always thought she was guilty. It wasn't anything she said, at least not at first. It was how she looked out the window when I brought up redemption.

Mattie

You probably think that in June I stewed about the trial coming up. Getting ready for it, worrying, maybe praying. No. My story got off track, way off. Here's what happened—a swindler named Annie Simpson almost bested me.

In early May, Annie, she was a stranger then, arrived at the Raymond Street Jail. Nice looking. Beautiful frock. The woman talked her way into my cell, claiming she was my cousin. Ridiculous. No kin ever visited me at that jail. But I was happy to have company. Annie told the guards and then she told me that she was an intimate friend of District Attorney Josiah Marean. Those were her words, intimate friend. She had met him in Madison Square Garden and dined with him. After two visits Annie sprang her flimflam. For a bribe of $250 to Marean and another $250 to some police official, money she'd deliver, she'd swing the case in my favor. She'd need some more to cover expenses too. I'd get bail on one indictment, so I could go home, and the other indictment would be dismissed. By the way, no one bothered with the charge of suicide anymore. Once the warden released me, if I needed a place to live, I could become Annie's companion—the two of us were getting along. In the mornings when Miss Meury visited in another part of the prison, that's when Annie came to see me. If Mrs. Handy stayed close by, then Annie and me whispered or used a few codewords we made up. Miss Meury and Mrs. Handy didn't know about the scheme. I should have run the plan by them, but at first, I thought it best to keep it to myself.

Annie's offer of influence was too good to pass up. We had four more meetings in May. I handed over to her $500 and my diamond earrings, the earrings Will gave me that Christmas after we got married, the same Christmas of Ross's first and last visit to Brooklyn. The visit where Ida was mean.

The deal between me and Annie was not simple. Clever, that one was. She knew not to ask for all the money at once. She started asking for little amounts, for little favors she could do. Annie would fetch some clothes or food for me, in return for a small payment. And the next time, more favors, with more payment. Seemed I could trust her.

Howard McSherry wasn't innocent in all this. Of the $500 Annie pocketed, I got $220 of it from him, and I told him just enough for him to guess what it was for. That money was part of the savings I gave to Peter and that Peter gave McSherry, to cover his legal work. If Annie was obviously a swindler, like some said, then why didn't McSherry, remember he's a lawyer, see that? Why didn't he tell me to keep away from her?

When I didn't see Annie for a few days, I started to worry, then to sweat. I needed the money back, the earrings too. I finally told my story to Miss Meury. She made sure I complained to Warden Bergen that day. Bergen was angry that Annie talked her way into his jail. He told me, ordered me, to file a complaint against her. After a week I got word that Annie was charged with grand larceny in the second degree. A few days later a messenger came to the jail and handed me a wad of bills. That took away part of the hurt, just part.

My old friend Judge Hurd presided at the trial on June 23nd, but with me as the plaintiff for a change. Much better that way. Annie had the nerve to plead not guilty. Her lawyers presented the receipt I signed, that I was foolish enough to sign, to prove she returned the money she swindled. Of course, she only returned the money after she learned I was suing her. The lawyers said Annie would return the earrings too, even though they claimed those were my gift to her, for all the trouble she went to on my behalf.

District Attorney Marean took the witness stand. That was a new one for him. He testified that he never communicated with Annie Simpson, didn't even know her. Annie's two lawyers were clever, but they were no match for Marean. He was a smart lawyer, married to his wife Elizabeth for thirty years, respected. And everyone knew he was about to be appointed to the New York Supreme Court. When Annie claimed she could influence an official, she showed bad judgment picking Marean.

For my turn on the witness stand, I talked in the quiet voice I used for court. It felt good to testify against someone.

Judge Hurd ended the trial at noon and sent the jury off to deliberate. Then another wrinkle, one of the jurors, Luhr Horstman, sent word that his place of business was on fire and he had to leave. Hurd adjourned court to the next day. Well, damn, that next day the jury returned with an acquittal. They knew I got my money back. They didn't see the harm.

I tried to figure out how I was duped. I had Emilie Meury visiting, and I had Mrs. Handy to talk to. I'd never had women friends before. It was like talking to those two opened up a dam, so I wanted to keep on talking, even to a swindler. Stupid.

The Trial

Mattie

After all the hearings and indictments and arraignments and inquests, the murder trial was about to begin. Marean decided to try me for Ida and not bother with Will. Why go for assault when you could get me for murder?

On July 5th, off to the Kings County Courthouse again. New court officers. George McCloskey was middle-aged and thick in the waist and William Eyck was younger but stooped over. They guarded me for the whole trial, three sweltering days, so I got to know them. I wore the same black silk dress, trimmed with black beads. The reporters liked it. I had taken in the seams. Since February I lost a few pounds, and I wanted to show off my figure, younger-looking than those gawkers expected. The same black kid gloves. I wore a different hat, this time a black straw sailor hat with an ostrich feather. And another difference—this time I brought along a folded black fan because I knew the courtroom would be stifling. But the biggest difference, by far, was that this time there would be a verdict.

Officer McCloskey led me to the chair between Howard McSherry and my newest lawyer, Six. From prison gossip and from Judge Hurd's sour expression when McSherry entered, I knew my New Brunswick lawyer was on thin ice. Probably had to do with the Annie Simpson mess. At least McSherry provided stability amid this changing line-up of lawyers. Those were Warden Bergen's words, not mine. Just before Hurd called us to order I smoothed out my dress and centered my hat. I asked my lawyers, first one then the other, if I looked presentable. They each gave me an odd look, then looked at each other. Maybe they thought I shouldn't care about my appearance. Foolish men. Ignoring their looks, I craned my neck to check the seats behind me. Crowded, as usual, every seat taken. I saw Edward Scheidecker sitting with the other witnesses. And I thought I saw a slightly familiar face behind him. Someone who looked like that lawyer, Wayne Knittle. The same man I thought I saw at the arraignment on February 15th. I turned back quickly. Didn't want to stare.

For a full day, John Maguire and Six questioned the pool of possible jurors, called talesmen. I listened carefully. I set my features, according to the papers my sharp features, to look calm, to hide my fright. Maguire wanted me to die. No question about it. He was just the assistant district attorney. But his boss, Josiah Marean, the man Annie Simpson claimed she could bribe, that man sat in the courtroom, watching. Six warned me that Maguire would try to impress Marean.

Maguire asked each potential juror the same horrid question: "Do you have conscientious scruples against capital punishment?" The week before, when Six met with me, he explained what capital meant. I knew I could be sentenced to hang, like that woman Bridget Deignan forty-one years ago in New Brunswick, or sentenced to have electricity kill me, like that poor fellow Kemmler eight years ago. Who could forget either one? Until the week of the trial, I managed not to think every minute of the day about dying in those ways. That changed. After talking to Six, pictures of execution took over my head.

The talesmen sitting on the benches probably dressed in their best, but they were not a fashionable group. Most were tradesmen who probably shaved and bathed for their appearance that day. Some had a bright look, but most squirmed, with their heads down. One by one Maguire called them up. All he wanted to talk about was the death penalty, which he explained he would call by the official term, capital punishment. "Do you have any conscientious scruples against capital punishment?" he asked, again and again, and again. The contrast must be clear to all the talesmen—Six never asked any of them about the death penalty, never asked about much at all. The first man fidgeted when he answered Maguire. "My minister told me the death penalty was wrong." The next three talesmen caught on quickly, expressing their scruples.

"My great-grandfather was hung in England. He was innocent."

"I don't believe in that form of punishment."

"I don't think a woman should be put to death."

By the fourth excuse, the talesmen waiting on the benches to be questioned started to snicker. The crowd lining the halls heard and snickered too. Judge Hurd rapped his gavel. He looked at me first, then at the crowd. His voice got deeper, dropped down a few notches. "The fact that this woman is on trial for her life should be no fun for any of us." With that, the snickers quieted down.

The fifth talesman to be questioned had a different problem. "I don't know, one way or the other, about capital punishment, but I was on the police force for thirteen years, working with Captain Ennis, and I believe anything that good man says." Six challenged him, of course. After a half-hour, not a single man had been selected for the jury. Then the tide turned.

John Krieger, a molasses manufacturer, said he accepted capital punishment if a crime was proven. The next man said the same thing. Then two more dismissals over scruples. Then another "all right with me." Then another dismissal. And on and on. Three hours of questioning, then a short lunch break, then three more hours. Finally, the jury was settled. The molasses manufacturer became foreman. The lawyers agreed on eleven other men—a painter, a butcher, a crockery salesman, a builder, a printer, a plumber, a real estate agent, a machinist, a box maker, a produce dealer, and an advertising agent. I smiled, something I didn't do much, because the list made me think of the nursery rhyme, the butcher, the baker, the candlestick maker. Then I looked over the men, hoping some of them would give me a sign, a sign that they understood, or at least that they cared about what happened to me. No sign. It was 4:00 p.m. Judge Hurd said he would see everyone the next morning at 10:00.

Mrs. Handy

The warden changed my assignment for most of Mrs. Place's trial. She'd leave in the morning and return late in the afternoon, so he redirected me to the general population of women inmates, down the hall. Back to their sweat and their swearing. But I was to oversee Mrs. Place in her preparations for trial and during the dinner hour, until the night matron arrived.

I felt anxious about my job that week. Afraid Mrs. Place might not be in her right mind. To my relief, she showed no sign of going crazy with fear. Like usual, she paid attention to how she looked. Asked me for a flat iron for her dress. I got permission from the warden to bring one to her and he ordered me to stand over her while she used it. Then she did her hair, took it down, and redid it three times. I thought she might want to skip breakfast. But no, she ate almost as much as usual. I thought she might spend longer in the bathroom. The jail had a bathroom, which the warden considered more secure than an outhouse. But no, her stomach seemed fine. The woman was made of steel.

When Mrs. Place returned from the courtroom, a guard summoned me back to her cell, to watch over her again. She was still fine. Ate a regular dinner. Told me what had gone on in court. I yawned while she talked.

Mattie

July 6th, 1898. Five months, minus a day since Ida's death. I saw my New York lawyer, Six, seated in the courtroom at 10:00 that morning. My New Jersey lawyer, McSherry, walked in thirty minutes late. I knew McSherry had a long trip from New Brunswick, but he had been on time before. Maybe he lost interest in me now that he saw his shenanigans irked the judge. Six was the better lawyer, but Six's style didn't fit me well. He was formal, stiff. Too late now to change again.

How could I be bored at my own trial for murder in the first degree? In truth I was. A combination of bored and disgusted. I had heard it all before, many times. As expected, Assistant District Attorney Maguire presented his view of the case. The usual talk about family quarrels over money and jealousy. "Martha Place," he said, "hated her stepdaughter, rarely spoke to her, and didn't want others to speak to her." He painted a picture of dead Ida, with blinded eyes, a protruding tongue, and discolored skin. Then he got even uglier. "Capital punishment protects life and property." When Maguire mentioned Will's injuries, Six stood up to object. Six wanted the jury to remember I was charged with murder, not assault. Even so, Judge Hurd overruled the objection. There would be a lot of that overruling business.

Six stood for his turn. He focused on that point about separating the charges. In our talk the week before he called it a strategy. Will more or less witnessed his own assault, Six explained to me, but no one witnessed Ida's death, so there should be doubt about murder. Addressing the jury, Six talked slow, drawing out his words. "The jury should remember Mrs. Place is on trial for the murder of Miss Place and not an assault on Mr. Place."

On to the long string of witnesses for the prosecution. Maguire led off with Patrolman McCauley. The man could barely fit into the witness chair. He testified how a neighbor summoned him to the Thompson home. There he saw William Place bleeding. Next, he saw Ida Place in her bicycle costume, in bed, with a scissors near her body. Last he saw Martha Place, me, on the floor of my bedroom.

That stupid scissors. The police thought Ida fought back with it, tearing my dress. I would not tell them that I purposely wore a torn dress that day, so I could send my better dresses in the trunk to Grace. Well, not all my better dresses. I don't know why the blasted scissors was on the bed. Maybe Ida needed to trim a thread.

McCauley kept talking. He saw a broken chair in the bedroom. Said it like that was a big clue. Ha. The chair had been broken for weeks. Will knew it too. Did they think I was foolish enough to leave a broken chair and a scissors? McCauley said he saw blood on Ida's pillow. Maybe seven- or eight-inches square. Not likely. I would have noticed. Six cross-examined McCauley, pulling out of him that Ida's face was not crushed down on the pillow and that she "lay in a natural position." Six's questions were good, but he was too quiet. Even though I sat up front I struggled to hear.

Nothing much changed when W. J. Maher took the stand. That stupid policeman said everything McCauley said two minutes before. But during Six's cross, Maher said the blood near Ida's mouth formed a square inch. Much smaller than McCauley's recollection. And Six got Maher to say Ida looked like she was asleep, in "a natural position." On that Maher agreed with McCauley. Then a lot of fuss about the broken chair again. Knew I should have had it fixed.

Next came James Desmond. I saw him twice before, once when he helped Will down the steps and once at the inquest. He complained he had to miss another day of work as a waiter. "Mr. Place was bleeding from the head and hand and leaned over the banister on the front stairs. Mrs. Place stood in the doorway." Desmond added that I held an axe and raised it about halfway, with both hands. Well, at least that was right. As I listened to Desmond, I felt sick to my stomach for the first time that day.

Now a familiar face, Frank Fairchild, wearing his formal undertaker's attire. Everyone in the neighborhood knew the undertaker. Kindly Mr. Fairchild. What could he say? "The body was cold, rigid, the face quite red. I saw crystals formed in the outer portion of the eye. Looked as if there had been acid that discolored the skin red, not blistered, but redder than the natural state." Six cross-examined him until Fairchild admitted there was no certainty of acid and that the body seemed perfectly "natural." But then Fairchild said the body had been dead twelve or fourteen hours when he got there at nine or ten at night, and that rigor mortis had set in. I saw Six's lips tighten. He got more than he asked for. "That will be all," he said, quietly.

Now more police officers. Cord Wilkin was full of himself. Said he was the first, well, then he corrected himself and said the second, to see Ida's body. Detective Frank Moore followed Wilkin. Moore testified, so damn proudly, that he found a bloody axe in a snowdrift, eight or ten feet from the rear of the house. Maguire smiled a wicked smile. Moore reached to the side of the witness chair and pulled out something large, wrapped in paper. "Take the paper off," Maguire said. Six was quick on his feet, objecting.

"This surprise, your honor, and indeed it is a surprise, has nothing to do with the crime my client has been charged with." Six and probably Maguire too, forgot that in truth the axe did have something to do with Ida. But Hurd didn't need to remember Ida's injuries for him to rule.

"Overruled. Mr. Van Iderstine, the axe is evidence bearing on the action, intent, and motive of the defendant on that day."

At least Six got Detective Moore to agree to what the others had said, to take the edge off the axe display. Ha. It's easy to be funny now. Moore said, "I didn't notice any marks of violence."

The parade of officers continued. Frank Maher, the little Maher, said the girl's face was disfigured. But he never saw any signs of violence. The painter on the jury and the machinist squirmed. They were hearing the same story, over and over.

The jury perked up when Maguire called Dr. Richardson to the stand. "She was just beginning to turn rigid." I wondered whose estimate of time of death would be more accurate, an undertaker or a physician. I looked over my shoulder. No sign anyone on the jury picked up on the different answers. As Richardson started to describe Ida's lips and face, the painter and the plumber sitting next to him had pinched looks. "Puffed and swollen." Richardson went on. "There was considerable froth and blood-stained mucous between the lips. Her tongue was slightly protruding." More pinched looks, now from the butcher and the builder. Then Six did his best, cross-examining Richardson in a sedate tone of voice. All the men on the jury looked puzzled when the doctor testified, "the face did not look as if acid had been applied to it, but some of the weaker acids would leave no sign on the face." Six pushed, quietly, until Richardson said, "I saw no signs of external violence on the body."

Now doctor number two. John Gormley, the youngest of the doctors by decades, reported that he examined Will the night of February 7th. Six objected, of course—what did that have to do with the charge of murder? The judge overruled the objection, of course. "Mr. Place suffered from two wounds, one at the malar and one at the temple. One of these was a compound fracture of the skull. Next, I was called to the parlor of the Place house. The defendant had passed out from inhaling gas. I adopted measures of artificial respiration. Then I was called upstairs. Ida Place lay on the bed. I pronounced her dead. Her lips were discolored, and some skin was rubbed off. Her face was badly bloated, swollen, and blueish. Rigor mortis had set in." Six again, pushing for Gormley to add something to help. "The appearance of her lips was not necessarily caused by acid," the doctor said.

Maguire called more police officers to the stand. I guess he thought he'd saved the best for last. Detective John Becker. Becker had been kind to me. I hoped he would be kind on the stand too. But no. He remembered everything I said on the day after Ida died. "At the Ralph Street Station, in the captain's office, with Detective Mitchell and matron Driscoll present, the defendant told us her husband struck her before he went to work. Then they quarreled. She went to his desk, took out some powder, and put it in a glass of water. Then she went to Ida's bedroom and threw it in her face." He blabbed on, all about Hilda and the errands. "Mrs. Place told us that when she went to the cellar to tend to the furnace, she noticed the axe and brought it upstairs in case Mr. Place wanted to fight with her when he came home, so she could defend herself. When she saw him enter the house, she thought he was going to strike her. She struck him first. Then she ran upstairs and threw the axe out the window. After that, she said she tried to kill herself." For the next ten minutes, the lawyers and Becker haggled over what I put in that glass. Becker said I told him it was acid, but then he admitted he told the coroner's jury that I said it was a powder, or a salt, then he said when he questioned me further, I said it was acid. I looked at the jury. They couldn't follow Becker. The printer looked at his new buddy, the butcher. Both, bafflement. Good. Then Becker talked about showing the axe to me on February 8th and testified that I admitted the axe belonged to our family. Now the tiresome up and back as Six made his usual objections to the axe, because it was connected to my attack on Will, and the judge overruled the objection.

Sarah Driscoll, the matron I thought I liked, was I ever a fool, came to the stand. She had done me only a little harm at the inquest, but I didn't know what story she'd tell now. She testified that on the day I arrived at the Ralph Street Station, I talked about my quarrel with Will and how after breakfast he and Ida were conniving. "Mrs. Place," she said, "explained to me that she put white powder or salts in a glass and threw the contents at her stepdaughter's mouth. Then Mrs. Place thought Miss Ida went out and she didn't see her again." Driscoll said she listened to my story twice, once before Ennis, Becker, and Mitchell arrived and once after, when they were in the room too. That testimony wasn't so bad.

At 1:00 Judge Hurd let everyone take a lunch break. I sat in the pen, with my lawyers just outside the bars. We ate sandwiches that Eyck, the stooped-over court officer, brought in from a street cart. I was hungry, but I noticed my lawyers were not. With all the testimony about no signs of violence and natural position, I thought they might look happy. Neither said much.

The bailiff called us back at 2:00, into the sweltering courtroom. Maguire was not at the end of his witness list. He dredged up another detective, Robert Mitchell. The one with the cough. Mitchell droned on about seeing me in the parlor and seeing the girl in the bed. Her eyes, he said, were "blurred, as if burned." Then he moved to the next day, that sorry conversation in the captain's office, where he said everything that Becker and Sarah Driscoll had just said—the argument, the powder, the door slamming, Hilda and the errands, retrieving the axe for protection, drinking liquor, striking Will, throwing the axe out the window, turning on the gas. The sun blasted through the west-facing windows. McSherry looked sleepy and my fan was no match for the heat. The jury drifted off. When they heard Mitchell say, "On the next day I went to New Jersey," they woke up. "The trunk was in the train station there. When we opened the trunk, we found jewelry, silverware, and clothing." But the twelve men drifted off again the minute Mitchell admitted that nothing in the trunk seemed connected to the murder.

Maguire stood a few feet off to the right, in front of the table where I sat. When I turned to see him, I saw beads of sweat drip from his scalp to his collar. The man was too busy trying to kill me to wipe his brow. He called to the stand Napoleon Bonaparte Thompson, that irritating neighbor. The minute N.B. started to talk about Will, Six objected. "This has nothing to do with the crime the defendant is charged with." And again, Judge Hurd overruled Six and told N.B. to continue.

N.B. was raring to go. You'd think he'd been everywhere and witnessed everything. "When I saw Mr. Place coming down his steps, with the help of James Desmond, I saw a lady in the vestibule of the front hall. I went to the Place house and saw Ida lying in bed. I identified her for the officers. Her face was discolored, her lips were swollen, her tongue was protruding, there was blood from her nose and lower lip, her arm was cold. Then I went into my own house and told Mr. Place of the death of his daughter." When N.B. said that I let my eyes drift to the side. To Edward Scheidecker. He squirmed, but there was more to see. Behind Edward I spotted Wayne Knittle, the first lawyer who deserted me, sitting in the section blocked off for the public. He was scribbling into his notepad.

Six cross-examined N.B, asking whether Ida—my lawyer reminded the jury that N.B. lived next door—was strong enough to fight off an attacker. I liked N.B.'s answer. "She was very vigorous. She was a large, strong, healthy girl." And answering another question, "There were no signs of a struggle."

Now Sarah McArran's turn. Hard to believe I gave this ingrate a rubber plant and a bicycle. Sarah testified that she rang the bell, looking for me, but no one answered. After a while, the maid came to the door. Then, finally, I came out. "We had trouble this morning, that's what she said to me, she meant with Mr. Place, and I am going to leave him for good this time. She said she was going to New Brunswick and I should take the bicycle. I asked for Ida but Martha told me she wasn't there because Mr. Place had boarded her out."

Sarah could have left it at that, but she had to go and mention that dumb letter I wrote her on February 8th. Maguire pulled it from his file and gave it to Sarah to read. "The horrible news is circulating. I should prefer death to it. Through Will's threatening, I was driven to desperation." The jury woke up.

The next witnesses didn't add much. A surveyor produced the diagram he drew of the second floor of our house, showing the bedrooms, maid's room, bathroom. The expressman said he took the trunk to the Annex at the foot of Fulton Street because Hilda told him I needed to make the 3:15 train for New Brunswick. Now the printer and the builder on the jury were sleeping and the molasses purveyor was fanning himself with his hand.

When those drowsy men heard Hilda called as a witness, they opened their eyes. Pretty, even prettier than Sarah Driscoll. Hilda's story was the usual one. Lots of people in that courtroom knew it by heart. Breakfast, hanging the laundry, hearing a scream. Then Mrs. Place saying that her services are no longer needed. Then all the errands—the expressman for the trunk, the postage stamps, the bank book. She added some new stories, damn. "Mrs. Place wanted me to leave the house before Mr. Place came home. I told her I should stay until the day after, to do the washing and ironing before I went. Wouldn't let me. She asked me to buy a ticket for her—a ticket to New Brunswick. Mrs. Place ordered me not to bother to say goodbye to Ida. But then she also told me if any people rang the bell and asked for Ida to tell them she went downtown." Hilda's testimony turned even worse when Maguire asked if I got along with Ida. "They seldom spoke. Hardly at all from Christmas to the time I left."

Six tried to undo the damage. "Miss Palm, you heard the scream when you were outside. Did you hear it again when you came inside? When you testified to the coroner's jury, you said you entered the house and listened, but didn't hear anything, correct? "

"Yes, the only scream was when I was in the backyard. I heard some noise upstairs, but I didn't hear any struggle going on or any moans. Didn't sound like anybody being hurt. Just sounded like a quarrel." The more the girl talked, the better it got. "I didn't notice anything unusual, anything different in the action of Mrs. Place from any other day. She went around the house as usual." And even better. "She said that Mr. Place had hurt her."

I wish the judge ended the trial there. Hilda did a good job for me. I'd been lucky with that one. She was a fine maid, but even more, she told the police about the trunk, just as I wanted, and about my destination, New Brunswick. And they believed her. It almost worked. If I had just swung harder.

Maguire called Edward Scheidecker to the witness chair. I hated that fellow. Even Will hated him. And I wasn't sure the girl wanted him either. The blockhead wore his uniform. Why was he proud of being a private? On the stand, he didn't repeat the awful things he said about me earlier, but he made no sense. First, he said he called on Ida in the afternoon, at 2:00, in the company of a young woman. He never came, and he never visited with someone else. "I could not say I saw Mrs. Place, but looking up I seen somebody at the window behind the curtains." Rubbish. Then he said he came back at 6:00, "to meet a young friend of mine." That made no sense either. He said he saw Ida's body, her swollen face, and one burned eye. He spoke slowly, without emotion, and he couldn't clean up his grammar like I could. I wondered if I should tell Six that Edward was lying, but everyone would notice if I whispered.

"I call William Place to the stand," Maguire said. No bored faces now. Will walked to the witness chair, bent over, with his bandaged head almost resting on his shoulder. The last time I saw him he was crawling through the vestibule, bleeding. My lawyers had told me Will went home from the hospital three months ago, but he made himself scarce. The lawyers also told me that at the March 2nd hearing—one of those pretrial hearings that went nowhere—Will hid in an alcove off the courtroom, thinking he might be called to the stand. The judge decided Will wasn't needed that day. Ha. He wasn't needed any day.

When I first arrived at the Raymond Street Jail, I asked Warden Bergen to ask Will to visit. The warden gave me a strange look. "If I could talk to him," I said, "I could tell him that I would never hurt his daughter." Bergen said he needed to check with Sheriff Creamer. A day later Bergen came to my cell to tell me Creamer said no, that Will's doctors would not let him leave the hospital. Did Bergen lie about checking? I'll never know.

Now Will sat in the witness chair, alive. I looked straight ahead, kept my chin forward. Moved my eyes. Will wore his best suit, the one I helped him choose last year from the tailor in Manhattan. He looked gaunt and weak. Was that contrived? I glared at him, one of the reporters wrote, a second wrote I was impassive, a third wrote I snickered, a fourth wrote that my posture as I sat was so erect that I made the people observing me uncomfortable. A fifth wrote neither husband nor wife looked at the other. The fifth was wrong.

Will's hurtful testimony didn't surprise me or my lawyers. The usual history. He hired me as a housekeeper, then married me. Relations among the three in the household were pleasant and affectionate for a year. Then malice, silence, quarrels. The morning argument was over money. When he refused for the second time to hand over my allowance, saying he would use it to pay my debts, he testified that I said, "If you don't give it to me, I will make it cost you ten times more." I couldn't remember threatening him, but I might have. "I did not hit her," he added. "There had been occasions in my past life with her when there had been some violent exchange between her and me; but not on that day." Violent exchanges, so that's what he called our battles. Then he testified that after he refused me money that morning I put on my hat and gloves and began to walk downtown, then, oddly turned back home as he left for work. When he returned in the evening, he entered the dark house, hung his hat and coat on the rack, heard a noise, and was attacked, twice on his head and once on his hand. Compound fracture of the skull.

Every few minutes he cried. The crowd looked away—maybe embarrassed. He buried his face in his hands, maybe to wipe the tears. His voice shook, sobs then words then, sobs.

A lot of objections from Six for this or that—hearsay, relevance, and so on—with the judge ruling sometimes one way, sometimes another. I couldn't say, looking back, that Six spoke forcefully when he stood to object. But he did his best in cross-examining Will. Yes, Will said, he sometimes gave me salts and pills for headaches. He told people that I was not Ida's mother because he wanted them to know that Ida was "better bred." Bastard. Hard to know if his slurs helped or hurt me with the jury. More questions, more answers. Will said I neglected to attend to his house for seven weeks in the winter of '96, '97. I prepared no meals for him. He said, too, that once, during a quarrel, he had to force me to the floor to protect himself. The butcher and builder were awake.

Will's anger at me was laughable. Such exaggerations. Such hate. He said he often sent his daughter to live with friends. Often? Hogwash. He said for two months Ida lived with Uncle Theodore to get out of the house. One or two weeks maybe. He said he repeatedly arranged for her to board elsewhere. Lies, except, maybe, for one summer. He said I barely spoke to Ida. How would he know? He stayed in his office all day. During a musicale at his home, I threw cake and lemonade out the window several times. Really—it was just lemonade, just once. I forced Ida to do menial housework even when I had a servant. Was it wrong for a daughter to help keep the house clean? I scolded Ida when she didn't clean properly. Of course. I chased Ida around the house and threatened to hurt her. Bull. I once tore Ida's hat to pieces because it made the girl look too pretty. I kept her away from her friends. Relations turned so bad that he told me I was no longer responsible for Ida. I accused him of taking Ida to a family wedding instead of taking me. An endless list of claptrap.

When Will left the witness stand, he walked out of the courtroom, still stooped. I never saw him again.

Judge Hurd should have dismissed us for the day, but no, he let Maguire call another witness, Henry Walker, a chemist. Walker said he analyzed the contents of two bottles in Will's desk. Six jumped up, objecting that the bottles had nothing to do with the charge against me. I knew that wouldn't work. "Overruled," Hurd said. Six looked exhausted from all that jumping up and complaining and getting shot down. Walker testified that one bottle contained pyro-gallic acid, and the other, muriatic acid. Useless information. After Walker's testimony, Hurd adjourned the court. As McCloskey and Eyck hurried me out, I glanced at my lawyers, trying to see what they thought. They were too busy to notice, talking to themselves. I was happy not to linger because by now I felt the sweat on my back and knew I didn't smell good.

Robert Van Iderstine

What a miserable day. I knew I had scored a few points. The jury, if they were awake, would realize there had been no struggle, no violence. How could a middle-aged woman hold down a younger and maybe stronger woman without making a racket? But the husband had done my client harm, a great deal of harm. He painted a picture of a shrew. That would stick with those twelve men.

McSherry told me there was no point in going home by train to New Brunswick and then back again in the morning. Much as I disliked the man, I didn't think he should have to pay for a hotel. I invited him to sleep in our home. That meant dinner together and drinking together. We agreed on our strategy for the next day—characterize the doctors as quacks. I'll give Howard credit. We play-acted and he was good at the doctor role. I cross-examined him. "Yup, I saw her lips were purple and her blood was blue." And five minutes later, after another whiskey, "Yup, I felt her chest. I felt it twice just to make sure." We had some good laughs.

Mattie

I guess McCloskey and Eyck never got a day off. They waited for me in front of the courthouse on July 7th. Led me through the hellish crowd and back inside again. "Court is in session." Judge Hurd wasted no time.

Maguire called Dr. Alvin Henderson to the witness stand. He walked up slowly. Seemed like he really did have an appendix attack the month before. The doctor may have had a medical license, but his testimony on the autopsy didn't differ much from what the men in the courtroom heard the day before from the police. Ida's tongue protruded, something Henderson called white mucous froth was on her lips, her eyes were hurt by a corrosive substance. Then something new. "Under the scalp on the left temple, there was a space about the size of a silver dollar, discolored, which resulted from violence of some kind." Discolored—everyone loved that word. When Maguire asked the key question, what was the cause of death, Henderson answered quick and easy, "asphyxia. You could call it suffocation."

I smiled to myself, thinking about the word asphyxia. I remembered a conversation a few weeks before when McSherry and Six visited me in jail. They fussed about which word to use—asphyxia, strangulation, or suffocation? Better to use fancy words or simple ones? Which word sounded more frightening? The lawyers couldn't decide.

Maguire sat down and Six started his questions. I squirmed in my chair, knowing Six would press until he got at least some of what he wanted. Not that I felt sorry for Dr. Henderson, why should I? I squirmed because I knew this part of the trial homed in on Six's strategy. Maybe the doctor knew what was coming. He didn't look happy. Six thought the jury would believe that if I strangled Ida, her organs would show signs of violence. Six made Henderson go through each of Ida's organs and other parts of her body, one at a time, telling the jury what showed up in the autopsy. Not much. The mouth, throat, tongue, larynx, stomach, heart, lungs, liver, kidneys, blood. I listened to see if Six asked about the uterus. Nothing. Just a vague question about pelvic organs. Only I seemed to notice. The men on the jury nodded off at the last organ or two, but Six got what he wanted. Even those twelve morons could see that Ida was a healthy girl. Then Six got Henderson to admit that if someone tried to suffocate a robust—remember, N.B. said Ida was strong—person, it would take three to five minutes to do that and the autopsy would reveal signs of a violent struggle. The victim's clothing would be in disarray. The position of limbs would not be normal. I was surprised Judge Hurd allowed Six to harass Henderson on the stand. Well, it was hardly harassment. Six was always a gentleman.

When Henderson testified about Ida's eyes, it didn't go as well. She lost her sight from the acid before she died, he insisted. Would the jury think a healthy, strong, young woman, who had just been blinded, was too disoriented to fight off an attacker? Henderson left the stand, looking tired. He had sat in the chair for a long, nerve-wracking hour.

Doctor number two. Maguire called Harry Enton to the stand. The man looked self-confident, handsome. Dark hair, prominent chin. He claimed to be an expert on the dangers of acid, but he talked more about suffocation. Death by that method took a long time, three minutes and fifty seconds on average, more than enough time for the perpetrator to understand what he was doing and to change course. Six sat next to me. I could feel him tense when Enton said "more than enough time." Enton went on to talk about acid in water and its effects on eyes and skin. Six stood, with questions. The doctor admitted that to determine the exact effects of acid he would need to know the temperature of the water and the ratio of water to acid. Six was trying to turn attention away from Enton's testimony about the time suffocation might take. We didn't know then how badly Six failed at his goal—six months later Governor Roosevelt would turn his mind to Enton's testimony.

After Enton, the judge adjourned us for lunch, a little early. He wanted everyone well-rested for what would come next. Witnesses for the defense.

That meant me.

So, for now, back to the holding pen. Six and McSherry, looking glum, waited for me on nearby chairs. Eyck delivered the usual stale sandwiches. I ate one, but the lawyers were more interested in preparing me than in eating, even though we had gone over everything ten times before. Six was not so worried about what I would say as about how I would say it. I should look at the jury. Use proper English. Seem humble. I knew what I had to do. "Enough drilling," I snarled. Court officer McCloskey was on the other side of a closed door, about twenty feet from my lawyers, but I'm sure he heard my voice rise. "I am not stupid. You know I am not stupid." The lawyers looked at each other, sheepish.

Then back to the courtroom for the defense part of the spectacle. McCloskey led me by the arm, like a lady. Maguire had called dozens of witnesses but Six had only two, and I would be the first of those two. The men on the jury were all eyes and ears. The murderess, at last.

Six was surprisingly loud. "I call Martha M. Place to the witness stand." I stood, fixed my posture, stuck out my chest, and walked to the stand. I kissed the Bible, a full kiss, as Six had told me to, and swore to tell the truth. My first lie was that I was forty-four, lopping off five years. Then I calmly repeated the story I had told before. Working as a dressmaker, going from family to family seeking jobs. Begging for my household allowance. Planning that morning to go downtown then changing my mind. Seeing Ida reading in the parlor. Arguing.

The men on the jury leaned forward. I used the sentences I had rehearsed. I said, "'Did your Papa give you any money this morning?' She said, 'None of your business.' I said, 'When he gives you money, he won't give me any.' She said, 'That is nothing to you,' and she picked up a cigarette box out of the basket and threw it at me and I went for her, and she jumped up and said 'I am going away. I won't stay here any longer,' and she went upstairs. I went in the back parlor and watered the rubber plant and after that, I went up to my room and I thought to myself I better go away from here, there is always so much trouble." I added more details, out of order, about packing the trunk and dismissing Hilda. Then back to the heart of the story, again using the words I practiced with Six. "Ida came up and I had just gone downstairs to get some salts for my headache from Mr. Place's desk and got a little bottle of salts, about that large, not very much in it, wasn't half full, and I took some out and put it in a goblet I had in my room. I dumped it out in that and went to the bathroom to put water in it and while I was there Ida came upstairs and she went to her room and after I had fixed the salts and I was just going to take it and my door was open and she could see my trunk and I stepped to her door and I told her I was going away and she said, 'Don't go, Papa won't like it. I will go.' I said 'No, I am going, there has been a great deal of trouble and I think I better go now,' and as she slammed the door shut I threw the salts at her and the door knocked the glass out of my hand and I went to my room. I thought I heard her going downstairs and I thought she would be gone for the day, as when we had words she would go out for the day."

Then more details about the afternoon, nearly accurate. Never seeing Ida again. Busy packing. Hearing Ida move in the basement later in the day. Sending away the trunk. Drinking whiskey. Planning to leave Will and take the train to New Brunswick, then to Princeton where I had a friend and planned to remain for a time. When I said Princeton, Six glared at me, then recovered in an instant. Right, he hadn't heard about Princeton before. I just figured that might be a good way to keep Peter out of this mess.

As I got to Will's return home that night, Six, my own lawyer, cautioned me. "You do not need to say anything about Mr. Place. That does not enter into the trial of this indictment." He knew that I sometimes wandered into that territory and needed a reminder.

A half-hour into my testimony, Six asked the key question. "Tell the jury, did you commit that murder?"

"I did not, as God is my judge, for I didn't do anything of the kind."

My muscles tensed, from my waist up to my neck, when Six sat down and Maguire stepped up to cross-examine me. He tried to make it sound like the quarrel was over a little twenty-dollar allowance, which made no sense to him since I had thirteen hundred in the bank. Then he badgered me about when I decided to leave, making it seem I decided only after I hurt Ida. I said I tried to leave a year before, but Will wouldn't agree to it and wouldn't give me the money I needed. More questions from Maguire. Why was I in a hurry to leave? Why did I dismiss Hilda Palm when the girl could have kept house for Will? Why did I tell Mrs. McArran that Will had boarded out Ida when that was not the truth? Why didn't I leave for New Brunswick, or Princeton, in the late afternoon? More questions about Will. Six popped up and down, as usual. "I object to this. I do not think it is at all relevant to the case, anything about Mr. Place at all."

"Overruled."

Then the expected question about the axe. Why did I take it upstairs when it was used to chop wood in the basement? I knew not to answer.

Maguire kept trying. I kept refusing. Then he switched to the day of February 8th. "Do you remember making a statement in the presence of Mrs. Driscoll, Detective Becker, and Detective Mitchell, saying you had thrown acid into the face of Ida Place?"

Now I had to answer. "No, sir, I didn't say so. I didn't throw any acid. I said salts or powder." Maguire wouldn't get me to say acid.

He moved on to the February 8th letter to Sarah McArran. "What did you mean by this, 'My dear friend, the horrible news is circulating. I should prefer death to it. Through Will's threatening, I was driven to desperation.'"

"I thought it was terrible to accuse me of things like that when I was not guilty."

"What did you mean by saying, 'I was driven to desperation'?" I didn't answer.

Maguire tired himself out. Or he saw the jury drooping. Or knew he had done enough harm. "No more questions your honor." My shoulders felt frozen. I took some deep breaths. Miss Meury had taught me that trick. I got up as quickly as I could. I forced myself to stand straight. I pushed my chest out again. Back to the chair next to my lawyers, as all eyes in that room watched me. My lawyers' eyes too.

Six had one other witness for the defense, Dr. Joshua Van Cott, a pathologist. For a few minutes, I didn't listen. Just tried to put to the side what I said on the stand. Then I heard Van Cott testify that he had performed over three thousand autopsies. This man was about to contradict Dr. Henderson. In the same way Six had gone over each of the organs with Dr. Henderson, he now went over each with Dr. Van Cott. The stomach, the heart, the lungs, the liver, the kidneys, the blood. The difference was that Van Cott, for each organ, pointed out what Henderson had missed. "Dr. Henderson has made some error," Van Cott testified. "He should describe the condition of the circulation in the stomach. A person who dies of asphyxia will show a livid stomach, just the same as the skin. If there had been asphyxia there would have been edema there, that is escape of serum from the blood. He failed to find that." And so on for each organ. Again, just a vague and meaningless mention of the pelvic organs. Then the key question about whether asphyxia was the cause of death. "I should say most certainly not."

"So, you disagree with Dr. Henderson?" Six asked.

"His findings are worthless. There is no evidence Ida Place died of strangulation." Six turned his head to stare at the jury, to drive home what Van Cott said. I smiled at the back of my lawyer's head.

Six wasn't through. He knew the jury might now doubt suffocation, but he had to deal with the bruise on Ida's scalp. Henderson left the impression that could have been fatal too. Van Cott helped. "In a wound, the condition must have necessarily left a black and blue spot, and if Dr. Henderson didn't find that, it is not competent for me to call it a wound at all." Seemed I was the only one who remembered that Henderson had called the spot discolored.

Next, time of death. Six was obsessed with that detail. "If the limbs were flexible and rigor mortis hadn't set in at about 6:30 or 7:00, when several officers saw the body, when do you think death would have occurred?" Again, was my memory—a dressmaker's memory—better than everyone else's? Six forgot or ignored the undertaker's testimony that Ida died in the morning.

"Death about four hours earlier," Van Cott said. "Maybe earlier than that."

For his cross-examination, Maguire asked just one question. "Isn't it a fact that rigor mortis in particular cases hasn't set in for twenty-four hours?

"Yes, sir, longer times than that where the body has been frozen."

And that was that. The trial part of the trial ended.

Six said, "Judge Hurd, I wish to make a motion to dismiss this case because there is insufficient evidence." That was part of the routine.

"Denied."

Emilie Meury

Each morning of the trial the other missionary ladies kindly covered my responsibilities in the women's annex so I could attend to Mrs. Place. After two streetcars and a seven-block walk, I felt hot and thirsty, even early in the morning, but I was set on bringing comfort to the poor woman.

I spent most of my time studying the jury. Turned out that I had a slight acquaintance with one of them, John Ahrens, who owned a small produce shop in my neighborhood. Like the other men, he sometimes drifted off, sometimes startled awake, and sometimes flinched. He never looked at Mrs. Place, except when she was on the stand, and then his eyebrows knotted together.

What little energy I had, I assumed I would direct toward Mrs. Place. But she held up well, remaining calm. Her lawyers needed me more than she did. When I offered to read a blessing as we were about to be called in to the courtroom, both nodded yes and listened respectfully. After studying juror Ahrens, I was not surprised that Mr. Van Iderstine was on edge.

Mattie

We limped to the finish.

I listened to the lawyers' summations the next morning, July 8th. Six did himself proud. He knew the evidence against me for the assault on Will was stronger than the evidence against me for what I did to Ida. "The jury must separate the charge of murder from the charge of assault and focus only on the alleged murder. For that, there is no evidence of strangulation and no evidence that Mrs. Place's actions led to Miss Place's death. She was not involved. No one saw her in Miss Place's bedroom. Moreover, Dr. Henderson's testimony is incorrect. There was no violent suffocation." He must have decided the word suffocation was the best choice.

Now Maguire. "Mrs. Place made life miserable for Miss Ida Place and was ready to do anything to get her stepdaughter out of the way. Mrs. Place was jealous of the beautiful, gifted Miss Place. The stepmother thought her stepdaughter stood between herself and her husband. The two women quarreled constantly. Also, immediately after the murder, Mrs. Place told Detective Becker and Matron Driscoll that she threw acid in her stepdaughter's face. But at this trial, she said it was headache salts. After she had five months to think it over. And what about the chair in the girl's room, the chair with a broken back? Maybe Mrs. Place struck her stepdaughter with the chair as well as with the axe." Then he brought up that letter I wrote Grace on September 20th, five months before Ida died, telling Grace to keep $200 of my savings for herself if anything should happen to me. "Points to premeditation," he said.

Third up was Judge Hurd, to charge the jury. The longest speech so far. "What was the cause of death? Asphyxiation, or death from natural causes? The People have produced testimony from Dr. Henderson who says positively it was a case of asphyxiation. On the other hand, the defendant maintains that the evidence does not show the cause of death, that it does not show it was a violent death or anything other than a natural death." He babbled on to say that if the jury found the cause of death to be suffocation, then they needed to determine if it was done by the accused and if so, what was her intent? I saw puzzled looks on the juror's faces. "The verdict can be murder in the first, murder in the second, or manslaughter, depending on intent." And more twaddle. "Even if there is no direct evidence, if it is all circumstantial, that could still be acceptable for a finding of guilt, especially if the circumstantial evidence is connected in a logical chain." Finally, "Members of the jury should have no pity on the defendant because she is a woman." Nobody ever had pity on me. For any reason.

At 12:55 the jury filed out to deliberate. I know because I looked at Six's pocket watch when he looked at it, when McCloskey walked over to get me. Newspapers later that day agreed on one thing—I showed no emotion as I left the courtroom to wait in the pen. The waiting wasn't as bad as you might think. Eyck dropped off another tasteless lunch, so I didn't go hungry. And I had a lot of company sitting just outside the pen—two lawyers and

Emilie Meury. I heard the three review the testimony and share what they saw on the faces of the jurors. No one asked what I saw. Of the three, Six was the most nervous, judging every detail. McSherry seemed puffed up, proud he had participated, even in the background, in a big city case. Miss Meury tried to lead the group in a prayer, but the lawyers fidgeted. She cut her blather short. Then McCloskey opened the door. "Jury's come in. Off to the courtroom." I joined Six in looking at his pocket watch again. 3:37. As we walked down a hall, past a window, McCloskey pointed outside. Hundreds of people lingered, jockeying for shade under the trees, waiting for the verdict. We could see a murmur pass from one gawker to another and now they rushed back into the courtroom, pushing, hoping for the same standing room they wangled in the morning.

Once everyone sat or stood quietly, the jury entered. I knew the men might not look my way. The lawyers prepared me. The twelve didn't just look away. Turned their necks away too. Bile came up in my throat. Judge Hurd addressed the foreman, John Krieger. That damn molasses manufacturer stuck his chin out high. Maybe smug. Pleased with himself. "Have you agreed upon a verdict?" Hurd was supposed to ask me to stand. Didn't. Probably thought I would faint.

Krieger, loud. "Guilty of murder in the first degree, as charged."

More bile. I struggled not to retch. Six asked for the jury to be polled, part of the ritual. This was not what Six expected. He expected a verdict of murder in the second degree, with a sentence of life in prison. He expected the jury to make concessions for a woman.

It took twenty minutes for McCloskey and Eyck to lead me through the crowd, back to the patrol wagon headed for the Raymond Street Jail. McCloskey's eyes met mine, but Eyck turned away. Some reporters wrote that I showed no emotion on the way out. Others said I cried. Lies. During the long slow walk through the crowd, I heard some of the black-hearted jurors talking to reporters. The only debate in the jury room was between murder in the first and murder in the second, and the men pushing for murder in the second caved when they remembered that I tried to kill myself. They figured I was not afraid of death. The other thing I heard was

182

what I already knew. Van Iderstine would appeal.

Back in my cell, I wondered if I could cry. When I saw the guards and even Mrs. Handy stare at me, I gave them what they wanted. Wails. Warden Bergen placed me on suicide watch, with an extra matron thrown in for good measure, and took away my hairpins and mirror. For two days, until I could convince Bergen I was no danger to myself, I looked like an old witch. I refused to talk to anyone, but I did read one of the Brooklyn papers. "For the first time in the history of Kings County, a woman has been convicted of murder in the first degree." Warden Bergen called on me as I was staring at the paper. "Mrs. Place, I have a responsibility to explain the process of sentencing. I believe you need to prepare yourself for a death sentence." He looked at me, expecting a response. I said nothing and feared he would wait until I did. He waited four seconds. I counted. Then he pursed his lips, stood up, and walked quickly out of my cell.

Peter Garretson

Shameful, I know, that I hadn't visited Mattie. Yes, I helped recruit Howard McSherry, for whatever that was worth, but that's all I did. Why make the trip to the Raymond Street Jail for a good-for-nothing? That's what I thought until July 10th, when McSherry called on me at home. He said the death sentence appeared nearly certain. I wouldn't call McSherry sentimental, but he seemed surprised I hadn't visited my doomed sister. Grace heard the talk between me and him. She sobbed and begged me to visit and to take her along. So the next day I had Matilda, she was twelve, take care of Ogden, he had just turned four, and me and Grace and my daughter Maggie took the train to New York, then streetcars to the jail. I had to ask a lot of people about the streetcars because I'd never been to Brooklyn before. When we got to the jail, I found the warden. "Hmmm. Surprised to see you," he said, in a snippy voice. "Not a single relative or friend has visited Mrs. Place, well, aside from Emilie Meury, the missionary lady. What brings you here now?"

I could not look at him. Grace answered. "My aunt has been kind to us. She led a hard life, but she always cared about me. I'm sorry we didn't see her before. We want to now."

183

The warden changed his expression. He looked at Grace. Smiled a little and gestured to follow him. We walked across a yard to Mattie's cell. She sat on her cot, reading. When she heard our footsteps, she looked up. First, she grinned. Then, it seemed like all her anger rolled onto her face. Her smile went away, fast. But Grace, dear Grace, she fixed it.

"Aunt Mattie, we want to visit. We're sorry we didn't get here sooner. Can you make time for us now?"

Grace reached her hands through the bars, to touch Mattie. The warden unlocked the door and ushered us inside. Maggie and I sat in chairs. Grace took a seat on the cot, hugging Mattie. None of us had much to say. I watched while the weeping spread, from Grace, to Mattie, to Maggie. I checked my pocket watch. I would handle five minutes of this. Waited. I checked again, then motioned to my girls—time to leave. I gave Mattie a kiss on the top of her head, almost undoing the knot, then I motioned to the guard and led my daughters away.

The Wait

Mattie

I thought about dying, looked at it straight. For weeks, even before the guilty verdict, I collected death stories in my head. I filled in a few things I didn't remember by asking the guards and reading the newspapers. Like I said before, I knew from my years in New Jersey about Bridget Deignan. Hung on a jerker. Pa talking about it, with Peter standing there. And I knew about William Kemmler. Fried, badly fried, in '90. And there were more women. Roxiana Druse. The woman shot her husband—he was mean to her—cut up his body and burned the pieces. In 1887 she hung for her crime. She was small, so the jerker didn't work the way it should. Her neck never broke. Took a long time for her to strangle. Even the officials didn't like that. Druse was the last woman they hung in the state of New York before they moved to the chair, but I didn't know that for a while. Then there was Lizzie Halliday. She killed at least four people in the early '90s, upstate. Lizzie liked fires and revolvers as her weapons of choice. She was the first woman they sentenced to die in the chair. But Governor Roswell Flower commuted her sentence to life in a mental institution. The newest case was Maria Barbella. That one had a happy ending, you could say. Barbella slashed Domenico Cataldo's neck with a razor in 1895. She was convicted of murder and sentenced to die in the chair. Her lawyers appealed. They said Cataldo raped her, promised to marry her, and hid that he was already married. The appeal worked. Hardly ever happens. Barbella got a second trial and was found not guilty. I would hear Barbella's name a lot, very soon.

After my guilty verdict, I didn't think about anything else except these cases. I drank my morning coffee, then my mind went to the gallows or the chair. I pinned up my hair with the pins I begged back from the warden. My head went back to the gallows or the chair. I sat with Miss Meury. My head went back to the gallows or the chair. I wondered which caused more pain. Most thought hanging.

Then it was sentencing day, July 12th—a God-awful day for me but a good day for Warden Bergen. "Can't wait 'til she's gone," I overheard him whisper to the deputy warden, John Wilson, when they stood outside the cell waiting for me to dress. "Too many crowds, too much publicity, for five long months." I picked the same clothes, still elegant, that I wore before, including my black kid gloves. Except this time, I removed the ostrich feather from my hat. I didn't feel flamboyant. Then the warden brought Mrs. Handy a plain canvas satchel and directed her to help me pack. I understood what the satchel signaled. The warden knew I would not set foot in the Raymond Street Jail again. Mrs. Handy opened the satchel wide as I carefully folded my possessions and placed them inside the dank bag.

We headed out to the Kings County Criminal Court, for the last time. A large party came along—Warden Richard Bergen, Deputy Warden John Wilson, Matron Handy, and two guards. No patrol wagons were available so we took a crowded trolly car. The other passengers didn't know who I was, but they stared because the guards were in uniform and holding my arms. "Do you really need these guards," I said to Bergen. "Do you think I'm going to run off through the streets of Brooklyn?" Bergen looked at me, pursing his lips and putting his finger perpendicular to them. "Requirement," he said, quietly.

At the courthouse, McCloskey and Eyck, like old friends, waited for me. They shooed Bergen and his entourage into the courtroom and walked me to the prisoner's pen. Emilie Meury—she wanted to be with me—and Six waited on chairs just outside the cell. McSherry was nowhere to be seen.

"Martha, I think you know the judge is likely to impose the death penalty. I suppose we can hope for a miracle." Six said this as quickly as he could, not looking at me. "I will appeal, but I'm afraid you will have the sentence hanging over you." He winced as he said those last words.

"Mr. Van Iderstine, would the judge be more compassionate if Mrs. Place confessed?" As Emilie Meury asked this, she looked directly at me. "Mattie, please think about it." Six saw me glare at her.

"Miss Meury, at this late point I don't think anything will matter," he said.

McCloskey announced court was about to begin. He escorted me into the courtroom, with Miss Meury and Six following. Right away Judge Hurd called me up to the railing in front of his desk. Warden Bergen and Mrs. Handy came to stand on either side of me. Each took an elbow. The judge asked if I had a statement to offer. I didn't dither. I shook my head no.

Hurd didn't wait another second. He delivered the hateful words. "The sentence of this court is that the sheriff, deliver you to the authorities at Sing Sing prison within a period of ten days, and that there, in the week beginning on August 29, 1898, you be put to death in the electric chair, in the manner proscribed by law."

This time the newspaper reports were correct, I did twitch and sob. Not at the mention of the chair, but the timing. Maybe forty-eight days to live.

Six, shaking for once, had memorized his response. "I suppose your honor has no discretion in this matter."

"None."

Two seconds later Sheriff Creamer walked up to me. I'd never seen him before. All I knew was that Warden Bergen claimed that Creamer wouldn't let Will visit me at Raymond Street when I asked. I glared at Creamer and he glared back at me and grabbed for my arm, rough like. I saw McCloskey on the sidelines, staring at the sheriff. I gave the officer a tiny smile. I was all right. Then I craned my neck to look at Six. "I will appeal," he said twice, just loudly enough for the crowd to hear. The sheriff led me to Bergen and then made a show of transferring me to the warden's custody.

The months from the day of the mayhem to the day of the sentencing had moved slowly, but the minute I walked out of the courthouse, time sped up. Eyck hailed a large hansom cab. I climbed in, followed by Warden Bergen, Deputy Warden Wilson who I hardly knew, Mrs. Handy, and Miss Meury. In twenty minutes, we were at Grand Central Station, where we boarded a train. I sobbed most of the ride. Felt I deserved the attention. Had to sit next to Wilson but thank God he looked out the window the whole trip. In two hours, too fast, the train pulled into Ossining.

The warden of Sing Sing sent a wagon to take us from the train station to the penitentiary. One of the newspapers reported that he sent a carriage. Ha. I didn't want to look as we got near, but when I saw the two men and two women seated beside me all turn to the left, I followed their glance. First, I saw the east bank of the Hudson, beautiful on this summer day. Then I saw a fortress-like hodgepodge of marble, marble I learned later that was hauled from local quarries by inmates. An ugly brick wall surrounded everything. I saw a guard tower with eight sides, higher than the six-story buildings around it, with men at the top looking down at everything. "Austere, isn't it?" the Deputy Warden Wilson said. Then he glanced at me, with a sheepish look. The others knew better and said nothing.

An old man, gray and stooped, wearing a formal suit, met us at the front entrance. He introduced himself as Warden Sage. Bergen had told me on the train to Sing Sing that Sage was a force among wardens. He brooked no resistance, put down riots firmly, handled matters fairly. Bergen sure knew a lot about Sage. I wondered if Bergen wanted that Sing Sing job himself one day. Later I learned that Sage's full name was Omar Van Leuven Sage. That name was one of the few things that brought a smile to my face over the next six months. Warden Sage led us to his office, wood-paneled and fancier than Warden Bergen's. I noticed Bergen eyeing the leather armchairs.

By now I was prepared for the humiliation of prison. With the Raymond Street group listening and watching, Sage asked me to hand over my money and jewelry, including my hairpins, to his clerk. When I pulled out the hairpins my hair fell, covered my chest. Streaks of gray. A guard led us—Sage allowed Miss Meury and Mrs. Handy to come with me—around the perimeter of the prison, not through the yard, to a cell on the third floor of Sing Sing's Old Hospital Building, on a hill just beyond the prison yard. They didn't usually jail women in Sing Sing, so there was no women's wing. Only women sentenced to death came here, to be locked in the hospital. The others went to the women's prison in Auburn. The guard opened the door to the same cell Maria Barbella lived in while she was under sentence of death for murdering the cad who dishonored her. Two strange matrons sat there, waiting for me. Mrs. Handy smiled at them. She gave me the satchel she had carried from Brooklyn and hugged me. Miss Meury did the same. The guard frowned and the new matrons stared, but no one paid them any mind. I wept, this time not for attention. Miss Meury cried, Mrs. Handy too, then they left. I never saw Mrs. Handy again. Three hours had passed since I heard my death sentence.

I looked around. The matrons Warden Sage hired to guard me introduced themselves. Annie Reilly was the day matron. Kathryn Coultry was the night matron. Then the two guards, borrowed from the men's quarters, said their names were Johnny Conyers and Albert Robinson. No need to get close to any of them if I had just forty-eight days to live.

The space Conyers locked me in was a cell, sort of, because it had bars. But the cell looked nicer and cozier than the Raymond Street Jail. Two rooms were connected, one for me and the matrons, one for the guards. I could enter the guards' space during the day, walking up and back between the rooms. Down the hall was a bathroom where the matrons said they would take me. Besides a bed—a real bed, not a cot—and a bed for the night matron, I saw armchairs, a settee, a small round table, and a screen. One barred window looked north to the prison yard. Another barred window looked south. Nice for a holding pen for the doomed. Sage knew, just like Bergen did, that his celebrity convicts would have lawyers visiting.

Warden Omar Sage

I had just about recovered from the fuss around one infamous and condemned inmate, Maria Barbella, and now I had responsibility for another one. By July 13th, just one day after the Place woman arrived, journalists were already swarming the prison courtyard looking for crumbs. Best check on her. I summoned the prison physician to come with me. Dr. Robert Irvine was young, spry, and up to the stress of a prison job. We found Mrs. Place sitting on her bed, twitching about the eyes, but otherwise fine. Robert checked her pulse and breathing and reported nothing amiss. No hysterics.

Warden Bergen from Raymond Street had given me a report. He assured me that Mrs. Place had not caused trouble in his jail, aside from the fact that he had to convey her up and back to court endless times. She had few visitors, he said. Almost no family. But she did welcome visits from a missionary lady and seemed to like her matron. Both women had accompanied her here. "No problem with those relationships, as far as I was concerned," he said. "Martha Place started off quiet, but then she trusted the two women enough to talk to them." He looked at me. "I know, she doesn't have much time left to talk, so what's the harm."

Ross Aschenbach

My Mama and Papa, the Aschenbachs, they knew. But after I did. I learned about the murder first from my cousin, Grace. Me and Grace were not friends, never even saw each other except for a few times when I was little. But I guess Grace heard from her Pa about how I was given away and I heard from that woman who's my Ma how Grace's own Ma died. Now Grace had to raise a brother and two sisters.

On Sunday, July 24th, the same day as one of my brother's birthdays, I heard a knock on the window of our house in Vailsburg, close to Newark. I saw a pretty girl, maybe fifteen or sixteen, motioning to me. She pointed to herself and mouthed her name. Grace? She moved her hand in a half-circle. I should come outside, around the back of the house.

Odd, but I thought it might be Grace Garretson. Made no sense. I hunched my shoulders in a question. She put her index finger to her lips so I would stay quiet. Now that I look back, isn't this every boy's dream? A pretty girl motioning to meet. I snuck out.

"Ross, you remember me, right? We're cousins. I'm Grace, Grace Garretson, Peter's daughter."

I guessed right. I nodded my head yes, waiting. She breathed fast, like she was scared.

"I can't stay. Need to get back soon. I had to wait 'til a Sunday when Pa stayed home, so he could take care of the little ones. Then I lied to him. Said I was going to a church concert in Newark. I snuck, well, I borrowed Pa's train pass to get here. I worried about finding the Aschenbachs' house, so I asked a policeman who helped me." She caught her breath. "I saw some of your brothers in the other windows, but they had blond hair, didn't look right. Then I saw you." She paused again, longer this time. "I reckon no one will tell you what happened to Aunt Mattie. Do you know?"

I froze. Was she dead? If so, maybe it wouldn't matter, much. But I didn't want her dead.

"Ross, I'm sorry to tell you this. She killed a girl. She killed Ida. You know, Ida Place?"

"No. Ida Place is her stepdaughter. Mr. Place's daughter. You're wrong."

Grace was ready for that. She reached into her satchel and took out three editions of the local New Brunswick paper. "Read these, but don't let your parents, your Newark parents, know that I'm here, and don't let them see these. I don't want trouble. Ross, I think you should go visit Aunt Mattie. Before it's too late. That's why I came to see you."

She reached out and gave me a hug. I pulled back, embarrassed. I'd never had a hug like that from a girl before. Then she turned and walked off.

A lot of boys and girls went into and out of the house that day, what with my brother's birthday. No one paid much attention to me. I managed to get to the cellar to read those newspapers. I was the maddest I'd ever been. I was mad at the reporters, what they said, and I was mad at Ma. For the next few weeks, I hid my anger, my embarrassment. But I needed to know more. I started to read the Newark papers Papa brought home. When I couldn't find much, I went to the Newark Free Public Library. I told the librarian I used to be a neighbor of a woman who committed murder, and I wanted to keep up with her case. The librarian had the New York papers waiting for me whenever I got to come in.

Mama and Papa said nothing about my Ma. I knew they had a letter from her a few weeks after Grace's visit. I saw them huddled over it one day. The next day I searched all their hiding places until I found it. Ma asked them to let me visit her, one last time.

I thought about sneaking out, taking the train to Sing Sing. I even checked the train schedules. But I knew I wouldn't.

Robert Van Iderstine

A reporter called at my house early on July 27th. "Is it true you're preparing an appeal? We heard Howard McSherry plans to move for a new trial on grounds of insanity."

I stood in the doorway, struggling to keep my reply at a respectable decibel level. "Howard McSherry is not licensed in the state of New York. He is not Mrs. Place's lawyer of record. He did not show up for her sentencing. He cannot move anything or appeal anything. I can tell you that I," I pointed to my chest, "am working on an appeal. As to insanity, I have no comment on that." I closed the door on the reporter, willing myself not to slam it.

I ignored the breakfast our maid set out and wrote a letter to Howard McSherry, without waiting to get to my office. In no uncertain terms I warned him not to speak to the press, not to mention insanity, and not to visit Mrs. Place. Enough! Surely my admonition would be sufficient. This case was impossible enough, without that dolt. Yes, I welcomed his companionship at times, but on balance I was happier solo.

After finishing the letter, I moved from anger to reflection. What had I said to the reporter? "I am working on an appeal." More like rubbing my fingernails over blank pages. What could I argue? Too late to introduce alternative theories of the case. Probably too late to try insanity, which wouldn't work anyway since our client never admitted guilt. All that was left was to pick at technicalities. No wonder I overstated my activities to that reporter. No wonder I was stalling.

Warden Omar Sage

Soon we would have one prisoner less to manage. That's what my guards thought. But I didn't like hanging days. Well, I couldn't call them hanging days anymore. Now, August 1st, it was Martin Thorn's turn. I could almost understand how Thorn shot William Guldensuppe. After all the two men had the same woman as a lover. But what none of us could understand was the way Thorn followed up the murder. He didn't just drag Guldensuppe's body to a deserted area and dig a hole, like most murderers. No, he hacked up the body into pieces, no doubt using skills he learned as a barber, and he hid those pieces throughout the city of New York. Parts of Guldensuppe were found in one river, parts in another river, parts in the woods.

We readied the execution chair, the same chair we used for William Kemmler in 1890. The prison guards who had been around for a while reminded me regularly about that one. Several of them had seen, heard, and smelled Kemmler fry, literally fry, for minutes. But the three men who we executed on my watch, one in '95, one in '96, one in '97, died painlessly in the chair, or at least the witnesses thought so. I wanted no bad publicity. For that matter, I didn't want pointless pain either. My goal was efficiency, not retribution.

A reporter hanging out in front of Sing Sing tried to connect my two prisoners on death row. The reporter was an idiot, writing in the *Brooklyn Daily Times* that Mrs. Martha Place and Mr. Martin Thorn spent time together in the penitentiary studying Spanish. My prisoners did not take language lessons. The women were separated from the men. And they did not socialize. I was certain that Thorn and Place never even met. What would Commissioner Collins, who ran the Department of Corrections, think of a prison as a college? I may have been near retirement age, but I didn't need Collins on my back.

While I was worrying about the reputation of Sing Sing, or more specifically about my own reputation, my wife Julia was worrying about the woman on death row. "What will she think when she hears that Thorn's date has been set for today? You know, Omar, she will hear the gossip from the guards and the matrons. You need to talk to her."

"Nothing to say. I can't tell her that her own date could be far off, maybe never if she wins her appeal. I don't know what to say. If this bothers you so much, you talk to her."

Julia Sage

I didn't call on Martha Place at first. As the warden's wife, I had no such obligation. But I did have a sense of personal duty, to minister to the lost soul. On the day of the Thorn execution on August 1st, a brutally hot day, I could put off a visit no longer.

When I reached Mrs. Place's cell, I saw a smartly dressed and coifed woman, about my age, standing to look out the barred window open slightly to catch the breeze. Thank goodness, I thought, that Omar didn't borrow a drab dress for her from the Auburn Women's Prison. She must be watching the male inmates across the yard, sweating in their striped uniforms. At that angle, their heads would appear large, their feet small. If she looked carefully at the prisoners gathered in the corners, she would see them talking, quietly, moving less than usual. She might notice, or at least hear, beyond the yard, the crowd of journalists, humanitarians, and curiosity seekers from the town out for a look. She would know it was a death day.

"Mrs. Place, I am Julia Sage, the wife of Warden Omar Sage. He asked me to visit you to see how you are getting along here, under his watch."

She stared, silent. I tried again.

"Mrs. Place, should we sit? I will ask the matron to bring us tea."

The woman remained standing. I sat down, ordered two cups of tea, and started right in. "Mrs. Place, you can see from the window that this is not a usual day here at Sing Sing, right?" The woman nodded. "Martin Thorn, the convict accused of killing and dismembering his rival for the affections of a woman, he will be put to death in an hour. Usually, I would leave the compound on such a day, but the heatwave is so intense that I don't want to travel." I watched the woman's face as I spoke. She remained standing. "But no woman has been put to death here at Sing Sing. You know that, do you not? Maria Barbella was confined in this very room, sentenced to death, and she is now a free woman. I spent time with her. I taught her English and crocheted with her. She held up well during her confinement here."

The woman slowly approached the other chair. She sat but remained silent. "What can you tell me about your appeal, Mrs. Place?" Still silence. "I understand you have a good lawyer. Do you have confidence in him?

"Mr. Van Iderstine, Robert Van Iderstine," the woman said. "I call him Six." I raised my eyebrows, in a question. "His initials, in Roman numerals, are six." I smiled. Stretched out the smile for a few seconds. "Yes, he has been kind to me. I'll tell you what I know, not much."

Martha Place talked for a few minutes. She stopped when the matron entered with tea. Then she started again. Had I opened a faucet? A lot about William, how her husband had been awful to her, holding back money, slapping her, favoring the stepdaughter.

Behaving like a victim, that's what I thought. After a half-hour, we both heard a roar across the prison yard. The protesters, making a racket with their feet. Then we heard clapping. The townspeople. Then we felt silence, from the prisoners in the yard. "So is it done?" Martha Place asked.

"Yes, it is done," I said. "See that your Mr. Van Iderstine, Six you call him, does a good job." As I finished the sentence I rose to leave. "You are a woman, I said."

State Electrician Edwin Davis

No one performed the work better than me. Later I would be known as the man who pulled the switch to execute Leon Czolgosz, President McKinley's assassin. But in 1890, when I was forty-four, people knew me by my official title. State Electrician. I hadn't planned such a career, as a matter of fact, such a career did not exist when I was a boy. First, I worked as a millhand. Then I worked as a carpenter. Then a photographer. I had a small gallery for my photographic work, and I installed a telephone there to aid business. Telephones fascinated me. One thing led to another and soon I was skilled with electricity. That led to a job with Edison Electric, and then with Westinghouse. I built electric plants in many parts of the country, especially in the East, and I installed electricity in Sing Sing and other prisons. I oversaw all those systems.

When I needed help to keep up with my increasing work, the state of New York hired me an assistant, Harry Tyler. We made a good entrepreneurial team. I was stout and getting stouter and Tyler was thin and getting thinner. He crawled into areas where I didn't fit. Together we invented the chair that a condemned prisoner sat in to be electrocuted. Soon officials called it the electric chair. In 1897 the U.S. government granted me a patent for that invention. Harry and I built it out of heavy oak, with a high back and wide armrests. On the headrest we fitted an inverted metal bowl containing an electrode in a leather harness, to go over the prisoner's head, on his shaved scalp. We arranged a second electrode to go on the prisoner's spine. We covered the electrodes with damp sea sponges to improve conductivity and we adjusted them to various heights. Eleven leather straps with buckles secured the convict to the chair, restraining his legs, waist, and chest. We added metal strips, extending from the bottom of the chair, so the wooden legs could be bolted to the floor to minimize shaking. A black wire ran from the base of the chair to the voltmeter that created the current.

I used alternating current, that was George Westinghouse's current of choice, not Thomas Edison's direct current. At the time Thomas—I knew him—fought with George—I knew him too—to dominate the electricity market. Thomas happily pointed to the lethal qualities of competing AC. In his lab in New Jersey, Thomas directed his men to use AC to electrocute stray dogs, a cow, and a horse. George, even though he loved AC, didn't want it used for punishment and resented Thomas for demonstrating AC's dangers. But don't worry if I've confused you because which current we chose, didn't matter much. What mattered was just that we used electricity. Most Americans then, and me and my assistant too, considered electrocution more humane than the noose.

I tried the chair on a human for the first time on August 6, 1890. William Francis Kemmler, a thirty-year-old fruit peddler living in Buffalo. Kemmler murdered his common-law wife in a drunken rage. He believed she stole from him and she planned to run off with his friend. Kemmler struck her twenty-six times with a hatchet. The physician in Buffalo did a careful count to get to that number. A jury found Kemmler guilty and a judge sentenced him to death. His two appeals failed, despite the record of his brutal childhood. I had the task of execution, the first-ever by electrical current. Kemmler dressed for the occasion. Suit and vest, with a white shirt and a bow tie. I adjusted the height of one of the electrodes, then attached the leather harness to his shaved head. After the warden cut holes in Kemmler's shirt, I attached another electrode to the base of his spine. Or maybe to his shaved leg. To be honest I can't remember. An attendant tightened the eleven leather straps across Kemmler's body, so he wouldn't lurch from the chair by the force of the current. That took a while. Next, the attendant put a blindfold over Kemmler's face. All seemed in order. Using the voltmeter, I administered 1000 volts for seventeen seconds. The physician in attendance declared Kemmler dead. Then the witnesses in the death chamber saw him groan and gasp for breath. I saw it too. I tried again, now with 2000 volts. That worked. Kemmler's flesh charred, his blood vessels ruptured, froth oozed from his mouth, smoke came out of his head and his jacket. I'm not sure what Kemmler felt, but the witnesses were in agony, smelling the stench of burning flesh. I wasn't happy myself. We never expected any stench since Thomas Edison's men didn't smell much in their experiments with the horse. Ignoring the witnesses' distress, the physician checked Kemmler again, more carefully now. The murderer was dead, at last. The Sing Sing warden paid me $3 for the job. By the way, my per head payments rose over the years. By the time I retired from my job I had earned over $70,000 for 278 executions, and that doesn't include what my assistant Harry earned. But I'm getting ahead of myself. Back to 1890, the warden offered Kemmler's clothes to me, but they didn't fit. As I said, I had become a little paunchy by then.

Don't think of me as heartless. I didn't like seeing Kemmler suffer. But I admit I ignored George Westinghouse's reaction, which made all the papers. I'm sure you heard it already. "They would have done better with an axe." For me, the execution was a deed done, and I didn't think anybody could have done it better. Not as though hanging's a walk in the park.

Nine years passed, nine years of more executions. As I said, I earned a nice salary, one death at a time, and I put on pounds with each one. The year after Kemmler, on a single day in 1891 I pulled the switch on four men. Then the pace slowed. In 1892 and 1893, each year I electrocuted a man. Then there was execution-free 1894. That didn't last long. In 1895, 1896, and 1897, each year I executed a man. Then Martin Thorn in 1898. The Thorn execution went well. It was quick and easy. Reporters claimed that Thorn's body contracted, that he made blowing noises like the neigh of a horse, that saliva dripped down his chin, that his carotid artery pulsated. They invented those details for newspaper sales. Warden Sage knew I was good. He trusted me.

Now it was 1899. I weighed two hundred and sixty pounds, and it was time for the next annual execution.

Robert Van Iderstine

News of Martin Thorn's execution on August 1st provided the final push I needed to overcome my near paralysis and to finish the paperwork. The next day I filed a notice of appeal that in effect served as a stay of execution until the Court of Appeals could rule. I had six points in my appeal, but only two of them had the least chance of swaying the appeals panel. First, I argued that the evidence to convict was inadequate. Yes, Ida Place died, but not necessarily from violence, and not necessarily from violence caused by Martha Place. Dr. Henderson and others testified they saw no marks of violence on the body. The witnesses said she looked natural. The rest of the poorly trained Dr. Henderson's testimony was insufficient and evasive.

Second, I wrote that Judge Hurd interpreted the law incorrectly when he admitted testimony about the alleged assault on William Place. That was a different and separate crime with no direct bearing on Ida's death. Only time connected the two alleged crimes—they occurred on the same day. No one had provided evidence that the defendant committed one crime to hide the other. Put more broadly, I saw no "unity of plot and design" that would be required to justify the admission of evidence about the assault. That evidence influenced the jury unfairly. These two points served as my best shot, but not much of a shot. Even though I knew we would lose, I took pride in my appeal. I didn't have much to work with. I lied only once, writing that Martha Place was forty. She was getting younger and younger.

The appeal totaled twenty-eight pages while the District Attorney's formal response to the appeal came to a mere seven pages. That said it all. I read the response with dismay and anger. Assistant District Attorney Robert Elder, writing for District Attorney Josiah Marean, contended that Judge Hurd thought Mrs. Place tried to get rid of a witness against her, and that justified allowing testimony about the assault on Mr. Place. Elder couldn't be bothered to say much about Dr. Henderson's evasive testimony. The Court of Appeals would begin to hear the case in three days, but it could take them a month to reach a decision. I had given up already, but I knew

Martha still hoped.

Reverend David Cole

Thirty-five years had flown by since I last saw Martha Garretson. You know her as Martha Place, or maybe Mattie Place. I once taught her in Sunday School in New Brunswick, not far from her family's farm. Now, I lead a congregation at the First Reformed Church of Tarrytown. In the winter and spring of 1898, I read in the New York papers that Mrs. Place allegedly murdered her stepdaughter. I followed the details of the case because I remembered the sad girl, poorly dressed, scoffed at by the other girls. A few months after her death sentence, I chastised myself for stalling. Sing Sing and Tarrytown are both on the eastern bank of the Hudson River, twenty miles apart. I took a ferry to the prison to talk to Warden Sage.

At seventy-six years, I remained active, still trying to bring the spirit of the Lord to my congregants. The warden looked about my age, though he had stooped shoulders and put a hand behind his ear. He needed me to speak loudly.

"I served as her Sunday School teacher many years ago. She would not remember me, but I remember her. She came from a poor family, poor and troubled. When I saw in the newspaper that her maiden name was Garretson, I made the connection. Is she receiving spiritual guidance here?"

"None whatsoever," Sage said. "I asked her if she wished to see a minister and she declined. More seriously, she has no visitors. I never had a prisoner headed for the death chamber who had no visitors. Both my wife—she's spent time with Mrs. Place—and the matrons who guard her tell me no one has come."

"Would you allow me to visit, to guide her soul?"

"Reverend Cole, forgive me for saying this, but like me, you are not a young man. Are you certain you are up for prison duty? Even in a limited way?"

"I could not do much for Martha Garretson when she was a child. With the war raging, my ministerial efforts turned in other directions. But I've been haunted by my memories of Martha, and the many other poor children in my flock. I would like one more chance to do right by her. Whether she is guilty or not."

Warden Sage shrugged his stooped shoulders. I could try. That day and for many more days leading up to the end, I called on Martha Place.

Robert Van Iderstine

The court finally sent me the $500 they owed me. The fee covered both the trial and anything related to it, so I received nothing extra for that twenty-eight-page appeal. I didn't share the fee with McSherry. After all, he never shared the money he got from Martha, funneled through her brother.

The ruling from the Court of Appeals took five long months, all the way into the new year, 1899. A messenger rang my bell on January 10th, handed me a large envelope, and asked for my signature. I ripped the envelope open, skimmed it, then sat down to read carefully. As predicted. Judge Martin, heading the appeals panel, denied Mrs. Place a new trial, affirming the verdict and sentence. I had to admit that Judge Martin considered my brief, took it seriously, and presented logical, if unfavorable, arguments sustaining the verdict. "It must be remembered," Martin wrote, "that homicidal suffocation is a crime which it is always difficult to detect, and the mere physical conditions of the body after death, as distinct and satisfactory indications of the fact, will seldom exist. Therefore, resort must be had to collateral proof to show that the death was not the result of natural or accidental causes." He acknowledged that two doctors had testified differently, but said the jury held the right to weigh believability. Martin also made short shrift of my contention that evidence of the assault on William was improper. "The evidence is material and relevant to the issue. The demeanor, conduct and acts of a person charged with a crime, such as attempted flight, a desire to elude discovery, an anxiety to conceal the crime, or evidence of it, are always proper subjects of consideration." And Martin didn't stop at that. He addressed each of the weaker arguments I had tried, and dismissed them too, easily, but respectfully. Well, I had done my job. Of all my lawyering, this is the case I would be known for, forever. I had not disgraced myself. I could move on, finally.

The last line of the letter that accompanied the Court of Appeal's judgment swore me to keep the decision confidential. Once the Court made it public, which might be in a couple of weeks, it would be the Sing Sing warden's responsibility to inform my client. I could hardly believe my good fortune on that front. I felt relief when I should have felt defeat.

Warden Omar Sage

Friends in Albany gave me the word on January 11th that Mrs. Place lost her appeal. She would have no new trial. Following the rules, I could not tell her until I received official word. I took extra care to ensure that the matrons stayed with her day and night, and that the guards remained vigilant. If by some chance Mrs. Place heard the appeal panel's finding unofficially, from someone other than me, she might try to end her life without help from Edwin Davis's chair. I would be blamed for negligence.

Official notification arrived by letter on February 4th, with the additional detail that I should schedule execution during the week of March 20th. For the first time in my professional life, I drank a glass of whiskey before going to tell Mrs. Place the news. I had given hardened criminals such news before, but never a woman. I also sent a letter to Edwin Davis, enlisting him to carry out the execution, and setting the per head fee for 1899 at $4.00, up from the fee of previous years.

The walk from my office to the Old Hospital Building took just two minutes. Usually, in the winter, I would step quickly, but now I took my time and welcomed the chill. The guards saw me, registered the slow stride, and looked away. Mrs. Place sat in a rocking chair in her cell, reading the Bible. Or, anyway, I saw the open Bible in her hands. I used the same words I had used before for condemned men. Short and to the point. Raced over the timing, forty-four days to go. I didn't pay a lot of attention to what happened next. I wanted to do my duty and to leave. But I can report that she cried, asked for Reverend Cole, and said she wanted to see Howe and Hummel. She would ask them to beg the governor. Hmmm. Howe and Hummel. I hated the thought of those men in my penitentiary again.

Mattie

Death stuck to my mind every minute. But those seven months from my sentencing in July in Judge Hurd's courtroom to the day that Warden Sage—he was twitchy—came to see me in February were more peaceful than you'd think. Yes, the matrons expected me to clean my cell and to wash my clothes. That took less than an hour a day. I had leisure, that's what I called it. Aside from the looming sentence, no one stood over me with a whip or a belt or a fist. And most of all, I had people to talk to—Mrs. Sage, Reverend Cole, and sometimes Miss Meury, when she could get away from Brooklyn. Did they see me as a murderess or as Mattie? I think Mattie.

In my cell, I favored the window that overlooked the yard. I could see the prisoners in their striped suits, shuffling in lines. I saw them from above, at an angle, their matted hair more than their faces. That day in February I sat near the good window, Bible tilted up in my hands. If Miss Meury came she'd see me reading. Instead, Warden Sage entered. I turned to see him. He made that twitchy face just so I'd know before he said a word. The judgment didn't hurt as much as the date he gave me. The week of March 20th. Forty-four days.

I liked the matrons—Mrs. Reilly and Mrs. Coultry—even Warden Sage, so I behaved. Just some crying, and I didn't have to work at that. The next few days, sometimes I got down on my knees, praying, especially when the matrons kept their eyes on me. My prayers were my own. Howe and Hummel and Hummel and Howe. That's what I chanted.

I knew from the newspapers that a notorious New York law firm, Howe and Hummel, had represented Martin Thorn. Howe and Hummel didn't save Thorn, but they did a damn good job at his trial. When Thorn's lover and co-conspirator testified against him, William Howe cross-examined that woman so well that no one believed her for long. Those lawyers might do better for me than dull Mr. Six, right? I needed to hire them, for a last-ditch try. Maybe insanity this time.

Warden Sage didn't like Howe and Hummel. The firm had a reputation for representing criminals and prostitutes. And for ruthlessness and flair, and that's what I needed. "Mrs. Place," the warden said, "I cannot in good conscience endorse Howe and Hummel, but I understand your wish to explore all remedies. Against my better judgment, I will call them for you." A few hours later the warden came to tell me the partners were inclined to take me on and wanted to meet. No need to tell Six, I thought. Let him read about it in the papers. He deserved nothing. The man couldn't even win a simple appeal.

Howe arranged to come on February 6th to discuss my case. I stared out the bars of my cell that morning. Warden Sage walked toward me, with a commonplace-looking man in tow. The reporters described William Howe as tall and fat and dressed in extravagant clothing and Abraham Hummel as short and thin. Which one was this?

"Mrs. Place, Mr. Joseph Moss of Howe and Hummel is here for you. I am afraid Mr. Howe was too ill to travel to Ossining," Warden Sage said, opening the cell door. My face tightened every place it could tighten. I stood up straight, pushed my shoulders back. Moss would be my seventh or eighth lawyer, according to my own count. Knittle, then McSherry, then Newman, then Ridgway, then Van Iderstine, well, Six, then Howe and Hummel, now Moss.

The lawyer saw my irritation. "Mrs. Place, I am the junior partner. Howe and Hummel, as you know, are the senior partners. Our firm is busy, representing clients throughout the East Coast. I assisted with the Martin Thorn case. Although we failed to save poor Mr. Thorn, no one could have made a better showing. And my understanding is that you are indigent, expecting us to work on your behalf for no payment. I am afraid, Mrs. Place, that you must take what you can get, and you are lucky indeed that I have come." He said "I" slow and loud.

The warden glanced at me. He was asking, did I want him to take Mr. Moss away. I did. But then I would have no one. No one, that is, aside from useless Six.

"All right, Mr. Moss. I'm miffed. But let's talk."

With that, me and Moss sat down while the warden went about his business. An hour later, Moss settled on plans. He would try the insanity route, first asking the Supreme Court for a stay of execution. He hadn't represented me at trial, so he needed time to review the trial transcript and prepare his brief. If not an appeal to the Supreme Court, then maybe a letter to the governor, arguing for clemency. Only Governor Roosevelt could commute my sentence. I liked Moss's ideas. Finally, a man of action. For a little while, I had hope.

Emilie Meury

Mattie was not the only prisoner I shepherded through trials and tribulations that winter, but I cared about her the most. She grew up in a Christian family, but I understood that their church attendance had fallen off. I talked to Reverend David Cole, her other spiritual advisor. We agreed that Mattie's soul could be guided to a better place, a place where she understood what she had done and sought forgiveness. Neither of us doubted she committed murder, but we doubted she accepted the fact of her crime. She continued to rant that she threw powder, not acid, and she said nothing about, well, about either hitting Ida or about suffocating Ida, and just a little about hitting her husband. If she had admitted murder and asked the court for mercy when the police arrested her, perhaps she would not be facing death.

Twice a week, with the consent of the Brooklyn Auxiliary Mission Society, I rode the train to Ossining for our visits. I knew I had made progress because Mattie no longer resisted the scriptures. But Reverend Cole and I wanted more than progress. When we heard that the appeal failed, we had only six weeks left to save Mattie's soul.

Clementine Swift

I loved to help the children who came to the Newark Free Public Library, usually along with their mothers. As head librarian, I pointed the children to suitable storybooks and taught them how we organized the shelves. I couldn't ever remember a child coming alone, with a request for newspapers. When Ross Aschenbach—I learned his name after a while—asked me to save papers that reported on the case of Martha Place in Brooklyn, I became curious. As I searched for the stories, I read them myself, and then I went back to the editions months earlier that covered the murder when it first occurred. I had a feeling that the poor boy may have been the child that the murderess gave up for adoption.

Understandably, Ross would be most interested in the fate of his mother, if she was indeed his mother. And her plight interested me too because I came to care about that lad. But another aspect of the case interested me even more. You see, in the evenings I carried out volunteer activities, seeking signatures on petitions for a woman suffrage amendment. We didn't get far, not then. Well, it turned out that the question of Martha Place's fate became part of larger discussions about the position of women. I might have read about her case even if I never met Ross, but because of him, I read with special interest.

Should Roosevelt grant clemency? Would he grant clemency? Men's clubs and women's clubs—I belong to two of the women's—we busied ourselves with intense debates about Martha Place. I never mentioned that I knew her son. Club members took sides on her fate, some arguing that a woman deserved special treatment and some arguing that women and men were the same before the law. The New York papers covered the debates, and we always collected those papers for the Newark library. So many stories, especially from New York clubs and associations. At a meeting of the Women's Health Protective Association, the President, a Mrs. Scrimgeour, asked whether the members wanted to prepare a petition in favor of clemency. Nine members said Mrs. Place deserved the chair, two advocated for life imprisonment, one hedged. At the Social Reform Club, the members, all men, argued against capital punishment, for any criminal. At a meeting of the Medico Legal Society, in the lovely Waldorf Astoria, members adopted a resolution that sex should not be a factor in sentencing. At a meeting of the Political Study Club of New York, members circulated a petition asking the governor for a reprieve. In Brooklyn, an ad hoc group of women organized to implore that women be treated the same as men and that the death penalty be carried out. These debates mirrored the debates I heard in my own women's clubs.

Famous people entered the fray. Elizabeth Cady Stanton wrote in the *Sun* that Mrs. Place should not be executed because she did not have the vote and so did not have a voice in setting laws. A *Brooklyn Eagle* editorial responded, arguing that if citizens followed Stanton's logic, women would always be favored. And we heard from a notorious poet, Cecil Charles. Despite the name, Cecil Charles was in reality Lily Curry, a woman known for espousing unfashionable causes. She collected over one hundred signatures for a petition to Roosevelt asking for clemency. "Mrs. Place's husband and daughter considered her socially inferior. Her husband would not let her son by a previous marriage visit her. These were conditions that would anger any woman," Cecil Charles wrote. So true. Of course, I noticed the reference to Mrs. Place's son.

The newspapers continued to capitalize on the hubbub, with editorials and letters to the editor running throughout the winter of 1898-1899. Opinionated citizens wrote in opposition to each other, with papers publishing their letters side-by-side. William Randolph Hearst's *New York Journal and Advertiser* ran a front-page article summing up the divergent views.

Then there were the officials. One assistant district attorney wrote that women should not be put to death. Another wrote that we must enforce the law whether the criminal is a man or a woman. Two politicians went beyond words, trying for action. Assemblyman Julius Harburger introduced a bill to amend the state penal code. No woman, he said, convicted of first-degree murder should face more than life imprisonment. Assemblyman Maher spearheaded another bill against capital punishment for women. The bills went nowhere.

Ross came to see me about twice a month that fall and winter. I handed him the papers I had collected, covering these stories and more. Then, in the spring, he stopped coming.

Robert Van Iderstine

Petitions flooded Roosevelt's office. He sent out word that it was useless for anyone to send him a petition for clemency unless it included new information on the crime or the trial. He would be influenced only by the merits of the case, not by what others said or wrote. Then, quashing many hopes, Roosevelt said it mattered little to him whether the criminal was a man or a woman. I felt relief that I had not made an issue of sex in my appeal. It would have been a wasted effort if Roosevelt had sway over the appeals panel, though I doubted he did.

Howard McSherry, true to form, remained an annoyance. In his local New Jersey newspaper, he blamed the New York lawyers, which meant me. McSherry claimed he had a petition from 12,000 women begging for clemency. More seriously, he claimed that Martha Place was insane and that he had letters from her proving that. I knew I should focus on saving my client but instead I fumed that this New Jersey ignoramus had challenged my reputation.

For a month I had remained little more than a bystander to the brouhaha over whether a female convict should be subjected to the same punishment as a male convict. But, eventually, I decided that to further my practice, I should enter the fray. I wish I could tell you that my decision was based on my compassion for the downtrodden, but that would be false.

I wrote a letter to Governor Roosevelt myself, arguing for clemency. I went all out—her childhood, her son, her sex, her insanity, definitely her insanity. I threw everything I could think of into that letter, ignoring the fact that some of these points were new arguments for me and that Roosevelt already said he would not listen to such entreaties. My letter could do no harm. I sent a copy to the *Daily Eagle*. Perhaps that was improper—the rules for such entreaties were non-existent. But the letter would keep my name in the news.

Reverend David Cole

Howe and Hummel must be clowns. Certainly, their junior partner Joseph Moss had failed Mrs. Place. I knew I should be more charitable, but right now I focused on Martha, who remained my charge, spiritually speaking. I would not offer kind thinking toward the men who made her promises and did not come through. Moss never prepared a brief, or if he had, no one ever saw it. So I took action myself. On February 16th I wrote Governor

Roosevelt, shamelessly touting my clerical credentials and appealing for clemency. I paid messengers to deliver copies of the letter to Martha's various past and present lawyers. My letter may have moved the governor. He replied that he would rule on the matter on February 20th.

You wonder why I could move the governor when others couldn't? Our church-going governor had, as a youth, attended services at the Collegiate Reformed Dutch Church of St. Nicholas on Fifth Avenue, though later he leaned toward the Presbyterians. Reverend Donald Mackay had just been installed as head minister at St. Nicholas. You see, Donald and I were friends. Donald had not met the governor yet but still carried weight because he now led the church close to Roosevelt's heart. Mackay asked the governor to read my letter with special care. And I will add more. Before St. Nicholas Donald spread the faith at the North Reformed Church in Newark. While there he befriended the reverend at the First Reformed Church in New Brunswick, where Howard McSherry worshipped. We clergymen are a tight-knit group. We help each other for a good cause.

Robert Van Iderstine

Howard McSherry and I had not talked in months. Unexpectedly he telegrammed on February 17th to request a meeting. I realized he must have written the Governor to argue that Mrs. Place was insane, despite my admonition against such futility. Then I remembered I had stooped to the same pointless effort myself.

We met in our usual pub. McSherry said he had spoken to an unnamed go-between, someone in the good graces of the Governor, and had pushed for us, the two of us, to lead the call for clemency. So, he had contacts in New Jersey who knew Roosevelt? Hard to imagine. But at least the bothersome yokel used the word "us." He knew that if he wangled an audience with the Governor, he'd better take along a heavyweight. A heavyweight who lived in the Governor's own state. And maybe McSherry was right to turn to insanity. After all, our client faced death, a fact I tried to ignore.

The day before I had learned that David Cole, that butting-in reverend, had intervened too, adding his own request for a reprieve. Maybe four entreaties for clemency or stays of execution sat on the governor's desk. One from me, which I had completed despite the humiliation of seeing Howe and Hummel claim to have taken over. That I heard from courtroom gossip, not from my client. One from Reverend David Cole. Perhaps one from Howe and Hummel's Joseph Moss, hard to tell. One from Howard McSherry. For all I knew hundreds of letters and petitions were piled up on the Governor's desk, even though he warned against them. Mrs. Place could claim she was represented by at least some of the lawyers writing Roosevelt. None of us would contradict her.

Howard's hunch that we would be granted an audience provided correct. I suppose the pressure became hard for Roosevelt to ignore. His secretary cabled us to come on February 20th to the executive suite in the governor's mansion, for a conference on the case. Howard and I rode the train together, each wearing our best suits. We had something else in common that day too—we were nervous.

The mansion looked imposing, even to me. Howard adjusted his tie and collar. I resisted the urge to do the same. As we entered, we handed our coats and hats to a liveried footman who led us to a butler or an aide who walked us down a hall smelling of furniture polish and lemon. Governor Theodore Roosevelt sat behind an enormous oak desk. I was surprised to see that neither Reverend Cole, nor Moss, nor Howe, nor Hummel joined us. I decided not to ask if they were invited. A second liveried servant pointed to armchairs but did not offer tea. Roosevelt took charge immediately, managing perfunctory introductions, then asking the first question.

"Gentleman, why do you say now that Mrs. Place is insane? Why did you not argue that at trial?"

As Howard and I agreed on the train, I would begin the discussion, but we both would participate. I didn't tell him that I would be all right with his participation, all right if he made a fool of himself because the governor would see who had the brains. Also, realistically, the case remained a lost cause.

"Sir," I began, "Judge William Hurd of Kings County assigned me to defend Mrs. Place. I always considered her insane, unbalanced." I tried to relax my facial muscles and to look straight at the governor. "But Mrs. Place kept to her claim of innocence, making it awkward for us to argue insanity."

"Does she continue to claim innocence?"

"When I spoke to her a few days ago, she no longer repeated that claim. Though she did not admit to guilt either. But she reminded me of what we presented at trial—the mitigating circumstances. Her husband treated her brutally, as a drudge, and gave her little money though he had the means to do so. And we learned from her brother that she fell from a sled years ago and became unconscious for a time. He thought she never fully recovered. The poor woman has no money. I am here at my own expense. She has no friends, and no educated or influential relatives to help or advise her with her case. Please remember, sir, that Mrs. Place, though uncultured, is a woman of good character and habits and that should have some standing toward leniency."

"What do you wish to add, sir?" Roosevelt asked, looking at McSherry.

I saw Howard reach into his pocket and dramatically flourish sheets of paper. On the train that morning, he never mentioned those pages. As he reached over to lay them on the large oak desk, he spoke, more clearly than usual. "I wish to make four points. The first relates to letters. On the day of the murder, Mrs. Place wrote three letters to her brother and one to her niece who resides at the same address. It might have been sane to write a single letter, but why write so many separate letters, on the same day, to the same people? These letters suggest we should consider Mrs. Place of unsound mind and conclude that she planned to commit suicide and nothing more." I saw that Howard had chosen not to share the letter Martha wrote to Grace, dated well before the murder, the one that suggested premeditation. "And let me point out another letter," Howard said, "one Mrs. Place wrote her husband while she was jailed, using endearing terms and saying she did not know what all the trouble was about. She was of unsound mind to have written him. Now the second matter. Mrs. Place showed indifference throughout the trial, barely helping with her defense. Also indicating an unsound mind. Third, consider the matter of Mrs. Annie Simpson. While Mrs. Place was in jail, she almost lost her small savings due

210

to that manipulative swindler. Only an insane person would let herself be the victim of larceny. Finally, the fourth matter, trivial as it might appear. On the day of her trial, she asked Mr. Van Iderstine and me how her dress and hat looked. No sane person in danger of being convicted for first-degree murder and sent to the death chair would ask such a question. She never recognized the seriousness of her position.

To my surprise, Roosevelt reached for the letters on the desk, pushed his wire-rimmed glasses down his nose, and began to read. Then to reread.

"Mr. McSherry, I believe these letters show she contemplated murder and flight, do they not?"

"No, Governor, I believe that is not the case because she did not flee."

The governor looked at us, shaking his head, not seeming to follow Howard's logic. "Please prepare a brief for me. I will read it and make a final decision. Good day, gentlemen. Oscar will show you out."

On the train back to the city, I hid my shock from Howard. Oh, I did thank him, offered him modest praise, but I didn't let him know I'd underestimated him. His points seemed weak to me, but he stated them well, and authoritatively. A heroic, last-ditch try. We returned to my office to condense our arguments into a final brief. A messenger delivered it to the Governor the next morning. A few days later, I heard stunning news. Our brief had some effect. Roosevelt appointed two physicians, alienists, to a commission to examine Mrs. Place, to assess her mental state. The first, Dr. William Mecklenburg Polk, served as President of Cornell Medical College. I never did learn anything about his neurology credentials, but his father was second cousin to President Polk. The second physician was Dr. Charles Loomis Dana, an expert on insanity who at the time was in private practice. I could not have asked for more.

Everyone knew I met with the governor. Everyone knew that as a result, we saw a glimmer of hope for my client.

Peter Garretson

Today, March 3rd, another trial took place, one that got no attention at all, just a little notice in the local paper. I went to court to defend myself against a charge by Dr. Ellis Hedges, an uppity physician who hailed from a family of physicians. Ellis lived and practiced in a pink Victorian mansion with a fancy French roof in the Crescent District of Plainfield. A high-class place. Theodore Strong was the judge. He lives two blocks from me and my four motherless children. He's uppity too. Came from a long line of Puritans, and let everyone know it, while we Garretsons, our branch of the Garretsons anyway, came from nothing. In court, Dr. Hedges told Judge Strong that I never paid the $82 I owed him for treating my wife Margaret, who died despite his expert services. That's what he said, expert services. I told the judge that my wife paid the doctor herself before her demise. The judge was hearing none of it. Judgment for Hedges. It was easy for me to let my anger against Hedges and Strong push out of my mind any worry about my sister. After paying McSherry and the Pinkerton he hired, I had just enough of Mattie's money left to settle the claim.

Mattie

Early on Wednesday, March 8th, Warden Sage said two men would come to interview me. Their fancy names were Charles Loomis Dana and William Mecklenburg Polk. That afternoon the warden led a man down the hall to my cell. "Mrs. Place," Sage said, "let me introduce you to Charles Loomis Dana. He's alone today. William Polk will come on Friday." For some reason, I thought Dana and Polk were friends of the warden's. Maybe journalists. I liked Sage, especially liked his wife Julia. I put on one of my fresher dresses for the visit.

Mr. Dana, in his mid-forties, sat down and motioned to the nearby chair for me. He was a thin, handsome man, with a trim beard and mustache. He said almost nothing about himself, just that today was his first trip to Sing Sing and he liked its beautiful location on the bank of the Hudson. I nodded in agreement, to be polite. I couldn't see the Hudson from my window. Mr. Dana began to ask questions, odd questions. "Warden Sage told me a little about your childhood, but I want to ask you about those years. Did you like growing up on a farm in New Jersey?" I bristled. There I sat, in Sing Sing, wondering if in a few weeks I would get life or that thing they called the chair, and the warden's friend asks me about my childhood. I didn't answer right away. Should I tell him straight about life on that New Jersey farm or clean it up a little? I decided to clean it up—he didn't need to know everything. A minute went by. While I thought about what to say, he asked me another question. "Maybe, Mrs. Place, do you remember particular days, events?" I started to talk, slowly. Then before long, I could feel myself talking too much, like I did sometimes with Miss Meury and Mrs. Handy.

"Well, I guess that day in December. Every December 26th, in the winter when the farm came the closest it ever came to taking care of itself, that's when we made the visits. Ma still tended the chickens and the cows and Pa still fixed the fences, but they had time for other things. So our family, the Garretson family, or I guess Pa, decided the 26th was a good time to pay our respects each year. The first year I remember, I was seven, even though I know I did the same thing on every December 26th of my life. I mean my life as a child."

I stopped there, wondering if I did too much droning on, making a bad impression. But I saw Mr. Dana listening carefully, looking right at me. Not blinking. "Good details, Mrs. Place. Close your eyes if that helps."

I went on, with my eyes closed, a little quieter but faster. "Up front in the farm wagon, Pa and Ma sit. That's what I remember. Ma holds the new baby, Eliza. Squeezed between Pa and Ma, holding the reins, there's Garret. He's fourteen or fifteen. The rest of us ride in back—Ellen, she's nine, Matilda, she's three, Peter's two, and like I said I'm seven. I find the wagon blankets and cover the little ones, even my sour older sister. The ride is short, but it's freezing. Flurries left from the night's snow. We're headed to Cedar Hill Cemetery. That place seems almost like part of the Garretson farm. All of us hop down, following Ma and Pa to the plot in the middle. We make a circle around the tombstones. They're granite. That's the only cost Ma and Pa never complain about. There's always money for slabs. We stand for a minute. We don't say anything. Just shiver." I stopped and opened my eyes. "Too much detail?"

"No, just fine, to help me understand your life. You may close your eyes again."

I tell more to Mr. Dana, the journalist, even though my story doesn't seem like much of a story for anyone but me. "Then, like he always does, Pa says the Lord's prayer. Pa says he's a man of God, but that's the only prayer he knows. Then Ma sings a psalm. Same psalm every year. She has a beautiful voice. That always surprises me. I can read already, so when Ma sings, I say to myself the names on three of the tombstones, stumbling a little in my head because they're hard names. Stephen, born 1841, died 1845. Cornelius and Abraham, the twins, born 1843, died 1843. See, I remember. And I remember the empty space around the tombstones."

As I say this to Mr. Dana, I wince a little. Then I say, "we need the extra space. More deaths are coming." I open my eyes. He has sort of a scared look on his face. I know he thinks I'm talking about my own death. "I mean Garret and Matilda and Eliza. But that's not 'til later." His look changes from scared to nosy. He's still not blinking. I keep going, my eyes closing.

"We don't have flowers to put on the babies' graves, it's the winter, but I remember Ma raising Eliza up to her shoulder and bending down to touch the dead grass peeping through under the snow. She sort of evens it out. Ma keeps a neat farmhouse and a neat graveyard. I learned from her. That year Ma didn't cry. She just hugged baby Eliza."

"Pa and Ma take two minutes for this ceremony. That's all we need. Pa gets us back to the wagon. No one says anything to me, or to Ellen or Peter or Matilda. Not even to Garret, the oldest.

I felt embarrassed at all I said. I didn't even talk to Miss Meury or Mrs. Handy like this. But when I finished Mr. Dana looked, well, satisfied. "So that's my first memory of something happening." He made a few notes in his leather notebook.

"That's excellent Mrs. Place. Very helpful. Tell me, do you have other memories, general recollections?" When I look back on that day, I think I should have stopped there, but by this time I figured it can't hurt for him to know more about my miserable life. I ramble, now with my eyes open. "Well, school. I go to school in East Millstone along with Peter and Ellen and sometimes Garret, but only a few months in the winter. Mr. Washburn, he's the teacher, he holds a short spring session, but Pa needs us on the farm then. Sundays, well, not every Sunday, we ride in the wagon to the Reformed Church, six miles away in New Brunswick. After the morning sermon, I stay on for summer school. Reverend Cole—did the warden tell you about him?—he remembered me. I didn't remember him, but I'll confess this to you, I pretended I did when he started to visit me here."

Mr. Dana's eyes wandered. I guess he wasn't curious about school or church. I try other stories. "I always think back on my chores. Even at seven and eight, Peter and I do our chores. I mean lots of chores. We help hold down the sheep while Pa sheers. We hold down the cattle and hogs when Pa butchers them. We pick up stones from the field while Garret and Pa plow. I churn butter 'til my arms get stiff and I watch over Matilda and Eliza when Peter feeds the livestock and fishes with pa.

When I told him the long list of chores, I saw from his eyes that he fixed on one of them. "Mrs. Place, tell me more about the butchering."

"First Garret hits the pig in the head with a sledgehammer or axe, to stun it. Then Pa slits its throat while Peter and I hold it down just in case it squirms. Then all of us roll the pig into a trough. Ma pours boiling water over the pig, so the bristles loosen up. I scrape the bristles off. Next Pa chains the pig, what's left of it, onto posts and cuts it into pieces. For the cows, same thing, almost. Garret stuns them with a blow to the head, Pa bleeds them. He makes a slit in the neck, I think in the jugular vein, and then we all string up the cow on poles. Garret cuts off the head and hoofs. Pa scoops out the guts, cuts off the skin, and cuts the carcass in half. Then he cuts each half in pieces."

For me, there is nothing strange about butchering. Farmers butcher animals just like they raise crops. But both times I talked about hitting an animal in the head, I saw Mr. Dana make a note in his little book. Maybe he grew up in a city.

After asking about my memories, Mr. Dana wanted to know about our kin, the Garretson kin. "I understand you had hardly any visitors in the Raymond Street Jail or now in Sing Sing. You have described a large family. I suppose there are aunts and uncles and cousins too. Do they want to come see you?"

I raised my shoulders and lowered my chin when Mr. Dana mentioned visitors. I sighed, buying a minute of time.

"My father, Isaac V.N. Garretson, he belonged to two big families, the Van Nesses and the Garretsons. Lots of them had money. One was a judge, one owned a mill, and it goes on. My mother's people, the Wykoffs, served as officials and owned property too."

I looked at Mr. Dana's expression. I knew he couldn't understand why these good people abandoned me. I didn't want to tell him that our kin saw us, the East Millstone Garretsons, as poor cousins, as outliers, or whatever you want to call people who are forgotten and ignored. Or maybe that my posh kin knew Ma and Pa were mean, like all us children knew. Or that Aunt Evelyn gave up on me. I stayed with a simple story.

"My Ma and Pa, they kept to themselves and didn't hobnob with other people when there was work to be done." Mr. Dana still sat in his armchair. He wanted more, I guess. He asked if any of what I had just said troubled me.

"I always wished we had more money," I tell him. That is the truth.

I didn't know until later that on his way out, Mr. Dana asked the warden to arrange a meeting with my matrons. He met with one at a time, so the other could continue the watch. Annie Reilly and Kathryn Coultry, she was night matron but ordered to come in that day, they both told him I always behaved, a model prisoner.

Two days after Mr. Dana's visit, Mr. Polk, Sage's other friend—that's still all Sage said—visited me. Polk was in his mid-fifties, older than Dana, kind looking with white hair and a white mustache. Before Polk arrived, the guard told me that this visitor served as a captain in the Civil War, under Stonewall Jackson, and that his father, Leonidas Polk, served as a lieutenant general under Braxton Bragg. I was on my guard. The day matron, Mrs. Reilly, added more. She told me that Polk worked as a gynecologist. Now I was more than on my guard, I was scared. Would he ask me about woman troubles? That I bled on and off? But when I met Polk, he seemed just as harmless and odd as Dana. More of the same questions about my childhood. After he left, I asked Matron Reilly why these strange men had asked about my childhood. The matron shook her head and opened her arms, palms up.

Warden Omar Sage

The second week of March I could not manage any of my regular work. I might as well have had just one prisoner under my watch, Mrs. Martha Place, and not fourteen hundred others. A pack of reporters badgered me. Most of their questions I answered easily. After all, I had overseen many executions by that point. But one reporter's question took me by surprise. "Will you have female attendants at the execution?"

"Of course not." My answer made the top of the reporter's story the next day.

Then I thought more carefully. Edwin Davis, the state electrician, needed to attach an electrode to a bare head and another electrode to a shaved leg. Did I answer the reporter too quickly? Commissioner Collins of the New York State Department of Prisons removed any doubt. He called on our new telephone to fuss about the newspaper story. "Omar," he said, "you must have women in attendance." Collins detested bad publicity.

While I worried about attendants, I carried out all the activities and errands on my execution checklist, beginning with a physical examination of Mrs. Place. I sent Dr. Irvine to her cell. He had examined her several times before, always pronouncing her in perfect health. This time he reported back that she remained healthy, perhaps a bit nervous, who wouldn't be. He said she chatted with him more than usual. "You know, Omar," Dr. Irvine said, "the woman thinks her sentence will be commuted. But stranger than that, she thinks she will get a pardon. Maybe she really is crazy."

All the men I had led to their execution knew what was coming. Some of them acknowledged their guilt, some insisted, forcefully, on their innocence. But they all knew what was coming. Now I needed to plan the execution of a woman, the first electrocution of a woman ever, and the woman thought she would go free. I am not sure, to this day, why that bothered me. Maybe because my wife planted herself in the middle of it.

Mattie

I liked Mrs. Sage's visits. The woman talked in a motherly way, more motherly than my Ma. Julia Sage was maybe in her mid-fifties, with grown daughters. Plump and pleasant. We gabbed a lot, sometimes about fashions, sometimes about the war, now in the Philippines. Made the time pass. The last few days the matrons had brought me a slim pile of newspapers—they said deliveries had been slow—so I welcomed the latest news from Mrs. Sage. When she visited on March 13th, she returned the sewing needles that the warden had taken away from me. The kind-hearted woman convinced her husband to return them, to keep my mind and fingers occupied I suppose.

But Mrs. Sage stayed quiet that morning. Before she said much, she finished half the tea Mrs. Reilly brought her. I felt my mouth twitch and I snapped at her. "Mrs. Sage, is something wrong? Don't keep it from me."

"Mrs. Place, I believe the warden may have neglected to tell you the identities of the men who came to speak with you last week. Did you understand the purpose of their visit?" She held the cup close to her chest.

"They were friends of the warden's. Curious friends. Maybe one was a journalist and one was a lady's doctor. But that one didn't examine me. They asked silly questions. About my childhood in New Jersey."

"Yes, I expect they did." She took a slow swallow of her tea. Cold by now. "They are acquaintances of my husband. He met them at a conference in New York. But you should know that both are doctors, what some call alienists."

"Alienists?"

"Governor Roosevelt enlisted them to examine you. To determine your mental condition. You know, to determine sanity."

I shuddered and ranted for a minute while Julia watched and listened. Then I thought, maybe she gave me good news. Could Roosevelt change his mind? What had I said to those men? Did I want to be sane or insane? I tried to remember my answers to their questions, especially the questions from the one named Dana, I guess Dr. Dana. Did I say too much? Not enough? Should I have told about the beatings? Not sure. At least I looked neat, I spoke decent, I didn't drool. If they found me sane, I'd die. If they found me insane, there would be no pardon, just endless days locked up. And still no

Ross.

Julia Sage put down her teacup and squirmed in her chair.

"Mrs. Place, you must not be annoyed with the warden. He knows, as part of his position here, to tell inmates as little as possible. When Governor Roosevelt hired the doctors, they asked Omar, the warden that is, to keep the newspapers from you for a while, so you would not know their identities. And please, do not tell the warden what I shared with you or he will be annoyed and forbid me more visits."

"Of course, Mrs. Sage, I understand. I'm not mad at the warden. He's been kind to me. But if the Governor stays my execution, that means I'd rot in prison for the rest of my life. That's no better than the chair." Julia Sage stared at me, saying nothing.

I picked up a scarf I wanted to embroider, threaded a needle, and started to stitch. I sewed, breathing deeply, waving out Julia Sage. My five weeks of hope had ended.

Reverend David Cole

On the afternoon of March 13th, I found Martha pacing up and back in her cell. Her lunch tray was on the table, most of the food still on it. I looked at Matron Reilly, who shook her head and raised and lowered her shoulders when Martha walked away. I asked Martha to sit with me. She paid no attention. The second time I asked she wouldn't sit either, but she started to talk. Almost spitting with anger, Martha repeated what Mrs. Sage told her that morning. How the warden had tricked her. The men who visited were alienists, in Sing Sing at the Governor's direction, to assess her sanity. She couldn't predict if they thought she was sane or crazy. Still pacing as I watched, she babbled, first this way and then that. She was sane, she was insane, she would fry, she would get life in jail. She would be pardoned. Then back to the same babbling. Finally, I convinced her to sit. With more difficulty, I convinced her to read scriptures with me. I chose the same passage we read the week before, a selection from Ephesians on redemption. She read slowly, with stutters and mistakes. But after a few minutes, as I stayed silent, her voice strengthened. I hoped she felt the power of the scriptures. But maybe the poor woman just wanted company. Her friends and relatives had deserted her.

Mattie

The day after Julia Sage told me those two men were alienists, their report came out. On March 14th, Matron Reilly didn't bring me any New York newspapers at all. Then I knew. By the third time I asked, she gave up. She walked far down the hall to fetch the newspapers, then left them on my table. She slinked off to a corner on the far side of the room. I didn't have to look beyond the headlines on the top paper. Mrs. Reilly cowered while I read. "Doctors Find Mrs. Place Sane." From the corner, the matron stammered. "Warden Sage, he didn't tell me to hide the papers this time. Just, I just wanted to myself." I spotted one tiny bright note in the papers. "Governor Roosevelt asks alienists for supplementary report laying out the evidence they used to reach their conclusion." But I guessed that wouldn't do much good.

Another bad story ran in the papers that day too. The legislators in Albany voted down a bill to abolish capital punishment for women. Seventy-two against, forty-two in favor.

I gave up that day, right then and there. I never really thought I'd be pardoned or get life in prison, but that's what I told people like Dr. Irvine and Reverend Cole. Not sure why. Maybe I thought if I said it, heard those words, then it might happen. Now I knew my life was over.

My mind stuck where I didn't want it. I survived pain before, the pain of beatings on the farm, the pain of the accident with the sled, the pain of Wesley's punches, childbirth, Will's jabs. But this pain I wouldn't survive. The guards must know more than the matrons. "Mr. Conyers, did you witness the execution of Martin Thorn?" I could tell by his quick response that he expected the question.

"No, but my friend Arnold Packer in the north wing, he stood guard there. He told me Mr. Thorn didn't suffer. Died without a whimper."

I went back to sewing. The next day I would ask the other guard, Mr. Robinson.

Julia Sage

On March 15th one of the Brooklyn newspapers reported that I visited Mrs. Place daily, sometimes more than once. Reporters often erred and exaggerated, but on this point they were correct. I felt pulled to the woman's cell. I could explain this easily, with the usual phrase, Christian duty. But if it was my Christian duty then I should visit the men in the death house daily too. No, something haunted me about this woman, this poor, wretched woman who had made a way for herself.

Since my marriage thirty-one years ago, I had been loved and cared for by Omar. My friends thought it dreadful that I called Sing Sing my home. They never understood. We lived in large and lovely quarters, set off in a corner of the compound with a nice lawn and wisteria over the front entry. Maids and gardeners served at our beck and call. I visited the men's tiers rarely, only when I saw a reason to do so. Omar, in my view, had earned the respect of the convicts, and certainly the respect of the guards, the politicians, and the officials. I grew up in a fine family—my father owned a small mill—but now I had an even better position in society and more comfort. What would I have done if Omar deserted me, if I could not see my daughters, if I had no money to feed and shelter myself? Martha Place prevailed against all odds, that is, until something snapped.

In the time I spent with Martha I noticed a change. First, she fidgeted, walking up and back across the cell as she chattered. Then, she slowed down. Kept talking, but not in the same ruffled way. She had a setback after the alienists visited, but that didn't last long. I wondered if my presence helped to calm her. Did I give myself too much credit? Or maybe Reverend Cole, that nice clergyman from Tarrytown, maybe he settled her. Or Miss Meury, the missionary lady. Or maybe Martha simply liked our company. She became the center of our attention.

Robert Van Iderstine

I knew nothing firsthand. But the New York bar had its own grapevine. My well-placed friends told me that the governor had met with Josiah Marean, the former district attorney who had just become a justice of the

Supreme Court of New York State. And they told me even more alarming news. Roosevelt also met with Maguire, the assistant district attorney, so the two could go over Dr. Harry Enton's testimony. Enton, you may recall, was the doctor Maguire called to the stand during the July trial. Maguire emphasized to Roosevelt that Enton thought suffocation would take over three minutes. If Martha Place started to suffocate Ida Place with a pillow, in a moment of madness, and then realized what she was doing after a minute, she could have found an easy solution. Remove the pillow. Maguire emphasized the case for premeditation, necessary for murder in the first degree. Those three or four minutes became the determining factor for John Maguire. And for Theodore Roosevelt. And for Martha Place.

I had to give credit to Roosevelt. He explored the question of sanity. When his alienists persuaded him of Martha Place's sanity, he explored premeditation. When his ADA persuaded him that Martha Place premeditated murder, he had nothing left to explore. He gave it his best, as did I.

William Place

My brother Theo had no chance to warn me. The reporter, a good-looking young man in his mid-twenties, ran to Theo's home on March 16th, just a minute after word went out that Roosevelt would not grant clemency. The reporter had heard a rumor that I was living with Theo because I didn't want to reenter what the papers called the house of horrors. Theo's wife Laura, not the brightest, explained that I had left her house months ago, returning to 598 Hancock Street. The fellow listened, then dashed the three miles from Theo's house to mine. All this Theo told me later.

So that morning I didn't expect a reporter, but no matter. My new maid Ellie and I both heard the knock. She opened the door and greeted the visitor. He must have glanced at the front stoop because as I hid at the top of the stairs, I heard Ellie say, "you won't see blood there. Neighbors tell me the police washed it away the day after." The reporter announced his name and newspaper and his wish to interview Mr. William Place. Ellie showed more interest in the handsome man than in protecting me. Even Martha would have taught a new maid better. Ellie told the man to follow her. I walked quickly to the rocking chair in the bedroom and rumpled my hair. Seconds later the reporter entered the room, looking uneasy. He must have known I had shared this room with Martha.

"Thank you for seeing me." His hand shook slightly as he pulled a notebook from his pocket. "I wonder if you are aware of Roosevelt's decision—no clemency."

I had not heard officially, but along with everyone else in Brooklyn, I guessed the outcome. "I don't care one way or the other what becomes of Mrs. Place. You see, I have become a spiritualist. In January I went to a séance, Mrs. Olmstead led it, Mrs. Lucille Olmstead, and I now commune with the spirit of my daughter, Ida Place." The reporter asked a few more questions, which I answered readily, with detail. When he left, I retook my hidden perch at the top of the stairs. The reporter stopped for a minute to thank Ellie. I imagined her rolling her eyes as she opened the door to lead him out.

"You know," she said, "he never went to no séance. He just thinks it sounds like he's off his mind with grief. But don't tell. Report it like he says."

Warden Omar Sage

On March 15th, Roosevelt's private secretary telegraphed me with an early notice. "The governor has decided. He found no grounds to interfere with the sentence." The next morning, after a predictably restless night, I read Roosevelt's lengthy memorandum in all the papers. "In the commission of a crime, a woman is deserving of the same blame as a man in a similar case."

Shameful that I could not take the next step by myself. I had managed to tell Mrs. Place in early February that the appeals panel denied her another trial. But at that point, she had forty-four days to live, not four—a number linked to sentencing and required by law. At breakfast, I confessed to Julia that I needed her. She looked at me with the strained look I had grown used to over our thirty-some years of marriage. "You ask me to go with you, to do your job?" She dwelled on the word your. "You complain I spend too much time with Mrs. Place. Now you may appreciate that time."

"Yes." Nothing more to say.

We dressed, more slowly than usual, not speaking. I took Julia's arm. We walked across the yard, to the Old Hospital Building, up the stairs to the top floor, still not speaking. The guard stared at us, then turned away. As we approached, we saw Mrs. Place sitting, sewing, looking through the bars.

I gestured to the guard to open the door. I paused to let Julia enter. She didn't move. She tilted her head a fraction of an inch. I should go first. Julia followed. Our movements were slow. The day matron, Annie Reilly, didn't look at us and walked away, into the room the guards used. Mrs. Place did look at us, but with no expression. "I have some bad news I'm afraid," I said, my rehearsed line. She teared up as I walked toward her. But she remained in control, and as I spoke, the tears stopped. I told her the date, March 20th, four days away. The tears did not resume. "I have sent for Reverend Cole. He will be here for you this afternoon."

"Send for my brother too, Peter Garretson."

I nodded assent. "And Mrs. Sage," I looked at Julia, standing in the corner of the cell, "will stay with you for a while." I continued to look at Julia as I turned to leave. Her features changed. She gave me a small smile as she walked up to Mrs. Place and embraced her.

I left, relieved this part had ended, relieved that Julia had stood by me. The rest of the day would be busy, but with less stress. I told the guard to once again remove all needles from Mrs. Place's cell. I called Edwin Davis, telling him the date. I reminded him to complete his inspection the day before. I began to draw up the witness list. So many details.

At night Julia read in the evening papers that the warden had asked her to accompany him to the cell that morning but that she was too nervous to do so. She threw the papers down in front of me. "You see, I said to her, we do the right thing, and they don't report it. This is what I go through all the time. Now you have a taste of it." With a clenched jaw, she blasted the articles, the governor, and even me. "Julia, come here." I hugged her. "I know what you did and no one knows better than I how you rose to the occasion."

Edwin Davis

After Omar Sage called to tell us the execution date would be the 20th, we decided that Harry Tyler, my young assistant, would speak for us both, to correct the rumors. Harry told the reporters that neither he nor the State Electrician, that's me, ever said we would resign if directed to execute a woman. We would never leave the warden to fend for himself. For us, the sex did not matter. A job was a job.

But both of us did have one worry. Would a woman's body respond to the standard voltage in the same way? Did different proportions of muscle and fat alter the way electricity would move through a convict? We had no way to experiment.

On March 18th, Harry and I made the familiar train trip from our homes in Corning to the prison in Ossining. The trip took the entire day, so we had to stay in one of Ossining's boarding houses, paid for by Warden Sage, or I should say, by the state of New York. The next morning we began our preliminary checks. The chair worked well, almost perfectly, we reported to Sage. Just needed a few adjustments.

Warden Omar Sage

I worked my way down the execution checklist. On March 17th I prepared letters inviting the official witnesses to the execution, giving them the 20th as the date but reminding them that the timing, by law, should remain confidential. The law specified other matters too. I must give the witnesses three days' notice—barely made that. I must invite a Supreme Court judge, the District Attorney, the Sheriff of Kings County, two doctors, twelve citizens, two clergy, and seven assistants. And obviously Edwin and Harry. And me. I also added my usual list of newspaper editors.

After finishing the invitations, I checked the path to the death chamber. Julia said the word chamber seemed ironic. As though the inmate simply went to bed. No woman had walked that path before. We confined Mrs. Place in the Old Hospital Building, across the yard from the main building. Before she could even get to the familiar part of the walk, she needed to descend two flights to the keeper's room, then go south through the old kitchen, across the yard to the principal keeper's office, then continue on the part of the trek familiar to the guards and to me, called the death walk—down the corridor lined with cells to the iron doors of the death house where we confine the condemned murderers, past those doomed men, through a second set of doors to the chamber. Maybe I could hang curtains across the cells so the inmates would not gawk at her. I took the path to decide what to do.

That day two newspapers I read lambasted Roosevelt for failing to grant clemency. One paper called the governor a monster. Another printed a cartoon depicting him and state officials—was one me?—dragging a woman to the electric chair. I knew that sort of publicity got under Roosevelt's skin. I had thicker skin.

Returning to my office after checking the death walk, I saw a letter from Roosevelt on my desk. He recommended I enlist a woman physician to check on Mrs. Place during the execution and that I limit press coverage to one press association and to *The Sun*, one of the few papers that had praised Roosevelt for doing his duty. Roosevelt's letter arrived just in time. I ruffled through the pile of invitations awaiting pickup by a messenger and threw out the three addressed to the editors of newspapers not on the governor's list.

I called my clerk in and dictated a telegram to Commissioner Collins. "Mr. Collins, the governor asks me to enlist a woman doctor to attend to Mrs. Place on Monday. I do not know any. Can you offer a recommendation?"

An answer came in a half-hour. "Not a problem at all, Omar. Jennie Griffin. She lives in Troy. She's not close, but she's a dandy one."

I went down the hall to check the name with Dr. Irvine. "Splendid. I met her at a conference in Albany last year."

Back to the clerk, to send a telegram to Dr. Griffin.

When I returned to my domestic quarters that evening, Julia cornered me.

"Her hair, Omar. Mrs. Place takes pride in her hair. It is still thick and she arranges it nicely in a knot, sometimes a twist, at the back of her head. With those other prisoners, I know you had a guard shave their heads. You cannot do that to her. You cannot. It would be humiliating."

I sighed. Was there no end to this business?

Mattie

Mrs. Sage came again on March 17th. Maybe she found her visits easier now that she knew they wouldn't drag on. Only three more days to watch over me. She acted kindly. Did the warden order her to come or did she want to? She talked, but not a lot. I fidgeted. What to do with my hands since they took away my needles? I bit my fingernails.

"How do you find the food?" Julia Sage asked. Why does everyone focus on how the condemned eat? The newspapers sometimes report that I eat well, and that's mostly true, or sometimes that I barely eat. Why does it matter? It's food that someone else purchased, cooked, washed up. No one did that for me when I had no food for Ross when I gave Ross away.

Reverend Cole entered my cell. Mrs. Sage looked up at him. I think she took his coming as a sign to leave. Did they have a plan that someone should be with me as much as possible? Someone besides the matrons and the guards? The Reverend put his arm around my shoulder and asked me what passages I wanted to read. I shrugged, so he selected one. We sat facing each other, taking turns reading. Every few minutes he stopped reading or asked me to pause and he asked a question.

"What do you think that passage means, Mattie?"

I hadn't paid much attention. Couldn't say. He interrupted the silence.

"The death of Jesus releases us from our bondage to our sins, right?"

I stared at him. He expected me to answer. "Yes."

He smiled and read on.

The Reverend left in the afternoon. Ten minutes later Emilie Meury arrived. She wanted to settle some business matters, she said. Seemed strange, a missionary settling business matters. Came down to the business of my diamond earrings—the same ones that damn confidence woman Annie Simpson had until her lawyers told her to return them. Last August I gave them to Miss Meury. Why not? Now she wanted to know what to do with them. Ah, a practical matter, something I could handle. "Keep them. Keep them for yourself. If you ever decide you don't want them, send them to my son Ross, and tell him to keep them someday for his wife. I'll give you his address."

Warden Omar Sage

On his way back home to Tarrytown, when he left Mrs. Place's cell, Reverend Cole stopped to see me. "How do you find her today?" I asked.

"Resigned to her fate."

"Yes, Mrs. Sage, and I think so as well."

"But she has lost her appetite."

Robert Van Iderstine

On March 17th, Howard McSherry traveled one last time from New Brunswick to my office in New York. The two of us had nothing more to do for Mrs. Place now that Roosevelt declined to commute her sentence. We met as a matter of formality, to close out our relationship. For me, the relationship could not have been odder. Most of the time Howard added little and plopped himself in the way. But he had his moments, including his valiant final fight for our client, in the Governor's office of all places. I knew Howard believed we fought the good fight, together in the limelight, more limelight than that country lawyer usually saw. Neither of us mentioned the awkward issue of payment.

Opening my credenza, I took out sherry and poured a glass for each of us. "To Mrs. Place," I said.

"May her soul find peace," Howard said.

With that ritual completed, we parted. For a few hours, I thought I had nothing more to do. But—can you accept sentimentality?—my brain and my heart interfered. Eleven months earlier, when Judge Hurd wrote me about representing Martha Place, he recognized that I cared about people who needed help. Poor children, Negroes, maybe even a woman accused of murder. I had almost forgotten my beliefs, focusing on the notoriety of the case and my own reputation. But a little of those beliefs remained. So I did what I didn't want to do. On March 18th, two days before the execution, I made my last trip to Sing Sing to meet with my client. I walked slowly, accompanied by a guard, to Martha's cell. She sat in a chair near the window, holding a Bible. No theatrics. I decided I could not bear to ask her how she was faring. I would just, well, conclude matters, hmmm, just say God be with you. I didn't know, but I would not ignore her.

"Martha, I want you to know that I believe I did, that Mr. McSherry and I did, all that could be done. We appealed, we met with the governor, we spoke with friends who had influence. I regret, deeply, that we failed. You may have heard a rumor that we would appeal once more, but we cannot. We have no grounds for another appeal. No legal redress." My words came fast, too fast. I took a deep breath and willed myself to stop talking.

"It is good of you to come to see me, Six. I do not blame you, not you and not any of my lawyers. I know I did not help much." She spoke in her most formal manner. "Now feel free to leave." You will notice that neither of us brought up the question of guilt.

"God bless you," I said. I stood up, gestured to the guard, and walked away.

Julia Sage

I felt tension in every part of my body. My back, my neck, my stomach. The woman on the chair across from me murdered her stepdaughter in the most horrific way. So why did I find this visit difficult? I had to hurry through what I needed to say, without seeming to hurry.

"Martha, do you know the rules that the wardens of Sing Sing established long ago, for their families?"

She stared at me, waiting.

"The wardens have their wives with them, and many times children as well, living on the compound. It is an easy life, in terms of comfort, but not in terms of the atmosphere at certain times. The wardens decided that when sentences were carried out, their families would leave, leave the prison for the day. The only reason I remained here when Martin Thorn met his end was due to the heat that summer—too hot to travel. Tonight, I leave for Albany, to spend the evening with my sister. I won't return for two days."

Martha looked stunned. She must have expected the warden's wife to be present, maybe even in the death chamber. How could she have thought that?

"I regret I will not be there to comfort you. The warden would not allow it." Convenient, but true.

Martha scowled. She stared at me, then beyond me. After a few seconds, her features softened.

"Mrs. Sage, do not look so uncomfortable. You have been kind to me, more than most. Go about your day. But first I have a gift for you." She motioned to the guard, asking him to bring the package.

No inmate had ever given me a present. Should I accept? What would Omar think? But I could not refuse. I opened the wrapping. Inside I saw a beautiful two-foot square Battenberg lace centerpiece. And an envelope.

"I made the centerpiece for you on the days they let me use my needles. I finished just in time. This is to thank you for keeping company with me. The letter, just take it. Don't open it until, well, until after."

"So kind of you." I must not cry. The guard and matron stared at us, at my tears. I reached for the Bible on the table, opened it to psalm 86:5. "One short passage before I leave."

"'For thou, Lord, art good, and ready to forgive; and plenteous in mercy unto all them that call upon thee.'"

Martha nodded.

I stood, embraced her, and motioned to the guard.

"May God be with you." I walked out, taking the centerpiece and letter with me but not turning around. That was March 19th, one day before the execution.

When I read the letter on March 21st, I suppose I expected a confession of sorts. "Mrs. Sage, I thank you for your friendship and I want you to know that I believe I have been forgiven for my sins." No detail on the nature of those sins.

That same day I read in one of the newspapers that the convicted woman had dined at the warden's table the last few days of her life. Ha. Is there no end to what these reporters dream up?

Emilie Meury

On March 19th I made my final train trip from Brooklyn to Ossining. The reporters called me the prison angel, but I did not feel angelic that day. I had guided prisoners for years. I had ministered to men accused of horrendous crimes, crimes I could not imagine. I had never comforted a woman sentenced to die the next day.

Martha Place murdered her stepdaughter. I never doubted her guilt. But I understood how a woman could be led to the brink of sanity, or over the brink. Growing up in Brooklyn, my best friend was Judith Masters, a lovely girl, popular, full of spirit. When we both turned seventeen Judith became sullen. Distant. I began my vocation by convincing her to confide in me. Then Mr. and Mrs. Masters sent Judith away, to a convent in upstate New York. She returned seven months later. For a few weeks, we talked again. She spoke of her despair at giving up Emily, named after me. Soon Judith left Brooklyn, headed west to a normal school in Illinois, far from her memories. She died before she could reach the school. I heard talk of a train accident, nothing specific. My first attempt at missionary work, at comforting, failed tragically. When I thought of Ross Savacool, or Ross Aschenbach, I understood despair. I would try again to comfort.

After I entered Mattie's cell, we sat for a few minutes, praying. I saw her look at me, intently. "Emilie, may I call you that, tomorrow I die, so today I'll tell you. It is simple. I killed Ida."

I froze. I succeeded. Now she would be freed.

"I tried to believe I hadn't killed her. But I suppose I did. I couldn't take it any longer." She stared at me, waiting. Only much later did I think back on that word suppose, and even then, not for long.

I patted Martha's hand. I hugged her. "Enough said. You will feel better now." I led the two of us in more prayer.

She did seem better, lighter. I told her I would stay in town that night and would return in the morning As I got up to leave, she spoke. "Keep this Bible, the one you gave me months ago, and take these pincushions I was using, for yourself. The book of psalms and hymns, here it is, that should go to Will, my husband. The warden has his address." This last request stunned me. Perhaps it served as her way of confessing to William, the only way she knew how.

I left the cell once Reverend Cole arrived. I headed for a boarding house in Ossining, but first I stopped at Warden Sage's office.

"Warden, do you have a minute?" He gestured for me to sit and asked me if I wanted him to call for tea.

"No, that is kind but not necessary. As you know, I have concern for Mrs. Place's soul, but I also have concern for her body. What arrangements have you made?"

"Miss Meury, I expected her brother, Peter Garretson is his name, to visit and planned to talk to him in person." The warden's shoulders stooped more than usual as he spoke. His eyes looked red, tired. "Mr. Garretson never came. I managed to reach Police Chief Harding in New Brunswick because he had a phone. Chief Harding fetched Mr. Garretson so we could talk. Not a warm conversation. I had to promise him that the state of New York would pay for transport of the body back to New Jersey."

I shook my head.

"So sad, warden. Also, I have some business to take care of for Mrs. Place. She requested that I keep her Bible, the one she'll carry tomorrow, and that her hymn book go to her husband."

The warden looked surprised as I handed him the book, but he agreed with the arrangements. Then he fidgeted in his chair.

"Miss Meury, I know that Reverend Cole and Matron Reilly will accompany Mrs. Place to the death chamber. Can I count on you as well?"

I had stopped at the warden's office to inquire about the burial and to tell him about the books. I had not expected the warden's question. But I was certain of my answer.

"Mr. Sage, I appreciate your request. I cannot. I know my own limitations, my emotional limitations. I will attend to Mrs. Place in the morning before you come for her, but I can do no more."

Already a small man, the warden seemed to shrink in his chair. "I understand. You have done what you can. I had no right to ask."

I felt proud I had not said a word about Mrs. Place's confession. That was a matter between the sinner, me, and God. For now.

Reverend David Cole

I had sat with hundreds of parishioners on their death beds. Some suffered too much pain to even think about the hereafter. Others were frantic, worrying about the abyss, the nothingness to come. Yet others questioned whether their souls would go up or down. Martha, Martha stayed calm. At times I wondered whether she enjoyed the attention. I knew that in her forty-nine years she had never before been at the center of anything. On March 19th, I read scriptures to her, the ones we read before and new ones. After twenty minutes she interrupted me.

"Reverend Cole, I need to ask you to take care of some of my things. I have a few clothes, just a few. I don't think my niece Grace would want clothes from Sing Sing. See that they go to the poor house in town or in Yonkers. Also, I have a letter for you. Don't read it until after, until after the execution."

"Of course, Martha. I will follow your instructions as best I can. Now let us continue reading." After a while, I stopped. I had done what I could. I considered asking her about her living relatives—her brother Peter, her sister Ellen, the son Ross. I stopped myself. Why add to the pain? At nine o'clock I wished her a peaceful night. "I am staying with Warden Sage in his quarters," I said. If you need me, send Matron Coultry or a guard to get me and I will be here. Otherwise, I will see you in the morning. I will walk with you."

"One minute, Reverend. Can you stay one minute?" She paused. "Reverend, tomorrow I die, so today I will tell you. It is simple. I killed Ida. I must have killed Ida."

I breathed in and out, deeply, closed my eyes, and opened them again. I took her hand. "God is forgiving. You have done right to confess before him." I led her in prayer, smiling. I succeeded at my mission.

She said nothing as I left the cell.

Kathryn Coultry

The only thing that kept me sane, well, me and Annie Reilly, the day matron, was remembering that our positions were temporary. In the summer of '98 Warden Sage sent around word in the town that he needed two matrons for a short time. He thought it might be a month. The month turned into almost a year. Me and Annie knew on March 20th we would be relieved of our duties, sent out with good references from the warden. But I had to get through the night first. Sitting with a woman who was about to be electrocuted. I steeled myself. Steel. What did that mean? I had to be hard, thinking about the goal, the next day, maybe with a bonus payment from the warden.

Then something I didn't expect.

"Mrs. Coultry. I need to ask you a favor. Would you cut a lock of my hair? And ask the warden to mail it to my son, Ross? The warden has his address. I don't want it to be the same lock the prison barber cuts off tomorrow—Mrs. Sage made sure it will just be a lock—to attach the electrode."

As a matron, I never helped Mrs. Place with any part of her dress, other than sometimes searches the warden required. I had never touched Mrs. Place's hair. I would need to divide, to touch. The warden didn't allow scissors in the cell, of course. Mrs. Place used her teeth to break thread for her handiwork. I spoke with the guard and he spoke to the warden. The guard returned with a scissors and a second guard to watch over the operation. The lank I separated and snipped had no smell, no curl, no oil. I blinked a lot. None of the four of us looked at each other.

The End

2:30 a.m. Mrs. Place went to sleep. Night matron Kathryn Coultry reported no problems.

8:00. Guard opened cell door for Reverend David Cole and Miss Emilie Meury.

8:30. Crowd of reporters outside gates swelled. Invited witnesses kept time of execution confidential, as required, but reporters noticed more men than usual entering prison in morning.

9:00. I met with State Electrician Edwin Davis and assistant Harry Tyler. They reconnected wires to chair. Also met with Dr. Jennie Griffin who stayed at same boarding house as electricians and entered complex with them. Small woman, young.

10:43. I called twenty-two witnesses into my office. Guard led them to death chamber. Too big a crowd for room. Not enough stools. Note for future.

10:50. Went to Mrs. Place's cell. Found her holding hands with Miss Meury and Reverend Cole. Miss Meury hugged Mrs. Place then slipped out.

10:51. Edwin Davis tested apparatus.

10:52. Edwin Davis attached wires to chair.

10:53. Death walk began. I provide more detail here than usual, due to extreme public interest. Want record to be precise. Mrs. Place carried Bible, leaned on my arm. Reverend Cole on her other side. She stood as tall as Cole, taller than me. Behind us walked day matron Annie Reilly. Two prison guards who had been with Mrs. Place for months, Johnny Conyers and Albert Robinson, completed procession. Mrs. Place wore black dress with wide sleeves, not dress she wore at trial. She sewed it herself from black wool Miss Meury gave her. Mrs. Place had hoped to wear it to a new trial if she got one. Now wearing it to her death. Reporters wrote she slept in her dress, but the only person who could confirm that was matron Kathryn Coultry. Coultry under my orders was not to provide information. I spoke for Coultry, said that matron read the Bible to Mrs. Place and prayed with her during night. Convict wore tan shoes, same shoes she wore when she entered Sing Sing. A reporter called them russet slippers. Incorrect. As convict walked, she muttered a prayer. She seemed composed.

I had walked path a few days before. At my instruction, prison workers strung curtains over both sides of tiers of cells, where men would have had sight line to procession. This helped, though guards reported on wide open eyes on other side of curtain.

Reverend and I guided convict into chair. She held Bible in left hand. She sat and said quietly, "Warden, thank you." She paused for a second then said, "God help me." I asked convict to close her eyes so she could not stare at witnesses. I motioned to day matron, placing her carefully in front of convict. Matron knew what to do. She faced convict and spread her own full skirt to hide witnesses' view of convict's legs. Dr. Jennie Griffin knelt between matron and convict. Doctor pulled down convict's black stockings, placed electrode on each calf, toward convict's ankle, and arranged black dress over apparatus. Matron quickly moved far away. Doctor moved away. Careful observer with good eyesight might notice that convict's head was shaved, just small patch at crown. For death walk her hair was combed over bald spot and pinned in low knot at back of neck. One reporter wrote hair was braided. Incorrect, matron says. Davis attached electrode to bald area of scalp. He buckled harness of leather straps over convict's face and attached pad against forehead, covering eyes. Witnesses could still see mouth. Davis and Tyler stood at side.

Eight amps for four seconds. Convict's body stiffened. Slow rigid twisting of hands. Strained against straps. Then two amps for fifty-six seconds.

Voltage: 1760 for four seconds, then 200 for fifty-six seconds. Convict appeared deceased. Bible still in left hand.

11:05. Davis turned off current. Prison physician Dr. Robert Irvine examined body, checking pulse and heartbeat. He conferred with Davis. Both said convict dead but wanted to be certain. I agreed. Davis turned voltage back on for five seconds, as precaution. Some foam oozed from convict's lips. Dr. Irvine checked again and repeated confirmation. He asked Dr. Griffin to check. She confirmed. Reverend Cole approached, took Bible from woman's hand, gave it to me. I will send to Miss Meury, as convict requested.

11:10. Guards removed body from chair. Carried body to room set aside for postmortem.

11:30. Doctors Irvine and Griffin began autopsy. Reported later that they observed slight scorching of skin on both sides of forehead from contact with electrodes. Brain was normal. Autopsy report was sealed and filed in Kings County.

Commentary. Mrs. Martha Place was twenty-sixth convict and first woman to be executed in electric chair at Sing Sing. She was first woman in world to be executed in electric chair.

Addendum. October 31, 1899. Dr. Irvine preserved brain in jar, stored in prison hospital room, intending to bring it to Columbia University for examination. Ruined in prison fire.

Peter Garretson

I did not want to hire our local undertaker, Mr. Lane, of Lane & Herbert, but I had no choice. Lane asked what casket he should bring to Sing Sing. When I told him that I didn't know, the state of New York was responsible for such costs, Lane said he guessed the state would authorize only one of his pine boxes. He stared at me, then said, "want to swap it out for something nicer?" I told him pine would do just fine.

Lane traveled by train with the empty casket to Ossining and traveled back with the full casket to New Brunswick, arriving at ten at night on March 21st. He took charge of the casket until the next day. I didn't go with him to

Ossining, and I told him to keep quiet about the trip. No need to remind the busybodies in New Brunswick about my disgraced dead sister.

Reverend David Cole

On March 22nd I arranged to take an early train from New York to New Brunswick, along with Miss Emilie Meury and Dr. Jennie Griffin. To my surprise, Dr. Griffin had expressed interest in attending the funeral when she talked to me after the execution, while she was waiting to assist with the postmortem. "Some may think me heartless, Reverend, but that is not so. I did my duty as a physician. My part in all this will help me as a lady doctor as I build a practice. And even though I accepted the warden's invitation, I feel badly for Mrs. Place. I understand she gave up a son, and that cannot be easy for anyone's sanity. I will feel better about this whole affair if I accompany you."

In a telegram, I asked Peter Garretson if he wished to invite Howard McSherry or Robert Van Iderstine to attend the funeral. Mr. Garretson responded, no, without explanation. Perhaps this reflected his anger that the lawyers failed to stop the execution, or, since Mr. McSherry resided in New Brunswick, perhaps Mr. Garretson wished to keep the funeral under wraps in the town where he and his family lived. I came to believe the latter.

In New Brunswick, our small funeral party took a carriage from the train station to Lane & Herbert, the undertakers. There we met Mr. Garretson, who helped Mr. Lane and his assistant lift the pine casket onto the bed of a wagon. Our carriage followed the wagon to the family plot in the Cedar Hill Cemetery. There we saw Mr. Garretson's daughters, Grace and Maggie, a few assorted Garretsons, and two clergymen waiting for us. The day before, in his curt telegram advising me not to invite the lawyers, Mr. Garretson asked me to preside at the gravesite. I declined. I had held up well under the strain so far, despite my seventy-eight years, but I did that for Mrs. Place. No need to test my strength further. Reverend Alan Campbell, the pastor of the Suydam Street Reformed Church, offered prayers. Reverend Arthur Peake, pastor of the East Millstone Reformed Church, also offered prayers. They did a competent job, though I would have selected different passages.

Only Grace Garretson cried.

Standing beside the grave, I wondered if I had done the right thing the day before when I wrote Roosevelt. "Dear Governor, I know you are subject to vitriolic attacks from newspapers about Mrs. Place's execution. I wish you to know that she confessed to me, the night before she died, that she had murdered her stepdaughter. I believe she was sane when she committed the crime and sane when she confessed to me. I hope that knowledge gives you peace." Martha Place had not asked me to treat her confession in confidence, though, as I served as her pastor, perhaps that was her intent. But I also had a responsibility for the governor's soul. I did not want Roosevelt to go through life wondering if he had erred.

At the time I wrote the governor, I did not know that Martha had confessed as well to Emilie Meury. The power of prayer.

Ross Aschenbach

On the day of the execution, after dinner, I told my parents that I knew, I knew what Martha Place did. I wouldn't tell them how I learned of the murder, or how I kept up with the case.

Mama teared up. "Ross, I'm sorry. You should not have had to go through this. You are just fifteen." I won't repeat Papa's words.

I had decided what to say. "No need to talk about her. I know the two of you don't want to talk about her. And I'll be all right. But just one thing—if she wrote me a letter, let me see it. That's all I'm asking." You wonder why I thought she might have written me at the end? Hard to answer. Well, there was no letter from her, but in her own way, she let me know she thought about me at the end.

On March 22nd, a small packet and a bulky envelope arrived, both for me. The packet held diamond earrings, with a note from a missionary lady telling me that Martha Place wanted me to have them, to give to my wife once I married. The envelope was from Warden Sage. Mama handed over both to me.

I never did give the earrings to my wife when I married. I didn't want her anywhere near anything of Martha Place's. That woman was my burden, not my wife's. For the most part, I tried to forget about Martha Place, but I did keep the lock of hair, encased in a small satin bag sewn by the warden's wife. Much later, I was drafted to fight in the Great War toward the end when the army ran out of younger men. I carried Ma's lock of hair into the muddy trenches in France. There, I tried to remember.

Wayne Knittle

I followed the case of Martha Place for thirteen months and twelve days, wondering whether her parade of lawyers would be better for her than I would have been if I stayed on for more than a day. Let's start with Howard McSherry, a pompous dolt with little to be pompous about. Though I suspect he was cleverer than he seemed. Then Henry Newman. He had a head on his shoulders, a smart head with a vivid imagination, but he didn't last long. Next Ridgway, well, Ridgway disappeared. Van Iderstine? Staid Van Iderstine. Wrong strategies. Howe and Hummel. Crap. I should have been braver, should have represented the woman.

One thing Newman and I agreed on—the insanity plea would never work. Martha Place was a sane woman who lived a lawful life for most of her years. The sleigh accident she had in her twenties left no lasting damage and she knew right from wrong. Though I did chuckle to myself about that rubber plant. Kill someone and then offer your plant to a neighbor? But that offering pointed to eccentricity, not insanity.

I had my own opinions on the right strategies. I attended every hearing and trial, sitting quietly in the back of the courthouse. I don't think anyone spotted me and if they did, they didn't care. I bought every newspaper I could get my hands on, *The New York Times, The World, The Brooklyn Citizen, The Brooklyn Daily Eagle, The Sun, The Times Union, The New York Tribune, The Standard Union,* and even the *New Brunswick Daily Times* when I could find it. The reporters were idiots. They couldn't get Martha Place's age right or spell my name correctly. But the papers included information not mentioned in court, and the testimony included information that never made it into the papers.

In my view, the lawyers should have highlighted a crucial extenuating circumstance. Harry Ross Savacool, now Ross Aschenbach. I tracked down the paperwork governing the adoption, and I spoke with the elderly pastor at the Colts Neck Reformed Church. His name appeared in the adoption papers. I said I represented Martha Place. Just a little stretch. He confirmed that the woman was destitute. Next, I met with Mr. and Mrs. Aschenbach in Vailsburg, near Newark. It took countless requests before they agreed, unhappily, to talk. The Aschenbachs loved their son and prayed he would be spared the pain of his first mother's life and death. They confirmed everything I had learned about the adoption. Mrs. Place's actual lawyers should have arranged such a meeting themselves. If the jury knew that she suffered through such straightened circumstances that she had to give up her son, and knew that William Place forbid Ross to visit, and knew that Ida seemed to have everything a girl could want, would that have prompted at least a bit of sympathy for the accused woman? Not a diagnosis of insanity, but of misery. No one mentioned Ross at the actual trial, not William Place, not Martha Place, not Van Iderstine. Maybe Martha felt shame that she gave up her child, and maybe William felt shame that he kept Ross at a distance. No mothers besides the defendant participated in the trial. The lawyers were men, the judge was a man, the jury was twelve men. But surely at least one of those twelve men would have understood the sorrow of giving away a child. Or the sad tale would have led Roosevelt toward clemency.

I might also have raised questions about the time of death and the fiancé's movements. Why had Van Iderstine not seen such a path? Even a dumb jury might have understood. The maid heard screams at 9:00 in the morning, when Martha Place threw acid in the girl's face and hit her head with an axe. But she did not die then. She died later, according to my reading of the autopsy. While we are on the subject of the autopsy, why did neither the prosecution nor the defense call Dr. William Moser to the stand? He was the pathologist at the autopsy. He might have had useful thoughts on Ida's organs and on time of death. What happens if we combine the uncertainty about timing with the changing story Edward Scheidecker told, once saying he came to the Place house at 2:00 and once saying his friend George came there at 2:00? Scheidecker acted, or overacted, or lied. The Place brothers, though hardly wise men, distrusted the fiancé, weren't even sure he was engaged to Ida. Scheidecker had enlisted in the 22nd Infantry as a private. I inquired about him to the lads in his regiment. Several had been promoted to corporal, but Scheidecker remained a private.

I continued snooping. Again, saying I was Martha Place's attorney, I interviewed Fred Fahrenkrug, the friend and young detective whose name appeared in one of the papers but never in any of the testimony. Here's how I got to him. I talked to a Place neighbor, N. B. Thompson, who referred me to Gertrude Hebbard, who in turn referred me to her own fiancé, Fahrenkrug. The four young people—Ida, Edward, Gertrude, Fred—were close friends. Fahrenkrug offered me many details and seemed more distressed about Ida than Scheidecker. Remember, the coroner pulled Fahrenkrug from the crowd on the street to join the nine others impaneled for the inquest on the night of the murder, and he remained a member of the jury for the official inquest. An odd conflict of interest. What was Fahrenkrug doing on the street that night? Here's my flight of imagination—he secretly kept company with Ida Place. If so, could Scheidecker have found out? Maybe Scheidecker planned a rendezvous with the girl, in her room, in the afternoon, to confront her about Fahrenkrug. Scheidecker might have seen the maid leaving to run an errand. He might have known that the Places rarely locked the back door to the row house. He might have known that Mrs. Place often had a drink too many in the afternoon. He might have snuck into the house, seen Mrs. Place, tipsy and drowsy, and crept upstairs. He would have seen a body lying on the bed, unconscious. He intended to confront Ida. Instead, he finished Mrs. Place's work by smothering the girl. Even if he didn't plan on a confrontation, maybe he saw Ida's ruined face, saw the blood, and decided to put her out of her misery. Death in the afternoon would be consistent with the time of death reported in the autopsy. Only the undertaker thought death came in the morning, and since he remained a lone voice no one paid attention to him. Martha's confession? Could she have confessed to something she didn't do? Or is it possible she couldn't remember?

The neighbor, N.B. Thompson, had more to say to me. He recalled that for better or worse, he told Mr. Place about Ida on the night of the murder.

But Edward Scheidecker said he was the one to tell Mr. Place, the next day. Theodore and Charles Place forbid Scheidecker from attending the funeral because they didn't think he should have been the one to tell William of his daughter's death. Or was that a convenient excuse to keep Edward away? And if so, why?

Bear with me, I have more. This is not the only criminal trial I have followed. Almost always, when a young woman dies, the autopsy report covers pregnancy. The report says, "There were no indications of pregnancy." Or sometimes "The deceased was three months pregnant." Why did I see no such mention in this report? When Van Iderstine questioned Doctor Henderson about Ida Place's organs, why did the lawyer not add the uterus to the list of organs? Just a vague question about pelvic organs. Henderson answered, "regular." But what does that mean? If Ida was pregnant, and Scheidecker found out, and let's say the girl had been, well, virginal, with Scheidecker, couldn't that give him a motive? Now, this may sound farfetched, extremely farfetched, but here goes. If Coroner Delap discovered the girl's pregnancy, and the Place brothers learned of that discovery, is it possible that one or all of the Place brothers could have bribed Delap to keep that out of his report? Delap was already under suspicion of bribery in connection with covering up suicides. The brothers would have had to bribe the other doctors too, but Henderson was a dummy, and Moser, well, interesting that Moser never testified, right? Farfetched, yes, but a lawyer needs just one member of the jury to buy into a fantasy. Most likely established lawyers would never think to blame a coroner, a coroner they might need to work with in the future. As an unestablished lawyer, I would have had less to lose. Oh, and if by some unlikely chance the Place brothers did think Ida was pregnant, they may have blamed Scheidecker, which would explain why they kept him away from the funeral.

Let's return for a minute to Gertrude Hebbard, Ida's best friend, the one engaged to the Fahrenkrug lad. As of today, Gertrude remains unmarried. Could she have fallen out with her beloved Fred Fahrenkrug? And if so, why? Fahrenkrug, meanwhile, wed another woman.

Or, and it pains me to say this, but what about the young and beautiful maid, Hilda Palm. The officers interviewed her once, I know, but just once. She could have been jealous of Ida Place too. What if Miss Palm testified correctly about the morning, but not the afternoon? What if she went to clean Ida's room, saw Ida half-dead on the bed, and finished the job. That's not likely, I admit, but why didn't those lawyers offer it as a possibility? Introduce doubt.

Yes, I heard the rumors that Martha Place eventually confessed, maybe to that minister who was with her, or maybe to the prison angel. Mrs. Place didn't yell on the chair that she was being executed unfairly. But maybe she thought she killed the girl, even if she didn't. Or, I knew, maybe she did.

Historical Note

I based this novel closely on a true crime. The main characters, including Martha Place and her family, the lawyers, and the judges, are historical figures. A few minor characters are creations of my imagination, but of those few only Aunt Evelyn has a significant speaking role. My thoughts about alternative theories of the crime are just that, thoughts. I have absolutely no proof that Ida Place was pregnant, that she and Fred Fahrenkrug had an affair, that Coroner Delap continued to accept bribes, that Edward Scheidecker misled anyone, or that Martha Place intended to disappear in the West. All the alternative theories have at least a slight foundation in the ambiguities of the case, but nothing more.

My sources include the newspapers of the era, particularly the *New York Times*, the *World*, the *Brooklyn Citizen*, the *Brooklyn Daily Eagle*, the *Sun*, the *Times Union*, the *New York Tribune*, the *Standard Union*, and the *New Brunswick Daily Times*. Coverage of the crime was uneven. One article would contradict another article. A name would be spelled one way one day and another way another day. Knittle may have been Nittle. Ridgway may have been Ridgeway. Palm may have been Talm.

My primary sources include the transcript of the July 1898 trial and the 1899 appeals brief and response. I culled most of the dialogue related to the inquest and various hearings from newspaper accounts, and most of the dialogue related to the July 1898 trial from the official transcript. At times I simplified the court record for readability. But I have imagined all dialogue unrelated to court proceedings, as I tried to fill in the gaps in our understanding of Martha Place.

I had difficulty researching Martha Place's siblings and parents. Her mother, Penelope, was often called Ellen. Some reports mentioned a sister named Ellen, while others did not. The sister who was her partner in a dressmaking business may have been Tillie or may have been Ellen. I opted for Ellen. The record on her brother Peter is thin. I based his emotional distance from his sister on his infrequent visits and no more.

I believe Martha Place was guilty of murder in the first degree. I also believe she was not well represented by counsel. When she first admitted to throwing acid at Ida, she had no lawyer guiding her. Then she had a series of lawyers, with uncoordinated approaches. Today, I believe she would receive a verdict of guilty and a long prison sentence.

Acknowledgements

My family provided endless encouragement and help for this book. My husband, historian Mark Wasserman, listened with empathy as I fussed over incomplete and contradictory records. My brother, Robert Dale Parker, held my hand through every stage of the writing and publishing process, providing invaluable guidance. My sister, Carol McConnell, assisted with research and suggested sensible and necessary cuts. My son, Aaron D. Wasserman, critiqued an early draft and my daughter, Danielle Blass, helped interpret legal matters. I offer thanks to librarians and experts on the New York City and State court system, including James Blain, Deputy County Clerk of Kings County, New York State Unified Court System; an archivist at Researcher Services, New York State Archives; and Katie Ehrlich, New York City Municipal Archives. I also thank Tom Glynn, Librarian at Rutgers University.

I owe heartfelt thanks to Verena Rose, Shawn Reilly Simmons, and Harriette Sackler at Level Best Books for their superb editorial, design, and publishing skills.

About the Author

Marlie Wasserman writes historical crime fiction. She and her husband split their time between New Jersey and North Carolina.